Lost in
◆ Jersey
◆ ◆ ◆ City

Also by Paula Sharp

THE WOMAN WHO WAS NOT ALL THERE
(A Novel)

THE IMPOSTER: STORIES ABOUT NETTA AND STANLEY

Lost in ◆ Jersey ◆◆◆ City

a novel

PAULA SHARP

HarperCollins*Publishers*

The excerpt from *The Earl of Louisiana* (copyright © 1961 by A. J. Liebling, copyright © renewed 1989 by Norma Liebling Stonehill) is here reprinted by permission of Russell & Volkening as agents for the author.

Except for Huey Long, the characters in this book are purely fictional, and any resemblance between them and any persons, living or dead, is not intended by the author, and should not be inferred.

HarperCollins books may be purchased for educational, business, or sales promotional use. For information please write: Special Markets Department, HarperCollins Publishers, Inc., 10 East 53rd Street, New York, NY 10022.

FIRST EDITION

Library of Congress Cataloging-in-Publication Data

Sharp, Paula.

Lost in Jersey City : a novel / Paula Sharp. — 1st ed.

p. cm.

ISBN 0-06-016564-2

1. City and town life—New Jersey—Jersey City—Fiction.

2. Divorced women—New Jersey—Jersey City—Fiction. I. Title.

PS3569.H3435L67 1993

813'. 54—dc20 92-56217

93 94 95 96 97 ❖/RRD 10 9 8 7 6 5 4 3 2 1

This book is for Yayo and Yaya,
and for Julio.

Acknowledgments

I wish to thank Gina Maccoby for making this book possible. I also wish to thank Margaret Diehl and Terry Karten for their brilliant literary insights and criticisms; Charlotte Abbott and Lesley Sharp for reading the manuscript and providing essential advice; Marge Horvitz for her superior copyediting; Brian Breneman, Andy Fox and Karl Wasserman for contributing significant words and phrases; and the *Jersey Journal* and the writings of Owen P. Grundy for verification of essential historical details. Special and grateful acknowledgment is made to The Writer's Room, where this book was written.

Contents

Part V: THE TRIAL

Part I

RUNNING AWAY

◆ Mrs. Terhune

If you venture too far from home, life will wrestle you to the ground; it will carry you off to troubling places you could not have imagined; it will alter you, against your will, into a person you barely recognize, into someone you would not even want to say hello to. This is what Mrs. Terhune would have told you, had she been able to put her muddled thoughts into so many words. When she allowed herself to consider, even for a moment, what she was about to do, she experienced a panicky feeling that she already had ceased to be herself.

"I can't believe you talked me into this," Mrs. Terhune said, as her Chrysler New Yorker, pale blue and monstrous, nosed onto the road.

"No one talked you into anything," her best friend, Betty Trombley, answered.

"I never even heard of Jersey City before you moved there. If you hadn't come to Baton Rouge for a summer visit, this wouldn't be happening."

"Where we going?" Mrs. Terhune's daughter, Sherry, asked from the back seat.

"I thought we was going to Pensacola on the Panhandle," Sherry's older brother, Skeet, said.

"Don't you worry, sweetheart," Mrs. Terhune answered. "That's our first destination. Now sit back, you two."

Mrs. Terhune told Betty Trombley, "Tomorrow's Skeet's ninth birthday. I promised him this trip to Pensacola. My goodness, look at that truck up ahead, backing right into traffic from a hidden driveway."

Betty Trombley watched Ida Terhune assume that imperious expression of hers. It made her look completely frumpish, together with her lack of hairstyle and godawful clothes. Ida was a bosomy woman with delicate wrists and ankles, but she chose to hide these attributes under a cranberry-colored polyester pantsuit, the kind that hadn't been seen since the mid-seventies. It was as if she had squirreled herself away from the world for the last seven years.

Ida honked at the truck.

"I hate being honked at," Betty Trombley said. "It makes me jump out of my skin and want to run into somebody. It's almost like a reflex."

Ida Terhune frequently honked at vehicles simply to communicate a sense of disapproval. If a car ahead of her forgot to signal, ran a yellow light, or passed her when she was driving at the speed limit, Ida would honk long and punitively. She herself had never received a ticket for a moving violation.

"No one should back onto a busy road," she answered, without hearing the sanctimonious tone in her voice. What irked Betty most about Ida was that she was rigidly moralistic in the way of people who have led sheltered lives. But then Betty felt a rush of tenderness for Ida: she never changed. She was probably the only predictable element in Betty's personal history. When Ida and Betty were girls, Ida had possessed the same sense of sureness in her view of things. Betty liked to think of Ida going forth unbending into the world, the world stepping back in surprise. Since Ida Terhune would never alter herself to fit reality, reality would just have to alter to fit her.

Betty dangled her arm out the window to feel the breeze and said, "Jesus F. Christ, Mrs. Terhune, that truck was fifty yards in front of you."

When she made fun of Ida, Betty called her "Mrs. Terhune," although in this instance, Ida had no idea what Betty found so amusing. "Don't curse in front of the children," Ida answered. "And roll up that window. You'll let all the a.c. out, and we'll bake to death."

Sherry leaned toward Betty Trombley and said in a singsong voice, "Don't stick your elbow out too far, or it might go home in another car."

Betty laughed and rolled up the window.

Sherry perched, grinning, on the fold-down armrest, and Skeet stared out his window, surreptitiously cranking it partway open. Neither of the children looked like anyone in the family but each other. They were both pale-haired as old men, with flat faces and narrow-set green eyes like two snapping turtles getting ready to fight.

Skeet had found a two-inch walking stick behind the house and had fastened the insect to a safety pin by a length of twine tied around its abdomen. He had stuck the pin in the center of his T-shirt so that the walking stick, smooth and yellow as amber, crawled back and forth between his shoulders. Sherry touched it enviously.

"Where's the trailer?" Skeet asked.

"We're picking it up first thing," his mother answered. "Uncle Myron has it all ready for us." She turned onto a narrow road in the direction of her brother-in-law's car dealership.

"Myron Pinkerton? Have you seen this trailer?" Betty Trombley asked. When Ida didn't respond, Betty shook her head. Her earrings, fish with scalloped metal scales, clinked and glittered. Sherry leaned forward to look at the earrings, and the seven or eight bangles on each of Betty Trombley's long arms. Betty Trombley usually wore jewelry on every possible place from which it could dangle. At different times over the last two years, her hair had been a shimmering platinum or a bright henna or black as olives, and her nail polish often matched her shoes. She was the tallest woman Sherry had ever seen: Betty Trombley's head bumped the car's ceiling. Beside her, Sherry's mother's puffy brown hairdo looked like an abandoned hornet's nest.

Betty Trombley abruptly leaned forward, peered down a side road, and said, "God, Ida, don't look back now."

Skeet and Sherry turned around and saw their stepfather in his business suit, his elbow crooked over the arm of a red-haired woman in a green wraparound dress. The children's mother had told them several weeks before that their stepfather was away on a business trip, but Skeet and Sherry had seen him driving by their house with their Uncle Myron several times in the last few days.

"Don't look back at what?" Ida Terhune asked.

"I could swear I just saw them. Your very own Harlan Pinkerton and that Carlotta Stroke. Maybe they've just been to visit Myron."

Ida peered in the rearview mirror, but all she saw was the empty road behind the New Yorker. "It probably wasn't them," she said. "Harlan's busy today with a big real estate deal."

Up ahead, a police officer was yelling at a red-haired teenager who stood spread-eagled against a vegetable truck. The children watched as a second officer poked the boy with a nightstick.

Betty leaned forward. She hated police on principle, and for the hell of it, and for the pure pleasure of tormenting them.

"Stop, Ida."

Ida obeyed, thinking Betty had seen a traffic hazard.

"Those peckers look like they're just aching to crack that boy's head open," Betty said. She reached her right arm over Ida's and pressed on the horn.

The children watched the officers turn toward their mother's car. The one with the nightstick stopped poking the boy. The second officer approached the New Yorker and leaned in their mother's window.

"And just who are you?" the officer asked.

"I'm Mrs. Terhune," Ida answered, looking confused.

"You keep moving, ma'am. This is the scene of an arrest."

Betty shouted over Ida: "People in this area have been complaining about two men dressed as police officers robbing and killing people. Do you have some sort of identification? Can I just take down those shield numbers?" Betty opened the car door and stood up, removing a pencil and paper from her purse. "You just can't trust anybody nowadays." She wrote on her pad. "So what's your name?" Betty asked the other officer, "How come you're sticking that boy in the back? I mean, isn't this just a traffic stop? Are you really police officers? Just what is going on here?"

The boy by the vegetable truck looked as surprised as the policemen. Betty shouted to him: "My name's Betty Trombley, if you need a witness or anything. I have these guys' faces memorized." She climbed back into the New Yorker.

"Onward," Betty said. "Oh, come on, Ida. Don't look so scandalized."

Ida collected herself and steered the New Yorker back onto the road. A few blocks later, she drove into Myron Pinkerton's car dealership.

A yellow sports car raced out of the driveway as the New Yorker pulled in.

"Careful!" Ida cried. She pumped on the steering wheel, and two short honks issued from the New Yorker.

"Isn't that Honey Perkins?" Betty asked.

"That was Honey, driving like a maniac?"

"You never should have told that motormouth anything," Betty answered.

"Oh, I trust her as well as anyone," Ida said. "Anyway, she doesn't know Harlan personally."

Harlan's brother Myron Pinkerton, whom Betty had known since childhood as Myron the Skunk, was dressed in the tieless suit that had given him his name: a shiny undertaker-black jacket, with a stripe of white shirt down the front. When Ida Terhune emerged from the New Yorker, he slipped out the back door of the dealership, carrying a lug wrench. A lanky young man with a beak nose and crow-colored hair, whom Betty recognized as one of Myron's nephews, came out of the office's front door, extending a hand toward Ida.

As a girl, Betty had seen Myron the Skunk and his brother Harlan frequently, because they often hobnobbed with her own father, over real estate. Mr. Trombley and the Pinkertons had speculated together, buying up property in the poorer parts of Baton Rouge, collecting slum rents and avoiding any repairs in order to profit as fully as possible from depreciation at the end of each tax year. The three men would sell the buildings to one another every five years and then redepreciate the same property. Betty Trombley's father always kept his family in one or another of his buildings, moving the Trombleys back and forth as he bought and sold his holdings. Her mother would egg him on continually to fix up their apartments, but he would answer that this would interfere with his "tax revenues." In his buildings, pipes dumped rusted water into the sinks, toilets coughed and died, and porch boards collapsed under Welcome mats.

Betty had been suspicious the day Ida mentioned the trailer Myron the Skunk intended to sell her. Betty did not have to look at the trailer to know that it could not possibly be new: probably it would turn out to be fifteen years old or rescued from a junkyard after a fatal accident, or maybe it would explode on the highway.

When Betty got out of the car, she saw a camper in the back of the used car lot, resting on cinder blocks beside a small sign that read: FLOOR MODEL. NOT FOR SALE. Myron the Skunk stooped in front of one wheel, picked up the sign, and threw it over the roof of the trailer onto a scrapped car in the junkyard behind the dealership.

"Ida," she said, "why don't you pass on this trailer and rent one or something?"

"Now don't start up again," Ida answered. "I told you Uncle Myron's giving us a reduced price, and besides, I don't want a rented trailer; I want something that's mine. If I can't have a house anymore, at least I want something that reminds me of one. I've been desiring a camper all year."

Who knew what war was going on inside Ida Terhune? Betty Trombley wondered. Betty was certain Ida had stayed with Harlan for seven years because of a terror of financial insecurity, because a beautiful home meant more to her even than love or adventure. Now that Harlan had reached such depths, Ida was able to leave him only through the kind of quirky compromise a portable house meant to her. Betty had long regretted that the deaths of Ida's father and first husband on the same day had scared the life out of her.

"I know what you're thinking, and you're wrong," Ida said. "Stop speculating about me. I'm going to buy this trailer because I want to take the children camping along the eastern seaboard after we leave the Gulf, and that's that. I intend to have some fun, if nothing else." Little does she know, Ida thought, that I'm absolutely worried out of my mind. I can't believe I'm going to go through with this. She walked into the dealership office and talked to Myron's assistant, who proffered her some papers to sign.

Betty waited, leaning against the New Yorker. She watched Ida settle in the plastic chair before the desk and rummage through a red patent-leather purse, a style, Betty noted, that hadn't been seen since the Dark Ages.

Skeet and Sherry burst like popcorn from the car and ran to the back of the used car lot. When Skeet saw the trailer, set on cinder blocks, his face fell. It was the kind people used when they camped out in the woods, horse trailer size, not the deluxe model Skeet had envisioned. Uncle Myron was kneeling before the axle with a lug wrench, turning some bolts on one of the tires.

"You see the police on television settin' those dogs on those demonstrators?" he asked the children, without looking up from the tire. The children did not know what demonstrators were. "They used to say they wanted the rot to stay home from the war and the rot to eat in a restaurant, and the rot to this and the rot to that. Hell, I worked all my life and I never ate in no restaurant."

Skeet and Sherry had seen Uncle Myron and their stepfather eating out several times together at a pancake house and once at a coffee shop, where the children watched the men shovel eggs into their mouths faster than they could swallow. Neither of the children answered their uncle. They watched him twirl the lug wrench over each tire bolt. The walking stick traversed the hollow in Skeet's chest to the tip of his shoulder blade in the time that Skeet and Sherry waited for Uncle Myron to finish.

When Uncle Myron had dragged the cinder blocks from under the trailer and returned to his office, Skeet opened the trailer's back door and the children looked inside. They saw two narrow bunks and a table that folded down between them, to sleep three. You could put cushions on the table to make a bed or take the cushions off the table and eat on it. Strips of duct tape had been stretched across a rip in one of the cushions.

"He'll still get Mama to buy it," Skeet told Sherry.

The children also inspected the outside of the trailer, and so it was they and not their mother who noticed and pointed out the paint scratches over the wheels, the screws whose heads had been worn and skewed, and the dents as big as a man's thumbnail where someone had rehammered old pieces of siding.

When Betty Trombley approached the trailer, she saw the children look at one another with knowing, disappointed expressions. She was about to ask them what was the matter, but Sherry jumped, pointed at a piece of siding on top of the trailer, and cried, "Get it! Oh getitgetitgetit! It's crawled over! It's running off!"

Ida's children climbed the cinder blocks piled before the trailer and looked over its roof. Betty Trombley admired their agility. Their spidery legs hung from the trailer's edge as they hoisted themselves on top.

Sherry wiggled something over her head and yelled down at Betty: "A mantis! A praying mantis!"

"Oh goddamn! Oh lucky goddamn!" Skeet shouted from the trailer roof. He socked the air, spun around, and did a little dance. Then he remembered himself and checked his string to make sure that the walking stick was safely positioned. He climbed carefully down from the trailer. Sherry handed him the mantis as if the insect were a piece of the sweetest fruit in the world. She dangled from the side of the trailer and jumped to the ground.

"It's a giant," Skeet said.

Betty Trombley approached to look at the mantis. She had never been squeamish around insects, and she also felt sorry for the children at the moment—little did they suspect what was in store for them.

The insect was flukily large, Betty thought, the largest praying mantis she had ever seen. "Well," she said. "I don't know where those insects get their names. They don't look a bit as if they're praying." Sherry shoved between Betty Trombley and Skeet. "Maybe some nun named them so people wouldn't look too close," Betty continued. "Look at that. They don't even have hands to pray with." The insect's arms doubled over at the wrist into spiked clubs. A long body stretched behind its head like a green tornado.

Betty Trombley thought of saying more, but she was afraid she was starting to sound like a teacher. She had been working at Immaculate Conception Elementary in Jersey City for only a year, but already her job cloaked her like a false personality, making her feel schoolmarmish and patronizing at the worst moments. She had never held a job longer than three years, and it would be time to change soon. (Perhaps she should try hairdressing. The last resident of her apartment in Jersey City had been a beautician and left the place equipped with a wall-to-wall mirror, a barber's chair, and a wide sink for rinsing hair.) Standing between Ida's two children in the used car lot, Betty noted to herself that her present occupation, dedicated to children, was enough to make most of them shun her. She grinned and said, "Let me see if your mother's done drawing up those papers." Betty retreated from the trailer and disappeared into Myron's office.

The children found a mustard jar in the car lot, and Sherry put the mantis inside and took it to the New Yorker. Skeet followed Betty Trombley. He slipped behind her as the assistant said, "It's a steal." The assistant smiled briefly at

Uncle Myron, who did not smile back but took off his jacket, fished in his shirt pocket for a ballpoint pen, and laid it down beside the papers. Uncle Myron ducked out the door.

Skeet listened to everything that was said: he heard the needling tone in the assistant's voice, watched how his eye rested on Skeet's mother the moment before she touched her pen to the paper to sign it, and how he waited a moment before he casually scooped up the papers and handed her a second batch, which he explained related to insurance. Skeet saw Betty Trombley raise her eyebrows as his mother read the papers. His mother's helplessness had so often been joked about by her friends and her husband that even at eight Skeet was painfully aware of it. As Skeet watched, anger coiled in his stomach. He hated, more than anything, to feel cheated, to know that someone who seemed to have given to him had in fact taken something.

"Would you like a cup of coffee?" the assistant asked.

"No, I wouldn't," Betty Trombley told him.

"Why, yes, thank you," Skeet's mother said, concluding the transaction. Skeet looked over her head and saw his sister outside in the junkyard, scavenging.

Although Ida Terhune had not told her children that they would soon be leaving the only home they remembered living in, Sherry felt uneasy. She sensed that she was on the brink of forfeiting things that belonged to her, and a magpie instinct fluttered in her and compelled her to collect something, anything she could claim as hers alone. In the junkyard, she had discovered a piece of metal script that spelled *adilla,* lying mangled on the hood of a Cadillac, where someone had tried unsuccessfully to pry the car's entire name from its body; a pair of needlenose pliers dropped or forgotten next to a truck with a shattered windshield; a card that said *Myron Pinkerton, Process Server;* a gold scarf and a ring with a glassy purple stone, left in the back seat of a sports car; and several small car parts of various sizes. She tied her findings in the gold scarf and returned to the New Yorker.

The car had been backed up to the trailer, and her family,

Betty Trombley, Uncle Myron, and his assistant had gathered around the vehicles. Sherry tucked the scarf under the driver's seat.

"Come on all you big strong men," she sang to herself in a reedy voice. She checked the mustard jar to make sure that the mantis was still alive, and then joined her brother.

Skeet kicked the trailer's left tire hard, as if trying to make it burst.

"Son," the assistant said, "them tires is sure to hold up. You can stop testing them now." The assistant turned to their mother and talked without pause. Uncle Myron stood to the side, saying nothing, his hands in his pockets. "This hitch will haul a semitruck without any trouble," the assistant said as he slipped a large bolt through a slot behind the tow ball. "I could of made you a present of the smaller hitch, but it's better to go with heavy duty." He lifted a drill, and even after he threw the switch that started its deafening racket, he continued to talk as he bored a second hole in the New Yorker's bumper. He turned off the machine, dropped a bolt in the hole, and twisted a nut underneath. "Son, you're going to break your toe on the sidewall if you keep that up."

The assistant tilted the trailer hitch forward, fitting it over the tow ball. "This is how you lock it, Mrs. Terhune," he said. "Easy as pie." He stood, leaned on the trailer hitch with all his weight, and bent an interlocking piece over the ball. "You could get hit by a cement truck and this will still hold."

"Well, let's hope that doesn't happen!" Ida tittered.

"Where you all headed?" the assistant asked.

Ida began, "A long way—"

"They're taking a one-week trip to Pensacola," Betty interrupted.

"That's right," the assistant said. "Harlan told us his wife needed this nice big camper for a little trip along the Gulf Coast."

Ida saw Harlan in her mind's eye, standing before her, dressed in the straw-colored suit he had worn before they married. "You're my queen," he told her. "I'd move mountains for you."

"Harlan helped find this trailer?" Betty asked. No doubt he

looked forward to bringing Carlotta to his house while his family was gone. Harlan probably assumed that a week's vacation would cool things off and Ida would beg him to come home. He wouldn't expect in a million years that Ida would even think of running off. Neither would anyone else, for that matter.

"This trailer's going to last all the way to Pensacola?" Betty asked.

The assistant shook his head, as if saddened by her lack of faith.

Harlan will never let me have anything again, Ida thought. Fear curled in her stomach like an old cat, familiar and secretive. Whatever happened, she would not let Skeet and Sherry know how frightened she was at the prospect of being on her own. Why, I'm scared stiff, she thought. I'm afraid of the whole world.

After Ida Terhune left the car dealership, she drove slowly, getting used to the weight of the trailer at the back of the car. The first thing she saw on the road was the last thing she had hoped to see. There, in the distance, was Harlan, with his arm wrapped around a female shape. He was picking his way among the weeds and rocks and had not noticed the approaching New Yorker. Betty Trombley leaned forward.

"Children," Ida said, to distract them, "that's the building where your grandfather, my father, was first introduced to Huey Long." She pointed to a large brown house with a sagging porch she had shown them many times before. "My father had just come up here from Cameron, and Huey Long approached him and said, 'Roy Daigle, you're such a handsome devil, I could use you in my campaign.' After that, they were off to the races."

Betty Trombley smirked at the brown house and watched Harlan Pinkerton and Carlotta. It always irritated her when Ida talked about the years her father had been a right-hand man to Huey Long. Roy Daigle had been dirt poor when he first moved to Baton Rouge from Cameron, and he was filthy rich by the time of Long's assassination. Ida's father had been almost fifty when she was born, and he seemed to speak with the voice of history when he related his autobiographical accounts of his days with Huey Long. Nevertheless, Roy Daigle had surely exaggerated his importance in Long's administration. Ida's delight in her father's stories was ridiculous.

"'Mr. Long,' my father said, 'I'd be honored. But I'd rather have you come work for me in *my* campaign.'" Ida laughed, but the children, missing the joke or not finding it funny, did not join her.

Skeet and Sherry watched two brindle hounds, wandering loose in front of the brown house, snuffle under the front steps. When the dogs disappeared behind the porch, the children faced forward and saw their stepfather and a woman walking toward them on the road. Sherry noted that the woman's green wraparound dress tied over one hip and that she was slender and wasp-waisted, with a tall, winding hairdo. Her necklace glittered in the hot sun.

The trailer seemed to pull the car to the right, and suddenly the New Yorker was bearing down on both their father and the woman. A branch lying in the road exploded upward and hit the car, then thumped against the side of the trailer.

"Betty," Ida cried, "let go of the wheel!"

Harlan and the woman jumped into the roadside ditch. Skeet and Sherry turned and watched them scrambling up the roadbank.

"I can't believe you did that, Betty!" Ida said, looking in the rearview mirror.

"Oh, they'll survive," Betty answered.

Ida drove on in silence to Betty's house. When they arrived, Betty turned around to Skeet and Sherry, her fish earrings glittering.

"You all have a nice adventure. Now, you know your mother is going to drive along the coast to Biloxi, then you'll continue on to Pensacola. Let's discuss rules. Out in Pensacola in the ocean, there's two sets of underwater dunes.

Past the first dunes are the barracudas, and past the second are the sharks. You may swim out as far as the barracudas, but you are not under any circumstances to swim past the second dunes, where the sharks are. Is that understood?"

"Yes, ma'am," Sherry said. Skeet snickered.

"We're going to stop in New Orleans and spend the night at Aunt Rosine's, and we'll head off tomorrow morning," Ida told Betty. "We'll stay in Pensacola about four days, and I'll call you after that." She did not tell the children that from there they would be driving along the eastern seacoast, stopping at Civil War monuments and Washington, D.C., and then heading north for their final destination. She wouldn't mention Jersey City just yet.

"Rosine?" Betty said. "Does she know what you're up to? She won't approve of this at all, Ida."

"Don't stare at me like that," Ida answered. "I'm not a crazy person." This was one of Ida's favorite phrases; she used it constantly, and Betty was never quite sure what she meant by it. "I'll handle Rosine just fine," Ida concluded.

"I don't know," Betty said, looking over Ida's head. "Well, you have directions to my apartment."

Betty had known Ida since fifth grade, and important turning points in their personal histories bound them together. When they were twelve, Betty had taken Ida exploring in an abandoned house, where they found the decomposing body of a local politician for whom the police had been searching. In the same year, Ida introduced her friend to her father, Roy Daigle, who smiled at Betty with his yellow teeth and, to Ida's dismay, pulled Betty onto his lap and offered her a puff on his cigar. Six years later, after she had pried out of Ida the story of her mother's death in childbirth, Betty convinced Ida to accompany her to a respectable yellow house where a doctor gave Betty an abortion that almost killed her. When Ida married her first husband, Dewey, Betty dressed in pale apricot and acted as bridesmaid. Betty sat by Ida's side at the hospital during Ida's three miscarriages and attended the births, ten months apart, of both her children. Betty was the first person Ida called when Dewey and her father died in a steamboat explosion while

Ida was still pregnant with Sherry. And when Ida announced her decision to remarry only nine months after Dewey's death, it was Betty who made Ida promise not to tell her new husband that she would inherit $7,500 after Roy Daigle's estate was parceled out to his debtors.

"It isn't much," Betty had counseled, "but it's enough to help you escape, if you ever have to."

"Escape what?" Ida had asked her.

Betty slid out of the New Yorker, circled the car, and leaned in Ida's window. Betty squeezed Ida's hand and whispered, "Mrs. Terhune, whatever you do is fine with me."

"Don't keep assuming I'll chicken out," Ida answered. She honked at a truck backing the wrong direction down the one-way street and headed toward the highway.

◆ Home

On July 24, 1982, Ida Terhune left everything behind but her children, four large suitcases, and her 1970 Chrysler New Yorker. Among the things she relinquished were a house on Tulip Street with two enormous mimosas in the front yard; a backyard with an ancient, exotic rose garden; rooms furnished with antiques and twenty-seven ebony crucifixes collected by the house's previous owner (twenty-eight if you counted the one over the bathroom door, missing the head and both arms); an entire year's supply of crab apple jam and pickled walnuts, her husband's favorites; and finally, a seven-year marriage and her husband, Harlan Pinkerton, the only things outside the confines of her home that Ida Terhune considered hers.

By the time the New Yorker was halfway to New Orleans, the children and Ida were all in good spirits. The highway spread out clean and black, and Lake Pontchartrain ran toward the New Yorker and backed off as they raced along. Ida maneuvered her nineteen-foot vehicle and its trailer gracefully. She reminded herself that she had always been an excellent driver. The New Yorker was as much a part of her as some shelled animal's house was inseparable from it.

Sherry, in the back seat, had taken out the praying mantis. It clung to her shirt like a tieclip.

Skeet had deposited his walking stick in the mustard jar, and climbed into the front seat to navigate. Even on an ordinary day, he loved plotting out courses he had taken: his room was cluttered with hand-drawn maps showing shortcuts to the drugstore, dirt trails leading to the highway, and secret paths into backyards enclosed by walls fringed with cut glass. Now he held on his lap a map of Louisiana, Mississippi, Alabama, Georgia, and the top of Florida and examined the route his mother had charted with a red marker, from Baton Rouge to Pensacola.

Ida fiddled with the radio levers until she found a station without static. A weathercaster predicted that a germinating hurricane off the Gulf Coast would die down before it hit Biloxi. A disk jockey played "If I had a ship, I'd sail away," for a boyfriend in jail. A woman called in to talk with the disk jockey and said that if another woman stole her husband, she'd shoot the woman but not her husband, because he didn't have any sense. This was followed by a talk show in which a local reporter interviewed the wife of a man sought by the police for swindling widows out of their money and then killing them.

"The day I found that box," the interviewed wife began, "I was clearing out the garage. I don't know what made me open it. Maybe it was just dumb luck, maybe it was fate. Inside the box was a green garbage bag, and inside that was a scrapbook. And in the scrapbook, photographs. With the photographs were mementos, notes written to him: 'Honey, this little gift is to show you that I appreciate how you've changed my life.' Father's Day cards, things like that. And then there were the snapshots of him." Now the woman interviewee's voice took on a strained, anxious pitch. "In one picture, he wore a tuxedo with a red cummerbund; in another, blue jeans, a bandanna tied around his forehead; in the next, a businessman's suit; in the fourth, he looked like a professor, dressed in a herringbone tweed. On each page was a different woman standing next to him, a society woman, a hippie girl, a housewife, a smart-looking lady seated at a piano. It was as if he had been trying to make of himself what each woman might have wanted. Over the face of each one, he had drawn a black X. And then there was a picture of me. Me and him at the Kiwanis Club annual dinner. He had drawn a black X over me too."

This was the last thing Ida wanted to hear about—all the eligible men who would be lurking out there, ready to take advantage of a woman on her own.

"He was a paradox," the interviewed wife said. She pronounced this fancy word in a self-conscious manner. Ida believed the woman had used "paradox" incorrectly. Ida had never liked the word, in any case, and did not use it herself. It sounded foreign. And the idea that a thing could be its opposite was so nonsensical that Ida could not imagine anyone ever needing to use the word, except to draw attention to herself. Ida had never spoken "paradox" aloud since Sister Florence had assigned it for vocabulary in eighth grade.

"Yes, he was a walking paradox," the woman on the radio pressed. Ida switched off the volume. It was for this reason that neither Ida nor the children heard any further reports about the progress of the hurricane until later that day.

"We can drive into Biloxi and take a look at the house where your father was born," Ida said.

"Stepfather," Sherry answered. Recently Skeet had started correcting Ida when she called Harlan his father, and Sherry had begun copying Skeet, as she did in everything.

Skeet did not respond.

"Would you like that, honey?"

"Mississippi is just a spot of grease on this map," Skeet answered. "We can get right through it in about ten minutes."

Despite Ida's efforts, Skeet and Harlan had a problematic relationship. Harlan ignored Skeet, and Skeet, Ida had to admit, wholeheartedly hated Harlan. During her whirlwind remarriage, Ida had had such high hopes that Harlan would warm up to the children.

Harlan Pinkerton had first taken an interest in Ida at her father's and first husband's funeral, when she had been big as a house with Sherry, on the very verge of giving birth. She had feared her water would break right over her father's and Dewey's graves. Beside her, Skeet, barely ten months old, had twisted and wiggled and whimpered in Betty's arms.

This was when the most embarrassing moment of Ida's life occurred: as she rose to throw a handful of earth on Dewey's casket, she lost her balance, her stomach pitching her forward toward the grave's mouth as if she were one of those hysterical widows who wanted to be buried with their husbands. From nowhere, Harlan Pinkerton appeared, grabbed her arms from behind, and steadied her on her feet.

"Whoa there, girl," he said, patting her back as if gentling an unbroken horse. Ida had mistaken him for one of the funeral parlor men, he was so well-dressed and polite. But when he gazed at her over his beaky nose, telling her, "Come sit down over here by me, pretty lady," the panic that had hardened and lodged under her rib cage at the news of her husband's and father's deaths shifted slightly inside Ida. She followed Harlan Pinkerton to one of the folding chairs. He fanned her with his homburg hat while a flurry of women surrounded her. Thick graying hair nestled over his forehead, reminding Ida of a dove's breast.

When Sherry was born, a week later, Harlan Pinkerton came to visit Ida at the hospital. At first, he made her feel uncomfortable. She worried that he had some perverse attraction to pregnant women. But then he introduced himself as a business associate of Ida's father, the late Mr. Daigle; he had worked with Ida's father since the day Harlan and his brothers arrived together in Baton Rouge from Biloxi. He had come to the funeral, he said, because he knew how Roy Daigle had loved his daughter and would have wanted Harlan and everyone else to look after her. Ida relaxed when she heard this. After she was discharged from the hospital, Harlan visited frequently, and her new life built itself around his arrivals like a pearl around sand.

Ida's first husband, Dewey Terhune, had not prepared her for Harlan. Dewey had been a childhood sweetheart, a quiet man who liked to spend his weekends hunting small game with his brother, Porter, and their coonhounds. "Why do you want to hunt raccoons and possums, things you can't even eat?" Ida would ask him when he called her long distance from small southern Louisiana towns, his hounds baying spookily in the background. "You should be here with me. If you really want a raccoon, why don't you just leave a can of garbage behind the house?" Over the years, Dewey had withdrawn more and more into himself, as if he were afraid of her.

Harlan, on the other hand, radiated a belief in his own mightiness and treated Ida like a flower he might bruise if he touched her too roughly. He was thirteen years older, almost from another generation, and when they went on walks, he took her by the elbow to help her over curbs. He sang to her in his easy accent, Baton Rouge city talk oiled over Biloxi: *Ida, I I-dalize ya.* When he introduced her to his friends over dinner as "Roy Daigle's pretty daughter," he hovered at her side, proudly, as if she were something valuable he could not get enough of.

One day, he announced to her that he had made a killing while speculating in real estate: a client, an old widow in a decorous house on Tulip Street, had died during the night, and he could place a down payment on her property for a song. Harlan gave Ida a tour through the house that afternoon, pointing to the high-posted cherrywood bed with its matching footstool, the crystal jars full of expensive candies shaped like folded ribbons, the hand-painted wallpaper, the dark, expensively upholstered furniture, and the grim ebony crucifixes in every room.

When Ida told Betty he had proposed to her there in the

widow's house, Betty looked at her strangely and said, "Harlan Pinkerton? Have you met his family? Just don't tell him about the money your father left you. If Harlan walks out on you, he won't have to pay child support, you know. Unless he adopts Skeet and Sherry, which I doubt he will. Just do it for Skeet and Sherry." Betty then made Ida promise to keep her small inheritance a secret. Thereafter, Betty had pressed further. "Christ, Ida, I should have known—you always did need to be rescued by somebody. But Harlan Pinkerton? What does he want with you, a woman with two babies, anyway? He must be up to something. The Pinkertons are lower than snakeshit, Ida."

For years, the two women did not speak with each other. Ida sold the modest home where she had lived with Dewey, used the proceeds to make a down payment that covered something over half the price of the Tulip Street house, and married in a courtroom, without a bridesmaid.

After the wedding, Harlan began bringing his business cronies home. He would lead them, as if he were a realtor making a sales pitch, through the house, ending in the nursery containing his new bride and family, where he would linger, receiving praise for his generosity in taking on a young widow with two children already. But when the guests were gone, Harlan retreated from his home. He preferred to roam loose in his own vast world, which Ida could not begin to understand, peopled by hard-drinking real estate men, lawyers and small-fry politicians, and Harlan's brothers and cousins—a loud, backslapping, winking, wolfish, leering crew.

Dewey Terhune's children were the only thing that made Harlan feel uneasy. He kept his distance from Ida's babies. Harlan demurred at the suggestion of adoption and offered no resistance when Ida told him she would continue calling herself Ida Terhune, so that she and the children had the same surname, if he did not give the children his own. For a long time she hoped the birth of a new baby would strengthen her marriage, but Ida never conceived again, and Harlan refused to see a doctor.

The living room was off limits to the children as they grew up: Harlan would reprimand Ida if he noticed tracks on the pale-green carpet or found that the ribbon candy in the crystal jars on the sofa-side tables had been pilfered. He seemed to view the children as diminishing him and grudgingly gave Ida money for their needs. He asked Ida to do some typing for his real estate business while she stayed home with Skeet and Sherry, and she felt as if she were earning her keep, obligated to pay him back for sheltering her.

But then, in her first five years with Harlan, when Ida was caring constantly for her two small children, she hardly had time to think, much less judge her marriage. Everything that had mattered to her before grew dim. She heard that Betty Trombley had married and moved north. Exhausted from doting on the children all day and Harlan every evening, Ida could not find the energy to meet new friends. Harlan resented Ida's friendship with Dewey's brother, Porter, and his wife, Rosine, whom Ida had seen almost every weekend during her first marriage, and so she restricted her contact with her former in-laws to phone calls and infrequent holiday visits. And even when she called, Ida never ventured to tell Rosine her troubles. Ida thought it an act of disloyalty for a wife to complain about her husband, and Rosine surely would have agreed.

In the end, Ida settled for occasional talks with her neighbor Honey Perkins. But Honey, a willowy blonde married to a trusts and estates lawyer and prone to gossip, seemed to relish any expression of dissatisfaction from Ida, rather than offer direction. What Ida craved was a friend who would sort through her bewilderment and advise her exactly what to do next. Except for weekly grocery runs and shopping trips, Ida rarely set forth into the world outside Tulip Street. When she did, she felt a panicky desire to return home as quickly as possible.

Once, while shopping for the children's clothes in a nearby mall, Ida glimpsed a tall woman wearing an ankle-length orange dress and a wide belt studded with turquoise.

At first, Ida mistook the woman for Betty Trombley, but then she reminded herself that Betty had departed years before. At that moment, and later, when the woman passed Ida several times in the mall, she was seized by a sense of her own isolation and loneliness so overpowering that she had difficulty breathing. She had to sit down at a pizza parlor, where she felt obligated to order something although it was far too near the children's dinnertime. She had never had pizza before and pronounced it "pissa" until Skeet corrected her.

The next day, Betty Trombley knocked on the door, wearing the same turquoise belt over a purple jumpsuit. Her nails were manicured with purple polish, and the eyes of peacock feathers stitched into beadwork dangled from her earlobes. She announced that she would be staying with her family in Baton Rouge for the summer before returning to Jersey City, which she now called home. Without waiting for Ida to invite her in, Betty Trombley walked through the house, making fun of the well-preserved antiques and guffawing at the ebony crucifixes.

"Is your husband visiting Baton Rouge with you?" Ida asked.

"Who?" Betty answered. She waved her hand dismissively. "We split up years ago. We were only married for three weeks."

"I'm sorry to hear that," Ida told her.

"Has anyone ever walked on this?" Betty Trombley asked, pointing at the living room carpet and testing it with her toe before setting a dusty sandal on the pale-green pile carpeting. She lifted the lid to the crystal candy jar, took a handful of ribbon candies, ate two, and said, "These are really weird. I can't even figure out what flavor they are. No, you know what it is? They taste like someone left an old cigarette in the jar and the stale tobacco smell soaked in. How old are these, anyway?" She stuffed the rest in her pocket. She told Ida that the living room's velvet settee reminded her of "a coffin with the lid open, just what Dracula would crawl out of," and when Ida showed her the high, four-poster cherrywood bed, Betty broke into uncontained laughter. "Do you fuck on that thing?" she wanted to know.

Ida led Betty back into the living room. Sitting down on the edge of the settee, Betty said, "Christ, Ida, I've missed you." Before Ida could think of an answer, Betty added, "This house looks like no one lives here. Where are the kids?"

"Why, outside," Ida said. The children usually spent all day on the neighborhood streets and only came in for dinner before racing back out to play until bedtime.

"Well, that's good to hear," Betty answered. She opened the candy jar again and, despite her bulging pocket, helped herself to a new handful. She examined the candy jar's crystal top. "The Pinkertons are all like this," Betty said next. "Flashy. But they're real tight underneath. Harlan and his brother Myron and all the Pinkertons are shrunken up inside. You know what I mean? What's the word I'm looking for? *'Smallhearted.'* " Betty looked right at Ida when she said this, as if hoping for a fight.

"The Pinkertons," Betty continued, "are the kind of people who think that every time they do something for someone, they've been suckered somehow."

Ida did not ask Betty to leave.

"Ida, when I saw you yesterday in the mall, I hardly recognized you. You look like you've been under house arrest or something. You're skinny as a chicken, and what the hell is it with your hair? When's the last time you went to a beauty parlor?" Ida touched her hair, trying to recall.

"No offense, Ida, but this house gives me the creeps. Let's go somewhere."

When Skeet and Sherry appeared for lunch, Betty coaxed the Terhunes into an untrustworthy Pontiac she had borrowed from a "summer boyfriend" named Buzzy. Betty drove them to a bar on the edge of town, where she plied Sherry with Shirley Temples and danced with a cowboy who gave Skeet enough nickels to play four consecutive hours of ninepins on a miniature bowling alley in the back of the lounge.

All that summer, Betty would arrive at Ida's door and take her and the children out anywhere at all: to a dog show for lapdogs only, where overdressed matrons tugged weasely terriers around a grassy oval; to a burlesque theater in New Orleans, where men dressed as women danced the cancan; to the Tabasco sauce factory, where Betty showed Sherry how to clean a tarnished penny with hot pepper juice so that the coin glinted like new copper; to a fancy department store, where Betty and Ida spent all day trying on clothes they had no intention of buying, while the children made themselves rich filching nickels and dimes and even quarters from a fountain on the first floor.

When Betty left at the end of the summer, Ida felt bereft, but now her life had a course. Her years in the Tulip Street house seemed like a long tunnel from which she was emerging. Both children were in school, and Ida had empty hours on her hands. She began to think of leaving Harlan, and then she became consumed with the idea of escape, although she was uncertain she would ever summon the strength to actually run off.

She bought an atlas and plotted several different routes from Baton Rouge to Jersey City. She researched in the public library all the Civil War sites she would pass if she traveled north, and imagined taking the children to each one and explaining the history that had unfolded there. She checked the bank account where she had kept her father's money, untouched, for seven years, more out of deference to his memory than because she had believed Betty Trombley's words of caution. Ida shopped in obscure parts of New Orleans, where she bought things essential to travel—compasses and heavy-duty raincoats, a durable four-part luggage set on sale, a portable cup that snapped down into a circular case, a Swiss Army knife, a canteen covered in khaki material, and various unbreakable containers for holding shampoo, toilet water, and hand lotion.

During the year, Ida talked constantly to Betty on the telephone. Betty promised to visit Ida in Baton Rouge for two weeks the following summer. When Ida announced that she had determined to relocate to Jersey City, Betty was encouraging: she mailed Ida a safari hat for her thirty-eighth birthday. When Ida wavered, confiding that she had no employment record at all and no job skills other than typing, Betty reassured her.

"Jersey City is not a meritocracy," Betty said. "A dead German shepherd could get a job working for the city government. We'll find you something."

Ida even set a departure date for the morning after Betty would be flying home. If Betty doubted Ida, she never showed it. Inwardly, Ida continued to feel that she was merely going through the motions of escape, and she still could not believe that she would actually leave when the time arose. Even when she felt bravest, the mere thought of her Tulip Street home seemed to pull her back, like a whirlpool, to the center of her life with Harlan. But her plans for flight, whether or not they were real, had become the sustenance of her daily life.

At the end of June, Honey Perkins, whom Ida had neglected for months, called her on the telephone.

"I don't know how to tell you this, but someone has to," Honey began. "All of Baton Rouge knows that Harlan's seeing a woman named Carlotta Stroke. He's getting so careless that he's showing up with her in public." Her words "All of Baton Rouge" shocked Ida as much as the content of what she was hearing. How could all of Baton Rouge know if Ida didn't? Wasn't she part of the city she lived in?

Ida looked up Carlotta Stroke in the phone book: the name seemed familiar. Ida remembered the Stroke family from high school. Dewey and his brother, Porter, and Betty had been in classes with some of the Stroke girls, who had reputations for being trashy and foul-mouthed. Dewey, Porter, and Betty had been considered a little trashy too, Ida also recalled. The address listed in the phone book was only a few blocks away, in a boarding house run by an old man who innocently showed Ida into Carlotta's rooms when Ida identified herself as a visiting cousin. (Who would ever suspect Ida Terhune, in her navy-blue pantsuit and deflating bouffant hairdo, of criminal mischief?)

Left alone to snoop, Ida felt confused. Carlotta Stroke's

was the kind of place Ida would have liked to live in: bright and cheery, with green gingham curtains on the windows and pretty crocheted knickknacks on the tables of a cozy living room. The queen-sized bed in the small bedroom was low and modern, with a Posturepedic mattress and a fat quilt the color of beeswax.

There was barely a sign of Harlan anywhere, except for a bedside photograph: Harlan at a picnic to which Ida had not been invited. He looked as handsome as a politician, with his senatorial smile and white linen suit. Next to the picture, dwarfing it, was a curious object: an ostrich egg painted with a miniature scene of a farm surrounded by fields of sunflowers.

All day, since she had listened to Honey Perkins, Ida had been waiting for some feeling to fill her, anger or jealousy at least, but what she felt now was admiration. Somehow, Lotta Stroke had managed to remain unscathed by Harlan. Her home belonged to her, while there wasn't a room in the Tulip Street house that felt like Ida's. Maybe this is what I should have done all along, she told herself. I should have made my own home and only let him inside to visit.

Before Ida left, she slipped the painted eggshell into her purse.

Later that day, Honey Perkins called back. "What will you do, Ida?" she pried.

"I'm going to ask Harlan to move out for a while. And then, when I collect myself, I'm going to leave with the children." As she said it, Ida felt disappointed that the departure she had been planning so long in secret would be interpreted as a reaction to Harlan's infidelity.

"Leave your house?" Honey Perkins asked. "Boy, I wouldn't walk out on a place like that for the world. I'd hire the best New Orleans lawyer I could find and sue that Pinkerton for every stick of property he thinks he owns."

Ida told Honey her plan to leave Baton Rouge, but as she spoke, Ida doubted her own words. Her plot seemed ridiculous. After she hung up the phone, Ida wrote a note to Harlan and tacked it in an envelope to the front door. That evening, he must have lingered on his doorstep and read his wife's message, which said:

Harlan—

What you are doing is immoral. You may not enter this house until you stop seeing Miss Stroke.

Sincerely,

Ida

Harlan had not been home since.

◆ Coonhounds

Uncle Porter and Aunt Rosine were the children's favorite relatives, but Aunt Rosine did not look happy to see them as the New Yorker turned up Prytania Street in New Orleans. Ordinarily, when the children visited Rosine and Porter at Thanksgiving and Easter, Rosine ran down the steps to greet them. Now she stood on her front porch, frowning, her arms akimbo, her eyes on the trailer as the New Yorker parked beside the house.

Uncle Porter was in the front yard, leaning into a wheelless station wagon, where he kept two coonhounds penned during the daytime. A large oak tree bent over the station wagon, dappling it in shadows, that rushed over the car's surface like running water. Elephant ear plants and moonflower vines grew around and over the car, and a thicket of vegetation spread back from the station wagon to the street. The battered old pickup Porter drove sat baking in the sun.

A sign in the house's front window read:

> PORTER TERHUNE WILL FIX ANYTHING
> EVEN REFRIGERATORS
> ALSO WILL FIX SEWING MACHINES
> AND VACUUM CLEANERS

The house leaned forward on its foundations, as battered as Porter's pickup and shucking large flakes of yellow paint onto the surrounding foliage.

Porter shut the station wagon door and waved at Ida and the children. Rosine remained on the front porch. She was wearing her work clothes: a white dress printed with dancing rows of corn on the cob. Aunt Rosine worked as regional manager for the Corn Dog Paradise chain. It was her job to travel to Corn Dog Paradise franchises all over Louisiana and Mississippi to ensure that they met designated standards regarding the age of frying oils and the number of weevils allowed in a bag of cornmeal. She was away a lot of the time, and Ida could not approve. Rosine also made more money than Porter, who had been laid off from his job as a security guard at Maison Blanche and now eked out an income from his repair business.

The corn ears on Rosine's dress had women's faces and skirts made out of corn husks, and when Rosine finally stepped down onto the walk, the corn women seemed to scuttle out of her way with fear. "There's a letter here for you from Harlan," Rosine said. "What's going on with Ida?"

"You come let the dogs say hi to you," Uncle Porter told the children, opening the station wagon door and holding it ajar. Skeet and Sherry rushed to the car to pet the coonhounds, who sprang at them, wiggling uncontrollably, insane with affection and moaning in low, melodic voices.

"How come the dogs got to stay in the car?" Skeet asked.

"Can't afford a fence," Uncle Porter answered. Uncle Porter was a tall, heavyset man with a long face and a high, square forehead that reminded Sherry of the Frankenstein father, Mr. Munster, on television. When Sherry leaned against him, she barely came up to his hip.

"Maybe you should leave that jar outside for now," Porter told Sherry. "Rosine's nuts about bugs." Sherry took the mustard jar, which now harbored both the mantis and the walking stick, back to the New Yorker.

"At least tell Skeet and Sherry hello," the children heard their mother say.

"Skeet and Sherry, get on inside, out of the heat," Rosine called. Uncle Porter shut the station wagon door and cut a path through the vegetation to the house.

"I want to be tall," Sherry said.

"Oh, no you don't, honey," Aunt Rosine answered as she let the children and their mother inside. "All of the Terhunes are tall like Dewey, even Porter's cousin Clara. And for her, it's just a tragedy: she never married even though she's pretty as anyone. It was the same thing with Betty Trombley. There isn't a man on earth who'd want to walk down the street with a woman who's six foot two. I'll never forget when we were in school and Betty's height started coming on her. She used to stand every day for a half hour with a heavy rock on her head, because we thought it would keep her from growing. And she drank coffee and smoked too, to see if it would stunt her growth."

Porter had a hard time thinking of Betty Trombley as self-conscious about her height or anything else.

Sherry imagined herself growing until she was larger even than Betty Trombley, too big to fit inside the Tulip Street house, towering over Tulip Street and looking down on its tiny inhabitants.

As the children walked through the front hallway, they heard their aunt say, "Jersey City? Where's that?"

"It's where the famous Carpentier-Dempsey match was fought in '21," Porter told her in a joking tone, but Aunt Rosine did not respond.

Lowering her voice, the children's aunt asked, "Who's the man, Ida?"

"What?" their mother answered.

"Who are you leaving him for?" Rosine continued in a whisper.

"Oh. Well, it's not that kind of thing. I guess I'm just leaving him for me."

"You little fool," Aunt Rosine snapped.

"Come down here into the basement where it's cool, Skeet and Sherry," Uncle Porter said. "I got a secret to show you."

They descended the basement stairs. The air was rich with the smells of epoxy, rust remover, and machine grease. Broken appliances lay on every surface, surrounded by the tools needed for their repair. Clock radios, vegetable slicers, an electric typewriter, and a lady's electric razor were herded together on a battered Ping-Pong table; a newly patched vacuum cleaner nozzle coiled around a wire spool and snaked over the back of an armchair; hammers, pliers, and wrenches hung, batlike, upside down everywhere, on nails driven into the walls; a black, foot-pumped sewing machine rested between cement blocks, its needle tongue, fragile as a moth's proboscis, hovering in midair, the machine's metal parts polished with oil, its gilt filigree painstakingly retouched.

"All us Terhunes is pack rats," Porter told the children.

Skeet and Sherry watched Porter arrange bottles containing a clear liquid on a shelf over the basement sink. He took one down and opened it for the children to smell. Sherry held her face over the jar.

"Hooo!" she said. Skeet slid his nose over the rim and breathed in deeply. The odor burned his nostrils.

"That's home-brewed corn liquor," Uncle Porter said. "A policeman buddy of mine raided a still near Shreveport and saved me some of the proceeds. Look at it." Porter held the jar up to the light. "It's the only thing on earth that's clearer than water." The liquid sparkled and glittered like the ocean on a hot day. "You can do everything with this. Clean grease off a carburetor, soak a paintbrush. Step on a nail, you can disinfect your foot sole. Only one thing you can't do with it—drink it," he concluded.

"It will kill you?" Skeet asked.

"It sure will," Porter said. "But not for the usual reasons.

Let me show you." He squatted and poured some of the liquid on the basement's cement floor. He pulled a kitchen match from his shirt pocket, struck it on the floor, and said, "Stand back." He lit the pool of liquid, and it flared orange and white and blue.

"See that? See how it burns blue? That's a sign corn liquor has lead in it. Lead's dangerous. If it don't kill you, it surely will make you stupid." The children watched the blue tongue of flame lap the cement, now almost disappearing, now extending upward and curling over the white center above it. When the flame had died down, Uncle Porter drew two more kitchen matches from his pocket and, handing one to Skeet, said, "Now you try it."

He pulled Skeet toward him, embraced him with his left arm, took Skeet's right hand in his massive yellow tobacco-stained fingers, and showed Skeet how to strike the match against the pavement. Porter's warm breath tickled Skeet's nape. Skeet lingered a moment in his uncle's arms before he lowered the match and touched it to the alcohol. His uncle's embrace felt at once wonderful and strange: Skeet had rarely known a grown man to hold him, and he savored the sensation in him, a blossoming he had no words for. He touched the match to the cement, and a blue flame flowered from the floor.

"Man who operated that still must have used lead tubs or pipes," Uncle Porter said.

Across the flame, Sherry, her green eyes glittering blue, watched her brother and Uncle Porter. Porter pulled Skeet closer to him, away from a burning trickle of alcohol near Skeet's shoe. Sherry skirted the fire's edge and leaned against Uncle Porter's right side.

"Now you, Ladybug," he said, holding out the other match. When he had poured a new puddle of liquor, Sherry set fire to it and watched a blue hand unfist and grasp at the air over it.

"You don't weigh more than a frog," Uncle Porter told her.

Sherry put the burned matchstick in her pocket.

She and Skeet heard Aunt Rosine and their mother arguing upstairs. A low baying arose outside the house.

"Those two are going to upset the dogs," Uncle Porter said.

He looked at the children for a moment, his hands in his pockets, and said, "Well, there's lots more down here." He walked to the back of the basement and riffled through a pile of wood scraps and papers. "This is nothing special," he said to himself, and then, "That old stuff? She must have stuffed it up here." He pulled down a cardboard box and muttered, "Oh, yeah, this is surely worth it," and dug around inside.

The children came up behind their uncle. He sorted through old pictures of himself as a boxer, leather-gloved, half naked, purple half-moons under his eyes. "You don't have to look at this junk," he said, but then stopped at one photograph and told them, pointing at his face, "That's how I got this nose." The children stared at the flat place where his nose angled off to the left.

"Here's what I'm looking for," he said, lifting a brown wrapper. He pulled out two thick pieces of cardboard and a thin gray square of paper, and then flipped the paper over for them to see: black corners held down a faded black-and-white photograph.

"This is your daddy," he said, handing the photograph to Skeet. Sherry looked over her brother's shoulder.

The picture showed a man kneeling on a grassy field, holding two coonhounds by their collars. The dogs' noses were black and prominent, but the man's face, bleached by sunlight and slightly out of focus, was barely discernible. Brown caverns marked his mouth and the shadows under his eyebrows.

"We don't have a lot of pictures of him. Dewey was camera shy. He'd cut up so much when your mother tried to take his picture that she just gave up trying. Skeet, you let your sister hold on to that for both of you," Porter said, passing the photograph to Sherry. "She'll take better care of it."

"How come Mama never talks about him?" Sherry asked.

"Oh, I don't know. I guess maybe she thought it would set off Harlan. He never liked us to see you all much."

Skeet pored over the photograph.

Uncle Porter put his hand on Skeet's shoulder and said, "If you was going off somewhere for a while, I sure would miss you both something fierce."

Skeet looked at Porter, puzzled, and said, "We're going to Pensacola. For my birthday."

"That's nice," said Porter. "It's pretty out that way."

Porter turned to Sherry. "When you was a tiny baby in your mother's stomach, your father used to talk to you. He would say, 'Be good now, stop kicking your mother, don't give her extra trouble.'" Uncle Porter took back the photograph and slipped it in the brown wrapping with two pieces of cardboard. "Put this somewhere where it won't get all bent." Sherry folded the wrapping carefully.

Skeet looked longingly at Porter.

"He loved the ground you peed on," Uncle Porter told him. "Let's go back outside and visit with the dogs."

As Skeet and Sherry climbed the stairs, the voices of Aunt Rosine and the children's mother grew louder.

"Why don't you open Harlan's letter?" Rosine said angrily.

"How did he even know I was coming here?" their mother answered in a quavery voice.

"He called and asked. Open the letter."

"I'm not going to give him the chance to try to talk me out of it."

"If you're that scared to hear him out, you must know how wrong you are," Rosine answered. "You're not thinking of Skeet and Sherry."

"Maybe staying is the worst thing for them." As Ida said this, she pictured her children in Harlan's house on Tulip Street, sidestepping away from him as he brushed against them, chilling the air around them. Why didn't I see this clearly before now? Ida wondered. He *haunted* us.

"Coming through!" Porter called. He led the children to the front door as their mother and Aunt Rosine, their mouths open, paused. Their mother was clutching a cream-colored envelope. When the screen door slapped shut behind them, the voices rose again.

Uncle Porter walked to the station wagon, and Skeet followed. Sherry opened the New Yorker's back door, unknotted her gold scarf, and laid the burned matchstick and the photograph inside. She looked at the station wagon, where her brother and Uncle Porter were petting the dogs, and then she backtracked to the house, opened the front door, and peered through the screen.

Her mother stood on one side of the table, her back to Sherry, and Aunt Rosine sat on the other.

"I don't care if he's going around with that skinny little rat with diarrhea," Aunt Rosine said. "All the women in that Carlotta girl's family sleep with everything that isn't nailed down. She won't hang on to him long. You can't just up and leave a good breadwinner. What will you raise the children on?" Aunt Rosine's forehead creased in the middle. "Even the twins have got more sense than you," she said.

"They're not twins. Why do you always call them that?"

"They act like it."

"Why are you trying to scare me? It took me forever to muster up the courage to leave."

"It don't take courage to run out on a marriage like yours. It takes pure stupid blindness. The truth—my heart goes out to you; I'm afraid for you. You've always been so spoiled and taken care of. You don't know any more than a child about supporting a family."

Uncle Porter called Sherry back to the station wagon. When she was only halfway there, her mother threw open the screen door and rushed toward the car. Aunt Rosine followed to the bottom step, stopped, and put her hands on her hips. The corn women on her dress danced, kicking their feet and laughing.

"It's time to leave," Sherry's mother called. "Into the car, you two." She sat down in the driver's seat and gunned the motor.

Uncle Porter let the dogs go, so that they loped past Sherry and leapt against the New Yorker. Skeet followed, lingering in the driveway until his mother said, "We have to get going, honey."

Porter opened the New Yorker's front door and guided

Skeet inside by his shoulder. Sherry crawled in the back. Porter leaned over Skeet and placed some crumpled bills in his mother's lap.

"Porter, I'm really all right. You don't need to give me this."

"It's only seventy dollars. I wish it was more, Ida," Porter said, and shut the door.

Ida opened her purse, stuffed the money inside, and then reached in her pocket and placed the cream-colored envelope on top of the money.

When she backed the New Yorker out of the driveway, the dogs galloped wildly around the car, bawling and lifting their noses high. Aunt Rosine remained on the steps and watched the New Yorker drive away. She wiped her eyes on her sleeve. Skeet and Sherry knelt backward on their seats and watched the dogs chase the car until Uncle Porter whistled them home.

◆ Hurricane Marguerite

As the New Yorker passed the first road signs for Biloxi, a large, hat-shaped cloud hovered over the scenery ahead of Ida Terhune. She turned on the radio. A local station was issuing storm warnings for small watercraft, and a weatherman explained the naming of hurricanes.

"Once there was this fella, in Australia I think it was, who named hurricanes after politicians he didn't like. That way he could bad-mouth them without getting in trouble. He could say things like politician so-and-so was 'causing great distress' or 'wandering aimlessly about the Pacific.' Well, now they just use ladies' names. Every year they start over and run through the alphabet. See, if the last hurricane began with a *B,* this one would have to be, say, Carol or Cynthia. See how it works?"

"Or Carlotta," Sherry volunteered, snickering. Ida looked

at her daughter in the rearview mirror. Sherry was sorting a pile of metal she had wrapped in a gold scarf. Could she know enough about Carlotta to resent her? Probably not.

"Or Cowhead. Or Coke Bottle," Skeet continued.

"What are you going to do with all that stuff, Sherry?"

"Keep it," Sherry answered. She lifted the mustard jar and tapped it. The mantis and the walking stick frantically butted their heads against the lid.

Ida blared her horn at an oncoming vehicle speeding as if it were being chased. "Why, he must be going eighty-five miles an hour," she said.

She looked out to sea. The tall cloud had darkened and thinned, but all around it, sunlight sparkled on the water. The sky tilted overhead like a man's lifted hat. She told the children, "I think the weather will be beautiful tomorrow."

Skeet kept his eye on the Gulf. He saw a dark-green thunderhead sucking the sky toward it, darkening and fattening. He saw, or thought he saw, the ocean hump at the horizon and then flatten.

"Maybe it's a hurricane out there," Skeet said.

"It certainly is *not,*" Ida answered. "The radio said that whatever storm is brewing is bound to die down over the ocean."

Skeet persisted. "I think we are going to all get killed."

"Oh, Skeet." Ida switched the radio to a local station playing country music. She noted to herself that there were surprisingly few cars on the coastal highway.

Sherry pressed her face against the back window. The cloud ahead of them thinned and stretched upward as if in response to her mother's pronouncement. A fan of sun rays spread open below the cloud.

"Have it your own way," Skeet answered, sighing.

Rain hammered on the cartop.

"The devil's beating at his wife's door," Ida told the children. She said this, without fail, whenever rain and the sun appeared at the same time.

A woman singer came on the radio, and Sherry joined her in a high, mewling voice. She sang melodramatically, mocking the song but also enjoying it. Ida felt awed by, and somewhat uncomfortable with, her daughter's proclivity for memorizing popular radio tunes.

"'I'm wild about your loving,'" Sherry piped. "'Got to have my fun.'"

A sudden wind tugged at the trailer. Ida turned deftly to the left until the trailer realigned itself. She drove for another thirty minutes through scattered showers. Lightning illuminated the tall cloud.

"A little rain won't spoil our trip," she said.

A radio announcer interrupted the music program to say that a hurricane was gathering off the coast between Biloxi and Mobile.

Skeet crossed his arms.

"That's just a warning for boats out to sea," Ida said.

Skeet looked toward the ocean, and now he was sure he saw a hump of water rise and settle along the horizon.

Sherry rolled down her window. A sultry wind sank into the air-conditioned car.

"Roll that back up, honey," Ida said. "Let's not let in the outside."

Sherry closed the window. Lightning flashed like a grasping hand from the tall green cloud, and for a moment Sherry wondered if she had actually seen or just imagined a glittering waterspout, slender and wasp-waisted, descend from the cloud, advance violently in a half-circle toward shore, and then disappear. She picked up her gold scarf and held it in her lap.

Water bucketed down on the windshield for almost twenty minutes.

The weatherman again interrupted a song. He opined that the approaching cyclone was headed straight for Biloxi.

Now the wind grabbed the car and wiggled it, and the New Yorker lurched to the side. Low green-and-purple clouds flocked toward the highway from the sea. Ida slowed the car.

"I can't keep straight on the road," she told the children. She turned the wheel all the way to the right, but the car continued to list to the center of the highway.

"It's the wind hitting the trailer crosswise," Skeet noted.

"You're going to have to unhitch it and leave it by the road." He sounded glad at the prospect.

"Skeet, that will hardly be necessary."

The announcer speculated that the hurricane would damage property for a hundred miles inland before losing momentum.

Ida slowed the car and pulled onto the road shoulder. "Show me the map, Skeet," she said, taking it from him and balancing it on the steering wheel. As she checked the map, hailstones hammered the windshield. "We can turn back and take I-59 inland."

"You'll never make it with the trailer," Skeet said.

Ida tried to turn the New Yorker around on the highway. As she pulled into the oncoming lane, a gust of wind socked the car and trailer, spinning them back into their original direction.

Ida turned up the radio, but static obscured an announcer's voice. "Don't be afraid," she said. Ahead on the road, she saw a green exit sign for Biloxi.

"We're not," Sherry answered. The mustard jar rolled across the floor at her feet. The walking stick and the mantis twirled inside the jar, clutching each other in a wrestlers' embrace.

"When Huey Long died," Ida said, "Judge Fournet and my father were with him. A young man with slick black hair approached them on the steps of the capitol building with a stubby black pistol in his hand. It was a hot night—this was before they had a.c.—and my father had removed his panama hat and was holding it. He always said he didn't know why, but he swiped at the man's pistol with his hat. The man shot Huey, and Huey gave a whoop and jumped like a hit deer. After he fell to the ground, my father bent over him and said, 'Don't be afraid, Kingfish, you'll pull through this fine,' and Huey said, 'I know no fear.'" Ida paused. "'I know no fear.' That's what he said."

The children had heard the story many times before. "But he died anyhow?" Skeet asked.

Abruptly, the trailer jumped up behind them and whipsawed in midair. Ida braked. The car shook as if in the jaws of a huge dog. Just as suddenly, the crosswind vanished and the car became still.

Ida maneuvered the New Yorker into a second U-turn and headed west. An ominous roaring rose on the car's Gulf side. Egg-sized hailstones shattered on the windshield, and the car again listed landward, the steering wheel seeming to lock in its rightmost position. Ida slowed the New Yorker but did not stop.

A burst of wind jolted the car from behind, and suddenly it seemed lighter. The children turned around in their seats, and Ida looked into the rearview mirror.

Delicately, the trailer rose in the air behind the New Yorker, shimmering in a sudden burst of sunlight, its metal siding iridescent as the green-and-purple chest feathers of a pigeon. It seemed to flutter ten feet off the ground, and then it soared seaward, steadily, perfectly level with the water. Below it, a creamy white ocean rose to meet a pale horizon. When the trailer was no bigger than a dove against the sky, the wind again slackened, as if appeased.

"It cost seven hundred dollars," Skeet told Sherry.

A few hailstones rattled halfheartedly on the windshield.

Now I've lost everything, Ida thought to herself. Absolutely everything. There's nothing left between me and the world. She slowed the car to a halt and shifted into neutral.

"What are you doing, Mama?" Sherry leaned forward on the fold-down armrest.

"Are we stopping here?" Skeet asked.

I can't do this to the children, Ida told herself. Whatever could I have been thinking? She was almost forty, ridiculously old to be setting forth on her own for the first time. Among the things she had never done in her life were: pay bills, apply for a credit card, and work for a salary. Ida shifted into drive and pressed the accelerator. She felt overwhelmed with relief to be heading back toward Louisiana.

She heard Harlan's voice on the day he took her home from the courthouse. "Ida," he whispered, "I'm the luckiest man in the world. You're the only thing left I needed. A pretty wife in a pretty little house."

To the south of the New Yorker, the sky cleared and then darkened. A torrent of rain washed over the car, obscuring Ida's view of the highway. Blurred shapes, pale and spectral, loped across the road ahead of her. Ida honked her horn and slowed the car again. As the windshield cleared, she saw Brahman cattle, white and humpbacked, move toward a clump of trees as if scraps of paper borne by the wind. It would be safer to turn north than to continue along the Gulf into New Orleans.

"Who's that? Ida? What did you come here for?" Harlan said. Now he sat on his brother Myron's desk, in an ivory summer suit. Myron, squatting on the ground outside the dealership, looked away toward the junkyard as if embarrassed for her. "It's none of your business where I've been. You think I'm a dog on a leash? Why'd you come up here dressed like that? Ida, you aren't half the princess you were the day I married you."

"It's a road," Skeet said.

"What, honey?" Broken branches and fence posts were strewn across the highway. When Ida drove over the debris, it felt as if someone were kicking the front of the New Yorker.

"It's the skinny little red road that goes up on the map."

Ida turned right and headed north.

Ida Terhune followed the interstate past Meridian, past the point where I-59 vanished into I-20, beyond Anniston and into Atlanta. When she arrived at Atlanta's outskirts, Skeet and Sherry were asleep. Ida had been driving eight hours, stopping only to feed the children at a Kentucky Fried Chicken in Birmingham. Ida had been farther north just once, as a girl, when her father had taken her to Washington, D.C. They had stayed in the same fancy hotel where her father had roomed with Huey Long. Ida's father told her that Huey had always greeted reporters in his pajamas. He had never been daunted by the world's opinion.

Ida hoped to stay in an equally grand hotel with her children in Atlanta, but the first few hotels where she stopped were full of people waiting out the hurricane before traveling south to the Gulf. The only vacancy she could find was at the Playboy Hotel.

The clerk at the hotel counter hesitated when he saw her: a dowdy woman followed by a little girl carrying a dirty yellow rag, and a boy with a jar full of bugs.

"This place ain't exactly designed for children," he said.

Ida broke into tears. "We almost got killed in the hurricane!" she told the clerk. "We're lucky to be here at all. Imagine a man not coming to the aid of a lone woman and two children!" Ida was embarrassed by the childish tone in her voice—even she could hear it. She felt a familiar sliding of embarrassment into shame, an impulse to hide somewhere dark and safe. Rosine was right, she thought. How am I supposed to look out for Skeet and Sherry when here I am acting like a spoiled little girl?

Nevertheless, her hysterics were rewarded. "Hey now, ma'am, hey now," the clerk said. "Let me help you with your bags."

"Where's your car, Buster Brown?" he asked Skeet.

Skeet took his mother's keys and escorted the clerk outside. When Skeet reached the New Yorker, he saw that it was badly mangled where the trailer hitch had been. The bumper looked as if a giant animal had taken a bite out of it.

"Hurricane tore our trailer right off the car," Skeet told the clerk.

The clerk admired the damage. "Christ in hell," he said, touching the ripped metal.

Skeet opened the trunk.

"Which one of these she want?" the clerk asked.

"Maybe just the big one on top," Skeet answered. The bottom suitcases were filled with things belonging to Skeet and Sherry. Skeet had known they would be moving when he saw his mother, thinking he was outside playing, enter his room and pack his set of Matchbox cars and his collection of hand-drawn maps.

The clerk hauled the suitcase into the lobby and led the Terhunes to a room that was like nothing any of them had ever seen. The two beds were large and round, surrounded by mirrors. Hot-pink shag carpeting covered the floors, walls, and even the ceiling.

"There's a Magic Fingers over there," the clerk said.

"What's that?" Sherry asked.

"It's to take the wiggle out of you," the clerk answered, winking at her as he closed the door.

"You two put on your pajamas and get on the bed, and I'll show you," Ida said. Sherry and Skeet hurried out of their clothes and into their pajamas. They lay down on the pink bedspread as Ida dropped a quarter into the machine on the night table. Sherry's eyes widened in astonishment when the bed began to vibrate.

"Earthquake!" Skeet said.

"What's this really for?" Sherry asked.

"It's to make people relax after a long, hard day." Ida reached for the bedside lamp.

"I'm scared. Don't shut it off yet," Sherry told her.

"I'll turn on the television for a night-light," Ida answered. She set the volume low to put the children to sleep and then switched off the lamp.

The late news showed pictures of Biloxi. "The hurricane campaigned inland," the anchorman said, "causing millions of dollars in damage." Skeet sat up and leaned forward to get a better view. Biloxi looked like a wood crate someone had kicked in. Houses were washing up in splinters on the beach, and stray dogs nosed around in the wreckage.

"Christ in hell," he said.

"Skeet!" Ida cried. "What a thing to say." When the Magic Fingers stopped, Ida lifted Sherry onto the other bed and tucked in both her children. "I love you more than I can bear," she whispered, kissing them on their foreheads. "Don't let the bedbugs bite." She brought Skeet a glass of water, lay down next to Sherry, and stared at the shag rug on the ceiling. Ida imagined couples in amorous positions above her, miraculously not falling. She pictured Harlan and Carlotta Stroke, belly to belly, Harlan biting his lip and screwing up his face as he customarily did when he was holding back.

The weight of Ida's lonesomeness hit her full force. She longed to be pressed against someone. But then, she was not sure it was Harlan she wanted to be pressed against. Why had she married him? Lying in her bed at the Playboy Hotel, she recalled the fear that had washed over her at Dewey's funeral as she had sat in her folding chair, ungainly in her maternity dress, thinking: No one will ever touch my breasts like that again. In a year, I won't even recall what it feels like. I'll just turn into a shriveled old prune.

Ida thought of the cream-colored letter in her purse. What had made her believe she would feel any different seven years later? That she would be able to lie in bed, night after night, solitary, self-widowed, aging into deeper and deeper loneliness? Rosine had said that Harlan would leave Carlotta eventually. And surely it was better to have someone, anyone, to touch than to have nothing at all.

"I was standing out here," a man on the television said. "And the gale come up and snatched that telephone pole out the ground like it was a pencil, and thowed it onto the road there, and then picked it up again and thowed it at my truck. Then the gale wandered over yonder and knocked down a house. I hid under my truck for hours, and all the while I was sure I was a dead man."

Ida switched off the television. Sherry and Skeet were both asleep. Ida pulled the pink spread around Sherry and slipped under the sheet.

When Ida awoke, a man stood a few feet from her bed, a tall shadow backlit by the bathroom light. For a few moments, she believed she was dreaming. Ida's dreams were often more vivid to her than her own life: the colors of things more vibrant, the characters who peopled them more dangerous or more forceful, and she herself always happier or sadder than she ever felt while awake.

"Harlan?" Ida asked.

The smell of stale beer filled the air in front of her. When Ida shook off a dream, fear grabbed her. She sat up, pulling the covers to her throat, and now saw, clearly, a man-shape at the foot of her bed: a chesty, square-shouldered man, nothing like Harlan. Ida looked at the clock dial beside her bed: it said 3:30. She reached her left arm protectively over Sherry.

"What are you doing in here?" she asked.

The man took a step backward. "Zenaida?" he answered.

Ida sat up. "Who are you? Why are you here?"

"I came in to fix the bathroom," the man said, holding up the silhouette of a sink pipe elbow in one hand.

I can't believe this, Ida thought. I've been through too much today already. For a moment, Ida willed the man to disappear. Then she said, "I think you should get out of here." Her words failed to form more than a whisper.

The man walked into the bathroom, closing the door partway behind him. She heard water running.

"What's he doing?" Skeet's voice rose in the darkness beside her. His voice expressed curiosity rather than fear.

"I said 'Leave'!" Ida called, loudly. The water turned off, and the man emerged from the bathroom.

"Skeet, honey, hand me the hotel phone on your bedside table," Ida said. "Can you feel it there, Skeet?" She heard him knock over his water glass.

The man opened the entranceway door, and slipped into the hall.

Ida jumped up and ran to the hallway, saw nothing, and then closed and bolted the door. The smell of stale beer lingered in the air outside the bathroom. She turned on the entranceway light.

"What did he want, Mama?" Skeet asked.

"I don't know, honey. Maybe he was looking for someone else. It's all right; go to sleep."

She covered Skeet up, toweled dry the bedside table, and called the hotel desk. Could she have left the door unlocked? Twice, she let the phone ring fifteen times, but no one answered. With each ring, she felt fear gathering in her, first as a vague anxiety, then growing to something larger, a controlled terror.

She would go back to Harlan and say, "I was wrong. How could I have been so foolish as to think I could make it without you?"

Dawn lit the window curtains. She took her purse into the

bathroom. She turned on the tub's faucet, pouring in the purple bubble bath supplied for hotel guests. Before she took off her nightgown to step into the water, Ida opened her purse and pulled out the letter from Harlan. She unfolded it slowly, thinking: I shouldn't look at this now; it will take away all my resolve. We've come so far. I can't let him persuade me to go home. She put the letter back into her purse and snapped it closed.

Then she reopened her purse, withdrew the letter, and read:

Dear Ida,

Don't think I don't know what you're up to. That little blonde down the street called and told me two weeks ago. And don't even pretend I have a mind to stop you. For seven years, I've put up with you judging every little thing I do, with your letting me know in every way how high and mighty and perfect you are, and how you don't like me or my buddies. You think I'm a bad husband, Ida, don't you? But next to you, who could ever feel good? You aren't going to get a goddamn dime out of me. I'm sick of supporting you and your children, and I put the house in Myron's name years ago, so don't even try to get title to it.

Love,
Harlan

Ida turned off the bathwater. Under the letter were some papers stamped *Myron Pinkerton, Process Server.* Ida saw they were divorce papers.

She clutched her purse against her stomach and returned to the bedroom. She picked up the telephone, removed a black address book from her purse, and dialed a number scrawled on the front page over a United States map divided by area code.

When Betty Trombley answered, Ida said, "This is Mrs. Terhune." No other words would come to her.

"Ida, is that you? Fuck a duck! I've been so damn worried!

I thought that hurricane wafted you all away. I've been sitting up kicking myself for letting you leave on that trip. Rosine called me."

Betty sounded so close, she could have been in the same room. Ida held the phone tightly. "Betty? Will you call her back for me? I don't want to talk to Rosine just now."

"Sure I will, Ida, sure I will. Where are you?"

"Atlanta."

"Atlanta? All the way up there?"

"You're going to laugh at me, Betty. I'm in the Playboy Hotel. The other hotels were filled up."

"The Playboy? You mean the one with the pink shag carpet on the ceilings?"

How did Betty know about the carpet?

"So you're still coming?" Betty asked, quietly, as if she were afraid of scaring away the answer.

"Yes. Yes, we are," Ida said. She felt Sherry turn over next to her. She lowered her voice. "The trailer blew off the car in the hurricane. We don't have it anymore."

"Small loss," Betty said. Then she added, "Sounds like a close call. You must have been scared shitless."

Sherry sat up on the bed, her gold scarf in her lap. Ida wondered if her daughter had been sleeping with the scarf. Carrying it with her, Sherry wandered into the bathroom. She leaned on the inside of the doorframe, to catch the rest of her mother's conversation.

When Ida thought her daughter was out of earshot, she said to Betty, "I guess we'll just stay in hotels all the way up to Jersey City. I'm still going to take the children to a beach somewhere, maybe in South Carolina."

"You'll like Jersey City, Ida," Betty answered. "It's the only place on earth as corrupt as Baton Rouge. You'll feel right at home here."

"Betty? It's such a relief to hear your voice. I feel so—I feel like a crazy person!"

Sherry ducked in the bathroom and snooped around. She took a sample of purple bubble bath, four miniature soap bars, and a bottle of cologne from beside the sink and wrapped them in a washcloth with a pink, bow-tied rabbit on it. She untied the yellow scarf and placed the washcloth on top of the items already in it. When she knotted the scarf, the ball it made was larger than a man's head.

Sherry untied the scarf again, sorted through all the objects inside, and removed the photograph that Uncle Porter had given her. She examined the dark caverns where her father's eyes must be and the dark hole next to his nose.

"Now don't you worry. I'll call you tomorrow," Sherry's mother said in the bedroom.

Sherry returned the photograph to its wrapper. All the faces she had seen in the past few days passed before her like pearls on a necklace: Uncle Myron's and his assistant's, and her stepfather's, with their bent crows' noses; the woman in the green wraparound dress; Rosine's narrowed eyes and the corn women dancing on her dress; Uncle Porter's friendly monster face, and the noses of his dogs, pressed against the station wagon's windows. Sherry sensed she was on the brink of losing something larger than she had a name for.

"Sweetheart, what are you doing in here?" her mother said, appearing at the bathroom door.

Sherry tied the scarf quickly, concealing the pink washcloth.

"My lord, look at that bundle of yours. You're going to become a hunchback, carrying that big old thing around." Ida turned on the faucet, splashed water on her face, and dried it with a hand towel. When she looked up, Ida Terhune saw her daughter's turtle-green eyes fastened on her.

"Where we going?" Sherry asked.

◆ ◆ Part II

JOSEPH

◆ Lords of the Land

From the throne of the raised barber's chair opposite her kitchen window, Betty Trombley liked to catch her landlord, Rupert Dixon, turning the corner of Jersey Avenue onto Grand Street. In this way, she could ensure that his visits never went unattended by strife. On the morning Ida Terhune would arrive in Jersey City, Betty watched Rupert and his son, Chicken, approach in their white Mercury Marquis with the flashing blue police light perched on the roof. Betty assumed they were coming to post an eviction notice on Henry Purdy's door.

The basement floor, where Henry lived, was flooded again. The storm sewers of Orestes Cleveland Road had backed up into Grand Street, and a foul-smelling water had forced its way into the rotting pipes of Betty's apartment building. Water ran down the steps to the basement hallway and on through to the lot behind the building. The lot was enclosed by a five-foot cement wall, which trapped the water, creating a smelly pond four feet deep and two hundred fifty feet square.

The stench of the water permeated everything. Even the fifth-floor tenants complained to Rupert Dixon that a noxious odor leaked from their kitchen and bathtub faucets. Betty Trombley had called the landlord regularly for weeks and had contacted the Health Department and the Division of Property Conservation, without results.

Henry Purdy had suspended walkways made from scrap wood over the sewer water in his basement hallway, running from the street entrance to his apartment and to those of the other basement residents. Before the walkways were laid, the building tenants had believed that Henry Purdy might be simpleminded or addled, perhaps because of his severely crossed eyes and his refusal to socialize. He was in his late twenties, had a forlorn, heart-shaped face, and supported himself doing odd carpentry jobs around the neighborhood.

However, after the floods came, the tenants began to think that Henry might be a genius, secretly, in the way of some people who appear stupid. Henry collected bricks from the vacant lot beside the building and laid dams at the thresholds of the basement apartments. The dams were attractive and ingenious. Each had a series of steps on one side, and a platform at the top big enough for a doormat, so that the basement tenants could walk up and jump down into their apartments without unusual effort, keep their feet dry even after heavy rains, and cease to worry about tides of sewer water soaking their living room carpets.

Shortly thereafter, Henry stretched a banner made from an old sheet across the side of the building:

RUPERT DIXON IS NOT A "LORD" OF THE LAND
(HE IS THE SCUM OF THE EARTH)
THIS IS NOT SOUTH AFRICA!!!!

Dixon retaliated by turning off Henry Purdy's water.

When Betty returned to Jersey City after visiting Baton

Rouge, she found hand-copied, scrawled personal messages in front of all the tenants' doors, announcing that Henry had stopped paying rent. Once each day since Betty had arrived home, Henry came upstairs to her apartment with a green bath towel, soap, a razor, and his dishes (always the same ones: a green plate, a cracked china teacup, three pieces of silverware, and a wooden breakfast bowl). Betty admired Henry Purdy's tenacity. As president of the building's tenants association, she had placed herself in the middle of his battle with Rupert Dixon.

Chicken Dixon turned off his blue police light as the Mercury Marquis halted outside the apartment building. Neither Rupert nor his son was a policeman. Chicken bragged that he was a civilian deputy of the local police department and held that he had been given the light for undercover work. None of the tenants believed this story. Instead, they recognized that Chicken was peculiar, and that the blue police light, along with Chicken's ogreish appearance, ugly blond loofah hair, and evident mental dullness, was Rupert's just reward for a life as one of Jersey City's worst landlords. Betty Trombley had once noted that, like her father, Rupert Dixon would just as soon burn out a tenant as evict one. He had the same "snaky slumlord blood" in his veins, the "will to suck people dry in exchange for the mere privilege of shelter in a pigsty," as she had written Rupert Dixon in the letter she enclosed with her last rent check.

When Rupert Dixon stepped from his car, he was relieved that Betty Trombley was nowhere in sight; he saw only Mr. Rodriguez, an irascible old man, seated on the stoop next to a tiger-striped dog with a wedge head. Usually, on weekends, Betty Trombley perched on the stairs as if guarding the entrance to Rupert Dixon's building, "like a gargoyle," he told Chicken. A long-boned, horse-faced woman, Betty Trombley did not believe in softening words or in anything that resembled diplomacy. She fought raucously and in such a way that she appeared to enjoy fighting.

"You know there's no dogs allowed in this building,"

Rupert Dixon said to Mr. Rodriguez, by way of greeting. Chicken, two heads taller than his father, peered over Rupert's Yankees hat at Mr. Rodriguez: both the Dixons were fair-haired men, with small lashless blue eyes, but while Rupert's eyes narrowed shrewdly under his baseball cap when he talked, Chicken's appeared to be too wide open, as if he were surprised by everything his father brought him to witness.

Mr. Rodriguez, whose eyes were bloodshot from constant exposure to the insecticides he used in his exterminating business, scratched the dog on the head. Mr. Rodriguez recently had become elected treasurer of the tenants association, because he was good at handling books, because he detested landlords in general, having worked for them for forty years, and because, as one of the basement tenants, he disliked Rupert Dixon with particular intensity.

"I don't see a dog in the building," Mr. Rodriguez answered. "Just one standing outside a building." He tickled the dog between the ears. He saw no point in explaining that the animal was not his. Henry Purdy had rescued the dog, a brindle part bull terrier named Joseph, from a dogfight. In the end, it would be the dog, Joseph, who would get them all—Henry and the Terhunes, as well as Chicken—in more trouble than any of them could have foretold.

Rupert took off his baseball cap, revealing a green-and-gold Dixon Ticonderoga pencil stub perched on his ear. His cap's Yankees insignia dangled from a long tear in the visor.

"What happened to your hat?" Mr. Rodriguez asked.

"Dog got it," Rupert answered dryly.

"Hate to see that dog," Chicken said.

"You won't," Rupert told him.

As Rupert and Chicken walked around Mr. Rodriguez, Joseph thumped his fat tail. Rupert descended the stairs to the basement, and Chicken trailed after him, carrying what appeared to be an eviction notice. Mr. Rodriguez picked up Henry's dog and rang the buzzer to Betty Trombley's apartment.

Both Dixons hesitated for a moment before entering the basement hallway: the foul odor of the sewer water assaulted them. Holding his nose, Rupert stepped onto Henry Purdy's walkway, trailed by Chicken, also holding his nose.

Chicken had on the Italian leather boots that were his hallmark. They were fancy boots, perhaps costing one hundred dollars, and made of leather the dark red of rooster hackles. He wore them whether he was dressed in a suit or in work clothes, as he was now. When the walkway dipped, allowing a small splash of water onto his left boot, Chicken stooped and rubbed at the dark stain on the oxblood polish.

Chicken followed Rupert to Henry Purdy's dam, ascended the four steps, stood on the doormat, and knocked. There was no answer.

Rupert Dixon took the eviction notice from Chicken and tacked it onto Henry Purdy's door just as Mr. Rodriguez and Betty Trombley appeared at the end of the hallway. Betty Trombley carried a clipboard and scribbled notes on a yellow writing pad. Rupert Dixon removed the pencil stub from behind his ear and underlined several sentences on the eviction notice.

"Be careful not to get your feet wet, Angel," Betty told Mr. Rodriguez. "That's sewer water. No telling what kind of diseases you could pick up from it."

Rupert tacked a second paper onto Henry Purdy's door.

"I was down here all day today, and I never saw you serve that notice," Betty said. "I never saw you attach it to that door. And I'm prepared to go to landlord-tenant court and testify that you never came here at all."

It was just like Miss Trombley to fall back on the most outrageous argument at her command. Rupert Dixon would not, however, engage seriously in a dispute with a woman before it was absolutely necessary. He stared slightly over her head and turned to backtrack along the walkway.

"She'll do what she says, too," Chicken ruminated.

"If I want any shit from you, Chicken, I'll squeeze your head," Rupert answered.

The board walkway was too narrow for Rupert and Chicken to bypass Betty Trombley. "Everyone clear the way," said Rupert, not addressing Betty specifically. "Get out of my way."

"This is not your way," Betty Trombley answered, blocking the exit. "Henry Purdy laid these boards. They're made from his wood, not yours. If you want out the door, you're going to have to go the regular route. I hope you brought your hip waders."

"Move," Rupert growled. The anger in his voice affected the dog, Joseph, in Mr. Rodriguez's arms. Joseph stopped panting, turned his nose toward Betty Trombley, and, scenting a possible battle, barked once.

"Whose dog is that?" Chicken asked.

Mr. Rodriguez carried Joseph up the basement steps. The dog turned and looked over its shoulder at Chicken until disappearing from view.

Betty Trombley walked backward after Mr. Rodriguez, stooped on the first step, and picked up the end of the board resting on the stairs. She pulled the board so that its far end, a few inches from Chicken, fell into the water, splashing him and leaving both Dixons marooned on Henry Purdy's dam in the stagnant basement canal.

A few moments later, Rupert appeared on the street, his feet dry, followed by Chicken, whose pants were wet up to the knees. Chicken held his socks and soft leather boots in one hand.

"I guess you can see something should be done about that water," Betty Trombley said. "It's just not sanitary."

Downtown Jersey City was the ugliest place Ida Terhune had ever seen. Treeless and grimy, Newark Avenue stretched through a ten-block shopping district and then lost itself below an underpass in the ravine segregating the western uptown part of the city from the downtown area. Recent fires had blackened windows of buildings, potholes wrenched the New Yorker's tires, and trash littered the gutters, as thick as leaves in autumn. Ida turned from Newark Avenue onto Grove Street, also treeless, and drove past city hall, with its sooty roof arching over the unrepaired top floor where arson had destroyed unsavory public records three years before. She turned right onto Grand Street.

"We're almost there," Ida told her children doubtfully.

Between Barrow Street and Orestes Cleveland Road, Skeet and Sherry saw four men sitting on a couch on the sidewalk, and beside the couch, two living room tables with lamps mockingly set on them, their cords dangling, and before the couch, a coffee table and two armchairs, and behind them, a pair of beds, neatly and sarcastically made, with hospital corners, and between those, a large green-and-white-striped barrel in which a fire had been built by the smirking homeless inhabitants of the sidewalk house, and over the barrel, a grill with larded catfish sizzling on it.

The catfish smell made Ida think of downtown Baton Rouge. A wave of homesickness engulfed her.

Large trucks seemed to be everywhere. Ida slowed as she passed a vacant lot across the street from the men, the New Yorker failing to absorb the shock of the cavernous pothole at the corner of Grand Street and Orestes Cleveland, from which the car's front end would never recover. Ida stopped before a narrow apartment building standing by itself in a grassy area filled with the brick rubble of recently wrecked neighboring tenements.

Gray tar-paper shingles, cut to look like bricks, covered the building's front. Its left side had been attached to a now demolished adjacent tenement, and the vanished building's right wall remained intact, a crazy quilt of colors exposing the private lives of its former tenants: a red parlor's wallpaper abutted the walls of a pale-green nursery and a yellow kitchen, a gaudy orange-and-purple bedroom, an old gray boiler room, and a hallway with a mural depicting the assumption of a wide-eyed Mary into heaven. Beneath this, a gaudy sea of orange cosmos flowers, planted by Henry Purdy, swirled around the Grand Street building. The flowers grew crazily, unbounded by any flower bed, and spread without design or plan into the vacant lot along a cracked walkway leading from Betty's building into a half-block of low August vegetation: weeds, escaped sunflowers, and ailanthus seedlings struggling through splintered wood and broken bricks.

Betty Trombley waved merrily to the Terhunes to welcome them to their new home.

When Ida stepped from the car, two inches of foul-smelling water soaked the cuffs of her pantsuit. She saw three men surrounding Betty; one of them appeared to be shouting angrily. Ida could not bear it when men shouted. It made her want to fall to pieces and become hysterical.

"Ida, you made it!" Betty called as Skeet and Sherry leapt from the car over a small river in the gutter. "Well, this is certainly a glorious day."

"You're undesirable, Miss Trombley!" the man behind Betty yelled.

"Ida, this is my landlord, Rupert Dixon. Rupert, this is Mrs. Terhune."

"I don't put up with garbage from my tenants," Rupert said.

Skeet watched with interest: behind Betty, a wiry old man restrained a bowlegged brindle dog who reminded Skeet of the orange-and-black-striped Gila monster he had seen at Stumpy's Lizard Farm in North Carolina, where his mother had taken him and Sherry after they complained about visiting too many Civil War sites on their two-week journey from Atlanta. The dog watched Betty Trombley, his pink tongue showing behind a jagged smile. When a third, yellow-haired man stepped toward Betty Trombley, Skeet alone noticed that the dog stopped panting and acquired that absolute stillness and concentration Skeet had noted before in dogs when they suddenly ceased to pant.

Chicken stared at Sherry with his pale, lashless eyes. She hugged Betty's long legs and buried her hands in Betty's skirt: a gauzy orange material that swirled around her ankles.

The dog growled.

"Now, Joseph," Mr. Rodriguez said, setting him on the ground but keeping hold of his choke chain.

"Whose dog is this?" Rupert demanded.

"He's his own dog," Mr. Rodriguez answered.

"You upset him," Skeet volunteered.

Rupert smiled down at Skeet. "He your dog?"

Rupert's smile made Skeet think of Harlan Pinkerton and Uncle Myron. Skeet did not answer, although he wished Joseph were his. He had never owned a dog, because Harlan

Pinkerton did not want pets in the Tulip Street house. Skeet remembered the walking stick and the praying mantis: how their jar had rolled out of his hands in Washington, D.C., splintering into a hundred pieces and sending the insects whirring onto Lincoln's knee at the Lincoln Memorial. Skeet felt a knot in his stomach just remembering it.

"Pit bulls are about to be outlawed in Jersey City," Rupert said. "And in any case, I don't let dogs in my buildings."

"Pit bull," Skeet said, without looking at anyone, privately savoring the words.

"He looks about half pit," Mr. Rodriguez explained. "The rest of him might be plain bull terrier, maybe a little something else. How can you outlaw a whole dog when half of him is legal?"

"That's not my boy's dog. We're not from here," Ida volunteered. "I've never rented before in my life."

"We were in a hurricane," Sherry added.

"We've only just arrived. It's our first day in Jersey City," Ida rattled on nervously. "We're from Baton Rouge. Have you ever been there? My father was Huey Long's right-hand man. I've lived there all my life."

Skeet stared across the street with embarrassment: there, he saw a man sitting on the couch in the sidewalk house, watching them. The man wore only one shoe and had a large hole in the front of his shirt.

Rupert Dixon looked at Ida curiously for a moment and then ignored her. He turned toward Betty Trombley, stepping over a tire tread lying on the sidewalk to shake his finger in her face.

"You mind your own business, you skinny bitch—"

"I don't approve—" Ida said.

"Because I'll have your ass on the street in two seconds."

"I don't approve of that kind of language around children."

"Surely this is my business," Betty said, looking, Ida thought, as if she were thoroughly enjoying herself. "I live here."

Joseph stretched forward on his choke chain and sank his teeth into the tire tread. He snarled and closed his eyes.

"Hold on to that dog!" Chicken shouted, sidestepping toward the curb.

"Now, Joseph," Mr. Rodriguez said, scratching the dog's spine. Joseph scissored his teeth deeper into the black rubber.

Turning toward his son, Rupert Dixon announced, "This is enough crap for one day. Let's go, Chicken."

"Chicken!" Sherry repeated.

"What's that smell?" Ida asked. "Is this where we're going to live?"

The two Dixons climbed into the Marquis. Once ensconced inside, Chicken reached through the driver's window and stuck his flashing blue police light on the car's top. As the Marquis drove away, the blue light darted across the tenement and then reeled skyward.

Ida had never said that she intended to accompany anyone to court. However, two mornings after her arrival, Betty perched on Ida's bed, thrusting coffee at her.

"Rise and shine!" Betty announced. "We've got a date with a judge this morning."

Ida felt disoriented. She had been dreaming that she was back home at Tulip Street and that Harlan had woken her up, asking for coffee and pickled walnuts. In her dream, she had felt so tranquil as she walked down the cool, dark hallways of their house in a diaphanous nightgown.

"I think I should stay inside today, just to get the children settled in better," Ida answered, her face pressed into her pillow. Skeet and Sherry were sleeping in a back room Betty had been using as a clothes closet, but Ida had been assigned to a couchlike thing Betty called a futon bed in the living room. Ida felt homeless and exposed, although she appreciated Betty's hospitality. Ida certainly did not want to be on her own right now.

"Oh come on, Mrs. Terhune," Betty said. "You've barely been outside yet. Don't stay here all cooped up in the apartment. You've hardly looked at Jersey City."

"I saw it when we drove in."

"I swear, Ida. You're such a recluse."

Ida could not think of a reply. "I wish I had some of that chicory coffee from the Café du Monde in New Orleans. I never had a chance to go there after Daddy died, but I always wanted to. And I always bought their coffee at the supermarket."

"You've never had the time to go back to the Café du Monde? What were you doing all those years in Harlan's house?"

"I was raising my children," Ida replied loftily. At least that's what she had done until Sherry started kindergarten, three years ago.

"Huh," Betty answered.

"This is no way to wake someone, Betty, but I'm getting up. I hope you're pleased." Ida threw off the covers and sat for twenty minutes clutching the coffee cup before she finally rose and dressed herself. When she found her way into the kitchen, Skeet was drawing one of his maps at the dining table. Sherry sat in the barber's chair by Betty's kitchen window as Betty's long fingers worked a greenish paste Ida thought might be henna into Sherry's neck nape.

Betty's trying to shock me, Ida told herself. But I'm not going to say anything about the fact that her apartment used to be a barbershop. However, Ida could not restrain herself completely. "I don't know about this, Betty," she said. "I don't condone little girls wearing any kind of makeup."

"It's just for fun," Betty answered. "It'll wash out before school starts." Ida looked doubtful, and Betty's outfit did not increase Ida's confidence in her friend's awareness of conventions—a bright-red skirt twirled around her legs like a square dancer's, and a black vest covered with tiny round mirrors sparkled above it. Perhaps she had decided not to go to court, after all.

"Yeah, Mama, don't worry," Sherry said. She leaned forward and looked at the muddy paste covering her hair. "It's hard to believe this doesn't come out green."

"We have to rinse your hair immediately," Betty told her. "When your natural hair's this light, it'll turn bright orange if you leave the henna on too long." She lowered the chair and led Sherry to the rinsing sink on the kitchen wall.

"That water smells funny," Sherry said.

"It's not the water. The water's fine. It's the air that comes up the pipes when the water's not running that stinks. I wonder what that assholehead is up to now." Betty sprayed Sherry's hair with a nozzle attached to a pink hose.

"Who?" Ida asked. "Please don't use that word in front of Sherry."

"That assholehead Mr. Dixon," Sherry answered.

"If the evil landlord knocks on the door today," Betty said, "let's put sugar in his gas tank."

While the landlord certainly appeared to be in the wrong, Ida wondered if things still couldn't be worked out peaceably. She did not, like Betty, see the world as a place full of adversaries. However, Ida did see the world as a place from which she was entitled to be protected, and she did not want to get involved in Betty's war with the landlord. After having lived with Betty only two days, Ida felt like a person tied to a mast in a storm at sea.

Betty set down the nozzle and toweled Sherry's hair. "I've always liked the idea," Betty mused, "that you could destroy a car, even a large fancy car like a Mercury Marquis, with something as pure and simple as sugar." Not that she'd do it, of course—she couldn't imperil the tenants association's position by committing a crime. But she would have liked to do it. "Think of the sugar melting in the gas tank, zapping through the car, coating its parts like peanut brittle stuck to a pan."

"You're rubbing too hard," Sherry said.

A barefoot young man entered the apartment without knocking, carrying a pile of dishes, a towel, and a razor. To Ida, he looked like a derelict.

"Betty!" she cried.

"Excuse me," the man said. He backed into the hall.

"This is my friend Ida. She just got here," Betty explained, as if reassuring him of something.

He nodded, and without saying anything further, walked into Betty's bathroom. Skeet recognized him as the man who had watched them from the sidewalk house the day they arrived.

"Is that a boyfriend?" Ida whispered.

"That's Henry Purdy," Betty answered. "He usually comes every day, but I guess he held off awhile when he saw you were staying here." She turned on a blow dryer, and Ida could not catch the rest of Betty's response.

"It's the same color as orange Kool-Aid," Sherry said, admiring her hair in the mirror.

"You're gorgeous," Betty told her.

"Look, Mama, I'm gorgeous," Sherry echoed.

Ida thought of the swath of orange cosmos flowers outside. She missed her garden on Tulip Street. She doubted roses could thrive in a place as northern and industrial as Jersey City.

"Don't ever let anyone tell you you're not sexy," Betty advised Sherry. "Even if they're working you to death at some awful job, and you don't have anyone special, don't let it kill the wild part of you. Just put on a risqué slip under your clothes, or a tight dress to show off your figure, and you'll know who you are." She pulled down her shirt's neckline and showed Sherry a scallop of yellow lace.

Sherry nodded, as if she understood perfectly.

Ida sat down beside Skeet. "Can I see the map, honey?"

"When it's done. When there's something to see," Skeet told her. He and Sherry had only had two days to explore. Shielding his map from his mother, Skeet drew a small, sharp-eared dog on the path opposite Orestes Cleveland that ran from Grand Street to the junkyard he and Sherry had discovered. Next to the dog, Skeet inserted Henry Purdy, a wiggly character wearing one shoe. Beside them, he inserted himself.

Ida opened the *Jersey Journal* and turned to the classified section. She read the first entry aloud: "'Masseuse wanted. At least five years experience. References required.' What's a masseuse?" she asked.

"I can never remember if it's male or female," Betty answered.

Ida waited for further information, but when she realized none was forthcoming, she returned to the classifieds. "There isn't much here," Ida told Betty after a few minutes.

"I don't know how to do anything except type. What does 'no steno' mean?"

"Relax, Ida. Live off your savings awhile."

"I don't think that would be responsible," Ida answered.

"Anyway, I'm getting a rent abatement until they fix the basement pipes. If you want to help out with expenses, come with me to court. We'll listen to Henry's case and see which way the wind's blowing."

"Why can't we just let Henry tell us what happens?"

"Henry's not going to court," Betty told her. "He doesn't believe in the legal system. But this lawyer the tenants association contacted is supposed to show up for him, to let the judge know that Henry's too far gone to appear in court."

"What do you mean, too far gone?" Ida asked, glancing at the bathroom.

"Oh, Henry's as crazy as the day is long. I'm supposed to appear as a witness, to describe the state of Henry and the state of the basement. Look, Ida, it'll be fun fighting the lords of the land. Our upstairs neighbor Mrs. Tutwiler will keep an eye on Skeet and Sherry for you."

Ida pretended not to notice that Betty was staring at her, waiting for an answer. Ida leafed through the national and local news in the *Jersey Journal* until finding the Family section, containing the horoscope and advice columns. She ignored the horoscope. She did not approve of horoscopes. She shook her head while perusing "Dear Abby" and then carefully read "Hints from Heloise" and an article titled "Wire Coat Hanger May Unclog Sink."

◆ The Devil

On Tulip Street, there had been little for Skeet and Sherry to do. They had hung out with a pack of neighborhood children, overturning garbage cans, setting loose watchdogs, and once stealing a lawn mower and leaving it dismembered by a drainage ditch. The Tulip Street house—its velvets covering the walls and furniture like a scarlet moss, its ubiquitous crucifixes haunting every corner like black widows—was a memory that made Jersey City seem wonderful by comparison.

Across from Betty Trombley's apartment building was the narrow path Skeet and Sherry had found, which stretched from Grand Street along a fenced-off field posted with no-trespassing signs (KEEP OFF—VIOLATORS PROSECUTED—HAZARDOUS MATERIALS) and which terminated in the best-equipped scrap-metal yard the children had ever seen. It put Uncle Myron's to shame. Three barking dogs guarded a lot filled with hundreds of cars compacted in a metal crusher and stacked like coins. Hubcaps, manhole covers, spools of copper wire, lead sinkers, grappling hooks, and other items of interest covered the ground outside the radii of the dogs' chains. Uncompacted cars—convertibles and Cadillacs, Lincolns and even an old Studebaker with a broken windshield—parked head to tail, formed a circular barrier around the lot. On their first day in the junkyard, Skeet and Sherry sat in the Studebaker for an hour, pretending to drive, without being detected by anyone.

"I'm Myron the Skunk, this is my junkyard, I'll sell you for scrap metal if you hassle me!" Skeet cried, as Sherry hooted in the seat beside him.

Beyond the junkyard, a path paralleled a small canal from the Hudson, where a colony of men lived in boats and jerry-rigged tar-paper shanties. The men were white and black, whiskered and thin, smelling of sweat and cigarettes. One of the men, wearing a stained bandanna around his forehead, waved to Skeet and Sherry on their first day out exploring and told them they were on "the Jersey City Riviera. If you take that path there, you'll end up in Liberty State Park." Skeet and Sherry peered down a trail leading to a road and a green area. "From there you can see Liberty Industrial Park and the Statue of Liberty out in the water, with her asshole turned toward Jersey City."

The other men laughed. Skeet and Sherry followed the speaker's instructions, and they did see the Statue of Liberty facing New York, her backside turned toward a group of men crabbing from an old creosote-smelling dock.

When Sherry revealed this discovery to their mother, she said, "I don't want you children leaving the block. This is not Baton Rouge. It's not safe here. You stay on the sidewalk in front of the apartment." The children's mother made them commit to memory the telephone numbers for Betty and the police. "And don't go anywhere alone," she added, "so that if someone grabs one of you, the other one can scream."

However, after Betty convinced Ida to come to court and leave the children with Mrs. Tutwiler upstairs, Skeet and Sherry neglected to communicate these precautions to the baby-sitter. As soon as Betty brought the children to Mrs. Tutwiler's apartment, they informed her that they were going to Liberty State Park.

"Does your mother know how far away you walked a few days ago?" Mrs. Tutwiler asked. "I watched you from my window. Don't go out of seeing distance, beyond those cars there, on the edge of the junkyard."

Mrs. Tutwiler was a small woman with a deep voice. When she stood, she was barely taller than Sherry, but when she spoke, she reminded Skeet of the minister at Park and Pray, the church near his Uncle Porter's. (A year ago at Easter, he and Sherry had followed Uncle Porter's coonhounds to the church's parking lot, and before the children could stop them, the dogs had picked up a smell that drove them wild with demonic joy, and they had run through the church doors and up the aisle, in the middle of the service. Skeet and Sherry had stopped at the door, uncertain about what to do. The entire congregation had turned their heads, staring at them. "You may fetch your hounds," the minister had pronounced in a sonorous voice: the voice of God, Skeet had thought at the time.) When Mrs. Tutwiler spoke, she tilted her chin upward, rather than looking down at Skeet and Sherry, and projected her voice to a distant point over their heads.

"Don't go down to the park by yourselves. Once, they found a little girl in Liberty State Park with her arms and legs and head cut off." Mrs. Tutwiler described for Skeet and Sherry a world of child-snatchers and murderers who would spirit them away if they strayed beyond her eyesight.

Filled with fear and excitement, Skeet and Sherry walked along the path to the junkyard, vigilant of adults.

A man emerged from the canal's boat colony and waved to them. The children bolted halfway back down the path. Seeing Henry Purdy standing on the edge of the path with the dog, Joseph, Skeet backtracked cautiously to the junkyard. Sherry ran across Grand Street into the field of cosmos on the side of the building, her orange hair rippling like a burning fuse over the flowers. She took the stairs two at a time. She burst into Mrs. Tutwiler's apartment, breathless, without knocking, and announced, "Skeet is talking to a crazy person."

Mrs. Tutwiler did not turn around from where she sat. Leaning over the windowsill, she watched Skeet closely, her back to her apartment. Mrs. Tutwiler wore her hair in two gray braids that hung past her waist, and tucked them into the belt of her skirt. Sherry found this a source of interest: was this a style in Jersey City? Did young people wear their hair like this, or only old people? And how did Mrs. Tutwiler avoid sitting on the braids when she used the toilet? Sherry asked if she could undo and rebraid Mrs. Tutwiler's hair, but the old woman demurred. Sherry crept up beside her and leaned over the sill in order to taste the sensation of being Mrs. Tutwiler.

Wilma Tutwiler had worked for half a century as a bookkeeper at Joseph Dixon Crucible Company and the Colgate factory and, later, at the Sabrett hot dog outlet, keeping track of boxes of hot dogs and hot sausage for distribution to vendors. She had never married, and in order to pay her rent she had supplemented her meager paychecks by doctoring records or authorizing the removal of toothpaste tubes or sausages never accounted for.

Since retiring ten years before, at the age of seventy-three, Mrs. Tutwiler had never walked more than ten blocks from the Grand Street building: she never strayed south of Grand Street, which was bordered with overgrown railroad supply yards and dumping grounds; never ventured as far east as the Hudson's decrepit, perilous docks or even beyond the west side of Grove Street, where she bought all her sausage at La Isla Meat Market; never wandered farther north than Newark Avenue, where she occasionally dined out at the Tripoli Restaurant; and never traveled farther west than Norman's Pharmacy on Jersey Avenue, where she bought the pills she took for a myriad of physical ailments. She had never, in the eighty-three years she had lived in downtown Jersey City, taken the ten-minute PATH train ride that terminated in Manhattan. Even so, her ambit was much broader than Ida Terhune's would be during her first several weeks in Jersey City.

Mrs. Tutwiler's knowledge of her territory was detailed and

profound, from networking among stoop-sitters, and the old widows and confined housewives who sat by their front windows, watching the street out of idleness or a deep-seated depression that kept them in housecoats all day. When not perched before her own windowsill, Mrs. Tutwiler would position herself in a chair on the sidewalk, a few feet from the pay phone used by the tenants who could not afford telephones or whose calls were of such a private nature as to require protection from their families' eavesdropping. Politely pretending not to listen, and staring straight ahead at the viewless view across Grand Street, her eighty-three-year-old hearing as acute as her eagle eyes, Mrs. Tutwiler would overhear the details of teenage romances and drug sales, mid-life love affairs, wives' teary requests to relatives for money to be kept hidden from irresponsible husbands, and complaints to the sympathetic about people upstairs who might have been offended had they been able to eavesdrop.

Mrs. Tutwiler was a repository of local news, whose particularities were as infinite as the infinitesimal permitted. She never displayed malice in her eavesdropping, or passed on damaging news to anyone who was not intended to hear it, and so she overheard everything, asked questions and got answers, and lived a rich and vicarious existence belied by the apparent drabness of her life in the ugly Grand Street tenement.

There was not a tragedy in her realm that she could not tell in startling detail if she chose to. She knew, for example, that Mr. Rodriguez came from Santo Domingo and had settled in Jersey City twenty-five years ago, in his forties, after sailing around the world in the Merchant Marine; that he had married a local girl and that their only child, a son, had died in infancy of causes attributable to Mr. Rodriguez's exposure to certain insecticides he no longer used; and that his wife had left him shortly thereafter. Mrs. Tutwiler knew that Henry Purdy had been arrested several times for vagrancy, as well as for stripping a stolen car abandoned under the overpass at the end of Second Street, a common dumping ground for stolen vehicles. She knew that Betty Trombley had come to Jersey City seven years before with a husband, almost her height, and that she had left him only three weeks later for the sole reason that he had yelled at her for serving him a plate of cold grits. Mrs. Tutwiler was of the opinion that there were few foods less appealing than congealed grits. She could well understand the husband's hurt and humiliation and believed that Betty Trombley had overreacted.

Mrs. Tutwiler also knew Jersey City scandals with the comprehensiveness of people who live for decades under the umbrella of a political machine. She had been seventeen when Boss Frank Hague was first elected and almost fifty when he stepped down, and although many mayors had come and gone since then, it was clear to her that his ghost continued to run the city. She kept up on every aspect of Jersey City politics without knowing or caring anything about state or national news. She knew, for example, that Rupert Dixon had been raised by an uncle only a few blocks away, in a squat building in the shadow of the Dixon Ticonderoga factory. He was no relation to the founders of Dixon Ticonderoga, and his uncle had in fact despised them and made a point of letting people know that he was from the Pine Barrens Dixons, not the rich Dixons of the Crucible Company dynasty. He had never spoken of them except with contempt and envy, and Rupert liked to brag that one day he would turn the factory into condominiums and charge rich people an arm and a leg just for the privilege of breathing in pencil dust. Despite Rupert's inherited contempt for the other Dixons, he was never seen without a yellow-and-green-striped Dixon Ticonderoga pencil in his pocket or behind his ear or in his hand, and Mrs. Tutwiler was not sure whether he wore the pencils ironically or because he secretly longed for people to connect his name with theirs.

Mrs. Tutwiler recalled when Rupert's uncle had worked for a time as a lesser bureaucrat in city hall, before he went on to organize a mayoral campaign for an anti-machine candidate who won the Democratic primary and so the election (thirteen Democrats ran that year, and no Republicans) and who, several elections later, as the incumbent machine candidate, was defeated by the new anti-machine candidate, whose campaign Rupert, by then in his late thirties, organized. She knew that Rupert owned not only her building but many of the tenements on her block, Bright Street, and Columbus Avenue; that housing inspectors visited none of his buildings; and that the police did not ticket him when he double-parked anywhere in the downtown area.

She knew smaller things also. She knew that the lawyer who hung around the tenants association, looking like a hungry fox, was the son of Percyvaldo Ribeiro, who had been jailed for eighteen months in federal prison for illegal trafficking in South American birds and who, upon his release, had continued to traffic in them with an ostentatiousness that betrayed a startling lack of reformability. Mrs. Tutwiler also knew that Henry's dog, Joseph, had been smuggled as a puppy in a woman's cosmetic case into the United States from the Dominican Republic, raised in kindness and indulgence by Olita Olivera, who ran a bakery on Second Street, and upon her death bought from Mrs. Olivera's brother by a local breeder of fighting cocks and dogs, who had just begun to make a good profit off Joseph when a New Yorker with an unheard-of Japanese dog that looked like a long-haired German shepherd arrived one evening in the vacant lot near Borinquen Home Improvement Center, where dog and cock fights were held. The foreign dog broke Joseph's front leg and would have killed him if Henry Purdy hadn't pried Joseph's jaws off the foreign dog's neck fur with a tire iron and paid seventy-five dollars cash for the privilege of removing Joseph's all but dead body from the arena. Mrs. Tutwiler did not know where Henry had found the seventy-five dollars.

From her window, Mrs. Tutwiler saw the tiger-striped dog and recognized Henry Purdy. Although she did not consider Henry to be dangerous, Mrs. Tutwiler thought him strange and unpredictable, and if Skeet had been within shouting distance, she would have called him home. She waved, but Skeet acted as if he did not see her.

When they smelled Henry Purdy's dog, the three guard dogs outside the junkyard lot barked cacophonously, tangling their chains so that they appeared to be one giant three-headed animal. Joseph barked twice and lost interest in them.

"He's your dog?" Skeet asked.

"Yep," said Henry Purdy, squatting down and scratching Joseph on his blunt lizard nose. Henry remained both shoeless and shirtless. He looked at Skeet cross-eyed, and Skeet was not sure whether Henry was studying him or focusing on some point behind him. "He's partly pit bull terrier. You ever seen these dogs before?"

Skeet shook his head.

"A bull will grab on to something and just hold on, come hell or high water." Henry picked up a greasy chamois cloth from beside the hull of a wrecked car and dangled it in front of Skeet. "Go 'head. Waggle it in front of him."

Skeet took the cloth and shook it. Slowly, almost politely, Joseph opened his jaw and clamped it shut on the chamois.

"Waggle it," Henry Purdy instructed.

Skeet tugged the cloth back and forth, and the dog's stumpy reptile tail wagged in reply. Joseph shook his head, pulled backward, and jerked the chamois out of Skeet's hand.

"You can drag him around by his teeth, and he'll still hold on. His jaws can take four hundred pounds of pressure."

Skeet nodded.

"He can drag a twelve-foot two-by-four for a mile. Go 'head. You can pet him."

Skeet rubbed the dog behind its ears.

"Do you live there?" Skeet asked, pointing toward the canal's boat colony.

"I was looking at a boat," Henry answered. "Is Betty Trombley upstairs?"

"She's going to court with my mother," Skeet answered, disappointed that the conversation had shifted so quickly to adult matters.

"Also, this dog can jump," Henry said. "He's all back leg. Watch this." Henry pointed at the hood of a Rambler's chassis and said, "Hey, Joe, Joe, come on, Joey boy, leap!" Joseph loped toward the Rambler, jumped straight up, and soared over the hood to the other side, the chamois cloth still tight in his jaws.

"Next week, me and Joe are going to take a boat over to Ellis Island. You want to come?"

"OK," Skeet told him.

Henry Purdy looked over Skeet's head. Skeet turned around and saw Mrs. Tutwiler spying on him from the highest window of her building. His sister's red hair danced like a flame beside her.

"Would you like to keep Joe for a while?" Henry Purdy asked, picking up the dog and holding him out toward Skeet. Apparently then realizing that the dog was too heavy for the boy to hold, Henry set him down again, in front of Skeet. "I have to go do something." Henry turned and ran back toward the canal as if chased. Skeet watched him jump over a piece of scrap metal and veer around a clump of marsh reeds.

Skeet took off his belt, fastened it to Joseph's choke chain, and led him jubilantly toward the apartment to show to his sister.

When Ida and Betty opened the door to leave for court, a leaflet, Xeroxed on green paper, lay on the doormat. Similar papers lay in front of all the other doors in the hallway.

Betty read the paper and then handed it to Ida, saying, "This must have been left by Henry." Ida looked at the handwriting. Some words were printed as neatly as typescript, and others were almost illegible. She read:

> Please try to understand this.
> An innocent life could be saved.
> Somebody could suffer, and if he does, it would be a very big mistake!!
> People have seen this person not functioning, sort of off in a daze, and, because of this, they were sure that he lost it.
>
> THEY ARE WRONG!!
>
> Sometimes he doesn't function and is in sort of a daze because the physical structure of his mind isn't

strong and he can't take certain things. He doesn't
lose it anymore.

In other words: People think he loses it
but they are wrong.
He keeps it.

Please spread this around.

"What does he mean?" Ida asked.

"I guess all this apartment business is getting to Henry," Betty answered. She tucked the leaflet into her purse. "He's usually a little more clearheaded than this. Maybe I'll bring it as evidence."

Downstairs, in the letter box, Betty found a cream-colored envelope addressed to Ida. Ida felt half pleased and half irritated that Harlan intended to dog her with letters wherever she went. She took the letter from Betty but then noticed that the paper had been scented with a lemony perfume. Ida turned it over, read the return address, and said, "It's from Carlotta Stroke!"

"Open it!" Betty told her, but Ida dropped the letter into the privacy of her purse.

The two women walked toward the New Yorker. A stranger would not have associated them with each other. Betty strode ahead in her gold espadrilles, her square-dancing skirt swirling around her long legs. Ida plodded behind in her mint-green pantsuit, her head tilted to the side as if she were lost in thought or as if her lopsided bouffant caused her to hold her head that way.

The New Yorker, pockmarked by hail, its bumper mutilated, leaned toward the curb, looking exhausted from its journey.

"It's got a flat," Betty said. "It must have been a slow leak."

Ida stared mournfully at the car. I'm losing everything, piece by piece, she thought.

"Well," Betty answered, "at least this way no one will steal it. We'll have to fix the tire later and take the PATH train to Journal Square, or we'll be late for court."

This might not have been the best time for Ida Terhune to come here, Betty thought to herself as they walked up Grove Street to the PATH station. There's nothing Ida hates more than a fight. If she had her way, we'd probably be living without heat or hot water, just as a courtesy to the landlord.

But then Betty smiled to herself as she watched Ida. If it hadn't been for Betty, Ida would have spent her life walled up in her father's house, making her own clothes and holding lonely conversations with Roy Daigle's mother, an angry old woman who spoke a garbled French-English and had come to Baton Rouge from New Iberia to care for Ida after her mother's death.

Betty had first laid eyes on Ida in morning Mass during the third week of fifth grade. Ida appeared at school three weeks late, she later explained, because she had been sick with a cold and her grandmother had kept her home. (Eventually, both Ida and Betty would be asked to leave Our Lady, Betty because she missed too many tuition payments, and Ida for excessive absences.) Grandma Daigle, slender in a flapper's dress, wearing bright lipstick and a hat with stuffed cardinals on it, led Ida into Our Lady's church and seated her in the pew in front of Betty. As the old woman turned to leave, Betty saw her move a plug of chewing tobacco from one side of her cheek to the other.

Ida had not yet bought her school uniforms, and this alone would have set her apart from her classmates, who sat sullen and immaculate in their white blouses and navy-blue skirts. But her clothes started her classmates whispering and giggling—a low-waisted polka-dot dress that looked like something Betty's mother might have worn in old photographs, a grown woman's patent-leather purse instead of a book bag, and old-ladyish gray pumps.

Mrs. Daigle's decision to bring Ida to school late made acceptance by her peers difficult in any case, since by the time of Ida's arrival, all the girls in fifth grade had formed partnerships and cliques. Betty alone had remained aloof. She had attended public school through fourth grade and resented her mother's success in cajoling an aunt into saying she would pay for parochial education. Her mother had been afraid Betty would never outgrow her tomboyishness, and Our Lady, an all girls' school, was Mrs. Trombley's final effort to convert her daughter to feminine ways.

The only daughter in a family of five brothers, Betty was unable to feign interest in schoolyard play at Our Lady. Longing to wrestle her new classmates to the ground in a game of touch-turned-tackle football, Betty watched sneering as they bumped fists in a round of one-potato-two-potato. She tried to convince them, unsuccessfully, to play ring-a-boy, a game invented by her brothers in which they would swing her around their heads and let fly, counting on Betty to land on her feet, once dislocating her collarbone. In the second week of school, Betty exhibited to some of her puzzled classmates a baby water moccasin, trapped by her oldest brother, R.E., in a jar with holes bored into the cap with a hand drill. The girls backed away and reported her to the principal, Sister Florence, a short woman with a round, boyish face. Sister Florence had taken the jar without betraying the slightest fear, placed it in her top desk drawer, and then waved Betty out of her office.

During Mass, Ida appeared unaware that the other girls were watching her, sizing her up. She stared straight ahead, listening to the priest although he spoke in Latin. She did not turn around when Betty tapped on her shoulder. Nor did Ida respond when Betty leaned forward and whispered, "Who are you?" Ida did not move a muscle when Betty took out a pencil and wrote on the soles of Ida's gray pumps after the class had knelt in unison: "hell hell hello" (on the left shoe) and "I am the devil" (on the right shoe).

However, as Betty walked down the aisle after taking communion, she saw Ida lift up her feet, one at a time, and turn them secretly, in her lap, in order to read what Betty had written. When Ida saw her left shoe sole, she looked bewildered. She then examined her right shoe, moving her lips as she read. Betty had been hoping that Ida would cry out and thrust her foot to the ground as if her shoe had bitten her, but instead, before Ida had puzzled out the words, the sister who taught the class snuck up behind her and read the message. She seized Ida's arm, pulled her out of the pew, and led her down the aisle and out the door, presumably to Sister Florence.

As the fifth graders filed into the classroom after Mass, they found Ida seated in a back row in her stocking feet. Betty inferred that Ida had not informed on her, because Sister Florence did not send for her later that day. However, Ida looked at Betty imperiously and later passed her a note, which said:

> If you were the devil, you would have turned into a poof of black smoke when the priest rang his bell during communion. I hate this school and I want to go home. I miss my cat Oogie and my electric fan.

At the end of the day, Betty saw Ida's grandmother in Sister Florence's office, arguing in a furious half-French and waving the gray pumps over her head as if threatening to throw them. Sister Florence watched unflinchingly, and Ida sat in a chair beside the principal's desk, saying nothing and staring out the window as if she wanted no part in the quarrel.

On the way to the PATH station, Betty and Ida passed a side street lined with decrepit and boarded-up buildings.

"You see?" Betty said. "Just like Baton Rouge."

Ida did not answer. Jersey City was not at all like Baton Rouge. Everything in Baton Rouge had been familiar, and everything here was strange. Ida looked at her friend and for a moment indulged herself in hating Betty for luring her away.

They crossed to a small rectangular area outside the Grove Street station, bordered by concrete benches and flower beds in which nothing had been planted. "Angel Rodriguez calls this 'Rat National Park,'" Betty told Ida. They descended an escalator into a tunnel, where an approaching train, its brakes squealing deafeningly, caused Ida to cover her ears.

She sat down a few feet from Betty inside the train. She read Carlotta's letter and said, "How inappropriate!" When Betty scooted closer to her, Ida returned the letter to her handbag.

A man slept on his seat opposite Ida, his chin resting on his chest. Most of the riders looked somber and miserable, Ida thought, the way people did when they had to go to work. Only Betty chatted energetically, joking with the passengers around them and then plunging into a one-sided conversation with Ida.

"What did that letter from Carlotta Stroke say?" she began.

When Ida did not respond, Betty continued: "Lotta was pretty wild when she was young. We hung around a lot together in my second year of high school, and she was always getting me into some kind of mischief. I remember once I was trying to bring her home by twelve midnight so that her mother wouldn't kill her—that was curfew time in the Stroke house. Lotta wandered into a bar, and they didn't stop her, since she was fifteen going on thirty; she never looked her age after junior high. I looked mine, fourteen, and I couldn't get in. I had to ask every cowboy who walked by, would he please look inside the bar for a girl in a sleeveless chartreuse dress?"

Ida made an involuntary horn-honking motion with her arm when the PATH train braked suddenly. The train emerged into daylight, and below her, Ida saw overgrown train tracks in a ravine, and a little yellow dog nosing a fallen telephone pole.

"Finally, after I'd waited an hour in the parking lot, Lotta wandered out of the bar and then straight into a boardinghouse next door. I chased after her, saying, 'Lotta, come on, we got to go.' She stopped and looked at this snapshot of a man taped to a door inside, with the name 'Sparky' written on it. 'Mmmmmm,' she said, and then walked right into the room and closed the door. It locked behind her, and there I was, left standing outside while these noises, moans and the like—both hers and his—start coming out of the room. Then a man's voice: 'Christ! Jesus! Jesus! Christ! I thought you were my girlfriend!' The door flew open, and this naked man came running out, with just a cowboy shirt wrapped around his waist, and made a beeline for a bathroom at the end of the hall."

A woman sitting across the aisle from Ida was staring at Betty, who did not seem to notice.

"Pretty soon, all the doors in the hallway were opening up, oil workers and cowboys spilling out. They peeked into Sparky's room. There, sitting on the bed, was Lotta, completely naked and laughing back at the cowboys. I thought I'd never get her out of there. The cowboys didn't react the way you might have expected. They were pissed, especially Sparky." Betty seemed completely absorbed in her recollection, as if she were back in Louisiana, where she and Ida belonged. "The cowboys threw her against the wall and out the door and tossed her clothes after her down the stairs. She didn't get her clothes on until we were both outside. Then she discovered her favorite jacket was missing and sent me back up to get it. I had to walk through this gauntlet of cowboys saying things like, 'Little Miss, ain't it past your bedtime?' I walked into the cowboy Sparky's room, where he was sitting on his bed between two friends, shaking his head and laughing nervously. I just pretended he wasn't there and fished around the bed for the jacket and then ran out."

The woman across the aisle moved to a seat at the front of the car. Ida reddened and stared out the window at walls of rock reinforced with ugly rusted metal rods. She felt as if Lotta Stroke were riding in the seat next to her.

When the train reached its destination, Betty led Ida through the back of the station toward a building that looked like a prison. Men dangled their arms and heads out of its high barred windows. Below them, women and children milled around a sign posting visitors' hours.

"I'm right here, Barney!" a girl called. A pale hand waved from a third-story window.

Betty told Ida, "The courthouse is right behind the jail. Hudson County Penitentiary is hell on earth. They say the men in there commit crimes just to get transferred to state prison. Henry Purdy told me he was there once waiting for a petty larceny charge to be dismissed, because he couldn't make bail. He said for days in the middle of summer, the plumbing wasn't working—they'd just haul in big garbage cans full of water for the men to wash their faces and chests in. It was about three hundred degrees inside during the summer. He says there's this roving goon squad of guards who take men into the prison basement and beat them senseless for no particular reason and that this has been happening for at least ten years."

"Mr. Purdy's been in jail?" Ida asked.

"You know," Betty said, "what I always think when I think of Lotta is that the wildest things you'll ever witness all happen before you're twenty, because you don't have the sense yet to know how to see them coming and get out of their way."

As they waited for a traffic light to change, Betty took out a bottle of blue polish and retouched her fingernails. Trucks and buses rumbled past, filling the air with exhaust.

"It has nothing to do with age; it's who you associate with," Ida said, and then thought: your whole life you've led me into trouble.

Ida unfastened her purse, shielding its contents from Betty. She sneaked a look at the envelope inside. It had never occurred to Ida to scent her envelopes. Lifting the purse flap higher so that Betty could not watch, Ida pulled out the single sheet of stationery and reread the note:

Dear Ida Terhune,

I am very sorry about whatever I had to do with the breakup of your marriage. I was never serious about Harlan, never. *I'm not even sure I liked him.*

Sincerely,
Carlotta Stroke

Imagine having the gall to write me now, Ida thought. She tucked the letter back into her purse.

When it became clear that the traffic light was broken, Betty grabbed Ida's arm and dashed across the street. A bus driver bore down on Ida with a look of astonishment.

"Make it snappy!" Betty cried as the bus narrowly missed them.

◆ The Law

As long as he was never awake and alone at the same time, Mike Ribeiro knew he would pull through the hard months following the breakup of his marriage. He rose that morning with a sense of joy and expectation, thinking of all he had to do for Henry Purdy's case. He threw off the shirt and tie he had fallen asleep in while watching *A Day at the Races* and headed for the shower. His *New Jersey Code of Criminal Justice* lay next to the toilet and was soaked before he noticed it. He hoped it would dry reasonably unwarped. He opened the code and blotted it on one of the Quality Inn's bath towels, overturning the bottle of Napoleon brandy he liked to keep next to the toilet for the occasions when he competed against himself in games of Scrabble solitaire. The hotel's bath towels were undersized and too thin to absorb much. Mike had made a mental note to buy some real towels on

Newark Avenue, but he kept forgetting—there was so much to replace.

When his wife had departed eight months before, she had taken everything with her: the furniture, her clothes, his clothes; she had emptied the medicine cabinet and removed the spices from the kitchen shelves; she had swept and vacuumed and then packed up the cleaning supplies. She had not even left a note of explanation, although the last angry thing Mike remembered her saying had been: "I can't stand living in the middle of the chaos you call your life."

Mike longed to believe that she had secretly fallen in love with someone else: the idea that she might have left him after six years of marriage for nothing at all made his stomach knot with fear. It was true, he did carry chaos around with him like a house. He enjoyed clatter and bustle. He always juggled far too many clients, divided himself among a dozen pro bono projects, and more than once he had made appointments to meet with two different friends at the same time, in opposite ends of the city. He gave away so much money to charitable organizations that his checks would bounce. His office was rich with the clutter of notes from investigations and idiosyncratically annotated case law. When Mike came home, he would take off his clothes immediately after shutting the door and leave them where they fell: he liked the surprise of finding a sock resting on the stove, his necktie entangled with his wife's stockings on the shower ring, an unpaid utility bill in his underwear drawer. He spread his papers out on the kitchen counter, in doorways, on the living room couch. The first thing he did when he awoke was turn the radio on full blast, to a spirited political debate or salsa or samba or klezmer music—it hardly mattered what, as long as it was lively.

Now that his wife was gone, Mike tied his toothbrush to the faucet so that it would not elude him. He had been delighted by his discovery of soap-on-a-rope in a downtown drugstore. He wondered with genuine puzzlement how his wife had kept the bathroom so neat and how she had maintained the laundry in a perpetual smooth cycle of clothes worn and cleaned. He allowed his laundry to collect in the walk-in closet. The left side contained dirty clothes, and he emptied newly laundered ones onto the right side. When his clean shirts came off the pile unacceptably wrinkled, he threw them back to the other side, hoping they would fare better the next time around.

Since her departure, Mike's wife had written him only once, from New Mexico, where she had procured new employment: she had been a professor at Rutgers but now worked for a research institute near Los Alamos. She studied vacuums. Her lawyer would send the divorce papers.

If the papers arrived, Mike never received them. After his wife left, he was unable to return to the empty apartment. He took a room at the Quality Inn situated at the mouth of the Holland Tunnel and ate all his meals in restaurants. Sometimes he missed cooking. Despite the messes he left in the kitchen, even his wife had loved his rice and beans and collards. But now that Mike's wife was gone, and with her the pots and pans, cooking hardly seemed possible. Mornings, the Quality Inn would vibrate with the flow of passing traffic, and sometimes the air was so thick with exhaust that Mike's lungs hurt with the effort of breathing. His wife had always complained that Jersey City smelled bad: the stink of the asphalt refineries and landfills rode the easterly winds into the heart of town and choked her.

Mike considered taking a vacation to Brazil, which he thought of as an opulent country, crowded with life. His father had migrated to Jersey City from the Amazonian state of Mato Grosso, and throughout Mike's childhood, he had been regaled with stories of his father's homeland: there, the soil in the rain forest smelled as if a human could eat it, like cinnamon and chocolate; Brazilian cane liquor was twice the strength of rum, and Brazil's Brahma beer made American beers seem like horse piss; the animals and plants of the Amazon were so various that many of them had no names yet. His father had once told him, "The lazies would move so thick and slow in the overhead trees that we could pull them off like fruit and drop them into burlap bags," and it had taken Mike years to understand that by "lazies" his father had meant a kind of animal, three-toed sloths, large arboreal creatures with squint-eyed human faces.

But in the end, Mike was unable to tear himself away from his clients in order to travel. He forgot his cares as he leaned toward the jury box, wooing the jurors. He lost himself in the wonderful moral complexity of the criminal law. He celebrated his clients' acquittals and mourned any sentence of imprisonment. He consumed his work, and it consumed him.

At night, back in his bed at the Quality Inn, Mike would be too exhausted from the day's business to think about his wife. However, he would awake early in the mornings, hearing her voice, and her criticisms of his character would mingle with his dreams and surface in a maddening tangle of thoughts. His wife had despised his work. "You take the truth," she would say, "scramble up the facts in evidence, put them together in a way that's pure lie, and then you sell your lie to the jury. You're nothing but a salesman," she had concluded, although Mike was unsure of the insult, because his father had been a talented salesman who at the time of his death supported his immediate family, a dozen friends who occupied the upstairs above his store, and countless relatives abroad. He had sold everything in his store on Columbus Avenue: alligator shoes and radios, encyclopedias and liquor, cooking utensils, hardware, and small pets. And, Mike had thought in response to his wife's accusation, wasn't it amazing the way the same facts could puzzle themselves together into so many contradictory truths? The idea of a world sparsely populated by absolute verities made him feel lonely.

Mike's wife had often attacked him for having no morals: she believed what she believed with conviction. Even about small points that touched her only tangentially she could be adamant. Once, for example, although she often stated that she had no desire to have children (he wanted dozens), she had trapped herself in their building's hallway, arguing furiously about the superiority of cloth diapers with a neighbor she had spied carrying a bag of Pampers. "In short," he had heard her pronounce, "disposable diapers constitute thirty percent of solid waste in landfills and take hundreds of years to decay." He had intervened, joking, "How can you argue against Pampers? Where would New Jersey get its topsoil, if not for Pampers?" The neighbor had giggled, but his wife had looked at him icily. Thereafter, whenever they chanced on a baby in a restaurant or on the street, she would grow still and frown as if reminded of an insult.

Now that she was gone, he found himself arguing continually with her in his mind, defending the things she had hated. As he shaved that morning, he heard her saying, "You dress badly on purpose!" In this she was wrong; he simply could not perceive, however hard he looked, why pinstripes clashed with horizontal stripes, or why houndstooth and plaid were incompatible. Perhaps there was a kind of color blindness for the patterns in things.

Today, as he shaved, he decided that he was not a handsome man. His head was too large, his chest stuck out like a prow. In fact, he was all chest; he was just a chest with legs stuck onto it. Once his wife had asked him, "What do you want the most in life?" He had answered honestly, "To be adored," and she had looked at him disapprovingly. Why? he wondered. He shifted the angle at which he viewed himself and saw that he was really quite handsome. And he looked a little devilish: his black eyebrows snaked upward, and his smile was crooked. A shadow seemed to rise under his razor even as he shaved. His tie was rumpled. "But this is my newest tie," he said aloud. "I like this tie."

He missed her terribly. The sensation of missing was as powerful as any feeling he had known: he could have opened graves with the crowbar of his feeling. His life had become too quiet. Often when he came home, he would talk aloud to himself, practicing a summation for an upcoming trial: he did not feel he was there unless he was reassured by the sound of his own voice. After all, he was a mouthpiece. He had doubled his caseload, joined several legal organizations and the Sierra Club (he hadn't had time to attend one of their hikes yet), and taken on the Grand Street Tenants Association case, which was bound to keep him busy for months. He knew he would prevail. He was proud to take on the notorious slumlord Rupert Dixon, proud to be a member of the human race and happy to be alive, happy to help anyone who crossed his path. As Mike stepped past his laundry pile and opened his door to the snorting sounds of Holland Tunnel traffic, the world rushed to greet him, full of promise, boisterous and overflowing with unnamed possibilities.

Outside the courtroom, a list of the day's cases was posted. "Let's see," Betty read. "'Dixon v. Kim, Dixon v. Mendez, Cunningham v. Moreno, Dixon v. Esposito, Dixon v. Williams, Dixon v. Hopewell, Dixon v. Castro, Dixon v. Olivera.' That's strange. This is definitely the right place—it says Judge Bundy's courtroom." She reread the notice that Rupert Dixon had tacked to Henry Purdy's apartment door. She pushed open the courtroom doors and walked past the tenants seated in the back of the court. Ida lingered near the doorway.

A case appeared to be in progress, but Betty nevertheless approached a clerk seated next to the bench and asked him a question, showing him Henry Purdy's papers. The clerk whispered something to her and gave back her papers without looking at them. She handed them to him again and said, loudly, "Just look at them. It won't take you a minute."

The judge, a large and daunting man, Ida thought, stared at Betty with a look of exaggerated perplexity and said, "Take a seat, miss."

"I just need to know where exactly I'm supposed to be," Betty answered.

"I said, 'Be seated.'" The judge seemed agitated.

"I have this paper with your name on it, saying we should be here today, but—"

"Wait until your name is called!"

"But then, we're not on the list outside, so I'm wondering if something is going on here."

Now the judge raised his voice. "I will have to ask you to leave this courtroom if you do not sit down." Ida stepped back toward the doors.

Betty seated herself beside the aisle, sighing audibly. She

turned around, her earrings tinkling, and motioned Ida to join her. Ida walked self-consciously down the aisle and sat behind Betty, next to a pregnant woman fanning herself with a magazine.

The judge heard several cases, and Betty shook her head after each decision. Throughout the proceedings, the pregnant woman whispered to her neighbor, a lady in a startling yellow suit, and Ida had difficulty following what was transpiring before the judge.

"What if that son of a bitch throws me out?" the pregnant woman said. "Who's going to rent to someone with a belly out to here?"

"They should have the death penalty for people like him," the woman in the yellow suit responded.

Ida thought of her own pregnancy and then of the moment when she had first viewed Skeet. His face had startled her: it looked collapsed on itself, chinless, with huge jowls and swamp-green eyes. But a moment later, when she had adjusted to his appearance, she experienced the strongest rush of love she had ever known. Immediately afterward, she worried that this might be improper and felt awkward and guilty. Her romance with Dewey had been passionate, but with a slow-moving kind of passion: he invited her out, they went steady, they spent their days together, and then they married. When Harlan proposed to her, Ida had been so overwhelmed with gratitude that she was unsure what else she might be feeling.

"That idiot!" Betty whispered beside Ida. "He's decided every case for the landlords!"

Ida clucked her tongue. She felt chagrined that she had not followed the proceedings. She was living in the past, she saw; would Harlan and the days of her marriage always seem more immediate to her than any of the goings-on around her? Betty seemed so engaged in everything.

Ida tried to pay attention to the courtroom drama. "There wasn't any problem with the heat or hot water in the building," a landlord was saying. "That girl is just a thin-skinned, bony little thing who needs twice as much heat as everyone else!"

"Concentrate?" the pregnant woman whispered beside Ida. "That jackass wants me to churn out my work a mile a minute. No way am I suffering through this again. It's just too much, this and working too. How am I supposed to concentrate when every third thought I have is: 'Don't toss your cookies, don't toss your cookies, don't toss your cookies'?"

The joy Ida had felt gazing at the newborn Sherry had carried her through the early dark days of her widowhood. Harlan's lack of interest in having children of his own had astonished her and made him inaccessible to her understanding.

Mrs. Terhune's not listening, Betty thought, glancing at Ida's profile. She's off in her own world, as usual.

Betty made a sound of disgust in reaction to something that happened up front in the courtroom. Ida looked up, to find the judge staring right at her, pointedly, as if he thought she had made the noise. Then he continued talking to one of the lawyers near the bench. Ida was mortified. Why was Betty always drawing negative attention to herself?

"This is enough for me," Betty whispered. "Let's get out of here. This judge is a jackass."

The judge rolled his eyes as Betty stood and Ida followed her.

"Good-bye, ladies," he told them.

Once outside the courtroom, Ida said, "I've never felt so put on the spot in my life, Betty! How could you act like that? Don't raise your eyebrows at me!"

"Ida," Betty answered.

"Why do you do these things? Why did you take me out of Baton Rouge, where I was safe, and bring me here, where I don't even know if I have a roof over my head? A place that smells? A place that's dirty?" Ida heard her voice take on an embarrassing high pitch.

"What do you mean, why did *I* take you? You're a grown woman."

No, I am *not* a grown woman, Ida was tempted to answer.

Betty looked down the court hallway, as if the discussion were over. "Ida, I don't want to quarrel. You know I only like to fight with real enemies—landlords and traffic police and boyfriends and boyfriends' ex-girlfriends, that kind of thing.

Real battles. I don't want to fight with *you*; you're my friend."

"But you didn't tell me what it would be like!"

"Oh, for God's sake. Nobody knows what's around the bend from one second to the next."

Ida began to sob. She had been afraid this might happen.

"Jesus, Ida! Who cares what the old-fart judge thinks? He's just a lawyer in black robes." Betty pulled a red bandanna from her skirt pocket and handed it to Ida, who took it without saying thank you.

"Look, Ida, I've got work to do here. Why don't you sit on this bench and pull yourself together while I go look for that lawyer of ours?"

Betty abandoned Ida outside the courtroom. Ida blew her nose. She opened her handbag and read Carlotta Stroke's letter a third time. Ida pursed her lips and returned the letter to her handbag.

Mrs. Terhune surely is a challenge, Betty Trombley said to herself as she sped down the court hallway. Betty remembered how she had felt as a girl in Ida's presence: as if she, Betty, lacked propriety, and all the good graces in the world were embodied in Ida Daigle. What did I have in mind when I invited her up here? Betty wondered. Betty Trombley, you know damn well you enjoyed the challenge of dislodging Ida from that awful house. And now that you have, what the hell are you going to do with her?

Ladies and gentlemen of the jury: before you pass judgment, I simply want you to ask one question, privately, of yourselves. What is the worst thing you have ever done? (At this juncture, he would pause, rustle the papers in his briefcase, and give the jurors time to think.) Is the act my client has been accused of any worse? And yet the prosecutor is asking you to condemn him to a long term of imprisonment. Are you prepared to condemn him?

Wouldn't that be a great speech for the opening of a criminal case, Mike Ribeiro thought to himself as he sped along the court hallway. If only I could get away with it.

As he rounded the corner, Mike Ribeiro spied Betty Trombley handing a bandanna to a weeping woman with a beehive hairdo. No doubt one of Rupert Dixon's latest victims.

Betty Trombley took off in the opposite direction, and Mike Ribeiro quickened his pace to catch up with her. She was freakishly tall, and to top it off, she was dressed in an outlandish red garment that billowed behind her like the robes of a charioteer. Imagine intending to walk into a courtroom in those clothes, Mike thought to himself. I would like to see that.

Ida Terhune noticed Mr. Ribeiro first out of all the other characters loitering in the hallway: a woman with seven children who would spend the next four years in foster homes because of their family's impending eviction; an arsonist; a landlord who that very day would be denied the right to evict a drug dealer, who would later kill him; the drug dealer; a future mayor's wife, who looked as if nothing would ever happen to her but who would be killed years later by the Shining Path in Peru while traveling with her husband to see Machu Picchu; a lawyer whose sole mission was to pass an envelope full of money to a judge; the judge; an influential uptown landlord who would eventually perish in the collapse of one of his own buildings; and Mike Ribeiro, who burst through the crowd, talking to himself with his hands, something Ida had never seen anyone do before. He carried an unsmoked cigar, and as he walked, he suddenly drew his right hand upward, brought down the cigar as if delivering a pointed argument, and then jerked his palm to the right in a dismissive gesture. He moved his lips slightly, muttering something that apparently delighted him.

He's not talking to himself, he's arguing with himself, Ida thought. It never occurred to her that he was a lawyer, however. His shoes were scuffed, and his shirt was as wrinkled as if he had slept in it. And his socks did not match, to say the least: he wore one brown sock and one argyle. As he sped past her, Ida thought that he must be one of those clients she had seen portrayed in television police shows, whose lawyers had brought them a suit for the occasion of a trial.

He was built the way Ida thought men should be built, however: broad-shouldered, although not as tall as Harlan, with her father's jet-black hair and Dewey's olive complexion. Ida caught herself: she had been separated only a little over a month, and already she was casting about for a new husband! She blew her nose on the bandanna and forced herself to change the topic of her thoughts. She sat up straight, holding her pocketbook firmly in her lap. "Whenever I feel afraid," she hummed to herself, "I hold my head erect." She wondered what Skeet and Sherry were up to. Of course, Betty assumed Ida was unaware that her children had secret dangerous lives of their own. Betty thought she had a special rapport with them. And perhaps she did. But Ida kept tabs on them, oho, yes she did. There was no doubt in her mind that that strange old woman Mrs. Tutwiler (how *did* she use the toilet with that hair?) had her hands full for the day.

"It's me, it's me, no need to worry," Mike said.

The man with the wrinkled shirt stood in front of Ida, with Betty Trombley in tow. This close to him, Ida could see that he had gravy on his sleeve.

"You must be one of Rupert Dixon's latest victims?" He opened his briefcase and handed Ida a large box of Kleenex, mashed and misshapen as if he had been carrying it for years. He snapped his briefcase closed.

"Well, not exactly," Betty explained. "This is my friend Ida Terhune, from Baton Rouge. This is our lawyer, Mike Ribeiro."

"Terhune?" he asked Ida. "As in Albert Payson Terhune, the famed writer of dog stories?"

"What?" Ida answered, blowing her nose.

"Don't worry about the case," he told Ida, apparently still under the impression that she was caught up in Betty's crusade against her landlord. "I guess you saw that Mr. Purdy's name was not on the roster today. I checked around, and it would appear that Dixon purposely erased the court date on the summons and wrote in a later one. Mr. Purdy lost by default three days ago. But I'll get the case back on the calendar. It isn't even legal for a landlord to serve his own notice."

Ida understood almost nothing he had said. "Take me home!" she directed, turning to Betty. "I would like to go home right now."

"Let me treat you both to lunch," Mr. Ribeiro told Ida. He picked up her hand and patted it.

Before Ida could answer, he was off. What could Ida do but follow? She almost had to run to keep up with Betty's long, loping stride.

The My Way Lounge was a dark bar with a twenty-five-foot fish tank behind the counter. Most of the customers were men, and Ida did not feel at all comfortable. Large shadowy fish swam behind the bartender's back.

Betty abandoned Ida to telephone Angel Rodriguez to come meet with them. As Mr. Ribeiro led Ida toward a one-table dining section, an unshaven man sitting at the bar called, "Mikey!"

"Tommy!" Mr. Ribeiro returned warmly.

Tommy approached, shook Ida's hand, and told her, "This man saved my life. If he hadn't helped me, I might be in Dannemora, behind bars, instead of here, in a bar."

Betty reappeared, leaned on the counter, and said, "What are those fish, groupers? Do they eat leftovers?" Tommy laughed and asked Betty if she wanted a drink. Ida could not hear her answer, because at that moment, Mr. Ribeiro pulled out a chair with an ostentatiously debonair gesture and said, "Please let me make you comfortable, Mrs. Terhune."

While Betty lingered by the counter, Mr. Ribeiro lit a cigar and talked. Ida felt she should be impressed by anyone who earned his living upholding the law, but he was the most garrulous man she had ever encountered. After seven years with a tight-lipped husband like Harlan, Ida was at a loss how to respond. She felt the lawyer's current of words spinning around her and flowing outward, as if he were a man shaped and defined by the sound of his own voice.

"It's amazing," he was saying when Mr. Rodriguez arrived at the bar and seated himself at the table. "If you stop to think how many things which are frail on the inside are so tough on the outside as to be unassailable or even dangerous—soft-bellied porcupines, fast-moving black cars with rich old ladies wearing minks inside them, oysters. Rupert Dixon has a weak spot; we'll find a way to make him knuckle under. If not by legal means, then perhaps by extralegal means." Mr. Ribeiro wiggled his eyebrows in a comically villainous way. "After all, the law in Jersey City is only a trapping. This is the wild frontier."

Angel Rodriguez studied the menu and said nothing: he didn't like lawyers. Among other things, they talked too much. He himself talked only when he had something to say, and sometimes even then he held back, polishing his ideas inside himself like dark gems. For example, he knew the lawyer purported to be Brazilian or part Brazilian, but Angel had no intention of announcing that as a young man, in his merchant marine days, he had spent a year in Brazil, sailing up and down its coastline. He had even eaten piranha.

Ida sensed an undercurrent of friction between the two men seated at her table. Mr. Ribeiro was probably the kind of man who raised other men's hackles. Her father had been that kind of man: women had loved him, but men often seemed to become argumentative in his presence. "Barnyard fowl behavior," Ida's grandmother used to say, clucking her tongue.

Sipping from a bright-blue drink with a paper parasol in it, Betty sat down and rescued Ida from the conversation, questioning Mr. Ribeiro about every item on the menu. "You should taste this, Ida," Betty said, handing her the blue drink.

"In the afternoon?" Ida answered. Ida almost never drank, even in the evening. She disliked the feeling of being out of control and couldn't abide the taste of any liquor, with the exception of champagne, and then only on special occasions such as weddings. The smell of bourbon made her positively ill.

They were the only people in the My Way Lounge who

ordered a meal. Ida wondered if the food was safe. Mr. Ribeiro ordered for her, and she was surprised when a motherly woman exited the kitchen wearing a checkered apron and laid the dishes on their red tablecloth.

Ida ventured a small bite. "This is really very good," she conceded. "I've never had eggplant parmigiana before. In fact, I'd never heard of it."

Mr. Ribeiro looked at her curiously, seeming to forget what he had been talking about.

"Ida just moved here from Baton Rouge three days ago," Betty explained.

"I really don't know much about landlords," Ida confided in Mr. Ribeiro. "In Baton Rouge, we had a beautiful house. It had twelve rooms, every one of them stocked with antique furniture. I had the most beautiful garden, with rosebushes in it. Ancient rosebushes."

"I've never been to Baton Rouge," Mr. Ribeiro answered sympathetically. He cut his meat with gusto; he had ordered a sort of steak wrapped around green paste and tied with string. He jerked the string, spinning the meat like a top in his dish and smiling as it flipped open. "I took this case because I thought Rupert Dixon would be a personal challenge. I'm not really a housing lawyer; I'm a criminal lawyer. I usually just defend criminals."

Ida frowned.

Angel Rodriguez ignored the lawyer and watched the fish over the bar. The piranhas he had eaten had been that big. They were ugly, underbitten fish with too many bones. "Your boy," Angel told Ida, "wanted to know where Ellis Island was."

"Ellis what?" Ida asked.

"I told him it was off grounds to visitors nowadays because they're fixing the place up. Maybe you could take him over to Liberty Island, to see the statue."

Ida didn't like to cross large bodies of water, and she was especially afraid of riverboats.

"Ida needs a job," Betty told Mr. Ribeiro. "She just broke up with her husband, and she's on her own."

"Betty!"

Mr. Ribeiro held up a large, hairy hand with a thin gold band on the ring finger. Ida was unsure why he wanted her to look at it. "I'm separated," he said, "but I just can't get myself to part with the wedding band. Jurors distrust old bachelors. Although, when I see I have an aging mother in search of an eligible son-in-law on my jury, I've been known to take my ring off. It makes them side with me and acquit the defendant."

Turning again to Ida, Angel said, "Your boy asked me what Ellis Island was, so I told him it was a place everyone used to go to get away from wherever they were. Sort of like Jersey City is now. Why people come here beats me. I mean, think of crossing half the world, coming from Russia or Pakistan or somewhere real, and ending up in this place. It boggles the mind. Every morning I wake up and ask, 'Why am *I* here?' but here I am."

Ida smiled politely.

"She's a good typist," Betty persisted, "and has a wonderful telephone manner. You must know some lawyer who's looking for a receptionist or a secretary."

Mr. Ribeiro pushed back his chair and looked at Ida. I could use her, he thought. An attractive, stuffy-looking woman who could give my office an air of efficiency. Noting Ida's embarrassment, he told her, "I greatly enjoyed *All the King's Men.*"

Ida gave him a blank look.

"About your former governor? Huey Long?"

Ida brightened and said, "Oh, Huey Long! My father was his close friend."

"Really?"

"Yes, he was with Huey Long when he died. It was an exceptionally hot day, back before they had a.c. A young man with slick black hair approached them, carrying a stubby black pistol. My father swiped at the young man with a panama hat when he fired. Huey jumped like a hit deer."

"That's quite a story," Mr. Ribeiro said. "Imagine your father standing there in the crosscurrents of history."

"She needs a job with benefits," Betty pressed.

Ida wished to continue talking about Huey Long and

frowned at Betty. "I don't know a thing about being a legal secretary," she said. "I've only been in a courthouse on two occasions: once to get married and once when I was a juror in a murder case."

Angel Rodriguez had been called to serve on juries seventeen times in his life. He thought this remarkable but saw no point in going on about it.

Mr. Ribeiro leaned forward. "You were?"

"Yes. I was the holdout vote."

"Ah, just like *Twelve Angry Men*! As a criminal lawyer, I've always been impressed by the moral fortitude of the juror who clings to his sense of justice despite the pressure of his peers."

"Well, I hung the jury," Ida responded. "They were going to let him walk the street, but I said, 'No, he's guilty. I feel in my bones that he's guilty.'"

Mr. Ribeiro set down his fork. "You were the holdout vote for *conviction*?"

"I knew it in my bones," Ida repeated. "He looked the type to burglarize a house with women and children in it. 'Ho, you don't fool me,' I said, and I held firm."

"Fascinating!" Mr. Ribeiro muttered, plunging back into his meal. "I myself believe that the inability to forgive always shows a failure of the imagination."

Ida had no idea what he meant.

"Dixon's weakness," Angel interrupted, bringing the conversation back to where he thought it belonged, "is fire violations. For one thing, that fire on Bright Street was in one of Rupert Dixon's buildings. Where all those children died? Our building is full of fire violations. The only reason it hasn't burned down is that it has a moat of sewer water around it." He gave Mr. Ribeiro a challenging look. Angel doubted there was anything in the world the lawyer could do to save them.

◆ Chicken

After lunch, Betty and Angel met with Mike Ribeiro at his office, and Ida demanded to be dropped off at Grand Street. However, once secure in the apartment, Ida saw her children playing with the tiger-striped dog on the sidewalk near the strange outdoor living room, and her anxiety concerning the animal's dangerousness propelled her down the stairs and outside. She crossed Grand Street. The men who were usually in the outdoor living room were gone, and Skeet and Sherry had appropriated their turf, turning the couch at a right angle to Grand Street and inducing the dog to run along the sidewalk and leap over.

Only the day before, Ida had seen the group of men who loafed in the outdoor living room leave it hurriedly as a police car rounded the end of the block. The car pulled up in front of the area, but by then the men had disappeared down the path leading toward the junkyard. Ida assumed the police had been trying to do what they could to keep down vagrancy. After the men had fled, Ida saw Rupert Dixon emerge from a white car parked down the block and talk with the officers: he must have summoned them, out of worry about his property values. As well he might. A short while after the police left, Ida had seen Henry Purdy sitting with the same men in the outdoor living room, cooking catfish and feeding them to his dog.

Now Skeet held the dog by his collar a half-block away and Sherry stood behind the couch. "He can be your big dog, I don't care," Sherry was singing in a brassy voice as Ida neared her. " 'Cause I can be your little dog when he's not there."

Skeet let go of the dog's collar, and Sherry yelled, "Joe, oh Joey boy, come on, Joe!"

The dog galloped toward and beyond Ida without noticing her and cleared the sofa by several inches.

"All right, Joey boy!" Skeet yelled, running past Ida to the dog, who lay down on the sidewalk, legs splayed and tail wagging, as both of Ida's children fussed over him.

"Are you sure that animal's safe?" Ida called. Her children drew together and faced her, acknowledging and excluding her at once.

"He's our buddy," Sherry answered. It was just like her daughter, Ida thought, to passionately imitate her brother's enthusiasm for the dog.

Skeet pretended not to hear the question, and Ida was sorry she had asked it. All his life he'd pestered her for a coonhound, and she'd never let him have one because of Harlan. Why couldn't I have stood up to him more? Ida thought. Why, Skeet's willing to keep insects, he's so starved for a pet. But then Ida pictured Harlan's house with its crystal jars and pale carpeting and remembered how ludicrous it would have been to keep a large, bumbling animal there. Imagine him robbing me of my own home! I hope the house burns down, Ida thought, and then felt horrified that she could have wished such a thing.

She sat down in one of the armchairs on the sidewalk.

"This outdoor living room is out of this world," Ida said to Skeet, in order to connect with him in some way. She thumped her chair's arms, and two puffs of dust rose in front of her. "Well, he *seems* like a nice dog," Ida said. "He's certainly very athletic."

Now Skeet looked up. He and Sherry dragged Joseph toward the armchair, where he stopped and grinned ferociously at Ida, with incongruously tender black eyes.

"Go 'head and pet him," Skeet said.

Ida reached down and touched the dog's forehead. He lifted his nose and licked her, and she jerked back her hand. "Oh!" she cried. "He startled me." Then, to prove to Skeet that she was not against him, she reached down again and scratched the dog's back. "Aren't you a sweet ugly thing," she said.

Skeet smiled.

"Well," Ida said, standing. "I just wanted to check on you to make sure you were all right. I'll be upstairs making iced tea if you need me."

Skeet and Sherry watched their mother cross back to the apartment. They both saw the same thing: a vulnerable, bewildered-looking woman holding her head high as if she were trying to be brave in the face of some imaginary enemy. The two children felt the same pangs of love and exasperation. They did not have to communicate to each other what they felt. They sighed at the same moment, and Skeet shook his head. Sherry fingered a metal sinker in her pocket, which she had found in the junkyard.

Skeet patted Joseph. "Ladies and gentlemen," he said. "This here dog will now perform a death-defying act that will put him once again in the *Guinness Book of World Records*. My dog Joseph will jump over that there couch while holding my sister's tennis shoe in his jaws." Skeet knelt and laid his head alongside Joseph's. "I'm counting on you, son," he said. "Don't let that shoe go."

Seated in the barber's chair near Betty's kitchen window, Ida sipped her iced tea. It had been a long day, and she was glad to be home. She watched her son feed Sherry's shoe to the dog. Sherry did not seem to mind. She hobbled along, tugging the dog to the corner. His teeth clamped on her sneaker, the dog raced down the sidewalk and soared over the couch. Skeet patted him, the dog dropped the shoe, and Skeet held it up victoriously. Ida had never seen him look so happy.

A week later, when Chicken Dixon came to padlock Henry Purdy's door, Ida was eating lunch with Betty Trombley and Mike Ribeiro at the My Way Lounge, Angel Rodriguez was fumigating a building on Bright Street, and Mrs. Tutwiler was asleep in her living room. Skeet and Sherry were across the street with Joseph. They baited him with a five-foot two-by-four and repeatedly encouraged him to run the entire length of Betty's block and, the board still in his mouth, to jump over the coffee table in the sidewalk house. Breathing heavily through his nose, Joseph scrabbled up to the table and tossed himself over it sideways.

The white Mercury's flashing police light preceded it. The light sent blue wings flitting across the street to the sidewalk house. It passed along the couch and the bedside table. It shimmered across Joseph's brindle fur, blinded Skeet and Sherry momentarily, and then settled on the Grand Street building. Skeet tied a clothesline to Joseph's choke chain and held the end in both hands.

Ida's children watched Chicken emerge from the Mercury Marquis, carrying a toolbox and a long, flat iron bar. Skeet and Sherry followed him down the basement stairs, pulling Joseph behind them. Chicken set down his toolbox on the dam outside Henry Purdy's door. From the box, Chicken removed a cordless drill, a bag of screws, and a heavy padlock. He opened the door with a key hanging on a large metal ring holding dozens of keys, ran thick fingers through his yellow loofah hair, and then picked up a nail and a hammer and tapped shallow holes in the door and the doorframe. He turned and saw Skeet and Sherry.

"Hey! Get out of here!" He thumped his boot on the dam, as if he were trying to scare away a small animal.

Joseph sprang toward him, barking.

"Joe!" Skeet cried, leaning back on the clothesline. Joseph landed in the water. He remained there, chest-deep, straining at the end of his tether and glowering at Chicken. He thrashed in the water, snorting through his blunt nose, swishing his tail and barking.

"He looks like an alligator!" Sherry yelled happily.

Chicken raised the metal bar and brought it down over the dog, and both children screamed. Skeet jerked Joseph sideways. Joseph lunged forward, snarling and snorting in the water. The bar fell again, just missing his head. Sherry covered her eyes and shrieked.

Skeet stepped into the water and grabbed Joseph's choke chain. He dragged the dog backward as Chicken, towering over him like a yellow-haired ogre, cursed and pulled the bar out of the water. Skeet wrapped his arms around Joseph's chest and lifted him partway.

"Take his rear end," Skeet told Sherry, so coolly that it steadied her. Sherry stepped into the smelly water and hugged Joseph's middle. Suddenly, as if he weighed nothing, Joseph was up near their waists, his nose pointed toward Chicken, a low growl in his throat. The children set him on Henry Purdy's walkway and crawled up after him.

Once on the walkway, they lifted Joseph again. Stepping together, their eyes on Chicken, Skeet and Sherry climbed back onto the stairway and up to the sidewalk. Stinking from the sewer water, they carried Joseph, still snarling but thrashing halfheartedly, up to Betty's apartment.

They locked her door behind them. They stood still just inside the door, dripping wet and listening. Through Betty's open window, they heard the sound of the cordless drill. Between them, Joseph shook himself, spraying water on Betty's couch. He sniffed her floor and lay down, his back legs sprawled behind him, his eyes focused on Skeet.

Skeet and Sherry stayed inside, looking out the window, until they saw Chicken emerge from the basement with his toolbox and drive away. The blue police light circled him, swooping along the fronts of neighboring buildings and flickering down the block.

Ida's children ran downstairs to the basement. There, they

saw that Chicken had installed the iron bar across Henry Purdy's door and bolted it in place with a huge padlock. A white paper with fine black lettering fluttered above the bar.

Its new tire snagging on potholes, the New Yorker inched through Newark Avenue's sluggish traffic. Ida drove while Betty scribbled on her yellow pad in the back seat and Mike Ribeiro read over some papers in the front seat. Cars large as Ida's, blaring a foreign, island music, approached and passed her, the songs rising, deafening, and falling like a siren. There were so many unpredictable drivers that Ida felt as if she had been honking the whole way.

"Ida, you're going to short out that car horn if you keep leaning on it," Betty answered.

"I'm not a crazy person," Ida said. "I'll thank you not to tell me how to drive, and I'm not about to let us all be victims of a negligently driven vehicle."

"Ida's never gotten a ticket for a moving violation," Betty told Mike Ribeiro.

"Well, she might get one here. The police don't always wait for you to break the law." Mike Ribeiro laughed. "A clerk who works for Judge Polk of traffic court told me that every morning the judge stacks all the contested parking tickets on his desk and writes 'Guilty' on every one from the top to the bottom of the stack. Then he sits there on the bench all day, listening with a good-natured look to the citizens of Jersey City as they explain how they didn't run a red light and didn't speed and did signal and so on, and when they finish, Judge Polk shouts 'Guilty!' and tells them to pay their fines."

"That's shocking," Ida said.

A whiskery man leaned in Ida's window, startling her and filling the car with the odor of gin.

"Mike, my man! It's me, Luther! I'm out of jail!" he called. "I'll come by the office for a visit." He looked at Ida and said, "He's the best criminal lawyer in Jersey City—'criminal' in both senses of the word, ha ha."

"Come by anytime, anytime at all," Mike answered, gripping Luther's hand so that Ida had to duck to see the street.

The man thumped on the New Yorker's top in a good-bye gesture. Ida drove on slowly.

Small stores with limited and eclectic inventories blocked pedestrians with outdoor displays offering, in a single area, plastic dolls from Puerto Rico, spices from Guyana, floor mops, metal dishes from South Africa, babies' clothes, Ax House rattraps, toy brass knuckles, and tricyles. Vendors selling Sabrett hot dogs barricaded the sidewalks so that pedestrians spilled onto the avenue. Repeatedly, Ida applied her brakes. Young men, their arm muscles bulging, shaved ice from blocks into paper cups and covered it with syrups labeled in large capitals with the names of flavors unfamiliar to Ida, like tamarindo and guava, calling what they hawked snow cones, although these were unlike what Ida had called snow cones up until now. Women Ida's age, trailing children, and wearing tight jeans, high-heeled sandals, and shirts shimmering with sequins, sorted through outdoor clothing racks. People were so thick on the sidewalk that it would have been impossible to walk a straight path, if Ida had ever descended from the New Yorker.

There was only one building of any beauty, with a rocket-shaped tower that said ROCKET FURNITURE on the side, but when Ida passed it she saw that it was a discount goods store and that all the upper-story windows had been covered with sheet metal. In the six-block business district, Ida counted seven stores that seemed to sell bridal apparel. She flinched inwardly, as she always did when she thought of her courthouse marriage to Harlan. She deeply regretted not having had a real wedding. She had been ridiculously eager to remarry right away, and Harlan had rushed things so. In retrospect, she realized that he had not wanted to spend the money a wedding would require.

Ida turned onto Jersey Avenue, where traffic stalled behind a convoy of trucks, before she finally reached Grand Street. There, she saw her children sitting on Betty's stoop, soaking wet. Sherry was crying.

Ida braked without pulling over to the curb, threw open her door, told Mike Ribeiro, "Scoot over and park," and abandoned the New Yorker as she ran to Skeet and Sherry.

"We stink!" Sherry said as she leaned into her mother's hug.

After Betty and Mike Ribeiro joined Ida, Skeet reported with great excitement what had happened: how Chicken had tried to kill Joseph, how Joseph had tried to kill Chicken, how Chicken had locked Henry Purdy's door. Betty and Mike walked into the basement to assess the damage while Ida took her children upstairs.

"Henry came to the apartment and got Joseph," Skeet told her. "He's keeping him safe over by the canal."

"You were alone with him upstairs?" Ida asked. "Where's Mrs. Tutwiler?"

"She's snoring on her sofa," Sherry answered.

Ida ordered Skeet to shower, and when he finished, she led Sherry into the bathroom and turned on the water, adding foaming gel. "This is Jean Naté," Ida said. "It will make you smell beautiful." Ida left her favorite nightgown, with the yellow bow under the collar, hanging on the bathroom door for Sherry.

When Ida later entered the living room, Mike Ribeiro was seated next to Betty and Sherry on the couch, talking about dogs. Skeet listened, standing off to the side.

"There was a recent case in the law journal of a pit bull owner prosecuted for assault with a deadly weapon." Mike Ribeiro snorted with laughter, although Ida could not tell what was so humorous. "The dog injured a man, call him Victor, who approached the owner, call him Owen, on the street about a bad debt. Victor provoked an argument and then knocked down Owen's bicycle, and the dog—well within his rights, if you ask me—attacked Victor. Victor later testified that he felt the dog had acted justifiably, but some busybody, a young woman passerby, called the police and served as the prosecution's star witness. Owen stayed in jail for eight months, unable to make bail before trial, his dog was sent to the ASPCA—dog jail—and Owen eventually was convicted and sent to prison."

"That sounds unusually unfair," Ida interrupted. "Come sit on the sofa, honey," Ida told Skeet.

Skeet would have felt more comfortable around a quiet

man, distrusted Mike Ribeiro's talkativeness, and stayed where he was, staring at the floor, his pale, old man's hair hiding his expression.

Sensing Skeet's unease, Mike Ribeiro turned to him and said, "The prosecutor argued, 'Jurors, this dog gripped that man's arm for ten full minutes before he let go. How long is six hundred seconds? Imagine this homicidal beast gnawing, gnawing, gnawing, that's only three seconds, gnawing, gnawing, gnawing, three more seconds, gnawing, gnawing, gnawing . . .'"

Skeet looked up and grinned.

"If it was my dog who did that," Skeet asked, drawing closer, "would I go to prison?"

"They can't send someone your size to prison," Mike Ribeiro counseled. "You'd just slip between the bars and escape."

"Children don't go to jail, honey," Skeet's mother followed.

When Ida tucked her children into bed that night, Skeet told her, "Sherry thinks Mrs. Tutwiler pees on her braids."

"Skeet!" Ida answered. "What a thought! Now listen, you two. For the time being, I want you to stay away from Mr. Purdy, and his dog, and that Chicken man. This is not your fight. I don't want to have to worry about you being hurt." Ida turned out the light and closed their door, leaving the children in pitch blackness.

Sherry wrapped herself in her blanket, turning around twice so that it held her like a cocoon. (Ida had given Skeet and Sherry separate sheets and blankets because she felt uncomfortable with the notion of a sister and a brother sharing the same bed, even if they were both under ten years old.) Sherry listened for her brother's breathing. She thought of the house in Baton Rouge, with its gloomy frightening crucifixes and blood-red velvets and her mother's high-posted bed she let Sherry crawl into in the mornings after Harlan left. Sherry was glad to be in a new place, where danger was not some unnameable fear, a ghost flickering in a shadowy room, but plain and palpable, where monsters were called Chicken and walked in broad daylight and failed to unnerve her brother.

Skeet watched the lights from passing cars move over the ceiling. Sherry heard her brother rustle under his covers and said, "I didn't know that children couldn't be put in jail."

Skeet answered that if you were going to commit a crime, you would have to do it while you were still young, before you lost your chance.

"I can't think of any crime I want to do right now," Sherry told him.

Skeet volunteered that putting sugar in someone's gas tank, as Betty Trombley had mentioned a few days before in the kitchen, might be a crime. "It has to be against the law to destroy a whole car," he reasoned.

Sherry wondered how you would get sugar in a gas tank. She knew enough to unscrew a gas cap, because she had seen a service station attendant show Skeet how to fill the New Yorker's tank. But she found it hard to believe you could pour sugar sideways. Maybe you would spoon it in, one spoonful at a time. But then it would take too long and someone would surely catch you.

She lay quietly in the darkness for several minutes. She pictured the molasses in Betty's cupboard. ("Mo'lasses for mo' flavor," Betty said at breakfast, pouring the tarry liquid into her coffee as their mother dropped sugar cubes into her own cup.) Could you pour molasses into the mouth of a gas tank? It would take forever; someone would catch you.

Sherry tugged on Skeet's covers. "Sugar cubes," she said.

Skeet sat up and peered into the darkness where he thought Sherry was also sitting up.

"If I wanted to do that to a car, I'd use sugar cubes," Sherry told him. "You could plop them in easy."

Skeet said, "You could plop them right into a big ugly car like the one Chicken drives."

Sherry felt a suppressed snicker shake her. "I'd put in *a whole box.*"

Skeet shrieked with laughter.

"Go to bed, you two!" their mother called from the living room.

They lay down and listened to the voices of the adults, rising and deepening and interrupting one another. Skeet and Sherry tossed inside their covers, unable to sleep, kindled by the outrageousness of their idea. They fell silent until they thought their mother would believe they had fallen asleep, and then they sat up again, whispering to each other.

They looked out their back window, toward the river. The moon lay like a new dime in the middle of the pond of sewer water trapped behind the building.

A small light beam, reddish, the size of a hand-held flashlight, moved toward them from the far end of the pond. The red beam pierced a circle of light cast from a street lamp beside Betty's building. Skeet and Sherry leaned farther out the window. Below them, ghostlike, a figure seemed to be riding in a small skiff, facing backward. It held oars in its hands and moved the boat steadily toward the basement window beneath them. Standing at the boat's prow was a shadowy being, anvil-headed.

"Whoa now, Joseph," Skeet and Sherry heard below them. Henry Purdy grabbed a protuberance on the side of the building and tied the boat to the wall with a rope. He stood up in the boat, holding a large screwdriver, and jimmied open the window. And then he crawled through. Joseph sat back in the prow, hurtled himself forward, and leapt into Henry's apartment. The window banged shut behind them.

All of the front windows of the basement apartments were barred with iron grillwork that predated Rupert Dixon's purchase of the Grand Street building. When he arrived the following morning to examine Chicken's work, Rupert saw lamplight coming through the grates over Henry Purdy's windows.

Rupert walked toward the basement. He passed Betty Trombley, seated on the stoop like a gargoyle next to a dumpy-looking woman whom Rupert did not recognize as one of his tenants, a little red-haired girl, and the boy who Rupert suspected kept the pit bull as a pet. Irritatingly, all of them followed him downstairs.

Rupert examined Chicken's work. He tested the bar and found it to be soundly mounted. He removed a green-and-gold pencil stub from behind his ear and circled a paragraph on the notice tacked to the door. However, as he turned to leave, a radio inside Henry Purdy's apartment blasted a jaunty Caribbean tune.

"What the fuck is going on here?" Rupert asked.

Ida clucked her tongue. "Language," she said.

Rupert wrinkled his forehead and looked at her briefly. He turned back to the door, removed the padlock, and pulled down the heavy iron bar. He opened Henry's door.

Before the landlord rose a smooth wall of bricks, extending from the floor to the ceiling and spreading from one doorjamb to the other. The wall was artfully, even ornately, made, with light bricks set next to dark ones in a chessboard pattern. Four large bricks decorated with carved cherubs were set in the corners. In the center of the wall was a hole guarded by a square of metal.

"I'll be dipped in shit and rolled in cracker crumbs," Betty said.

"Purdy!" Rupert yelled.

The metal square was lifted, and behind the small hole, Henry Purdy's crossed eyes bobbed into view and then disappeared as the metal square shut.

"What the hell is this?" Rupert spoke into the metal square. "Have you lost your mind, Purdy?

Henry Purdy laughed on the other side of the door: it was a diabolical laugh, but sarcastically diabolical, as if Henry enjoyed appearing demented.

Betty Trombley and the Terhunes followed Rupert to the end of the walkway that led to the back of the building. He forced open a doorway leading into the backyard. There, thirty feet away, in the swamp behind the building, a skiff floated, tethered to the wall next to Henry Purdy's back window.

◆ Sulfur Bombs

In the afternoon, three men arrived at the building in a black van with tinted windows. They knocked on Angel Rodriguez's door, wanting to buy a case of sulfur bombs from him.

"You know what I mean by sulfur bombs?" Angel asked as he sat at Betty's kitchen table across from Ida, waiting for Betty to come home. "The kind where you light a wick on fire and it burns slowly, letting off a stink that will kill all the roaches and mice and rats within smelling distance?"

"My," Ida said, trying to show interest. "I've never heard of that, Mr. Rodriguez." His eyes were terribly bloodshot, as if he had been drinking. She read the pockets of his gray work shirt. *Exterminator* was stitched in orange thread on his right one, and *Angel* on his left one.

"It's a joke," Mr. Rodriguez said. "You know, like 'angel of death.' My first name is Angel. Call me Angel—you keep calling me Mr. Rodriguez."

Ida seldom felt comfortable using first names when addressing older people or people in positions of authority, even after she had known them for a long time, unless they were family or she felt a special connection to them, as she did to Huey Long, whom her father had always called just plain Huey or Kingfish or, jokingly, "The Earl." Even when such people insisted that she use their first names and Ida complied out of politeness, she would continue to call them Mr. or Mrs. So-and-so when she spoke of them privately. At times, she even thought of herself as "Mrs. Terhune."

"Anyway, the thing about sulfur bombs is that you can't stay in your apartment after you light them. You have to go out for a good long while. Take an afternoon at Sandy Hook. Do your laundry *and* go shopping. You can't breathe in the fumes."

"I see," Ida said.

"So, soon after I shut the door, I said to myself, Why would anyone want a whole case of sulfur bombs? Those things are strong. I began to worry. Well, maybe they work for a landlord somewhere. Maybe they're fixing up a new building and need to hit a lot of apartments at once. Only they didn't look it. You know, they had black leather jackets on. Dark glasses. Big guys. Up to no good. So I went to my window and looked out, and there they were, still sitting in their van, parked across the street from here, just staring at the basement. Then it hit me. They do work for a landlord. You know. *Our* landlord."

Ida wasn't sure what Mr. Rodriguez meant to imply.

"They intend to use those sulfur bombs here. *All* of them."

Was he complaining that the men were encroaching on his territory? To think I live in a building that has to be fumigated, Ida thought. But she did not communicate this sentiment to Mr. Rodriguez, for fear of offending him. After all, he was an exterminator.

"Get my drift?" Angel asked.

Ida nodded. "I believe I do, Mr. Rodriguez."

"Well, just pass it on to Betty, will you?" Angel said. "I'm sorry to trouble you," stuffy lady, he added mentally, "but it's important."

A rotten yellow smell crept over Betty's kitchen windowsill during dinner as Ida told her, "Mr. Rodriguez came here today to say that he thought Mr. Dixon had hired some men to exterminate your building."

"Hired exterminators? Why would he do that when Angel has always done it so cheaply? This must be a retaliatory action on Rupert Dixon's part."

"It stinks in here," Skeet said.

Sherry breathed in and confirmed, "Yuck."

Betty walked over to the sink, sniffed the faucet, and said, "It doesn't seem to be coming from the pipes."

A little later, someone knocked on the front door.

Betty opened it, and before her stood Mrs. Tutwiler, her braids wrapped around her ears like the horns of a ram.

"Some thugs broke the windows in Henry Purdy's apartment and threw sulfur bombs inside, and now it smells like death itself down there," Mrs. Tutwiler announced. "Angel can't get in his own apartment for the smell, and the other two families who live down there left for the night to stay with friends. You better come see." Betty and the Terhunes followed Mrs. Tutwiler down the steps.

Only then did Ida realize what Mr. Rodriguez must have been telling her.

By the time they reached the front steps, yellow smoke was billowing from the basement hallway and curling from the cracks under the basement windows in a dozen yellow whirlwinds. Angel stood on the sidewalk, chatting with some other tenants.

"Stay on the pavement," he told Skeet and Sherry. "You don't want to breathe that stuff in."

A yellow miasma floated across the vacant lot, swirling over the broken bricks and gliding around the building until dissipating across the street a few yards from the black van.

"Dixon's trying to smoke Henry out," Angel announced.

"I've never seen anything like it. They must have twenty of them burning at once in there."

"That pigfucker. He's going to kill Henry," Betty said quietly.

"No he won't," Angel answered. "I warned Henry right after I talked to that Terhune lady." He nodded at Ida. "He got out this afternoon with his dog and is hanging out by the Morris Canal boat colony."

Skeet and Sherry slipped away onto the road, in the direction of the junkyard.

"You come inside," Ida commanded, and the children returned to the sidewalk.

The men in the black van stayed until after nightfall. Angel climbed the stairs to Betty's and watched the van from the kitchen, waiting for the smell to diminish. At nine o'clock, when it was too dark to see, the van's headlights blazed on and it drove away.

In the morning, before the adults awoke, the children pulled on their clothes and tiptoed past Betty Trombley's door, the foldout couch, and Mr. Rodriguez, who had fallen asleep in the barber's chair after shifting it to reclining position. Skeet and Sherry turned the locks and knobs on the front door with infinite slowness and left it open as they soundlessly stepped into the hallway and down the stairs.

Sherry carried a box of Domino sugar cubes tucked under her shirt. "I'm having a sugar baby," she said, tittering and pointing to her stomach.

"Shh!" Skeet told her.

Outside, Grand Street looked desolate in the early morning light. The Mercury Marquis was nowhere in sight, but the van had been reparked across the street, half a block from the sidewalk apartment.

The children heard men speaking in the basement and peered around the basement doorjamb. There, Chicken and three men in black leather jackets stood outside Henry Purdy's apartment, talking. Henry Purdy's door had been taken off its hinges and propped above the neighboring dam, and a head-sized hole had been broken through the brick wall Henry had built in his own doorway. Chicken looked through the hole. He raised a pickax, and the three men stood back. Chicken swung the ax and knocked a layer of bricks loose above the hole. Bits of cement flew into the water.

Skeet and Sherry walked back up to the sidewalk, crossed the street, and circled the van. They opened the driver's door. There was nothing of interest inside, nothing to match the curiosity the black-tinted windows evoked. There were just two front seats, and behind them an empty carpeted area.

Skeet shut the door and searched along the van's side for the gas tank.

"They're coming!" Sherry said, ducking behind the van. But it had been a false alarm: no one emerged from the basement. The children heard the pickax crashing against Henry's wall.

When Skeet and Sherry stood up straight, they saw the Mercury Marquis, three cars down, behind a double-parked station wagon.

Skeet, a whoop held back in his throat, crept alongside the row of cars between the van and the white Mercury. The Mercury's back door was unlocked, and Skeet opened it partway. Inspired by his daring, Sherry slipped inside and sat down on a maroon plush seat. Skeet slid in beside her and closed the door after him. He looked at the leather steering wheel cover, the black stereo speakers, the open ashtrays piled with cigarettes, and Chicken's blue police light lying on the floor before the front seat.

Skeet's stomach tied itself into a knot, and he felt as if he would die from happiness and fear, from the terrible and beautiful realization that rules, any rule and every rule, could be broken by anyone, even by him. He could be dragged from one end of the country to another, tied to a useless trailer, led into a hurricane, and forced to live in a stinking apartment, but he could also set in motion things just as unexpected by the adults who ran his world in their accustomed chaotic way.

"I'm going to go through with it," Skeet said. "I'm really going to go through with it."

He opened the door and crawled on his hands and knees to the gas tank. Sherry leaned over the front seat and lifted the blue police light. She pulled out the box of sugar cubes and tucked the light inside her shirt. She followed Skeet and closed the Marquis's door behind her. No one could see them. The junkyard lay to their rear, and the double-parked station wagon blocked their view from the street.

Skeet pried open the gas tank door and unscrewed the cap.

Sherry tore the top off the Domino box and set it on the ground. She and Skeet grabbed at the sugar cubes and pushed them through the gas tank's mouth, one by one, their fingers bumping one another, spilling some of the cubes onto the pavement.

They emptied the box. Skeet screwed on the gas cap and snapped the tank door shut.

They walked toward the junkyard with studied slowness and nonchalance, in search of Joseph. Sherry felt borne alongside her brother by a passion she lacked the words to describe, and Skeet was too exhilarated to talk.

After Skeet hid Chicken's blue police light under the chassis of the junkyard Rambler, he and Sherry sought out Henry Purdy. They found him lying in his skiff on the edge of the boat colony, rocked gently by the waves, his eyes closed and the dog Joseph curled at his feet like a cat.

Did Henry still plan to take him to Ellis Island? Skeet wondered.

Joseph thumped his fat tail, and Henry's eyes popped open. Staring at his own nose, he said, "Hi, Skeeter." To Sherry, he said, "Hi, girl."

"Those men who stunk out your house are still there," Sherry told him.

"They're in your apartment," Skeet added, looking longingly at Joseph. "They took off your door and busted a big hole in the brick wall."

Henry lifted Joseph from the skiff and crawled out himself. He lay on his stomach and groped under a tarp in the boat until his hand found something. He pulled out a long knife.

"This is called a machete," Henry told Skeet. Skeet saw that the blade was dull and rusted.

Henry and the children walked along the path to the junkyard. They stopped when they spotted the three men climbing into the back of the van. Chicken sat in the front and drove the van away, leaving the Marquis behind.

Henry waited a few minutes, as if to reassure himself that the men would not return, and then he headed toward the apartment building, the children and Joseph following.

Mrs. Tutwiler watched them from her fifth-floor window. She had always been sensitive to smells, and the gunpowder odor of the sulfur bombs had kept her up all night. She had risen at four and drunk a pot of tea in her accustomed perch by her window, and so she had seen Skeet and Sherry looking in the van and crawling into Rupert Dixon's white car. She knew they were up to some kind of mischief when they got out and disappeared alongside the Marquis, and she watched them sneak off to the junkyard and squat behind a car's hull as a ghostly blue light fluttered over the junkyard around them. Mrs. Tutwiler recognized Chicken's police light. She also knew that Chicken and his thugs had arrived only an hour before in the van and that Rupert had tailed them in the car and then disappeared into the store he owned at the intersection of Grand and Orestes Cleveland. She would have called Betty Trombley and woken her up had the children not reemerged so soon.

Mrs. Tutwiler poured herself another cup of tea and unraveled one of her braids. However, before she had lifted the brush to her hair and just as the children reached the model living room on the sidewalk, the black van reappeared to the east of the building and parked down the street. Mrs. Tutwiler called Betty Trombley.

Ida picked up the phone.

"Betty," Mrs. Tutwiler said, "I think you better come downstairs quick. Chicken's about to snatch Henry." Only after she had hung up did Mrs. Tutwiler see that Henry was carrying a meat cleaver.

Ida put down the phone and, feeling muddled, snuggled back under her covers. She saw Mr. Rodriguez asleep in the barber's chair, and recalled the night's events. She had slept in her quilted bathrobe, because wearing only a nightgown felt too risqué with a man present.

The front door was open.

Ida sat up and stuck her feet in her fuzzy blue slippers. Before she could formulate a thought, she entered Skeet and Sherry's room. Their beds were empty.

She looked out their back window and saw them walking along the path across the street, right beside Henry Purdy. He carried a long vegetable knife and moved in a half-shuffle like a crazy person, his dog trotting in front of him. Suddenly, the sinking sensation in Ida's stomach, which had been there since she left Harlan, bottomed out, and she realized that she would never miss Harlan again, because the mere flicker of a thought that she might ever lose her children or that any harm might come to them dwarfed every other feeling inside her.

The ringing phone summoned her back to the couch. Ida picked it up, returned it to its cradle to clear the line, and called the police.

Henry and the children were on the basement stairs before they noticed Chicken. Joseph scented him first. He turned his nose to the east and snarled.

Chicken came alone down the street, his boots whacking the pavement, the three men skulking a half-block behind him. Chicken carried his pickax.

Joseph lunged forward. Henry held him by the collar and dragged the dog across the street to the sidewalk house. Chicken and the three men, still at a distance, also crossed the street.

"Stay there, you two!" The children heard their mother call behind them. "Don't you dare move an inch."

Sherry skittered back to the curb, but Skeet, obeying his mother with literal perfection, halted where he was, in the middle of the road.

"Get back on the sidewalk, young man," Ida told him. He returned almost to the curb, staying several feet away from his mother. She grabbed him by the shoulders and pulled him toward her. Skeet saw that she was wearing her bathrobe and ridiculous furry blue slippers.

"I called the police, and they're on their way here."

"Why?" Betty Trombley asked, coming up behind Ida in a red slip. "Why the police?" Mrs. Tutwiler loomed beside Betty, looking like a banshee with one half of her hair unraveled.

"Why?" Ida answered.

Now Chicken was only a dozen yards from Henry, who had seated himself on the sidewalk couch, his fingers gripping Joseph's choke chain. Chicken stopped when he saw the dog.

"You're undesirable, Purdy," Chicken called to him. "We're not taking any more shit from you."

Henry let go of Joseph. The dog strode halfway to Chicken and stopped. He sat on the pavement, spreading out his back legs behind him and pointing his nose toward Chicken.

"This is your last day here." Chicken raised the pickax, cocked it back as if it were a baseball bat, and said, "I'll give you to the count of three to disappear. Strike one." He swung the pickax in slow motion. The three men stopped halfway down the street, talking among themselves.

Henry balanced his knife on his knees.

"Strike two," Chicken said, swinging again in slow motion.

Joseph remained calm, but he stood and took a few steps toward Chicken.

Chicken swung the third time, hard, as if really hitting a baseball. The pickax flew out of his grip and across the street, smashing into the side of the New Yorker. The ax bounced off the curb, and its wooden handle went *thonk* as it hit the street. Chicken stepped back, watching the ax, surprised his weapon had separated itself from him.

Joseph sensed that an acceptable human limit had been transcended. He shot toward Chicken. Chicken kicked at the dog, missing him. Joseph opened his jaws as if in a silent roar and shut them on the ankle of Chicken's right boot.

Chicken shouted and shook his leg in terror. He stamped his foot and hobbled across the street, pounding on the pavement with each step, but Joseph held on. When Chicken reached the other curb, he kicked out ahead of him, slamming Joseph's body into the side of the New Yorker. Joseph's mighty jaws scissored into the boot like a Gila monster's, heat-seeking and perhaps for that interval even bloodthirsty, capable of withstanding the pressure of several hundred pounds. By the time Chicken began striking Joseph's head with his fists, the dog was lost in a primeval trance, deeper than instinct, tighter than the force that held the universe together before it burst apart, more tranquil and steady than the eye of a cyclone, more blissful than Eden.

The three men ran toward Chicken.

A siren rose in the distance. The three men halted in midrun and looked at one another. Behind them, Rupert Dixon emerged from his store, wearing his torn baseball hat, a green-and-gold pencil perched behind his ear. He walked unhurriedly toward his apartment building.

A police car, red lights reaching far beyond the parsimonious radius of Chicken's blue light, rounded the corner of Jersey Avenue and parked on Grand Street. Two officers emerged from the vehicle and approached the small crowd accumulating on the sidewalk in front of the Grand Street building. The police slipped through the crowd, and seeing Joseph, his wedge head pointed toward the earth, his jaws embedded in Chicken's boot, they retreated to their patrol car. Rupert Dixon spoke to them, and Skeet watched one officer unhook his car radio and ask for the fire department.

Several passersby stopped to watch, thickening the crowd.

Chicken shouted and smacked Joseph on the shoulders and head, stomped his boot on the curb, dragged the dog across the sidewalk to the vacant lot, and slung him into the crazy-quilt wall on the building's right side. The mural of the assumption hovered over them, Mary wide-eyed and still as death, as Joseph continued to cling to Chicken in dead silence. The crowd yelled and hooted as if at a spectacular dogfight.

Now the huge man cursed and tried to kick Joseph with

his free leg. Losing his balance, Chicken toppled onto the dog, his head knocking the wall of the apartment building, his body crumpling onto the rubble of the lot. Joseph crawled out from under the fallen Chicken, still holding on to his boot. A second siren blared in the background, and a medium-sized fire truck turned the corner of Jersey Avenue and stopped at Orestes Cleveland Road. "The big guy's fainted," an onlooker said.

"Smacked his head," someone corrected.

Two firemen, in black-and-yellow jackets, disembarked from the fire truck, carrying a canvas hose. The crowd stepped back. The firemen stopped in front of Joseph and Chicken and signaled to a third man on the fire truck. The hose coiled upward, like a tornado in slow motion, and then a waterspout shot upward from it, high into the air. The firemen aimed the hose at the rubble-covered lot, and a blast of water hit the ground, carving a wide, mud-filled hole before the current was turned off. The men turned the hose, which now seemed to have a life of its own as it twisted and coughed a burst of leftover water. The hose pointed at the dog's hindquarters.

"Don't worry," one of the firemen told Chicken's unconscious body. "I've got perfect aim."

The crowd laughed. The firemen once again signaled toward the truck.

A battering ram of water hit Joseph. For several seconds, he held on as his feet were lifted from the ground by the force of the water. Then he whirled backward. Instantaneously, he regained his feet, a piece of dark-red leather in his jaws, and faced the hose as if it were another animal.

Skeet broke away from Ida and darted toward the dog before an onlooker grabbed him away from the column of water. He yelled and thrashed as the water again moved toward Joseph.

Behind Skeet, Sherry cried, "Stop it, stop it, stop it, stop it!"

The water caught the dog in the ribs, and miraculously, he stayed on his feet under the full force of the hose, and stepped to the side. The current shifted, hitting Joseph in the chest and jaw. He spun backward and lay stunned while the water continued to pummel him.

"This is excessive." Ida Terhune's voice rose over the fracas. She stepped right up to the mouth of the hose, apparently willing to interpose herself between the dog and the firemen, if necessary. The water, as if responding to her sensibleness, or perhaps just aware of its victory, lessened to a column no bigger around than a garden hose, worried the fur on Joseph's neck, and splashed Ida's fuzzy blue slippers. Finally, the water crept backward, arching and narrowing to a trickle.

Now the police sidled from their car. Rupert gestured at the sidewalk house, where Henry Purdy still sat, watching the action before him unfold, the rusty knife balanced on his knees. The police walked across the street toward him. He dropped his knife as one officer unholstered his gun and walked behind the couch. The other policeman, his right hand resting on his nightstick, stopped in front of the couch. Henry's terror held him like a halter: the first officer had to pull Henry's hands from where they gripped his thighs in order to handcuff him.

"Let him go! What did he do?" Betty Trombley yelled, following the police as they led Henry like a wobbly calf to their patrol car. But when one of the officers raised his gun and held the barrel against Henry's temple, even Betty grew motionless. The officer slid into the patrol car behind Henry and told Betty, "You're obstructing the law." The door closed behind him.

Rupert whispered to one of the black-jacketed men, who descended the basement stairs and then reemerged, carrying the door to Henry's apartment. The two other men lifted Chicken onto it. He looked dead, stretched out on the door, his ankle curiously revealing no injury. Like pallbearers, the three men carried Chicken to the van and laid him in the back. Two of the men crawled in after him, and the third slammed the doors shut and climbed in the front seat. He started the engine and drove Chicken homeward or to the hospital, whichever Rupert Dixon deemed best.

The scene of the fight pulled apart, piece by piece: the fire truck drew away from the curb, its hose's golden head folded neatly over its canvas coils. The crowd widened and divided into small groups interested in exaggerating or diluting the drama through discussion. The police car, its siren blaring gratuitously, sped toward Hudson County Penitentiary, with Henry in the back seat. Rupert Dixon stepped into his Mercury Marquis and turned on the ignition. Sherry tucked her hand into Ida's, and Skeet stroked the dog Joseph where he lay on his side, breathing shallowly, tiger-striped, his jaws still clutching the dark leather.

Part III

STEALING

◆ Shoplifting

He knew he delighted the children. He would come to the Grand Street building carrying an overfilled briefcase in one hand and flowers in the other—exotic hothouse flowers from Manhattan, which he proclaimed were for Betty or Ida or Sherry, whichever woman wanted them. Skeet and Sherry would attack him from behind when he sat on the armchair in the living room, and he would snatch them, one-handed, and toss them over the chair back and tickle them to the floor. He would let them puff on his cigar, and he would carry them by their feet in front of him, their skulls bobbing precariously over the linoleum, as they objected in pleasantly terrified voices, or he would let Sherry sit on his shoe as he walked, goose-stepping high in the air so that she shrieked in mock terror.

Ida would listen as Mike Ribeiro sat in the kitchen,

describing his criminal cases with gusto and amusement at their lurid details, or debating with Betty Trombley over politics and legal matters, which Ida found incomprehensible.

"Impeaching a witness can be a hair-raising process," he had told Betty yesterday, while Ida was scouring the top of the refrigerator. "If you're too good at it, even a truthful person will appear to be a liar, so that, standing up there, you yourself begin to believe that the truth is a lie, that truth is something that can be altered through verbal intimidation." These words had been jumbling around in Ida's head all day. She had found his statement difficult to follow, but what she did understand, she did not approve of.

Ida was unsure what the lawyer's motives were: she had never met anyone like him. Was he interested in Betty? A married man! (Ida did not consider a man who was merely separated to be unencumbered.) Ida felt uncomfortable around Mike Ribeiro. She was careful to remain on formal terms with him, to avoid attracting him in any way.

Betty had invited him for Sunday breakfast, ostensibly to discuss Henry Purdy, and Ida intended to occupy herself in the kitchen when he appeared. Betty could chat with him in the living room. She evidently enjoyed sitting with him on Ida's futon couch, talking about the landlord and Henry Purdy's defense and raising money for the Free Henry Fund. Ida hoped that Betty had the sense not to become entangled with a man who was newly separated. Betty had always had flighty relationships. Even now, Betty spiked punch for block parties, brought her radio down to the front steps, and danced on the sidewalk in front of the apartment building with men she'd never met.

However, if Betty was attracted to Mike Ribeiro, she wasn't showing it: as far as Ida could tell, Betty never let the topic stray to anything romantic. The one time Ida had implied that the lawyer was interested in her, Betty had answered, "Christ, Ida, we're just friends. Can't a man and woman be friends?" But Ida did not believe that a man and woman could just be friends, and her curiosity was piqued.

Betty had secured a job through Mike Ribeiro as an investigator for the municipal public defender's office. For this job she had purchased a man's white shirt and brown trousers and wing-tip shoes, and she wore an ID photo clipped to her front pocket. She was obviously in love with the drama of the job. "They said it was too dangerous for a woman," Betty had announced to Ida, looking absolutely thrilled.

Betty was seldom home. When she was not working at the court, she rushed from one tenants meeting to another, and as if this was not enough, she had begun attending a hairdressing course two nights a week. Her classes did not end until ten o'clock, and often she did not return home until after midnight.

As Ida mixed a bowl of flapjacks, Betty padded into the kitchen wearing red long johns. She looked like one of those lanky hillbillies that had been so popular on television at one time. "Mo'lasses for mo' flavor," she announced, pouring molasses into the cup of coffee Ida set in front of her. Betty added, "I wish you'd reconsider Mike Ribeiro's offer to work as his legal secretary."

"I'm not going to help criminals," Ida answered. "We're out of maple syrup," she followed. "Skeet!" she called, and then, louder, "Skeet and Sherry!"

Skeet's dog trotted into the kitchen, his barrel chest still wrapped in the bandage the veterinarian had taped to his shaved ribs three weeks before. His mouth half open, the dog stared at Ida inquisitively, as if she had summoned him. In the end, Ida's natural tendency to indulge her son, and the lawyer's persuasions, had won out over her belief that the dog was dangerous. Mike Ribeiro had argued that Joseph had attacked only when provoked, to protect his owner. "If anything, the dog makes Skeet's life safer," he had concluded, Skeet grinning beside him conspiratorially.

"If you won't work for Mike," Betty persisted, "what about teaching? Jersey City's crawling with parochial schools."

Ida tested the skillet, dropping some pancake batter from a spoon into a puddle of corn oil. She watched the little islands form and darken too quickly. Ida turned down the flame, slid the pan off the burner, and said, "Stop distracting me, Betty."

"Stop distracting yourself," Betty answered, sitting at the kitchen table. Her long legs bumped the chair across from her. "The sisters at Immaculate are always looking for lay teachers. The diocese pays peanuts, so you don't have to be certified. You don't have to be very intelligent, either. Or like children. You don't even have to be Catholic anymore. All you have to do is—"

"I'd like to earn a little more than peanuts, thank you," Ida said. She did not want to be a schoolteacher: a sharp-chinned spinster preoccupied with obedience.

Ida still had every intention of acquiring work, but her expectations collided with her fears, causing her to feel paralyzed. She rarely stepped outside. When she did, the ugliness of downtown Jersey City and the hot August air made Ida feel grimy and lethargic. She kept her shopping trips down to weekly excursions, and when something was needed in the interim, she sent her children to the corner store.

Ida reasoned that she could not take a job where she had so little prospect of landing a husband: she imagined Immaculate was full of young single women in shabby clothes, tittering in the presence of a handful of priests and almost priests and those unmarrying bachelors she associated with parochial schools.

"You might consider living without one for a while," Betty told Ida.

"Without what?"

"A husband."

"That's what I seem to be doing at the moment. Stop trying to read my mind. I'll never understand why you never remarried." Ida immediately regretted her tactlessness.

Betty answered: "When I was twenty, my mother confided in me that every Wednesday for thirty years she had told my father she was going out to visit my aunt. All those years, she was lying. She was really going out by herself. Sometimes she would just walk around all day, or she would take herself out to eat or go to a movie. Sometimes she would go to a store and try on dresses she didn't have the money to buy. The point was, my father didn't know what she was doing. It was, she said, her only free time, the only time when she felt like herself. Well, that really gave me the willies. I never could see taking the risk of marrying for keeps."

Just what point was Betty trying to make? Ida wondered, but she was relieved that Betty's feelings had not been hurt. If anyone had thought to ask Ida whether she wished to remarry, she would have explained that she did, because now that she had come unmoored from Harlan, she was afraid of losing all ties with the world. She was so naturally retiring that she could easily have spent her whole life in one room.

"Skeet and Sherry!" Ida called again. "Run down to the corner store and get some maple syrup. Make it snappy so the pancakes don't get cold."

Ida's children burst into the kitchen, smelling like gunpowder and carrying unwound rolls of red caps. Skeet took some money from a jar on the table. Sherry, her henna hair faded to a pinkish color, tossed her gold scarf over her shoulder and clattered down the stairs after him.

Ida slid the skillet back onto the burner and stole a look out the window. Since vandals had meddled with the landlord's car three weeks before, Ida worried perpetually about the New Yorker and always parked it in plain view of the apartment. Mrs. Tutwiler sat on the sidewalk near the car, her head cocked in the direction of the pay phone, where a young man in dark glasses stood, his hand cupped over the receiver.

Ida's children passed the New Yorker, and the dog galloped beside them. Instead of going directly to the store, they detoured up the path to the junkyard, disappearing behind an abandoned car under a tree. Moments later, Ida saw blue light pulsating inside the car, and passing eerily across the underside of the tree. Ida recalled a newsreel she had once seen of flying saucers that had illuminated the vegetation around them as they landed and left nothing but a circle of scorched grass beneath them after they departed.

The children emerged on the path back to Grand Street. The dog plunged ahead of them into the orange sea of cosmos flowers, which had multiplied and doubled in height. The flowers made Ida think longingly of her garden on Tulip Street.

Persaud's Corner Store was not really on the corner: it stood a dozen feet from the path to the junkyard, where the long arm of Orestes Cleveland Road terminated, abruptly and empty-handed, at Grand Street. The store had been run for several years by the Guyanese man after whom it was named, until Rupert Dixon jacked up the commercial rent, forced out his tenant, and purchased the store's goodwill for a song. On the store's back shelves, customers could still find five-pound packets of unlabeled spices, mixed by Mrs. Persaud and meant to increase and enrich breast milk; assorted curries; homemade ginger beer bottled by Persaud and his cousins; calendars printed in Hindi and tiny figurines of eight-armed goddesses wearing pointy hats; and old blue coolers where Persaud had kept a curry made from goat giblets and pancreas. Now these objects lay gathering dust, since they were foreign to Rupert and of uncertain value. In Persaud's day, a group of men had collected in the store's back room on Friday nights, playing circular Eastern music, drinking, talking, and eating the goat curry, and inviting Betty Trombley and any customer to try the ginger beer or a little Caribbean rum.

Now only Rupert could be seen on some days in the back room, going over his books with a green-and-gold pencil stub and drinking one-quart bottles of Pepsi-Cola, a gigantic ceiling fan whirling directly above him, seeming to derive its energy from him. He employed a man named Bob Paper at the register, who had never spoken aloud in anyone's recollection, and who looked like a Dixon but evidently was not one, as if Rupert's tendency toward nepotism had failed to articulate itself completely in the clerk. Rupert kept the front of the store stocked with milk, kitchen matches, beer, baby formula, cigarettes, Popsicles, mousetraps, a powdery white rat poison, pencils, television guides, and other small necessities. He charged twice and even three times the ordinary retail price but kept the store open all night and on Sundays and holidays, and Bob Paper did most of the business at those times.

Even before the Grand Street floods, Betty Trombley had avoided the store on principle, because she missed Persaud and his loud, merry Friday nights. Skeet and Sherry used the store only when their mother sent them there, and they always checked first to ensure that Rupert was not inside. Because Skeet now went nowhere without Joseph, the children observed this precaution religiously, although on the one occasion they had run into Rupert when he was visiting the Grand Street building, he revealed no interest in them or the dog. Rupert had looked down at Joseph and smiled slightly, as if the dog's fight with his own son three weeks before somehow tickled the landlord and had earned Joseph his admiration. No one had seen Chicken since the fight, and so the tenants speculated that either he had been so badly injured he was still not ambulatory or he had been hurt so little he was ashamed to return to Grand Street.

Or perhaps, as Betty opined, Rupert, having banished the dog's owner, no longer cared one way or another about the dog. Not that Rupert had backed down after the fight. It was only that he had moved invisibly, his retaliations creeping up on his tenants like the yellow smoke of the sulfur bombs. Only moments after turning on the Mercury's ignition, Rupert had snapped it off, emerged from the car, and surveyed the ground near its back wheels until finding stray sugar cubes, as if an extra sense permitted him to elude such easy destruction. Thereafter, he had called a tow truck from his store, and two days later, the Mercury returned to Grand Street with new white-wall tires, hubcaps ornate as cathedral windows, and one of the black-jacketed men chauffeuring. The chauffeur was rumored to have the same pale, lashless eyes as Chicken and Rupert, although no individual tenant could claim to have seen, even after nightfall, the man without his dark glasses, which were tinted an unusual veridian green that reminded Mrs. Tutwiler of the stagnant pond behind the building. Mrs. Tutwiler did not believe the chauffeur was related to Rupert Dixon, except by obligation or common desire. The man always remained in the front seat, guarding the car, so that the Grand Street tenants felt watched as they entered and exited their building.

The sidewalk living room also had vanished the night after the fight, and everyone attributed this to Rupert, for only a week later a city road crew had begun widening the sidewalk where the sofa had been and laying cement for the base of what appeared to be a monument to a petty historical figure of Jersey City. Periodically, Rupert would leave Persaud's Corner Store to talk to the foreman as the road crew milled slowly around them, five men taking two weeks to mix and pour a few batches of cement that a man like Henry Purdy might easily have prepared in a few hours.

The basement and backyard remained flooded, although in the August heat, the water level had dropped significantly, so that now only three or four inches of greenish sludge lapped at Henry Purdy's dams. Finally—and all the tenants attributed this to Rupert, although without a shred of evidence—Henry Purdy's bail had been denied. Although initially he had been charged with a petty offense, unlawful possession of a weapon, "to wit, a dagger, dirk or stiletto," the Municipal Court refused to release him when the prosecutor revealed there was a warrant out for Henry's arrest on theft charges in some godforsaken Pine Barrens county where Henry swore he had never been.

Brandishing a sink pipe, Joseph emerged from Henry Purdy's gaudy orange cosmos flowers. The dog continually brought things to Betty's apartment, depositing them at the front door or under Skeet's bed: a new baseball bat; a large, unopened bag of butter mints; a five-pound reel of multicolored telephone wire; and a man's homburg hat—objects that suggested a story with a struggle in it or a discovery made in solitude. Joseph dropped the pipe at Skeet's feet. Skeet threw it at a trowel left by one of the cement layers, so that the trowel clanged pleasantly and leapt into the air. Skeet had been surprised several times recently by the accuracy of his throwing arm—he had knocked out the lamp of the corner street light two nights before with a rock tossed high in the air. He had been startled when the air suddenly grew dark above him, seeming to swallow the rock and everything around it.

Skeet pulled Joseph to the monument, and the dog watched compliantly as Skeet lifted his paw and pushed it into a square of soft, wet cement to the left of the brass plaque reading F. H. EGGERS: SON OF JERSEY CITY, so that forever thereafter the name appeared to refer either to a dog or to a man who had been eaten by one. Sherry entered Persaud's Corner Store, waving Skeet inside after checking for Rupert's absence. Bob Paper did not look up from where he stood behind the counter, intent on winding a spool of paper into the receipt compartment of Persaud's antiquated cash register.

"Where's the maple syrup?" Skeet asked, solely for the pleasure of proving again to himself and his sister that the clerk would not answer. Bob Paper gestured in the general direction of the right half of the store. Skeet headed for a far aisle, and Sherry walked nonchalantly behind him, searching for something to pocket.

The first thing Sherry had shoplifted had been a long brown root labeled "manioc" at the Shop-Rite on Grove Street. She had slid the root inside her pants pocket with the hole in it and then held her breath, thinking that the world might stand still or, at least, that a punishing hand might reach out and grab her by the back of the neck. But nothing had happened. She had accompanied her mother, somewhat stiff-legged, up and down the aisles, stood by her as the cashier rang up her purchases, and then followed her out to the car, big as you please.

"I can't believe that supermarket," Sherry's mother had said. "The meat section smells like a slaughterhouse. And they don't have greens, and the vegetables they do have are all shrunken and spotty. The lettuce is criminal. How do people here stay healthy?"

Sherry had had trouble sitting in the New Yorker's back seat, because the root dug into her thigh. It was also difficult climbing the stairs to the apartment, because the root poked farther and farther out of the hole in her pocket. But Sherry had arrived safely in her room and wrapped the root in her yellow scarf.

Since then, she had collected several other oddities: a card from the stationery store that said *Condolences: Your friends are with you in this time of need;* a Ramses ribbed condom in a gold packet, from Palace Drugs; and a pair of pinking shears from J&G Fabrics, which she had pushed up her sleeve while her mother discussed the prices of various velvets. (Her mother had loved the store, exclaiming that it carried dozens of fabrics she hadn't seen in ten years.)

Skeet paid for the maple syrup, frowning under his pale, old man's hair as the clerk rang up the price; Skeet was distressed by his mother's obliviousness to the costs of things. After Skeet turned to leave, Sherry saw the clerk reach over the counter into a box printed with the words TIGER BALM and take out a small octagonal jar with a gold cap and a turquoise label. The clerk opened the jar, dipped in his thumb, and rubbed circles of red ointment onto his temples. When he turned his back, Sherry approached the counter, pilfered one of the unopened jars, and wrapped it in her yellow scarf. She wanted to know what the clerk had felt when, a moment after rubbing on the ointment, he had stared vacuously ahead of him as if savoring an overpowering sensation.

When the children mounted the stairs to the apartment, Betty's voice, tendentious and cheerful, rose to meet them.

"Why don't you at least go down to the elementary school and register Skeet and Sherry? It's open all week."

Joseph, sensitive to changes in the children's moods, growled with his mouth closed. Skeet and Sherry looked at each other in shared resentment at the adult intrusion into the world they were concocting together. They associated their new life in Jersey City with a fetterlessness they had hoped would not end.

"I had every intention of doing just that," Ida said. "Give me that hand towel to keep the pancakes warm."

"Good," Betty answered as Joseph and the children entered. "We're having a tenants meeting here this afternoon. We're preparing for a rent strike. I've decided to hold all future tenants meetings in my apartment. I thought I might scare you out of the house by bringing the outside world in."

Ida answered, "I thought just Mike Ribeiro was visiting." She was surprised by the disappointment in her voice.

"Ida," Betty answered, "you're going to start collecting lint if you don't get out. You've barely budged from that piece of the kitchen floor for weeks."

"I'm not a crazy person," Ida answered. "I know exactly where I've been and how long I've been there." When she saw the children, Ida said, "Look, perfect silver-dollar pancakes!" She did not mention school.

Skeet and Sherry exchanged looks and sat down at the table. Sherry fingered the outline of the Tiger Balm jar in her scarf. Abruptly, the jar slipped from the scarf to the floor and rolled under the table between her mother's feet. Sherry retrieved the jar and rewrapped it in the scarf. Her mother did not seem to notice: she was staring ahead of her with a blank look.

On the nights when Betty came home late, after the children were sent to bed, Skeet and Sherry could hear their mother roaming the kitchen, sobbing unexpectedly as she rearranged Betty's knives in the silverware drawer. Sometimes they would find her at the kitchen table in the morning, right where they had left her the evening before, bowed over the classifieds and drinking coffee black and thick as oil, bitter with chicory.

Confessions

In addition to having sacrificed everything else, Ida had lost her privacy, the thing in the world that she valued most highly. Mike Ribeiro, once again, had spread his legal papers on the kitchen counter and table. The tenants meetings, held at a moment's notice at any hour of the day, were going to drive her insane. Ida clattered the dishes loudly in the sink and vengefully permitted the sudsy water to spill on the floor, beside the lawyer's briefcase.

Even my children have nowhere to be, Ida thought melodramatically, although Sherry was in the living room, enjoying the noise, and Skeet was drawing a map at the kitchen table. Joseph lay beneath the table, gnawing on an empty wallet he had obtained somewhere outside and thumping his tail against the rungs of Skeet's chair.

"We could drain the sewer water into old soda bottles and

ship them to Rupert Dixon one at a time," Ida heard Betty say. The tenants association hooted and howled. They were a strange collection of people who obviously were unable to find lodging elsewhere: old men and teenaged couples, families who spoke languages Ida had never heard, pregnant girls, odd fish like Henry Purdy and Mrs. Tutwiler, and a young woman who played the harp.

Mrs. Tutwiler's low, eerie laugh lingered after the other tenants quieted. Ida believed that Mrs. Tutwiler, although responsible with the children, was slightly senile. Ida's grandmother had been slightly senile during most of Ida's childhood, although Ida had not realized this until she was in her early thirties, years after Grandma Daigle had died. Ida had often wondered if this was why she felt so baffled by the world—it had been interpreted to her through someone who only remembered to tell her about part of it. For example, Grandma Daigle had been fond of saying, "Don't marry a man unless he's good between the sheets. Because if he's not, the marriage won't last." She would wink when she said this, but she never told Ida what went on between the sheets, much less how Ida could tell if a man was good at whatever did go on, especially if, like Dewey, he refused to sleep with her until their wedding night. It was not until she had married Harlan that Ida realized just how good Dewey had been, and by then it was too late for her to feel thankful about it.

Mike Ribeiro's voice intruded into the cacophony of the tenants meeting. "It's not a matter of raising bail. They simply won't let Henry out, with the warrant waiting for him elsewhere. We'll take one hurdle at a time and first just get him acquitted here." He then told an anecdote about a client who had committed an armed bank robbery. "He had almost pulled the whole thing off, fully disguised by a mask, but then he looked up and saw a partially hidden security camera. He reached up to the camera to cover it and left a full set of fingerprints right on the lens." The tenants association laughed appreciatively. Mike Ribeiro's voice was loud and lively. It reverberated inside the pot Ida had turned on its side to clean, so that the metal seemed to come to life. Although Ida did not approve of Mike Ribeiro's profession, his ties to the criminal world did make him seem somewhat mysterious and attractive.

Sherry appeared at the edge of the sink and said, "Mama, I need some pennies."

"Look in my handbag," Ida told her.

Sherry opened her mother's beige purse where it lay on the table, and peered inside. She almost did not dare to stick in her hand. The purse seemed the repository of her mother's most private possessions: her broken circle of blush, a tin of adult aspirin, a kidney-shaped coin purse, an opened envelope with a letter inside, a package of Wrigley's spearmint gum, and red mouths of lipstick on crumpled tissues. Betty Trombley sometimes carried a drawstring suede bag like Robin Hood's instead of a purse, and she wore lipsticks with names suggestive of adventure: Carmine Dream and Ruby Desire. But when Sherry turned over her mother's lipstick, the case invariably said, simply, "Red." Sherry withdrew the package of gum and the letter and hid them in her pocket. Then she emptied a handful of pennies from the coin purse and laid them on the table, end to end. She opened the bottle of Tabasco sauce that stood beside the salt and pepper and let a drop of the red liquid fall on each coin. Skeet looked up from his map to watch her wipe each penny as it transformed from a dark brown to a radiant copper.

"Meanwhile," Ida heard Betty say, "there are several things we can do to make our landlord's life less comfortable while we're preparing for the rent strike." This was followed by a knowing laugh from the crowd, as the tenants stood up, disbanding for the evening.

Thank God, Ida thought.

"You're an unlikely pair," she heard Mike Ribeiro say to Betty as he shut the door after the last tenant.

"Ida and I get along because she's impossible to argue with. Otherwise, we'd argue all the time." Feeling insulted, Ida chose to ignore the lawyer when he entered the kitchen carrying a stack of papers. Ida saw that he had written at the top of the first page: "Speak briefly, try to sound respectful, and do not fiddle with your necktie."

He grinned at her with an expectant look. Ida willed him

to disappear. However, when he dropped the papers into his briefcase, took out a book, and turned away without even greeting her, she felt annoyed.

"That's quite a map," he told Skeet. "I've never seen a more beautifully depicted sausage company. The monument is spectacular. The dog is terrifying. Henry Purdy would be flattered. I've brought you a book, Skeeter."

Ida knew that Skeet never read unless he absolutely could not avoid it, but his interest was apparently aroused by Mike Ribeiro's interest in him. Skeet laid down his map, and when the lawyer set the book in front of him and placed a hand on his shoulder, Ida saw Skeet grow still: whether with embarrassment or delight, she was not sure.

"It's called *Bruce,* by Albert Payson Terhune, and it's about a great dog of war, a collie dog. I thought Joseph might like having it read to him. Mr. Terhune happens to be one of New Jersey's great writers."

Skeet felt guilty for a moment for the recurring thought that coursed through his mind: I hope Henry Purdy won't get out of jail, so that he can't ever take Joseph back.

Ida had never heard of anyone named Terhune outside of Dewey's family. "Is the book's author still alive?" Ida asked.

"No. He died a long time ago, but his spirit lives on, hovering above the landfills." Before Ida could take in the lawyer's answer, he added, "I also brought something for you, Ida." He pulled out a book titled *The Earl of Louisiana.* "It's about Huey Long. I had to search high and low for it. I have to congratulate myself for finding the book; it's a miracle, given that the second-largest city in New Jersey has no bookstore, unless you count the magazine stand in the Journal Square PATH station."

Ida flushed with pleasure. "When I was a girl," she responded, assuming a girlish expression, "my father used to take Betty and me to breakfast at the Café du Monde in New Orleans on Sundays. We would sit at the same table he and Huey Long had always shared."

"I thought you might enjoy reading about the Earl of Louisiana while you're just sitting around whiling away the hours."

Ida promptly took offense at the judgment implicit in this statement—she hardly sat around. In fact, she would soon be cleaning up the mess left by the tenants association. Mike Ribeiro was certainly bookish, Ida noted. He seemed incapable of holding a conversation without citing two or three titles.

Betty entered the kitchen with a mountain of cups on a tray, left over from the tenants meeting. She was smirking, and Ida knew this was because the lawyer had shown an interest in Ida's father and Huey Long. This increased Ida's general sense of annoyance. Her father had always been nice to Betty, and it seemed gratuitously nasty for her to find his historical significance to be a laughing matter.

"Don't smirk, Betty," Ida commanded.

Hearing the hurt in Ida's voice, Betty suppressed her continuing desire to smirk. Betty could recall a few occasions when Mr. Daigle had taken her and Ida to New Orleans: he had spent each outing jumping up from his chair to shake hands with political cronies, thumping their backs, and flirting with women at other tables. When Betty reached age sixteen, he had begun to flirt with her, but Ida never noticed and Betty ignored him. She knew from the gossip of her mother and aunt that Roy Daigle was a charming, seductive, secretive man who avoided weak, martyrish women who would dote on him and accept his infidelity and tyranny. Instead, he sought hardheaded, fiery women whom he could sweet-talk and conquer and then drive into the ground until they became weak and doting and martyrish. Betty had never known the "infuriating slip of a girl I fell in love with the first time she made me mad" Mr. Daigle liked to tell about on the few occasions when he spoke of Ida's mother. Betty found such a woman, who could stand up to Roy Daigle, difficult to imagine.

"You're doing it again. Stop smirking, Betty," Ida said. "Betty has no pride in the state of Louisiana," Ida told Mike Ribeiro.

"When I was little," Betty said, "my grandmother used to tell me stories about the Civil War as if she had been present to witness it. She told me 'The Time the Yankees Stole the

Silver,' and 'How the Slaves Hid Under the Veranda so They Would Not Have to Be Freed,' and 'I Dug Sweet Potatoes with My Own Hands to Keep from Starving.' It wasn't until I grew up and saw *Gone With the Wind* for the first time that I realized she had simply appropriated whole sections of the movie and made it part of her own personal story. It didn't occur to me until late in life that the Yankees never made it to New Iberia, Louisiana, and that my grandmother wasn't even born yet when the Civil War ended. It takes a special kind of mind, the mind of a southern flibbertigibbet, to appropriate history and distort it for her own private reasons like that."

"Betty, just what is your point?" Without waiting for an answer, Ida turned to Mike. Although as a rule she did not read nonfiction books, she told him, "I am grateful for your thoughtfulness, and I intend to thoroughly enjoy *The Earl of Louisiana.* I'll have to read it right away, since I'm sure to start working any day now."

"That's just what I've come to the kitchen to talk about," Mike answered. He looked at Ida as if he found her to be a fascinating personal challenge. Ida again felt annoyed. "Betty told me you weren't interested in working for me. She said you don't approve of criminal lawyers." He smiled mischievously. "Nothing could persuade you? You could spare me a lot of trouble looking for an administrative assistant if you just tried—"

"No, thank you."

"I'd like to hear your reasons for rejecting my offer."

"Because if I accepted it, I wouldn't be Mrs. Terhune anymore. I'm not going to help criminals."

Mike laughed delightedly. Ida opened the *Jersey Journal* and began reading to show that the conversation had ended. However, she was unable to focus on the advice column, because the lawyer persisted in talking.

"Well, I really did come with other news. I have the perfect employment for you, in the Municipal Court's Office of Complaints. The job would entail typing up summonses for crime victims who wish to press charges for nonindictable offenses—petty violations and misdemeanors. You sit there, listen to them, and match up their stories to the offense in the criminal code that best fits each complaint."

Ida inwardly admitted that it did sound like a good job for her. But then she was distracted by the sudden recollection that her own grandmother had related the same stories that Betty's grandmother had told her. Ida had never thought to question their accuracy.

"The minute I heard that the job had opened up, I thought of you," Mike said, batting his eyes jokingly. Ida was unsure whether he was mocking himself or her.

"All right," Ida conceded, partly out of politeness but primarily to avoid criticism should she reject another suggestion for employment. "I'll try it."

"Good," Mike answered. "It will be nice to have a friend in the enemy camp."

Ida did not like the sound of that. "Look here," she said, pointing at a headline in the newspaper: DO YOU CONVICT INNOCENT PEOPLE? ASKS KILLER ARSON SUSPECT. A man in this very neighborhood confessed to committing arson."

Mike leaned over to study the article. "Oh, Mr. Clinton. I haven't seen him in years."

"If I ever committed a felony," Betty said, enthroning herself in the barber's chair, "I'd *never* confess. I used to take pride in the fact that I kept everything to myself during confessional, when Ida and I were in parochial school together. I'd count off all my sins for the week—disrespecting my father, committing murder in my thoughts—and then I'd turn to the priest and say, 'I'm sorry, Father, but I don't believe I did anything wrong this week.' It would make the priest so angry! What about you, Mrs. Terhune?" Betty asked. "What the hell did you do when you went to confessional? You used to spend forever in there."

"I never knew what to do in confessional," Ida answered, after frowning at Betty's language. "I was so embarrassed not to have any sins to tell about. I'd grope around, trying to come up with something to confess. I finally resolved to tell a white lie and invent a sin every week so that the priest would give me some kind of penance." Ida saw Betty smile at the lawyer with a bemused expression.

"You'd make a good criminal, Betty," he said, launching into one of those speeches on the law that made Ida uncomfortable. "Most of the time, my clients get caught simply because they can't resist boasting to someone, often a girlfriend or drinking cohort, about what they've done. Imagine your typical man: every day he goes to the same job on the same bus and does the same things. He comes home to dinner, and he has nothing of interest to report to his family. If anything at all happens that day—someone at work got fired, the bus broke down, he ran into an old acquaintance—he's sure to mention it. Now, just imagine that this man committed a crime one day. Imagine the irresistible temptation he feels to say to his wife, 'Yes, honey, something did happen today. I embezzled thirty thousand dollars.' Or better yet, 'I stabbed someone to death.'"

"Heavens," Ida said.

Ida dreamed that Mike Ribeiro proposed to her. He drove her to a church for the wedding, but when they entered the building, Ida saw that it was not a church at all—it was a cafeteria. "We're in the wrong place," she told him, but he rushed her on, piling onto her tray dishes she had never seen before—candied okra and pickled chicken and pork parmigiana. A priest greeted them at an altar set up near the lemon meringue pie.

Ida awoke feeling disoriented. She took all Monday morning to prepare for the outing to the local elementary school. She washed the dishes thoroughly first, scouring the fronts and backs of the skillets and bleaching the plates and coffee cups in Dutch cleanser dissolved in water.

"How disgusting," Betty told her.

"My grandmother always bleached the coffee cups."

"That figures," Betty answered, an image of Ida's grandmother looming suddenly in her mind's eye: Mrs. Daigle, smelling faintly of apricot brandy, apronless in a bright-green dress and heaping overspiced jambalayas and gumbos into her son's and granddaughter's bowls.

Ida also thought of her grandmother at that moment,

quarreling with her father about his messes while he ignored her with an affable expression. Grandma Daigle had fought with Ida's father relentlessly, although he never replied to any of her arguments or even appeared to notice them.

Ida pressed clean clothes for the children and shook out her sky-blue pantsuit, a drip-dry polyester hard to find nowadays, which never needed ironing. She polished her beige pumps and buffed them. She emptied the contents of her purse, culling out the necessary items and throwing away the bits of Kleenex, receipts, a melted lipstick, hair balls, and an empty envelope she found in the dark underbelly. She was such an orderly person, the disorder of the nether regions of her handbags always disquieted her.

Although Betty pointed out that the children probably did not have to come with Ida to the school, she did not want to make the journey alone. She and the children cruised the five blocks to the school inside the air-conditioned New Yorker. Joseph sat on the fold-down armrest. He yelped once, in pain, when the New Yorker dipped into a pothole, but then he wagged his tail stoically, as if to demonstrate that he found his own yelping amusing.

"Please don't let him lick you on the mouth, honey," Ida told Sherry. But then the children's mother looked out the window, lost in thought. She passed the school without seeming to notice.

"What will I do when you all are gone all day?" Ida asked.

Sherry told her, "It's that ugly building with the bob wire behind it. Me and Skeet already looked it over."

Neither Skeet nor Sherry informed her that when they had walked down to the school, they had seen a group of boys fill a soda bottle with gasoline, stopper it with a cloth strip, and then toss it over the fence onto the blacktop, where it sparked and exploded in a swirl of fire.

Ida circled the block twice, looking for a parking space big enough to hold the New Yorker.

"You just missed a spot," Skeet said.

Ida parked three blocks from the school, and Skeet rolled down the windows and locked the car doors for Joseph's comfort and protection. Skeet pressed his nose against the outside of the window until Joseph wagged his tail. Ida remembered how she used to smile at Skeet when he was a baby, tickling his neck until he would break out grinning. Skeet thought of his Uncle Porter's coonhounds, spending their days inside the old station wagon in the only shady spot in the yard. He wondered whether Joseph wouldn't like living in the New Yorker. Perhaps Skeet and Sherry could move in with him and just visit the apartment at meals.

Once inside the cheerless cinder-block building, Ida felt challenged at every step. When she tried to register Skeet and Sherry for third grade, the registrar, an imposing woman with turban-shaped white hair, peered down at the children and told Ida, "We have a policy against sticking twins in the same class."

"They're not twins," Ida said. "Skeet and Sherry are ten months apart in age."

The children's narrow-set green eyes peered at the registrar from identical flat faces. The registrar handed Ida two forms. "Please use their full names here. 'Skeet' and 'Sherry' are nicknames?"

"Oh, no," Ida said. "Skeet's father just called him 'Skeeter,' but then he died and I never did know what name he had in mind behind Skeeter. Skeeter is usually just short for mosquito, and I could hardly call him that. So I just wrote Skeeter on the birth certificate." After seven years of Harlan's censorship, Ida still felt uncomfortable when she mentioned Dewey. And she was never at ease talking about her family with a stranger. "Sherry is my daughter's real name. It's not short for Cheryl; it's Sherry. I named her after something I found in my community college English book, a line written by a Yankee poetess, Emily Dickinson: 'And my eyes like sherry in the glass that the guest leaves.'" Ida felt herself blushing and desisted defending her children's names to the outside world.

"Why don't we just try him in the third grade and the girl in the second?" the registrar suggested.

"She reads too well to put her back a year," Ida said. "And Skeet's not far enough ahead to skip third grade."

Sherry leaned forward and studied a clear plastic paperweight with a monarch butterfly frozen in flight, positioned on the registrar's desk.

"Did he fail a grade?" the registrar asked, turning toward Skeet and examining him. "What if we let him do second grade over? And we'll put the girl in third grade."

The registrar's suggestion was so bizarre that Skeet was uncertain whether he had heard her correctly. He was older than Sherry. How could he be in a lower grade?

"He's never failed a grade," Ida said.

Sherry pocketed the paperweight.

"He was sick in kindergarten, and I had to keep him home. He missed too many days for them to pass him, and so I had to start him over again the next year." Ida continued: "My children are very close. They stick together and like being in the same classroom."

"We'll have to see about this. I'll have to talk to the vice-principal," the registrar said with an unshakable smile, adjusting a placard bearing her name, Mrs. Winfidle, printed in gold. Mrs. Winfidle had retained her lowly position through the buffeting currents of several mayoral administrations and the continuing school board scandals of recent years. Only that summer, a board appointee had been found to have a prior conviction for embezzling; and all last year a jury had been investigating the supervisor of social studies for bribery and two high school deans for attempted extortion. Now accusations were flying that foul food had been served regularly in elementary school cafeterias during the preceding year. Mrs. Winfidle had remained unmoved when, only a week before the Terhunes entered her office, the deputy mayor uncovered the misappropriation of school funds totaling millions of dollars. At that time, Mayor Gerald McKann, who himself would be convicted of extortion several years later, had announced his hope that several municipal employees would be fired and arrested. The mayor publicly deplored "the long-held attitude" of people in Jersey City who "decide they themselves will get their piece of the pie." The mayor had declared, "Well, we are not going to protect them." Not until 1987, when the manifest impossibility of achieving a public education in Jersey City would lead to its school system's decertification and takeover by the state, would Mrs. Winfidle relinquish her post and retire to Atlantic City.

Mrs. Winfidle smiled and said, "Skeet, sweetheart, would you like to take a look at our second-grade classroom? Mrs. Flaherty is one of our favorite teachers."

"No," Skeet said. "I'm in third grade."

"I'm going to put you in Catholic school," Ida announced at dinner that evening. Betty had declared it was her night to cook, which meant no one had cooked at all. Betty had bought what she called "pizza bread" from Pecoraro's bakery, declaring, "Nothing I made could possibly taste this good." Sometimes the pizza bread contained cheese or sausage and once even whole hard-boiled eggs, and Ida was uncertain of the correct way to eat it.

"Tuition at Immaculate is only six hundred dollars a year for both of you," Ida told the children. "And besides, I want you to grow up with a proper moral education."

"We never had to have one before," Skeet said. "Not in Baton Rouge." He stirred his water glass with a spoon, creating a gray tornado that swirled from the surface until touching bottom. He thought of the trailer soaring over the Gulf and smiled. He did not want to go to any school where the boys wore clip-on neckties. On the other hand, he thought he would be able to hold his own better against a bunch of boys wearing clip-on ties than, for example, the boy he had seen throw the Molotov cocktail into the schoolyard.

"Having taught at Immaculate," Betty said, "I'm not sure I'd send my kids there. You might do better at All Saints."

"Immaculate is right around the corner."

"But we're not Catholic," Sherry said.

"Well, you would have been if I'd made you go to church. That makes you Catholic," Ida explained.

"Was Daddy Catholic?" Skeet asked.

"Harlan? Yes, although he's somewhat lapsed."

"No. *Daddy,*" Sherry repeated.

"Oh," Ida answered.

"Dewey was a Holy Roller," Betty Trombley said, slicing a loaf of pizza bread containing a reddish sausage that burned Ida's tongue. "His grandmother used to go to a church where you had to bring your own rattlesnakes."

"Betty!" Ida cried.

Skeet and Sherry looked at Betty expectantly.

"But Dewey himself wasn't churchy," Ida told them. "He and Porter always went hunting on Sundays. Let's enjoy dinner."

"Ida, I'm sure they'd give in at the public school if you just pressed a little harder."

"My mind's made up," Ida said. "I can't see raising a ruckus. A rule is a rule."

It did not occur to Betty to suggest that Ida consider splitting up the children. Betty watched their hands hover in tandem over their plates. It was as if they had fashioned each other out of themselves, their identical drawly voices and snickering sense of humor prodding one another into the world and through childhood. Raised by a stepfather who barely noticed them, and a mother who rarely strolled outside her own yard, Ida's children had entered life in a partnership. They went everywhere together, leaning on each other when circumstances required it: when larger children on Grand Street accosted them, when adults irritated them, and when they were asked to move from the only home they knew to a place as crazy as Jersey City.

Sherry felt the paperweight in her pocket and pulled it partway out under the table, revealing to Skeet the coppery wings of the monarch butterfly. Skeet smiled secretively at her. He had seen the paperweight on the registrar's desk and was comforted by the fact that his sister had managed to lift the item without any adult noticing. All day since visiting the school, he had felt irritated and threatened, as if some theft of his person or property were imminent. Now the balance of things had been restored. He felt elated, his heart poised like the monarch's wings, lifted in unalterable flight.

◆ Moral Education

By the end of Skeet and Sherry's second week at school, the third grade at Immaculate had run through two lay teachers. Mrs. Leahy had departed in the first week after learning that she would have no assistant to help instruct her forty-one pupils. The second teacher, Mrs. Hardy, had been surprised by the principal exhibiting her caesarean scar to the class during math period. The third grade's new teacher, Mrs. Julietta Feeley, had settled in to stay.

Mrs. Feeley wore a brown velvet hat that looked like a collapsed devil's food cake, which she bobby-pinned down and never removed. Sherry speculated that Mrs. Feeley was hiding a bald spot. She kept a long-stemmed hand mirror on her desk, and periodically during the first day of class, Mrs. Feeley paused in the lesson and examined herself for as long as a minute. She would make faces as she did this: sometimes she would grin sheepishly at herself, as if she were a pupil who had invited a gentle reprimand. At other times, she would scowl and furrow her brow judgmentally, or she would smile with a look of practiced kindness. She also kept a small plastic case containing pink pills on her desk, which Sherry called her "mustache-removing tablets" or, alternately, Mrs. Feeley's "deworming pills," after the tablets the veterinarian had ordered for Joseph.

On the first day, during reading, Mrs. Feeley asked Skeet to begin reciting the textbook's opening story. However, as soon as Skeet had sounded out the title, "The Headless Horseman," Mrs. Feeley commanded, "Stop!" and laid her hand dramatically over her eyes.

"Children," Mrs. Feeley said, closing her own book, "I see this is a kind of ghost story here. I don't approve of horror stories. Life is full of far too many tales of woe and horror without us inventing more. Let us proceed to something different." She then stared for several minutes at a cutout of a black cat left by the former teacher, Mrs. Hardy. Mrs. Feeley failed to name the new story from which Skeet should read.

"If you really wanted to hear a scary story," she said finally, "I have one of my own, but"—she stopped in midsentence, leafing through her teachers' book—"I would not want to frighten you. Instead, I think I'll ask you all to write me a little something about yourselves. Out with your composition notebooks." Skeet felt on edge, chafed by a sense of expectancy as he wondered what story could be so frightening that Mrs. Feeley would find it untellable.

When Mrs. Feeley failed to elaborate on her instructions, Sherry wrote in her composition book:

A Story of Terror

> Once a little girl was at home by herself and a postman came to the door with a package for her and inside were three white Sunday school dresses and no note on it. So she put the dresses in her closet before her mother came home. That night when she was in bed the dresses left her closet and crept onto her, one two and three. They woke her up and she couldn't

> move, they were so tight on her. Too tight to call for help. In the morning the dresses went back to the closet. She couldn't tell anyone because her mother would get mad if she knew she hadn't told her about the package. So every night the dresses came and wrapped her up. So she was afraid to touch them in the closet in the day time. So one day a friend of the girl came to their house, and the girl said, Take these pretty dresses home with you! They don't fit me! The friend said, oh thank you! Yes thank you, oh thank you. You are so kind. HA HA HA HA HA HA!!!

When Mrs. Feeley leaned over Sherry's shoulder to correct her paper and made no objections, Sherry was disappointed—the composition was clearly a horror story. Under Sherry's writing, Mrs. Feeley noted in red pen, "Very good, but try to use 'so' less frequently."

Often during the school day, Mrs. Feeley would mark papers and ignore the third grade, requiring them to be deadly quiet, reading at their seats or completing their homework. Skeet, who had never read more than a few paragraphs of anything unless required to, kept the Albert Payson Terhune book Mr. Ribeiro had given him on the corner of his desk, and opened it periodically to examine the pictures of collies. He spent most of his time drawing maps and sending messages by brain wave to Joseph: *Hey, buddy, I'll be home right soon;* and *I'll get you a Sabrett hot dog;* and *If I was a dog, I'd be a coonhound. If you was a person, what kind of person would you be?* Skeet paid as little attention to the class as possible, content to stay somewhere near the middle of the middle reading group. Except during math circle, which he enjoyed and in which he excelled, whenever the teacher addressed the third grade, his mind would scamper elsewhere.

Sherry paid attention every minute, regarding Mrs. Feeley's quirks with amusement. She was well aware that Mrs. Feeley was more than a little strange. She noted that Mrs. Feeley's dresses were often too small, that she wore the same pair of hose with snags at the knees every day, that her slip showed, and that her manner toward the boys in the class was way too flirtatious to be appropriate.

In the ensuing weeks, Mrs. Feeley revealed several notable preoccupations in addition to ghost stories. One was crime stories in the newspaper, which she would relate to the third grade as cautionary tales while the students filled in their social studies workbooks during fifth period.

"Never," she would say, "climb into the trunk of a car at the behest of a stranger. Here is a story of a little girl who smothered to death after doing just that."

After reading to the class for several days from the continuing news coverage of a series of child murders in Atlanta, Mrs. Feeley arrived in class one morning looking particularly perturbed and wearing a green ribbon bent into the shape of a mustache and pinned to her collar.

"This," she explained, "is a symbol. It is through the symbol of this green ribbon that I am voicing my objection to the inactivity of the Atlanta police in finding the man who is killing so many children in that city. It is quite obvious that the problem is racial prejudice. It seems that the victims have been predominantly black children. Throughout Jersey City, teachers are wearing green ribbons in protest."

Mrs. Feeley described the Atlanta police investigation until Tarsheika Pulley, one of several black students who appeared to be growing restless, raised her hand.

"I don't see why you have to tell it that way," Tarsheika said. "Why does it have to be black people?"

"Stand up when you speak," Mrs. Feeley answered.

Tarsheika stood: she was taller than Mrs. Feeley, with a high ponytail and eyes that tilted upward. She crossed her arms and said, "Why can't you have it be white people's children getting killed?"

"You may sit down. The answer to your question is that this is not fiction," Mrs. Feeley said. "I do not control the facts. This is a true current event."

"Well, I still don't—" Tarsheika continued.

"I did not see you raise your hand," Mrs. Feeley said. "However, there is no more time for questions, because I have an announcement. And here it is: we are going to do something about this terrible event, instead of just complaining. I suggest that we get out our pencils and write the mayor of Atlanta immediately." Mrs. Feeley lifted her eyebrows and surveyed the class. "If you have any questions about the spelling of particular words, raise your hands, and I will write the words on the blackboard." Tarsheika waved her arm ostentatiously in the air, but Mrs. Feeley pretended not to notice. "Remember to indent," she said. " 'Dear' at the beginning. 'Signed' at the end." Tarsheika doodled on her paper without writing anything and then stared out the window at a calico cat that had trapped itself on one of the wrought-iron decorations of Immaculate Conception convent.

In response to questions about spelling, Mrs. Feeley wrote "prejudice" and "serial killer" and "murder" on the board, and these words thereafter resurfaced relentlessly in the third grade's letters.

Sherry showed Skeet her paper:

Dear Mayor of Atlanta:

I am sorry to hear about the serial killer lost in Atlanta. We are told it's a special deal of prejudice going on. We will try our best to work on it by wearing green ribbons every day. We hope that you will do something soon.

Signed,
Sherry Terhune

Skeet showed her his:

Dear Atlanta:

Will you do nothing to make the Atlanta serial killer killings stop? We believe that they should stop as soon as possible. We will murder the man when we find him.

Signed,
Skeet

Mrs. Feeley walked around the room correcting the letters and asking students to copy what they had written onto thick white paper usually reserved for tests. She collected Tarsheika's blank page without comment. When the class had finished, Mrs. Feeley inserted the letters in an oversized envelope, which she addressed and exhibited to the third grade after applying several stamps.

The forty-one students in the class were from Vietnam and Haiti, the Dominican Republic and Korea, the Ukraine and Ireland, Jersey City and the Deep South, India and the Philippines (half of Grove Street had been renamed Manila Avenue only two years before). Several children spoke foreign languages, and Edgar Elwardani, whose father was Egyptian, entertained his classmates by speaking false Arabic on the playground. Imitating his father, he would yell made-up syllables interspersed with guttural noises, pretend to lose his temper, and then choke on his words. When his father arrived at the playground, Edgar would be subdued and still; the animation would disappear from his features, and he would speak plain English.

Sherry liked Edgar. He had hair as black as Betty Trombley's blackest hair dyes, and dark eyes like M&M's, which revealed no distinction between the iris and the pupil. He was loud in class and rough on the playground and generous. After Halloween, when he brought a special pen to class, he passed it around the room and let his seatmate experiment with it. The pen, which he explained he had borrowed from his father, was exotically designed, with an almond-shaped top, clearly not American. It had a jet-black body with a brass tip and two golden rings that reminded Sherry of a hornet's abdomen. Inside was a metal cartridge, which Edgar filled with an eyedropper he dipped into a bottle of India ink. Before lunch, Edgar left the pen in the pencil trough at the top of his desk.

At the beginning of religion period, Mrs. Feeley took her break and Father Spooner taught the class. Even Sherry was surprised when Edgar, without raising his hand, made a mournful, inhuman sound. He repeated in an expressionless, dull way, "My father's pen. My father's pen. My father's pen." He stared at the empty gutter where his pen had lain. "Someone took it."

The priest, a broad man with shiny black hair and a wide, bull-like nose, scanned the third grade, looking for a cough or gesture betraying nervousness or guilt.

Sherry crossed her ankles. She was wearing striped pinkish-orange knee socks that matched her hair and clashed extravagantly with the green plaid of the school uniform. She despised having to wear the ugly required jumper and white shirt with its Peter Pan collar. She hummed to herself, "my mama told me, Son . . ." Father Spooner glanced sharply in her direction but, unable to detect the source of the humming, looked away. ". . . always be a good boy; don't mess around with guns," Sherry concluded.

"No one," Father Spooner said in a booming voice, "will say or do anything until the person who stole Edgar's missing pen fesses up. Feet on the floor, hands folded on your desks, and not a word."

The forty-one third graders obeyed, at first. After five minutes they grew fidgety, and after fifteen, the class was alive with muffled noises. Skeet raised his hand and stated that it was unfair to punish the whole class when only one person had done anything wrong.

"Tell that to your peer who took Edgar's pen," Father Spooner retorted.

Edward Elwardani volunteered that at least he should not be punished—after all, it was his pen. Father Spooner silenced him with a look. Fifteen more minutes transpired. Father Spooner surveyed the room, student by student. When his stare had passed over Sherry, she looked at Skeet and rolled her eyes. *I tried to lift my leg when I was peeing yesterday,* Skeet beamed to Joseph. *And I fell over and conked my head on the toilet. How do you do it, boy?* Sherry opened her jar of Tiger Balm under her desk, dipped her finger into the exotic, cinnamon-smelling ointment, and rubbed it onto her temples. They burned with a contradictory coolness.

Father Spooner again surveyed the class. Sitting on Mrs.

Feeley's desk, he said, "I stole something once when I was about your age." He held out his arms and stared at the hairy backs of his hands. "It was the first and last time I ever stole anything. My brother Francis and I had found a truck full of building materials on a road off Communipaw Avenue. I climbed inside the truck, and there I discovered a paper bag full of beautiful Spanish tiles, with blue and green and yellow patterns on them. I carried the bag outside the truck and was making my way back down the street, when suddenly Francis began running. A policeman had appeared out of the blue. He stood in front of me, the butt of his gun raised. And then he whacked me in the side of the head with it. I lost consciousness. When I came to, I was lying on the sidewalk, my brother Francis was standing over me, and the tiles were gone. For years afterward, I heard a buzzing in my left ear and experienced bouts of dizziness. After this incident, I never again took something that didn't belong to me."

Religion period had now ended, and Mrs. Feeley's devil's-food-cake hat popped through the doorway. She received the news of the theft with some excitement: she interrupted Father Spooner several times, and her eyes narrowed and seemed to look inward.

After Father Spooner departed, Mrs. Feeley sat at her desk for several minutes without speaking. She thumbed absently through the religion book that Father Spooner had left on her desk. When something caught her eye, she exclaimed suddenly, "Oh, the saints! Saint Paul the cowboy and Saint Anthony, full of arrows and looking like a porky-pine."

She tapped a green-and-gold Dixon Ticonderoga pencil a few times on her desk and then stared into space. Eventually, she took an empty Kleenex box from the trash can, placed it on her desk, and addressed the class.

"I have devised a plan," she announced, rising from her desk. She paced before the third grade, rubbing her chin with one hand. "You will now line up at the far end of the hallway, away from the door. You will then return one by one into the classroom. Whoever has the pen may drop it into the Kleenex box, no questions asked. Walk around my desk once and then come outside and return to the back of the line."

Sherry appreciated Mrs. Feeley's cleverness, as well as her ability to throw punishment to the wind in order to reach the heart of the problem, getting the distraught Edgar his pen. However, when the third grade had lined up in the hallway and Sherry's turn to enter the room came, she could not bring herself to drop the pen into the Kleenex box. As she approached Mrs. Feeley's desk, Sherry fingered the brass nib and black barrel, lifted the pen partway out of her jumper pocket, dropped it back in, and then withdrew her empty hand, feeling genuinely sorry for Edgar. There was still too great a risk of being caught—the student who entered the room next might see the pen through the slit in the Kleenex box and suspect that the person ahead of him had left it there.

Sherry filed by the Kleenex box and circled back into the hallway, terror washing over her as she reached Mrs. Feeley's desk and then receding as she passed the box and resisted the temptation to deposit the pen inside.

When the last student had paraded by the box and Mrs. Feeley had instructed the class to return to their seats, Edgar again slumped over his folded arms, sobbing with abandon. Nobody ridiculed him; the event had taken on a solemnity enjoyed and respected by everyone.

"I am very sorry, Edgar," Mrs. Feeley said. "You should assume at this point that your pen may never be returned. I think that we have all learned a lesson about the nature of crime today," she concluded, but did not communicate the lesson she had in mind.

The final bell rang, and after Mrs. Feeley dismissed the class, Sherry walked to the coat closet to get her jacket. When she turned around, Mrs. Feeley was standing behind her. Sherry maneuvered by her, but as she reached the door, Mrs. Feeley stepped in front of her, holding the pen by some sleight of hand.

"I believe," she whispered, "that you should remain here a few minutes after the other students have departed."

When the classroom was empty of every student except Sherry, Mrs. Feeley sat down at her desk and withdrew a metal box from one of her drawers. Motioning Sherry to approach, Mrs. Feeley said, "Is this the first time you have been caught stealing? We will have to fingerprint you." Mrs. Feeley removed a blank index card and a black ink pad from the box and, leaning over the desk, took Sherry's wrist. Mrs. Feeley uncurled Sherry's fingers and pressed one of them into the ink pad, lifted her hand, and brought her fingertip down on the index card. Then she lifted up the next finger and the next and the next, and finally the thumb, rolling each from left to right onto the card.

"Girl child," Mrs. Feeley said out loud as she wrote the words on the card. "About four feet tall, strawberry hair." She showed Sherry the card. "You're very young," she said, "but already you have a criminal record. The next time you are caught taking anything, the police will just check their files against this card. You may go home now. I caution you against stealing in the future." Mrs. Feeley dropped the card into the metal file box, slapped it shut, and banged once on the top.

◆ Public Offenders

In her lifetime, Betty Trombley had held over two dozen jobs. Sometimes at night, when she was unable to sleep, she would enumerate them in her mind, focusing on each like a rosary bead and then moving on to the next: investigator, teacher, snake-farm tour guide, candy wholesaler, fur-coat transporter, short-order cook, manicurist. (Once she had tried to remember the name of every man she had slept with, but when she hit one hundred, she grew even more restless and desisted.) Each job had a mystery to divulge, its own special knowledge.

For example, how else would she have known that all candy had a shelf life, that most chocolates you ate were reasonably fresh, while others, the waxy sweets like corn candy, were immortal, that they could lie in warehouses for decades, that they could be older than your mother by the time you purchased them from the retailer? And who would have known that under the streets of midtown Manhattan lay a network of tunnels as complicated as the subway system, through which racks of expensive clothing were transported; that groping, molelike workers tugged quivering minks underneath the sidewalks? That the sisters at Immaculate raised a third of the school's overhead by plying parents with overpriced mixed drinks at bingo games and raffles, sending them home stinking drunk to their children?

On the other hand, nearly every kind of work offered up its kernel of noteworthy information within a few days or weeks. After a short time on any job, Betty longed to slip away as carelessly as someone exiting an apartment after a one-night stand. Her job as an investigator, however, held her interest. This was a shame, because while she felt wholly satisfied ferreting out the endless details behind her clients' arrests, alibis, and motives, Betty suspected that she would be fired from the public defender's office before long.

She had found out too much too quickly, not about her clients, but about her employers. There was the matter of the receipt book she had discovered in a former investigator's desk, for instance. During her first week on the job, Betty had learned that the public defenders were charging their clients a nominal fee of fifty dollars each, money supposedly destined for the coffers of the municipal government, and a story spread that one of the past investigators had made off with thirty thousand dollars in nominal fees. Betty had started the story. She had been cleaning out the old investigator's things and found a receipt book with all the white pages ripped out but all the yellow pages blank, although these should have contained carbon copies of each transaction. She deduced that someone had been pocketing clients' fee money, and failing to record the amounts in the receipt and audit books.

Early that Friday morning, Betty felt a familiar feeling rise within her as she climbed the steps to the public defender's office: a shiver in her spine, a tightening in her shoulders, a feeling that, if she had been a ferocious wild forest animal rather than Betty Trombley, there would have been fur rising along the back of her neck. This was the sensation that always imbued her when she found herself irresistibly drawn into a dispute likely to goad an employer into the irrational, frenzied, furious state so many of her employers had experienced in her presence.

When Betty reached the office, the public defender who had been assigned to Henry Purdy's case, Ronald Preakness, was standing at the door, rummaging through his briefcase. Of all the public defenders, Ronald Preakness irked Betty most. He had a problem with authority, in that he enjoyed exercising it often. He talked down to his legal secretary and to Betty, an unfortunate attribute, Betty felt, in light of his evident mental dullness. He bragged that he had gone to Dartmouth and then attended an Ivy League law school. Betty surmised aloud that she had "seen better heads come out of a zipper," and that Ivy League education was evidently not what it was cracked up to be. She watched Ronald Preakness carefully and felt especially called upon to ensure that he did his duty, because Henry Purdy was at his mercy.

"How extraordinary to see you so early this morning, Ronald," Betty greeted him. It was eight o'clock. Preakness usually arrived at the Municipal Court around ten-thirty, although by eight-thirty the courthouse steps were packed with clients awaiting trial and their families. By the time Preakness drifted in, his clients filled the few benches in the waiting areas, lined the walls, and covered the stairwell. On hot days in late summer, his clients occasionally fainted from the heat of the assembled bodies and the sweltering August air before Preakness had uttered a solitary word to a single defendant. Now clients stomped their feet with cold for hours on the courthouse steps before conversing with their court-appointed counsel.

The lawyer answered, "That's Mr. Preakness to you." He looked irritated, and Betty suspected that a chief source of his irritation was the odd employment policy of the Municipal Court, which gave the court's administrative body, rather than the public defenders, hiring and firing power over their own staff. This meant that unfortunate souls such as Preakness, who were engaged on a contractual basis, had to plow through considerable red tape to discharge an underling whose tenure was likely to be secured by nepotism or patronage or the sheer inertia of Jersey City bureaucracy.

"Ronald, Ronald, Ronald," Betty said. "There's something I've been meaning to tell you. I get so scared, sitting up here alone in the office with the criminals walking in and out and that cash from their fifty-dollar nominal fees sitting in my desk. So I've decided to start going around the corner to the bank each day at lunch to have the fees turned into money orders."

Betty must not have looked convincingly frightened to Ronald Preakness, with her height, her artificial snow leopard coat, her men's clothes. "You'll do no such thing," he told her.

"Why not? Just explain it to me, Ronald. I'm a good listener."

"Yours is not to reason why," Ronald Preakness retorted. He really did not want to enter into a discussion with Betty Trombley. Far from fearing that she would not listen, he felt that she listened too intently. The minute his words were spoken, she snatched them and twisted them into arguments against themselves.

Was he one of the ones pocketing the cash? Betty wondered. "I guess I'm just too stupid to understand how it's legal to charge someone for a public defender," Betty said. "I mean, aren't public defenders supposed to be free? I tell our clients, 'Oh, don't bother with that silly little fee. If you can't afford a lawyer, I don't see why they should make you pay a fee. The career criminals know better than to fork over that money. Only the first-time offenders and innocent people believe they have to pay it.'"

"You tell them what?"

"Well, it's true; they have to be represented anyway. Just the other day, didn't you plead out Mr. Williams, and he hadn't paid his fee? So I tell our clients, 'Anyhow, in a place as corrupt as this, who knows whose pocket this money is lining?'" Betty looked pointedly at Ronald Preakness and tossed him what she thought of as her most charming smile:

the one where her mouth was partway open, covering her bottom teeth but not her top teeth, which were especially attractive, large and straight.

"Miss Trombley, I'll handle the fees henceforth." Ronald Preakness flashed Betty a look that made her wish to be someplace else. Even back at Immaculate, reading her fifth graders Doctor Dolittle during religion period. If she stayed here, she feared it was just a matter of time before she ended up at the bottom of the Hudson, heavy with the details of corruption.

Betty decided not to reveal too much of what she knew to Preakness. She found herself playing that game she always fell into when she was trying to restrain herself from saying anything further: if he were an animal, what kind of animal would he be? The secret to linking the right animal to a person's face was to ignore the person's nose and concentrate on his other features, because an animal's nose is in his chin. Preakness had golden eyebrows, a broad chin, wide-set eyes, a pale-yellow tie that made her think of chest markings. He looked at her as if he wanted to jump on her and tear out her heart.

A rottweiler.

This association reminded Betty of a joke Angel Rodriguez had told her. She smiled falsely at Preakness again and asked, "What's black and brown and looks good on a lawyer?"

Ronald Preakness did not respond.

"A Doberman pinscher, ha ha ha," Betty answered.

A woman wearing a neck brace entered the hallway outside the office. The public defender jumped up, extending his hand. "Mrs. O'Connor, please, please have a seat here in the foyer. I've already outlined our claim for damages. Just let me look through my notes, and we'll discuss your case in a minute." Mrs. O'Connor, a delicate woman who looked thin even in her winter coat, seemed to bow under the weight of the brace. She opened a battered purse shaped like an oyster and removed some papers.

"Ah," Betty said loudly, as the public defender retreated to his office. "A paying client. That explains why you're here so early, Ronald." Was it legal for the public defenders to practice on the side, when they had too heavy a caseload of indigent clients already? "I imagine Ronald here will work hard on your case, Mrs. O'Connor. He certainly has a lot of free time on his hands. It's hard for a capable, intelligent lawyer like him to be unoccupied."

Ronald Preakness frowned at Betty as he closed the office door.

Betty sat down in the foyer opposite Mrs. O'Connor and said chattily, "I'd like to tell you, Mrs. O'Connor, I had this theory that if a public defender read his client's case file before walking into the courtroom, the public defender would have to open the file folder first? The one containing all the confessions and police interviews and investigator's notes? So I started stapling some of the file folders closed with one little staple? And sure enough, at the end of the day, all of Preakness's files came back with the staples still in them. Even when a client, say, spoke no English, so that Preakness couldn't discuss his case with him in the courtroom. Now, I thought, either he's so smart that he doesn't even have to know anything about his clients' cases before he advises them to plead guilty or whatever, or he's got ESP, or he's one hell of a lawyer. So you're sure to be impressed by him."

Ronald Preakness emerged from the office and noted the look of bewilderment on his client's face. "I'm ready for you now, Mrs. O'Connor. Don't worry; I'll have things straightened out for you in no time. Don't you have work to do, Miss Trombley?"

"Sure, Ronald. I'll hop downstairs for a minute to check with one of our clients in the bullpen. Do you know you have a client named Henry Purdy? He's eager to meet you, Ronald."

A shrewd expression passed over Mrs. O'Connor's face as she tucked her papers back into her battered purse and snapped it shut.

Betty headed for the bullpen, hoping to catch Henry Purdy there before the office opened. She had relayed her fears about the incompetence and corruption in her office to Mike Ribeiro the night before over dinner with Ida and the children. "It's hard to know," Betty had said, "how to blow the whistle in a place like Jersey City. You have to have someone to blow the whistle *to,* and finding an honest person in the city government is like looking for a pubic hair on a baby." Ida, bustling around the stove, had frowned and pointed toward Skeet and Sherry, who had not reacted in any noticeable way to Betty's word choice. (They were too preoccupied smuggling pieces of Ida's smothered pork chops to the dog: Betty watched Skeet wrap his serving in his napkin when he was sure no one was looking and then smile to the area to the left of his chair, under the table. Skeet was crazy about his mother's smothered pork chops, and so this act betrayed just how deeply he loved the dog.)

"If you're really going to blow the whistle, try talking to Judge MacFarland," Mike Ribeiro had responded. "She's the only person in the courthouse I'd trust. You know for someone that honest to have gotten so far in the Jersey City government, she must have a mind like Einstein and the dauntlessness of Amelia Earhart." Mike had leaned back, and his eyes had become unfocused, a sign that he was about to launch into one of his impassioned speeches. "When you walk into her courtroom, there's a deep hush, spectators leaning forward on their seats, this sense that something important is coming to pass. Maybe it's not justice, but maybe at least order, competence, a semblance of trying at fairness. This comes as a shock to any lawyer who works in Hudson County. In most of the courtrooms, you wouldn't be surprised to see a herd of spotted cows dancing on the ceiling or a judge jumping through a fiery hoop and twirling a baton.

"Well, be careful, Betty," Mike had concluded. "Lawyers have a way of protecting themselves. If you just feed them contaminated potato salad at a picnic, they'll sue you. Imagine what they'd do to you if you told the truth about them. Also, if you plan to talk with Judge MacFarland, do it soon. There's a rumor she's going to be promoted to Superior Court."

Betty had arranged to meet with the judge in a half hour and looked forward to the encounter. She had worn her artificial leopard-skin coat and two-tone wing-tip shoes especially for the occasion.

Henry Purdy's narrow face appeared in the darkness of the bullpen—a dank, shadowy area on the Municipal Court's first floor, where defendants waited to be arraigned or tried. He slipped Betty a note, although he could have spoken to her through the bars in the small window where defendants communicated with their lawyers.

SO WHERE IS HE, THE PUBLIC DEFENDER? the note said in ragged capitals. I HAVEN'T SEEN HIDE NOR HAIR OF HIM YET.

"Look, Henry," Betty answered, "I doubt you'll meet your public defender anytime soon. Why don't you let Mike Ribeiro take the case?"

"No way," Henry said, leaning his forehead against the bars. "I have the right to remain silent. If I can't afford a lawyer, I have the right to have the court appoint me one, and I aim to force whoever my lawyer is to do his job." Then, raising his head, Henry said, "Wait a sec," and receded into the bullpen's shadowy corners. Betty crossed her ankles and waited for him. She heard a toilet flush twice in the rear of the bullpen.

When Henry returned, he said, "There's a commode in here that looks like a pharaoh's tomb. It's set on a platform and has turquoise and gold tiles looping around in back of it. It's got this big ole brass pipe that swirls out behind it. Like a tuba. This guy here says they built the bullpen over some judge's office when they redid the courthouse. It's a judge's toilet."

"You know, Henry, you could plead guilty and they probably wouldn't give you more than a fine, or you could get time served."

"Oh, no," said Henry. "No way. I want justice." He looked at Betty solemnly from his crossed eyes.

"Maybe you don't want to take this one on, Henry. That guy Preakness who's representing you is really a penis brain."

For a moment, Henry looked worried. Then he said, grinning, "Life at the public defender's is getting you down, huh?"

"Just talk to Mike Ribeiro, OK, Henry? I've got to get back upstairs to the office before it opens."

"Hokeydokey," Henry said slyly. "Absolutely."

After meeting with Judge MacFarland, Betty climbed the top flight of stairs and entered the foyer abutting the office. Several people were waiting for the public defenders. Preakness, however, had disappeared.

"Hi, everybody. I'm the investigator," Betty announced, beginning her usual morning speech. "Take a good look at me, because I'm the closest thing you'll see to a lawyer before your case begins." She interviewed each client methodically and patiently, taking down the names of their crimes (flag waving, fraud, assault, and a downgraded armed robbery) and noting alibis and defects in police procedure. An old Slavic man wearing a leg cast had come to the office to press police brutality charges, and Betty directed him to the complaints office. Betty found it curious how many people confused public defenders and prosecutors, as if all criminal justice were just one big mixed-up swamp of laws.

When she had just finished with the armed robber, Ronald Preakness ran up the stairs, two at a time. He entered the office bellowing, raised his briefcase above his head, and threw it on the ground.

"Why are you so agitated, Ronald?" Betty asked.

The armed robber returned from the staircase and leaned in the doorway. "You safe, lady? You want me to get this guy out of here for you?" He was a large robber, weighing perhaps two hundred seventy pounds and standing six feet two. Betty was tempted to ask him to hold down Preakness until the police could arrive to subdue him. However, she said, "Thanks, but the sad fact is that this is one of our public defenders, Ronald by name."

Ronald Preakness closed the door. "Are you telling clients to press charges against the police? I don't ever want to hear of you encouraging criminal defendants to file police brutality charges. I don't ever want that to get back to the police department!"

"You don't ever want that to get back to the police department?" (If someone says something really stupid, don't answer, just repeat what they've said, was one of Betty's choice aphorisms.) "Could you be referring to the old man whose thighbone was broken by an arresting officer?" It was definitely time to change jobs, Betty thought, and again that familiar sense of intoxication, uplifting and gleeful, coursed through her veins. Jobs were like relationships: if you let yourself get too bound up, they were sure to compromise you in intolerable ways. Although Mike Ribeiro is surely sexy, Betty mused, he might be too serious. Loneliness radiates from him. But sooner or later I'll probably sleep with him, even though we're just friends. That moment will come when I have my diaphragm in my purse and we're both in the mood at the same time. Mike would probably be great in bed, when I think about it. But in the meantime, I have Ida to keep me company, to keep me from getting involved in some doomed love affair. She's the closest thing I'll ever have to a family. She's the closest thing I'd ever want to a family. What man could be so accommodating? Who else would bleach my teacups?

"You pay attention to me, Miss Trombley!" Preakness said. "Don't you realize we have to keep good relations with the police?"

"We have to keep good relations with the police?" Betty answered.

"That's right, we do."

"That's right, we do?"

The phone rang, and Betty picked it up before Ronald Preakness could say more. "It's for you, Ronald," Betty said. "One of the judges downstairs wants to compliment you for your work yesterday and take you to lunch. Judge MacFarland. She says meet her in five minutes."

In fact, it was Ida Terhune on the phone, but Preakness believed Betty, because he retrieved his briefcase from the floor. "Later for you!" were his last words to her as he exited the office.

"I really don't like Chinese food," Ida said over the telephone. "But Mike Ribeiro insisted on joining us for lunch in my office, and I didn't feel it would be nice to turn him down. We're supposed to meet him in a half hour. Good-bye. I've got to get back to work."

"Ida?" Betty said, but Ida had already hung up, conscientious to a fault about her job. Betty wanted to talk to her. During Betty's first weeks at the municipal public defender's office, she had often longed for Ida Terhune. It was impossible for Ida to see the gray areas between questions of right and wrong, and so she was incorruptible.

What I need right now, Betty said to herself, is a spoonful of Ida Terhune.

Mike Ribeiro burst through the front doors of the Municipal Court, buoyed by a tidal wave of optimism. He would visit Henry Purdy and convince him to abandon his plan, made out of sheer perversity and craziness, to insist on a public defender. It was apparent that the prosecutor's office owed some favor to Rupert Dixon, to be spending so much time on an insignificant misdemeanor case. Mike longed to be Henry's lawyer. He had never lost a misdemeanor case in his fifteen-year career as a criminal defense attorney, and he was certain he could prevail in Henry's behalf. Already Mike had helped as much as he could. He had composed a fictitious witness list and given it to the prosecutor. The young prosecutor had wasted days hunting down imaginary members of the crowd that had watched the dogfight and arrest.

"You think you don't have to play by the rules," Mike's wife told him, appearing in his mind's eye, dressed impeccably in a royal-blue dress that held her in place, a neat center to focus on. "But you do, because the rules will get you in the end. They'll hunt you down like wolves."

Carrying several cartons of Chinese food, Mike approached the bullpen. He leaned into the single barred window allowed for clients who needed to speak with their lawyers and called Henry's name.

Mike heard Henry's voice at the other end of the bullpen

and a toilet flushing several times. After the toilet quieted, Henry called, "Mr. Lawyer! Mr. Ribeiro. There's a guy here I want you to talk to."

When Henry appeared at the bars of the bullpen window, a tall, gaunt young man with red hair stooped over behind him.

"This is my bullpen buddy, Stanley Shipley," Henry said.

The young man stepped forward. "Henry says your lady friend Betty's from Laoosiana. So'm I," he told Mike in a drawl so much thicker than Betty's or Ida Terhune's that Mike wondered whether the young man was exaggerating his southern accent on purpose. Jersey City was full of southerners who had fled the South, mostly black but sometimes white. Betty had told Mike that as a girl she had often heard Jersey City spoken of as a sort of mecca of the North and had imagined it as a glittering city of wide avenues and flickering lights, something like the French Quarter.

"I had that guy Preakness as my lower once," the young man Stanley affirmed. "Henry here'd be better off on his own than with one of these free Jersey City lowers." The boy's slow manner of talking was surely calculated to test the patience of any listener. "Once, I was accused of stealing this car, when all I done was to find it out on Route 9 and strip some wire out of what was left of it." He cleared his throat. "The battery and the hubcaps and radio was already gone. But the police just come along, tussle me to the ground, carry me down to the Superior Coathouse, and charge me with robbery. Then they downgraded it to theft and sent me here to the Municipal Coathouse. Well, that Preakness guy, my public *offender*—"

Henry leaned forward and wiggled his eyebrows, looking intently at Mike to see if he liked Stanley's joke.

Stanley paused out of respect to Henry and backed off into the darkness, making Mike think of the groupers in the aquarium at the My Way Lounge. The boy Stanley continued speaking somewhat faster but from the darkness, as if it were easier for him to talk that way. "My lower somehow got it in his head that the charges was only criminal mischief, vandalism. He didn't even read that little paper with my name on it where it said in plain bold obvious letters: 'Car theft.'"

Now the young man approached the bars again, with Henry smiling wildly beside him as if he had heard a joke from an inner voice no one else had been privy to. Henry looked at Stanley expectantly, and then, too restless to sit through another retelling, Henry continued: "So Mr. Public Offender walks right up to this man the complainant, who'd rented the car, and says, 'Mr. Cardozo, what did the Pontiac look like when you left it in the parking lot?' and Mr. Cardozo said, 'What did it look like? Well, it had a little dent on one side, but it was that way when I rented it. I didn't put it there.' 'And what did it look like when you came back?' Mr. Public Offender says. 'What did it look like?' Mr. Cardozo answers. 'It was gone!' Henry paused and wiggled his eyebrows again. Stanley bowed his head and laughed, as if overcome by the image of his lawyer's incompetence.

"So then," Stanley returned to his story, "my public offender wakes up. He runs back to his little desk and opens up my file with my name on it and for the first time sees they were saying I took that old car.

"I knew I was lost then," Stanley concluded. "That's why I aim to defend myself this time. Me and Henry both have decided to go *pro se.* It's been nice talking to you," the boy said, sticking out a bony arm to shake Mike's hand.

Henry followed Stanley away from the window.

Mike felt forsaken. "Henry! Henry, wait a minute!" Mike called into the cavernous darkness of the bullpen. But no one answered.

Ida loved her job in the Municipal Court. Perhaps she would have begun working years earlier if she had known that such perfect employment had been out there in the world, waiting for her. Her boss was an efficient, pretty young woman married to a city councilman, and Ida sat in a small, tidy office and listened to complainants who came to press charges against relatives, friends, and neighbors. The drama of other people's lives! Ida would never have guessed how readily some people pursued battles and nursed minor injustices. (Offenses that proved to be serious in nature required police authorization, and Ida referred them elsewhere.) Nor would she have thought there was a job from which she could so safely observe such tumult.

After hearing crime victims' stories, Ida scrolled a pink form into her typewriter and boiled down their tales of barroom brawls, domestic violence, and petty thefts into laconic sentences. She had already committed the pertinent sections of the *New Jersey Code of Criminal Justice* to memory and found an inexplicable delight in matching the best crime to the complaint at hand. "Complainant alleges said Harold Sims socked him in the eye, purposely, knowingly, or recklessly causing said complainant bodily injury," she wrote, after typing the word "Assault" at the top of the pink summons form. "Terroristic threats" she underlined twice over the sentence: "Complainant states that Cindy Owen did call her on the telephone on seven different occasions, each time threatening to 'tear out her hair,' with the purpose of terrorizing her." Many people who entered the office simply had grievances that they wished to air, which were really not legal in nature. Ida would listen attentively to them, sometimes giving advice and sometimes withholding it, and always passing judgment.

For the first time in her life, Ida felt independent. The feeling was new and exhilarating. The fleeting thought crossed her mind that she never wanted to remarry, but she dismissed it as impractical.

Just before lunchtime, after Ida had cleared a place on her desk where she, Mike Ribeiro and Betty could dine, her office was intruded upon by a broad-shouldered young woman with a quiet, composed manner, and an angry, whiskery old man with a leg cast that extended from his ankle to his hip. Once they had seated themselves before Ida's desk, the young woman explained that she was the man's daughter and that she would interpret for him.

"He wishes to say," the daughter translated, folding her small, pale hands in her lap, "that he is a law-abiding man."

"Is that Spanish?" Ida asked pleasantly, to set the old man at ease.

"We are Poles," the girl answered. "We were sent here by

the woman in the public defender's office upstairs. My father has never been arrested before, not in Poland, not here. Until last Friday, when a police officer hit my father in the back with a garbage can because he was drinking beer on the front steps of our building."

The girl's father shouted the next part of his story, banging his fist on Ida's desk and staring indignantly at her.

The daughter sat up straight and spoke forcefully, like a medium invaded by her father's spirit. She translated with an indignation that echoed his, although her face retained its composure, as if her voice were no longer hers. "My father has drunk one beer every night on the front steps of every house he has lived in since the first day he ever worked! Is this a crime? The officer dragged him to his police car and took him to jail." The daughter stopped and pointed at the cast. "There, two officers beat him with their police clubs, and he did not get to a hospital until two days later. They broke his thighbone."

Ida wrote this down on a pink pad she kept on her desk.

The man interrupted his daughter's translation and again shouted furiously. The daughter watched him, attentive and composed, her hands still folded primly in her lap. Her voice rose, and her face contorted with her father's rage. "Cossacks! We wish these officers to die," she said. "We wish them to be tried in court and then shot."

"I'm so sorry," Ida answered. "I'm only authorized to issue summonses for petty offenses."

The father looked questioningly at his daughter, who translated for him. He answered with a bark. She gazed at him placidly and continued: "How do we press charges against them?"

Ida answered, "Well, you can't just come to this office and charge a policeman with a serious crime. It's my understanding that you have to lodge a police brutality complaint first."

"And where do we go to do this?" the daughter said quietly, without waiting for her father to speak.

"The police department," Ida answered.

The daughter translated, and the father raised his fist and banged on Ida's desk, muttering under his breath.

"Then we will do that," the daughter said.

"I wish you the best of luck," Ida answered, although she was somewhat taken aback by the old man's behavior. "I only do little crimes," she added apologetically.

The young woman rose after her father and looked down on Ida under heavy, luxurious eyelids. "This is regrettable," she said, bumping into Mike Ribeiro as she and her father attempted to leave. Mike Ribeiro stood in the doorway, loaded with white cartons. His grin caused a small leaping sensation in Ida's stomach, which startled her. Ida wondered how long he had been eavesdropping.

And then, suddenly, Ida's domain was overrun with people. Betty arrived, followed by a young man whose face was red with fury. Mike stepped forward, setting down the cartons on Ida's desk and splashing brown and yellow sauces on her calendar. The older man and his daughter backed against the wall.

"You goddamn bitch!" the red-faced young man yelled. Ida reached for the telephone: she had been warned that criminal defendants sometimes came to the office to air grievances against complainants. I will not be intimidated, she told herself. She dialed the number for the courtroom's emergency line but heard a busy signal. The old man hobbled after his daughter into the hallway.

The red-faced young man shouted, "How dare you reveal confidential information about the public defender's office to Judge MacFarland!"

Ida felt confused, until she saw that the young man was speaking not to her but to Betty. Of course, Ida told herself. Betty has gone out and found herself a new enemy. Ida set the phone back in its cradle.

"I didn't report anything to Judge MacFarland that wasn't common knowledge already," Betty answered. Turning to Ida and Mike Ribeiro, Betty explained, "Ronald's upset because I think he's an asshole."

Ida almost felt sorry for the young man, despite his vocabulary and poor manners. She saw that once again, Betty was pushing an adversary beyond the limits of his endurance.

The public defender leaned over Ida's desk toward Betty

and said, "If you come near the office, I'll toss you out bodily."

"Hey, hey," Mike said. "Calm down. Why don't you let me take you bodily out of here? This is no way to talk to ladies." Ida sighed with relief. If nothing else, Mike Ribeiro was a gentleman.

"Now now now now now," he said, taking hold of the public defender's jacket sleeve and steering him out the door into the hallway. "Don't let the ladies get to you." Mike pulled the public defender through the door by his sleeve.

Betty snickered through her nose.

"Cunt," Ronald Preakness told her.

Ida blanched. Several people congregated on the courthouse stairway stopped talking to stare at the public defender.

"Oh, go suck farts out of a dog," Betty responded.

One of the court officers watched Ronald Preakness with an amused expression and jangled a heavy key ring. He entered Ida's office with a self-important swagger, brushing Ida's pink forms so that they swirled in a little whirlwind to the floor.

"Time was"—the court officer addressed Ida, as if she had caused the commotion—"there was two guys up in that office doing the work the whole mess of them upstairs are supposed to be busy doing now. But the two guys kept winning their cases, so the city got rid of them. Now they got these new ones, and they still win about half their cases, since the prosecutors are just as dumb as they are."

Ida nodded politely.

"Do you hear that?" Betty asked. "What's that noise?"

The court officer stopped talking and listened. The people seated on the courthouse stairway stood up. A low roaring arose in the hallway.

"What in hell?" one man said. "Water?"

Ida followed Betty and the court officer to the threshold. A rivulet, about the size formed in a gutter when a car is washed at the top of a hill, coursed down the steps. The court officer ran up the stairs.

Ida stepped back, upsetting one of the food cartons on her

desk calendar. Water washed along the hallway and wet the rug under her desk.

"We'll need a mop," Ida said.

"OK, OK, we're evacuating the building," the court officer said from the top of the stairs. "Everyone out the side exit."

Ida obeyed. Suspecting Betty would run upstairs to investigate, Ida took her by the arm and said, "Betty, will you come with me?" She and Betty slogged down the hallway to a fire exit and descended to Montgomery Street, where a crowd gathered.

Eventually, the court officer appeared on the fire escape to communicate what had happened: several court officers had converged outside the bullpen, from which water was now flowing freely. No one knew for certain which of the defendants awaiting trial was responsible, but when the officers burst into the bullpen, they found that the toilet in the back, an old commode with corroded joints, had been pulled from the wall, leaving a hole large enough for a police dog to slip through. From a pipe over the hole, water coursed torrentially into the hallway on the other side of the wall, barreling down the corridors into the courtrooms and flooding two floors. The plans for the building could not be found, and no one could locate the valve for turning off the water main. The rest of the trials for the day had to be canceled, an event that had not occurred since Judge Sharpless, more drunk than usual, had fallen off the bench.

◆ Highway Robbery

After an old caretaker for the court building had been located and telephoned and the water turned off, the police handcuffed the defendants who remained, obedient as cattle, huddled shin-deep in water inside the bullpen. Several other defendants had taken the opportunity to disappear through the hole where the toilet had been wrenched loose.

Mike Ribeiro located Ida and Betty outside the Municipal Court. "Henry's escaped," he told Betty, his back to Ida as if he did not expect her to be interested. Then, turning to Ida, Mike said, "Well, it looks like you get a holiday. Why don't we all go down to Ducky's and have a fancy lunch?"

His solution for everything seemed to be a lavish meal. "I really wanted to take a brief lunch," Ida answered. "I need to finish filling out some forms before I go home today."

"They aren't letting anyone back on the first floor," Mike Ribeiro said.

"Oh dear. Well, it must be permissible to leave, then," Ida said, but stood still, deciding whether it was really all right. She thought of the Chinese food lying on her desk calendar all weekend. "All right," she said finally. "I'll drive. I'm parked right around the corner." She led Mike and Betty toward the corner of Boland and Fairmount.

The car, however, was not where Ida had left it.

Mike felt a surge of compassion for Ida, sensing she was embarrassed at having forgotten her parking spot. "We'll just take my car," he said.

"No. You don't understand," Ida insisted. "I know where my car was. I always park it on this block, and this is exactly where I said good-bye to my New Yorker this morning." She pointed to a space between two cars.

The space was as long as a New Yorker, conspicuously long, Betty thought, in light of the fact that cars were lined up front to tail all down Fairmount Avenue: parking near the courthouse was notoriously difficult in the middle of the day.

Could someone steal a car that size in broad daylight? Mike wondered. Right around the corner from the police station? "Are you sure it was here?" Mike asked. "Could it have been towed?"

"I'd never park in an illegal spot," Ida answered, her voice quavering.

"This space is clearly legal." Mike put his hand on her shoulder.

"When it rains, it pours," Betty said. She volunteered to walk around the block. "If that house on wheels is anywhere around here, I'm sure I'll see it," she said.

As Betty strode toward Kennedy Boulevard, Mike told Ida, "I'll tell you what we'll do if Betty doesn't find the car. We'll just walk down the fire escape to the precinct office in the courthouse basement and report your car missing."

Betty reappeared shortly thereafter, rounding the corner of Bergen Avenue and shaking her head. "It's nowhere in sight," she announced. "Imagine the guts it would take to steal a car that size in broad daylight, right outside the courthouse," she added in a tone of admiration. Ida glared at her.

Mike took Ida by the elbow and led her down the fire escape to the flooded basement floor. Betty followed, smacking her shoe soles on the water and splashing loudly. "It's raining, it's pouring, the old man is snoring," she sang. She stopped when she saw the despondent look on Ida's face.

However, once they had waded to the precinct office, they found the door closed. An officer was sitting at the front desk but did not look up when they knocked. Betty rapped sharply and rattled the doorknob, trying to get his attention. Eventually, he rose and disappeared into a back office.

"Ida," Mike Ribeiro said, "I'll come back here first thing tomorrow morning and fill out a report on your car."

Overwhelmed by her loss, Ida leaned into Mike Ribeiro and burst into tears. His smell reminded her of Dewey. Dewey's smell had always reminded her of something musky—a wild boar or a swamp animal.

"A car like that's hard to hide, Ida. The police will find it," Mike assured her, although he doubted she would ever see it again. If the thief took the tunnel into Manhattan, the Jersey City police would never trace the car.

"They could have driven it a hundred miles by now," Ida answered in a despairing voice.

"Don't worry, Ida," Betty said. "It will turn up. Crooks in Jersey City are so provincial they never think to take a car to New York City to sell it. Once, someone stole the station wagon at Immaculate, and Sister Andrea just got in the school's other car and drove to the river, then zigzagged north to south along every street until she found the station wagon. She sighted it less than an hour later. Of course, they had the whole school praying for them. Sister Andrea came over the intercom and said, 'The first through fourth grades are already praying for our station wagon to be returned to us. If the upper grades would join in, all the bases would be covered.'"

"This is not a joking matter," Ida said. They arrived at Mike's car, and Ida felt a pit in her stomach when she saw the rusting Buick with torn seats, littered inside with old candy wrappers, unopened bills, and crumpled legal documents. When she sat down in the front seat, objects knocked against her ankles: a child's pair of inflatable water wings, an unopened six-pack of beer (wasn't it illegal to keep beer in the front seat?), a thick book titled *The Handgun Bible,* a paperback thriller, and a yellow legal pad with a dusty footprint on it.

A mere mile away, cruising downtown along Newark Avenue, Stanley Shipley gunned the New Yorker's motor. After Stanley had curtsied through the hole behind the courthouse toilet and strolled into the crisp, blinding daylight, Ida Terhune's New Yorker seemed to him like a message from fate. Stanley had rarely seen a New Yorker that size since he had been a boy and his father had owned one. Its Louisiana plates glittered darkly, like a letter with his address on it, and the car's chassis was the color of an expansive summer sky. Dipping into the shadowy ravine segregating downtown from uptown Jersey City, Stanley felt transported back to his childhood: it was as if he could remember all the names of everyone he had met, as if everything he had ever lost had found its way home.

Mike Ribeiro drove Betty and Ida to Ducky's, an Italian restaurant with red velvet wallpaper. After they entered, Mike walked around the restaurant, raucously greeting several people who Ida assumed were lawyers. After Ida sat down, a man wearing a long black robe stepped up to their table. He looked like a lunatic, but Ida blushed at the thought when he introduced himself as the bishop of a neighboring diocese. Ida wished to give him the courtesy he deserved, but she was in a state of shock and found that she could barely mumble out a proper greeting.

"So how did you ladies meet Mikey, here?" the bishop asked, seating himself without being invited. "I've known him since he was the star pupil at Saint Peter's. Amanda!"

the bishop called, waving at one of the waitresses. "We'll have bourbons all the way around." Turning toward the women, he said, "I sought Mikey out for Saint Peter's Prep, because of his Brazilian background, and insisted they give him a scholarship. I myself had just returned from my priesthood in Brazil, charting the Amazon in a boat. Little did I know they would suspend Mikey six months later for having 'no moral fiber.' I saved his neck then, and it wouldn't be the first time. 'Don't worry about that,' I told them. 'He'll make a good lawyer.' And I was right. Even if you weren't good enough for the Jesuits, you were good enough for the bar." He and Mike laughed.

The bishop leaned toward Betty Trombley and continued: "Riding down the Amazon River, I and another priest had the most challenging time. We were attacked by some insects called *miquim,* which burrow into your skin and make you itch horribly. The only thing that kills them is to hold a flame over the bites to smoke the *miquim* out." Turning to Mike, the bishop added, "Well, you can imagine what an experience that was, since those little bugs like to migrate toward the hairy portions of the body. There I was with no clothes on and Father Spooner leaning over me with a lit cigarette."

He leered at Mike, and they both laughed again. Imagine a bishop talking that way! Ida thought wearily, almost failing to feel affronted by his lewdness.

"Sounds like chiggers," Betty Trombley said. "These little bugs they have all over the South? We used to smother them by painting over the bites with fingernail polish. The next time you're in Brazil, give it a try."

The waitress deposited four bourbons on the tablecloth. Ida pushed hers away peevishly: even the smell of bourbon gave her a headache.

"I envy you," Mike told the bishop. "All my life I've wanted to travel in the Amazon."

"I've never understood the desire to travel," Ida said.

Betty snorted into her drink.

Ida stared vacantly at her menu until the bishop waved to a group of men at a far table. He excused himself, talking to the men across the restaurant as he walked.

Ida was seized by the urge to follow the bishop, to grab him and say: Pray for me. Pray for me to get my New Yorker back. She had never felt so full of despair.

When Skeet and Sherry came home from school, they found a few dollars and a note from their mother in the jar on the kitchen table: "Children—please let Mrs. Tutwiler know you're here. We need to purchase two pounds of Virginia ham." Skeet and Sherry walked to the store, with Joseph huffing behind, carrying a yellow alarm clock he had found somewhere. Sherry entered, and seeing Rupert Dixon in the back room, bent over his books, his green-and-gold pencil stub moving slowly in his hand, she motioned her brother to retreat with the dog.

Skeet crossed to the F. H. Eggers memorial, stopped to admire Joseph's pawprint, and walked toward the junkyard. For a moment, he thought he saw Henry Purdy, standing in the distance by the old Rambler. Skeet's heart leapt as if he'd seen a ghost: he was pierced by the recollection that Joseph did not really belong to him. But then he wrestled his imagination back into place, remembering that Henry Purdy was in jail. When Skeet reached the Rambler, no one was there.

Sherry stood at the counter of Persaud's Corner Store, her arms akimbo. When the clerk, Bob Paper, did not appear to notice her, she said cockily, "Ham, ham, thank you, ma'am."

The clerk walked over to the meat slicer without so much as looking up to indicate that he'd heard her order. For all Sherry knew, he might have been making himself a sandwich.

"Slice three pounds," she told him, ordering an extra pound for Joseph. Still unsure that the clerk had heard her, she added, "Extra-extra thin."

Sherry headed for the back aisles, which were filled with dusty packages of unlabeled spices. Several weeks had gone by since she had shoplifted: whenever she remembered that she had a criminal record, she felt a mixture of fear and pride, and both served to diminish her desire to steal. On the one hand, she was too scared to shoplift, and on the other she felt a sense of accomplishment in having achieved a criminal record so early in life. She doubted any other third grader at Immaculate had one.

However, as Sherry loitered by the spices, she saw a row of miniature eight-armed ceramic women on the bottom shelf. Their black hair flowed over the shoulders of their orange gowns. Their jewelry lay thicker on their arms than Betty Trombley's. Sherry heard the clerk turn off the slicer. She leaned over and stuffed one of the Hindu goddesses into her knee sock.

She paid for the ham, asking, "Three pounds, extra thin, right?" The clerk nodded. As she stepped out the door, Sherry saw her brother sitting on top of the Rambler in the junkyard. Joseph stood on the Rambler beside him, a hubcap clenched in his jaws.

She felt a hand grab her ponytail.

"You're the one whose mother lets you dye your hair," Rupert Dixon said, looking down at her with his pale, lashless eyes. Still holding on to her ponytail, he stooped and slipped his cold fingers into Sherry's knee sock. He withdrew the Hindu goddess. The clerk came out from behind the counter.

"Let her be," Bob Paper said. His voice was surprising, clear and sweet. Sherry saw red circles of Tiger Balm on his temples.

Rupert pretended not to hear. Still holding Sherry's ponytail, he told her, "I guess I'll have to call the police on you."

"It's just junk from the back shelf," Bob Paper said. "Let go her hair."

"Quit piping up," Rupert told him. "Where's your parents? They just let you run wild around here?"

Sherry refused to answer.

Mike drove Ida and Betty home, his car jumping at every pothole. Ida looked out the window, feeling hollowed out, as if she had just received a telegram announcing her own death.

After Mike turned onto Grove Street, Betty leaned forward

and said, "There's Jersey City's next little slumlord." Betty had heard that Chicken was married, but it was a shock to see him with his family. Somehow, he did not seem human enough to have spawned human offspring.

Ida recognized Chicken Dixon, in his blood-colored boots, standing on the sidewalk with a bottle-blond girl who looked no older than a teenager. He held a dark-haired baby in his arms and leaned down to kiss it on the back of its neck. Ida felt simultaneously moved by this display of affection and stabbed by the thought that Harlan, in his eight years with her children, had never made even so small a gesture toward them. I'll never have any more babies, Ida thought then, longing for the year that Sherry had been an infant crawling around on the carpet on her belly, her head raised like a turtle's. I may never have a husband again, either. Or live in a pretty house. Or drive a car!

Mike turned onto Grand Street.

"Why, that's Sherry," Betty said. "Why would Rupert Dixon be talking to her?"

Ida's daughter was in the doorway of the corner store with the landlord. What is it now? Ida thought. Will my children get in trouble every time I let someone else supervise them? When Mike stopped, she opened her car door and approached Sherry. Her son stood across the street. The dog was barking, and Skeet held him by the collar. High above them, Mrs. Tutwiler leaned out her window, watching.

"Are you the mother?" Rupert Dixon asked. "Is this your daughter?" Behind him, Ida saw the pale, lashless eyes of the clerk watching her from his expressionless face.

The landlord tugged Sherry's collar a little roughly. Ida saw that he was unaware that he held a sharpened pencil, which grazed Sherry's neck. She placed her hand on Sherry's shoulder, and he moved his hand slightly. "I'm Mrs. Terhune."

"Your daughter was shoplifting in our store." Rupert said, in a tone indicating that all adults agreed with one another when it came to matters regarding children, "She's a little young for that, don't you think?" Sherry rolled her eyes.

"Sherry?" Ida asked, stepping back. She felt beleaguered: she was too upset about the New Yorker to deal with another crisis right now.

"My clerk Bob here and I caught her red-handed," Rupert continued. The man standing behind Dixon did not speak or nod or otherwise attempt to corroborate the accusation. "She was stealing this little figurine." Dixon held up a ceramic ornament that reminded Ida of something she had once seen in Stuckey's. "Tell her to stay out of our store," the landlord pronounced.

Sherry stared off to the right, trying not to hear what he said. She suppressed a smile.

"You shoplifted?" Ida asked her. "Oh, Sherry, how could you disappoint me like that? I brought you up better. How could you disgrace our family? How could you steal—steal, of all things? Steal in a town like this, where people can commit highway robbery and not even go to jail for it? How could you ruin our good name like this?"

Sherry grew still, and the sardonic tuck of her mouth disappeared.

"What do you mean, shoplifted?" Betty said to Rupert Dixon. "Did she walk out of the store with whatever that is? Isn't the law that you have to actually leave the store?"

"That's the law," Mike Ribeiro asserted. Ida saw that the bottom edge of his tie was red, as if he'd dipped it into tomato sauce. Mike withdrew his wallet and removed a white card, which he handed to Dixon. On it was printed: *Michael Percyvaldo Ribeiro. Specializing in Criminal Law.* "I'm this family's attorney, and I'm sure you don't want it said that Rupert Dixon can't keep his hands off little girls."

Dixon let go of Sherry, snatched Mike's card, tore it in two, and threw it on the ground.

"I'm very sorry, Mr. Dixon," Ida said, although she felt grateful that Mike was coming to her defense. "I'm sorry and ashamed."

"What's a goddamn figurine to you?" Betty asked the landlord.

"I can handle this, Betty," Ida said irritably. "I'll thank you to let me discipline my own children."

"I don't even want to say out loud what you are," Betty told Rupert Dixon, "because it reminds me of cat shit."

Ida took Sherry by the wrist. "You come with me right now, young lady. You're grounded." Ida led her daughter away.

At breakfast, Sherry retaliated against her mother by refusing to speak to her. Ida's daughter sent her messages indirectly, through the others. "Betty, pass the sugar cubes," Sherry said, although the sugar cubes sat right at Ida's elbow. And later, Sherry announced to Skeet, "I don't see how I can be told not to watch TV as part of my punishment when we don't even have a TV." As Ida began the dishes, Sherry looked at Joseph and said, "How can she ground me when I don't even have a room of my own? All I have is a closet with a bed in it."

After breakfast, Ida sat at the kitchen table, staring out the window toward the street where she had kept the New Yorker parked. She barely looked up when Angel Rodriguez arrived. Betty had invited him over to try a new haircut she had learned in her beauticians class.

"I'm going to give you a high-top fade," she told him once he had seated himself in the chair.

"No frills," he answered. "Just make me beautiful. Cut it short all the way around to show off what a pretty shape my head is." Sherry handed Betty an electric barber's shaver and a white cloth.

"This is my assistant," Betty said, fastening the cloth behind Angel's neck.

He nodded at Sherry and told her, "Me and my brothers used to steal from this store near our house all the time as kids." Ida was distressed to see that the news of her daughter's conduct had traveled so fast. "The thing is, we were scared of going to hell, so then we'd worry about it so much we'd go put the things back. It got to be a kind of challenge. It was much harder to put things back without getting caught than it was to steal them."

"Who told you about Sherry?" Ida asked.

Sherry scowled as Betty turned on the barber's shaver, drowning out Angel's answer.

When Betty had finished, Angel examined his head in the mirror, thanked her, and left. Sherry crawled into the barber's chair, which was still warm from his body. She thought she should alter her appearance: she wondered how long it would be before Rupert Dixon ran her name and description through police records and discovered that she had a criminal history. "Don't put any dye in it," Sherry said. "It's almost back to Skeet's color. And I want bangs," she added, although she knew her mother thought bangs were tomboyish. "Bangs and a part on the side."

"Let's do Joseph next," Betty answered. "Let's dye him pink and green and give him a punk hairdo."

"Not on your life," Skeet said. "I don't want no skinhead dog."

"He's already a skinhead dog," Sherry said, referring to the area on his chest shaved by the veterinarian, which had grown back only partly since the bandages had been removed.

When she had finished shaping Sherry's bangs, Betty announced that she was taking both children out. She wanted to see the new *Star Trek* movie, and Skeet and Sherry were the only people she knew who would go with her. Ida did not put her foot down and require Sherry to stay inside, as she felt she should. She looked back out the window to the street where her car was not parked, and felt weak.

Betty failed to ask Ida to join them. Not that she would have accepted. Ida did not admire science fiction. Moreover, she was genuinely frightened by pictures about monsters and alien beings. Ida had seen *Rosemary's Baby* almost fifteen years before and still had not recovered. The idea that someone good—no matter how good—could be made a vehicle for evil was so terrifying she could barely stand to think about it, even for a moment.

"I'm staying here," Ida announced, although no one had invited her. "Mike Ribeiro has promised to come by and assist me in finding the New Yorker." He had offered to help search for the car, using Sister Andrea's method of beginning at the Hudson and driving back and forth along the street grids. Ida felt strangely secure that you could find a car that way. It made Jersey City seem small and homey.

Mike arrived before Betty left for the matinee. It was the first time Ida had been alone with a man since her separation, and she felt self-conscious sitting beside Mike in his car as he turned onto wide, empty Columbus Avenue.

Fires had blackened the windows of almost every building on the avenue. "Arson," he said, thumping the steering wheel emphatically with his hand. "I always thought Columbus should be the main street; it's so much wider than Newark Avenue. But as you can see, slumlords have torched everything on Columbus except the rectory." He laughed and continued: "Councilman Lopez thought we should have legislation compelling gas station owners to register all sales of gasoline cans, as an arson control measure. Only in our beloved city."

Ida smiled courteously.

Mike stopped and pointed to a burned-out building in a row of burned-out buildings. "That's where my father kept his store. It was there for twenty-two years."

"Your father?" Ida asked. "What did he sell?"

"Everything. At the time the store burned down, right before he died, he was doing a heavy trade in South American birds. Macaws and parrots and parakeets. His connection used to smuggle them in knee socks. The socks kept the birds' wings tucked in place and hooded them at the same time, keeping them calm in woolly darkness. My father would get them in hand luggage, laid head to tail like sardines. When the store went up in flames, he opened all their cages, and some of them flocked above it for days. They were spectacular birds, especially in flocks. My father said it reminded him of his home in Brazil, where whole crowds of those big macaws would pass overhead all the time, as if they were ordinary as pigeons."

"So he didn't die in the fire?"

"No; he died a few years ago, of emphysema. The doctor

said his lungs looked like he'd been smoking six packs a day. But he'd never smoked in his life—it was just the effects of Jersey City air. He liked to say it was from breathing in the smoke from so much arson."

"I'm sorry," Ida said. "My father died several years ago, in a steamboat accident with my first husband, Dewey."

"Both of them at the same time?"

The death of Mike's father made Ida feel closer to him than she ever had before. "Yes, my father invited Dewey to an inaugural held on the Mississippi River. The steamboat was a replica of the ones they used in the antebellum, and it was going to carry a group of state senators into New Orleans. My father and Dewey climbed onto it early, when no one was looking, hoping to play some kind of trick on the senators, people said. They were doing something with the boiler when it exploded."

"Your mother must have taken it hard."

"My father was a widower. My mother died in childbirth."

"Ah," Mike replied. "Mine took the proceeds from my father's cash register and ran off before I could talk. Lucky for her, ho ho. She had come out here from Traverse City, Michigan, with her sister to join the Rockettes and took the PATH into New York City every day. She never could stand the idea of ending up here."

"So we have something in common," Ida said after a few moments.

"We do?" Mike asked absently. Ida saw him move his right hand as if arguing with himself.

"Loss," Ida answered. "Every time I ever stuck my arm outside, I lost somebody. Just coming into this world, I pushed my mother out of it. And I had three miscarriages. Then I lost Daddy and Dewey and even my husband Harlan. And now the New Yorker. I've lost so many people, there's hardly anything left of me." Ida drew herself up abruptly. Why, she hadn't thought of her mother in years. She was drowning in self-pity, something of which she could not approve. But when she looked up, Mike, who was still gesticulating with his hands, appeared not to have heard her.

"Let's get going to the river, shall we?" she prompted.

Ida was deeply moved by Mike's offer to try to locate her car. However, he seemed to regard this task less seriously than she did and to entirely forget his mission almost as soon as they set forth. From the moment they arrived at the Hudson, Mike took it upon himself to give Ida a tour of downtown Jersey City, stopping several times to show her various sights, which were not at all interesting after the Civil War monuments Ida had seen with the children. Because the car had been stolen uptown, Ida felt they should progress through downtown as quickly as possible.

In addition, Mike did not progress in the systematic way prescribed by Sister Andrea, going street by street. His route seemed random—he passed several blocks at a time, then lingered in unlikely places. When they were a mere fifty feet from the river, Mike pulled onto a deserted cobbled street behind the Colgate factory, rolled down his window, and said, "Smell!"

Ida discerned a faint minty taste in the air.

"Toothpaste," he pronounced happily. "It smells like this for blocks."

As they turned around near the river, Mike pointed to some rotting boat docks and said, "Our former governor Cahill once took a tugboat tour of our waterfront and said, 'I get sick when I look at one side of the Hudson and then at the other.'" Mike thereafter threatened to drive Ida into Manhattan.

Only a few streets later, Mike parked beside a large red-brick building, sniffed the air again, and said, "Pencil dust. Dixon Ticonderoga." He showed Ida a green-and-yellow-striped pencil protruding from his shirt pocket. A black mark, perhaps from a felt-tip pen, had discolored one of the pocket's corners.

"Orestes Cleveland, after whom the road by your very own apartment building is named, was the son-in-law of Dixon of Dixon Crucible Company. Cleveland stole from the company, drove it into bankruptcy, and then got elected mayor shortly afterward."

Again Mike laughed delightedly, and again Ida smiled courteously.

Mike thought Ida looked uncomfortable. Did she suspect him of having designs on her? Did he have designs on her? He would have been happy to take out Ida Terhune if she ever revealed any interest. He was sorry she did not seem to be enjoying his tour.

A man crossing the street waved at Mike and called out, "Hey, Ribeiro, stay out of jail!"

"Mr. Soap!" Mike waved back.

The man cupped his hands around his mouth, took two steps back, and called, "Take her home, take her home!" Ida turned crimson.

"An old client," Mike told her.

"What did he do?" Ida asked, collecting herself.

"Burglary."

"Was he innocent?"

"No, but he's not a bad guy." Mike Ribeiro saw it as part of his personal martyrdom that he had chosen a profession others scorned. Even his clients tended to avoid him after acquittal, because they associated him with a terrible period in their lives. With the exception, of course, of career criminals like Mr. Soap, who stayed in contact with him because they might need his services in the future.

Ida watched Mr. Soap turn the corner. To think, she mused, that you might pass right by an armed robber or a murderer and not even know it.

Shortly thereafter, Mike cajoled her into getting out of the car on Brunswick Street. He led her into a fish distributor's, which he called "The Lobster YMCA" as he escorted her toward a three-tiered fountain in the back, where hundreds of lobsters lay, sorted by size. He leaned over the middle tier, talking to the lobsters and teasingly waving his fingers within pinching distance of their claws. He ordered Ida a cardboard cup of clam chowder, although she had never liked the murky taste of clams.

After two hours of driving and stopping, Ida felt agitated and exhausted. When Mike proposed that they scout around the back streets under an overpass west of the My Way Lounge, she looked fretfully into her lap.

"It's sort of a graveyard for stripped and abandoned vehicles," Mike said mildly. "Don't lose hope. We'll find that car. It stands out like a sore thumb."

"Please," Ida answered. "Please, drive me home."

She didn't like my tour at all, Mike thought a little dejectedly. He drove her back to Grand Street.

He pointed out the monument being built across the street from the apartment building and said, "F. H. Eggers was Boss Hague's nephew. Hague stuffed the ballot boxes and got him elected mayor, and then couldn't keep his hands off the reins. They had an unequal relationship, sort of like Huey and Earl Long." Ida looked up at the sound of Huey Long's name, but as Mike continued to regale her with the history of Mr. Hague, she grew weary.

"It does not seem that our search has been very fruitful," she interrupted. Ida attempted to restrain herself but was unable to: loud sobs rolled from her of their own accord.

"Ida, I'm sorry," Mike said, placing his arm on her shoulder and drawing her near him. He stroked her hair. Ida imagined turning toward him and kissing him. In her mind, he kissed her back and continued to kiss her long past the point where she felt comfortable. She had never kissed that long in her life.

Ida sat up, pulling her face from his. She opened the car door. Once on the sidewalk, she leaned in the window and said, "I appreciate everything. Thank you very much."

Ida was asleep when Skeet and Sherry returned from the movies. Betty had taken the children to a historic uptown theater, soon to be a landmark, where the floors were so sticky that Skeet's shoe came off as he walked down the dark aisle. All the spectators had to sit in the balcony, because the seats had been ripped out of the first floor and the first-floor doors were covered with plywood and nailed shut. Sherry had never sat so far from a film screen. During the movie, she kept glancing at the seatless floor below, an empty expanse of cement divided by two thin red carpets.

Ida slept right through dinner and the children's bedtime. She awoke once, in the middle of an erotic dream in which she was making love to Mike Ribeiro on a circular pink bed at the Playboy Hotel. During the dream, he kept shifting into Harlan and back to himself and then into Dewey. It was as if Ida were making love to three men at the same time, and even in the dream she found this shocking, although she did not want it to end. When Mike Ribeiro had assumed his own shape, Ida saw in the large mirror by the bed that he was covered with coarse brown hair, like a badger. She was sorry when she awoke. She tried to fall back asleep so that the dream would continue, but was kept awake by the sound of the children talking in their room.

Sherry looked behind the pile of objects Joseph had left under the children's bed, and she retrieved her gold scarf. She untied it, and she and Skeet sifted through the contents, stopping to admire the monarch frozen in plastic. Sherry unfolded the picture of Dewey Terhune from its wrapper. Skeet studied the dogs on either side of his father: the hound on the left looked like a blue tick; the other was a black-and-tan.

"If anyone ever tries to take this, I'll bite him," Skeet said.

Sherry opened the Tiger Balm jar, and they both rubbed its contents onto their temples and lay down, savoring its frosty burning.

After Sherry turned out the light, she tucked the retied scarf into the hollow beside her stomach, feeling afraid of the dark. She could not avoid fearing the familiar monsters: the ones beneath the bed and behind the curtains, the ones that would drag you away into other worlds and those that would eat you instantly, the ones with half-animal faces and the frozen, genetically engineered supermen on *Star Trek* whose deaths preserved the universe from being overrun by greed and power and selfishness. As Sherry drifted into sleep, she saw the monsters without faces, and the shrunken ones, and those with pale, ghostly complexions, and also the ones with angry, rejecting expressions that looked like Mrs. Terhune, with her cross face under its crooked hairdo.

Part IV

AN ACCIDENT

◆ Huey Long

On a Friday in March, an unknown denizen of the boat colony liberated a whole live hog from a meat truck destined for the Sabrett factory. The hog's cries as her throat was slit could be heard as far as Bright Street, but no one other than Ida Terhune's children followed the path beyond the junkyard to determine the source of the shrieking. When Skeet and Sherry arrived at the boat colony, they saw the hog lying peacefully on a plywood board, surrounded by admiring men.

Skeet was unable to determine who the owner or the killer had been: the men, exclaiming under their breaths in different foreign languages as well as English, closed around the newly killed pig and then made preparations for a roast. Skeet watched, spellbound, his sister beside him, as three men threw scalding water on the offering and scraped the hog's hair from the body with two jackknives and a switchblade. He and Sherry witnessed the quartering and disemboweling of the hog also, a sight that sickened and fascinated them and made Joseph pace excitedly, barking at the ground.

The men filled a squat barrel with slabs of pigskin, and the smell of cracklings bubbling over a low fire thickened the air until both children were able to taste the wind that lifted their jacket collars. From late afternoon through nightfall, the hog's body roasted over coals as men brushed the skin lovingly with long sprigs of parsley dipped in vinegar.

When Ida Terhune's children returned home, wielding a hog jawbone with the teeth still intact, Betty Trombley greeted them on the front stoop and asked them where their mother was.

Skeet looked at Betty with consternation: his mother's whereabouts had never been a mystery to anyone before. "She must be upstairs," Sherry answered.

But Betty had searched the apartment already. Several hours had passed since the children's mother had left the My Way Lounge in a huff, halfway through a meal.

Betty followed the children back upstairs and checked the bathroom a second time, to ensure that she had not missed Ida. It was unthinkable that Ida would not have called if she was able, she was so utterly predictable. Not like Betty: when she disappeared for seven days after her three-week marriage, her husband had not even thought to notify the police. He had simply packed his things and departed.

When Ida still had not returned home by eleven, Betty called Mike Ribeiro. A half hour later, he drove to the police precinct to file a missing persons report. The police had seen countless possessive males seeking runaway girlfriends and faithless wives, and the officers on duty treated Mike with sympathy, offering him milky cups of coffee but declining to take any action until the next day. After twenty-four hours, the police assured him, they'd issue an alert.

By midnight, Betty had not heard from Ida. Skeet and Sherry fell asleep on the futon couch, refusing to let Betty turn off the living room lights. Betty stayed awake all night in the barber's chair, drinking coffee with chicory and holding the telephone in her lap. In the morning, Ida still had not called. Betty told the children that their mother had food poisoning and had been taken to the hospital but would be out soon. They listened to her with angry, suspicious faces.

Mike arrived at the apartment at nine-thirty, and Betty sent the children upstairs to Mrs. Tutwiler's. Betty and Mike spent all morning calling hospital emergency wards in Jersey City and neighboring counties and, finally, New York City. Then they called morgues. In the afternoon, Mike returned to the police station. The police agreed to issue a missing persons report in the evening. Betty checked local papers and kept the radio on all day into late night, listening and waiting for news reports she did not want to hear, of unidentified persons found injured or dead.

By Sunday night, the police had no leads on Ida's disappearance. The children were distraught. Skeet wondered out loud if he and Sherry would be sent back to live with Harlan Pinkerton.

"Not on your life," Betty told him. "You're both staying here with me until your mother comes home."

Mike contacted a friend at the *Hudson Dispatch,* and the Monday-morning issue ran a short article under a small headline, WIDOW LOST IN JERSEY CITY:

> A Louisiana widow vacationing in Jersey City with her two children vanished without a trace Friday evening near the corner of Second and Brunswick streets. Ida Terhune was last seen at 4:45 P.M. wearing a light-blue pantsuit and carrying a beige handbag. Friends describe Mrs. Terhune as slightly built and approximately five feet four, although her hairstyle may make her appear taller.

Ida would like being referred to as a widow, Betty mused; it sounded more respectable than divorcée. And Betty herself enjoyed the idea of Harlan Pinkerton's history being wiped out with a single word.

Betty worried that the newspaper's description was too

general. There might be half a dozen old women on Brunswick who dressed like Ida. However, a commercial dry cleaner responded to the article, saying he had seen a woman matching Ida's description walking through the brush beneath the overpass on Merseles Street. While the children were in school, Betty visited the site below the overpass, a deserted and overgrown area that kindled her worst fears. Ida was so naive, she was an easy target for any criminal. Betty wandered through the brush, hoping and not hoping to find Ida's purse or some other sign of her passage. Broken glass glinted on the ground, and rusted machinery parts twisted through mats of vegetation. Inside a cast-off truck tire, Betty found a girl's red high heel, decorated with sequins and filled with small foreign coins, and the discovery seemed less strange to her than her failure to find Ida Terhune.

Mike visited the precinct again to pester the police, and they agreed to drive to the overpass to look around. He returned to his office and made several calls to hospitals and to Betty's. In late afternoon, as he was preparing to return to the Quality Inn, the phone rang.

Mike's old client Mr. Soap was on the other end. He explained that he had spent the morning at the Superior Court and that a woman named Mrs. Ter-somebody had been brought from the county jail into Central Judicial Processing for arraignment. When she had heard him mention Mike's name to the court clerk, she had asked Mr. Soap to call Mike. "Funny lady with a messed-up hairdo," Mr. Soap said. "She was worried about her kids."

Mike called Betty Trombley. "He said she wasn't sure what they arrested her for. She said she thought it might be murder." Mike laughed into the telephone. "I'd like to hear the whole story behind this. I'll go right down to the courthouse and straighten things out."

But Betty Trombley had been calling Mike all afternoon, unable to reach him because his line had been continuously busy. As he spoke, she was looking at a photograph of Ida on the third page of the *Jersey Journal:* a mug shot portrayed a gruff, matronly woman with a heavy hairdo, who looked more like a prison warden than a criminal.

"Pick up a newspaper, Mike," Betty said, sounding, for the first time in his experience, as if she were afraid. "It says Ida's been arrested for drunk driving. That she ran over Chicken, 'the son of ex-mayoral campaign manager Rupert Dixon.'" Betty felt like laughing and crying at the same time. It was as if the world had turned upside down. "Is this possible, Mike? Where would Ida have gotten a car? They must have her mixed up with someone else."

The story of how Ida Terhune found her New Yorker would be told and retold. Since the car's theft, she had carried her car keys everywhere, like a talisman. However, she had given up hope of ever seeing the New Yorker again when, two months after its disappearance, Betty Trombley announced that she wished to celebrate quitting her job at the Municipal Court.

It had been a noteworthy accomplishment for Betty to remain so long at the public defender's office. In the end, the city had decided not to fire Ronald Preakness but simply to let the term of his contract expire. Following Judge MacFarland's promotion out of the Municipal Court, those in charge feared that if Ronald Preakness were fired immediately, he would sue the city for breach of contract. Preakness barricaded the door to the municipal public defender's office with a filing cabinet and later changed the locks and refused to admit Betty Trombley. Betty had been reassigned to a new job, reorganizing court files. (Warrants were stored unalphabetized in topless cardboard boxes.) The only part of the job that appealed to her was her lunch break, when she would sit in the foyer outside the public defender's office, chatting with Preakness's clients.

Ida thought it was irresponsible to celebrate the loss of a job, but she agreed to come along with Betty when Mike Ribeiro announced that he would take both women out to the My Way Lounge. Betty ordered champagne and pressured Ida to have some, saying, "Come on, Mrs. Terhune, you're becoming an old sour ball."

Ida was surprised by how much she enjoyed the champagne. She had been feeling depressed since her New Yorker had been stolen, and did not realize just how dispirited she had become until the champagne went to her head. It was a relief to feel lighthearted. She refilled her glass. She listened to Mike talk about one of his murder cases, his face aglow like that of a person in love. Was he flirting? Really, he was an attractive, manly-looking man.

When they were halfway through the meal, Betty pulled out Ida's book on Huey Long and wiggled it over the table. For two weeks, Betty had been reading *The Earl of Louisiana,* snickering as she went and irritating Ida, who had not yet availed herself of the opportunity to enjoy Mike Ribeiro's gift. At the My Way Lounge, Betty opened the book with a sly expression and said, "Listen to this, Ida."

Betty read: " 'A young man came up on his'—that's Justice Fournet's—'right side and passed him, walking fast.' " Betty smiled and continued:

> What attracted the Justice's attention was that he had a stubby black pistol in his right hand. "It was a hot night—before air conditioning—and I perspire exceptionally," Justice Fournet said. "So I was holding my panama hat in my right hand while I wiped my head with a handkerchief in my left. Without thinking, I hit at the man with my hat, backhand. But he reached Huey and fired, and Murphy Roden, a bodyguard, grabbed his gun hand and got a finger inside the trigger guard, else he would have killed Murphy. Huey spun around, made one whoop, and ran down the hall like a hit deer."

Betty's eyes glinted with amusement.

"Why, that's exactly as my father told it!" Ida said, although the book left out the best part, where Huey pronounced, "I know no fear." "That's just what my father used to say, that Mr. Long whooped and ran like a hit deer. Only it was Daddy who swiped at the man with his panama hat. To think of Justice Fournet taking credit for that. What does he say about Roy Daigle?"

"Oh, Ida, Ida," Betty said. She appeared to be tipsy. Ida felt a little tipsy herself. "He doesn't mention Roy Daigle, because Roy Daigle was not there when Huey Long was shot." Betty's last sentence was broken by spurts of laughter: "Your—father—must have stolen—Judge Fournet's story!"

As soon as she looked up from *The Earl of Louisiana* and saw Ida's face, Betty regretted the joke. She had always had too wicked a sense of humor.

But when Ida rose from her chair, looking stately and indignant, another loud laugh escaped from Betty.

"I think I'll just go home, thank you," Ida said.

Mike stood and said, "Oh, Ida. It's just history anyway. At least wait until I've paid the tab, and I'll take you home personally."

"I'm not a crazy person, thank you. I'm a grown woman, and I'm perfectly capable of finding my way home!"

When Ida strode from the My Way Lounge, she turned, disoriented, to her right and walked the wrong way for more than a block, along Second Street. The sun was setting over the overpass, and as trucks drove before it, they cast the street into shadow.

How could Betty say such things about Roy Daigle? How could she find such pleasure in ridiculing a dead man? She had always had a mean streak. But no, that wasn't really true: Betty just thought Ida's Huey Long stories were ridiculous. And wasn't Ida Terhune ridiculous? She was the silliest woman ever born. Why, her father had raised her to be silly.

"You never let her go anywhere by herself," Ida heard her grandmother saying in a quarrelsome voice. "She's like one of those little Pekingese dogs."

A stream of sunlight freed itself from the dark form of a truck rumbling above, and Ida saw several abandoned cars ahead of her, nuzzling the underbrush near a fence encircling what appeared to be a high school. Imagine building a school under a highway, Ida thought, realizing simultaneously that she was walking in the wrong direction. She had definitely never been here before.

But then, after she reversed direction, something about the cars bothered her like a stone caught in her shoe. She turned back and saw the ragged bumper of a dirty blue automobile, looking as if some animal had taken a bite out of it. The license plate was the wrong colors—New Jersey's, not Louisiana's—but the bulkiness of the car's silhouette was as familiar as the faces of Ida's own children.

Ida walked quickly, so that she was almost breathless when she reached the New Yorker. She touched the car affectionately. She looked through the window: on the front seat were a baseball mitt, a pair of high-top tennis shoes, some racing car magazines, and a bottle labeled BOONE'S STRAWBERRY WINE.

Ida withdrew her car keys from her purse. She experienced a moment of doubt when her door key would not fit. Then she saw that a piece of wire had been jammed into the lock. And the door was unlocked! She just hadn't noticed in her excitement. She slid into the car seat and placed her hands gently on the wheel.

Was it proper for her, she wondered, to drive her own car away? Or should she call the police first, since she had reported it stolen? And then, she had drunken that champagne. But what if the car thief saw her and she was in danger? Shouldn't she get away as quickly as possible? Ida had difficulty pushing her ignition key into place, as if the ignition had been tampered with. However, the New Yorker came through and started. She backed slowly onto Second Street. A rush of exhilaration overtook her. Early dusk was shifting into twilight, and now that she had stolen safely away from the school fence, Ida turned on her headlights.

"I'm home!" Ida said to herself, then flushed because she had spoken aloud. She had never done anything so daring. She turned around, and the New Yorker moved forward in a stately way, like a car carrying a beauty queen in a parade. It dipped gracefully over the potholes. She passed the My Way Lounge. A slight drizzle fell on the windshield, although the setting sun illuminated the sky overhead.

"The devil is beating on his wife's door!" Ida again spoke aloud, but this time she felt too elated to care.

A horn blared ahead of Ida. An angry man in a semitruck was waving at her and pointing at a sign ahead. Ida realized that all of the parked cars on the street were pointed in the opposite direction. She pressed on the accelerator and drove onto Brunswick toward Newark Avenue. She saw that the cars were still pointing in the wrong direction and that she had begun to run a stop sign from behind. She retreated, throwing the car into reverse. Her heart was thumping wildly. She had committed two terrible moving violations at once. She steered toward the curb, waiting to hear a siren. But no one paid her any notice.

A limousine pulled up beside Ida. The driver leaned out his window, making a semicircular gesture indicating that he could not fit around the New Yorker. Ida proceeded onto Newark Avenue. The feeling of exhilaration rose impossibly high in her. She passed Jersey Avenue before she saw it, and continued onward. She felt giddy as she maneuvered her way around delivery trucks and kept abreast of the slow-moving traffic. When she reached Grove Street, an approaching car unaccountably honked at the New Yorker.

Grove Street stretched ahead of her, empty and inviting, and the New Yorker cruised toward the skyline. Ida turned right onto Grand Street. The sky was a purply blue, and the street lamps were casting a dim light that mingled with the half-light of the evening. The asphalt was too dark. She felt confused. Ida glanced at the knob that controlled the headlights but saw that they were on.

The asphalt became darker. Ida switched on her brights but discerned no change in the pattern of light in front of her. Were her headlights broken? She removed her foot from the accelerator and pulled into the left lane to avoid a double-parked car. She could barely see; a pale light from the corner store drifted over the street. Was the street lamp at the corner of Orestes Cleveland Road not functioning?

A shape, heavy and enormous (Ida thought suddenly of a Brahman bull), lurched from behind a van parked on the left side of the street and struck the New Yorker. Ida veered sharply to the right, stepped on the brake, and killed the motor.

Mrs. Tutwiler, who would later testify as a key and perjurious witness at Ida Terhune's trial, overheard the accident.

She heard the sound of Ida Terhune's headlight breaking as the New Yorker's front end struck Chicken Dixon. However, it was too dark for Mrs. Tutwiler to see who was driving, or the color and make of the car involved, or even that it had struck a person. She was already thirty yards up the path to the junkyard, looking for the Terhune children, who had not returned home yet despite her instructions that they be inside before nightfall. From her window, she had seen the underbrush near the junkyard suddenly turn a ghostly blue color, and she had concluded that Skeet and Sherry were playing with the police light they had taken from Rupert Dixon's car. As Mrs. Tutwiler approached the flickering light, she saw a small fire burning near the junkyard and smelled roasting pork. She found the children and a group of men gathered around a whole pig laid out on a grate over hot coals. For a moment, Mrs. Tutwiler thought she saw Henry Purdy, but when she peered again into the darkness, no one was there. Skeet was sitting next to a bowl of some kind of marinade while Sherry helped one of the men brush the pig with a long green sprig. A caldron of melted lard boiled over a second fire. It had been over fifty years since Mrs. Tutwiler had seen a pig cooked like this, and she stopped to watch before disturbing the children. She and the children remained there for half an hour and were not lured away by the sounds of approaching police sirens: police appearances were common enough on Grand Street.

When Ida stepped on the brake, the New Yorker's seat belt cut sharply into her shoulder, and her forehead struck the top of the steering wheel. She felt dazed and wondered if she had lost consciousness for a moment. She heard the cries of sirens, as red lights swooped like angels along the street. Moments later, her door opened and a police officer pointed a flashlight into the New Yorker.

"Please tell me what happened," Ida said.

"Lady, you tell me," the officer answered. He took her arm and helped her out of the car, although Ida did not want to leave the New Yorker. She believed she had read somewhere that it was dangerous to move someone who had been in a car accident.

"There's liquor in here," the police officer said next, his light settling on the front seat. He leaned forward and withdrew the bottle of cheap wine from the New Yorker.

Unscrewing the cap, he said, "It's opened and half empty. Been drinking?" he asked Ida.

"Yes, yes I was," Ida told him. But then, realizing the misimpression she had caused, she said, "But that's not my bottle."

"Lady, I can't force you to take a Breathalyzer test," the officer said. "But if you refuse, we'll arrest you and keep your license."

"I don't understand," Ida answered, but she agreed to the test, compliantly pressing her face against the Breathalyzer's half-mask several times when each successive reading came out well within the legal limit.

A second officer approached as Ida's face was buried in the Breathalyzer.

"We've called an ambulance, Starkweather," he said. "But I doubt it will do any good."

"I'm sure I'll be fine if I can just lie down," Ida told Officer Starkweather.

"You can lie down in the patrol car," he answered.

"You aren't going to believe this," the second officer called to his partner. "That car has stolen plates and was reported missing only two months ago. I'm radioing for someone to come impound it."

"It's my car. I reported it missing myself," Ida explained, but the officer backed away again. She felt groggy. "I believe I struck something."

Officer Starkweather spoke into his car radio.

Ida felt a hand wrench her upper arm and push her into the patrol car. "Please!" she said. "Please!" But the hand thrust her firmly into the seat. The patrol car door shut.

"Grand theft auto and vehicular homicide under the influence," Ida Terhune heard Officer Starkweather say into his police radio. The siren turned on overhead; from within the car, the noise sounded distant and tinny, not at all the way a siren did from the outside.

I wish, Ida thought, that I had never come to Jersey City.

* * *

After Mr. Soap called him, Mike Ribeiro drove to Central Judicial Processing, in the rear of the Superior Court building. He learned that Ida had been arraigned already and her bail set ridiculously high. The police had booked her under her proper name on Friday night and taken her to Hudson County Penitentiary to await Monday arraignments. Evidently, there was no communication between the branch of the police department that booked her and the branch that issued the missing persons report. And, Mike assumed, the inmates' pay phone at Hudson County Penitentiary was probably not working, as usual. He drove to the county jail.

Mike had visited clients at almost every prison in New Jersey and New York, from Trenton to Dannemora, but Hudson County Penitentiary gave him a special chill. One of his clients had been murdered inside its walls while awaiting trial, and only that year a fire on an upstairs wing had killed seven inmates. He arrived at the jail as the guards were changing shifts, and waited two hours before Ida was brought down to the counsel room. He loitered in the hallway, holding a cigar that crackled in its cellophane wrapping as he moved his hands, arguing with himself over what to tell her.

A hand-lettered cardboard sign near the visiting area said:

PROLONGED KISSING OR PETTING
NOT ALLOWED.
MAY EMBRACE BEFORE <u>OR</u> AFTER VISIT.
HANDHOLDING IN PLAIN VIEW ALLOWED.
HEAD ON ANOTHER'S SHOULDER
NOT ALLOWED.

Whenever Mike visited clients in prison, a need to escape as strong as instinct overcame him. As soon as he stepped inside the walls, he plotted how he would get away if he were imprisoned: I'd have to knock those five guards on the heads and seize the controls to the double electric gates, then I'd run across that courtyard there, dodging bullets from the guard towers, then I'd slink like a snake through those coils of razor wire. I'd leap like a salmon over the thirty-foot wall and land on my feet.

The counsel room was a gray windowless and airless cell with cracked cement floors and air thick with stale cigarette smoke. When Ida entered, she greeted Mike politely and formally, shaking his hand. Her clothes were rumpled, the belt to her dress was missing, and her shoes had no laces in them. Mike realized he had never seen Ida dressed even in casual disarray.

He could not really believe that Ida Terhune was sitting across from him at the counsel table, as a criminal defendant. If he had dreamed such a scene, he would have woken up amused at its absurdity. On the other hand, he had sat across from clients at that table so many times that nothing seemed more natural than being here, discussing homicide charges against Ida Terhune. He felt his two selves, the personal and professional, shift inside him, separating and joining.

"I want you to tell Betty to call the children's Uncle Porter and ask him to come up here and fetch them," Ida said. "And she should just say to the children that I've been in a car accident. I won't have her bringing Skeet and Sherry here to visit me. I don't want them to see their mother in jail. How long will I have to serve?"

"Ida, you haven't been tried yet," Mike answered. "You haven't even been indicted. If you are, I'm going to try to get your bail lowered when they ask you to come back and plead guilty or not guilty."

"Oh, I'm guilty," Ida interrupted. "Guilty as sin."

Mike had never defended someone who was more likely than any jury to condemn herself. He thought that Ida Terhune might be one of the greater challenges he had faced in his long career.

"Who represented you today when you appeared at Central Judicial Processing? Did the judge appoint a public defender?"

"I'm not sure. I thought the judge was representing me. He was a very nice man. I tried to plead guilty, but he wouldn't let me."

Ida watched Mike talk to himself with his hands; he sliced

the air, pointed downward emphatically, and then turned up his palms. Ida felt that she would be interrupting if she spoke.

"You don't know whether you're guilty yet," Mike said finally. "I have to look at the medical and police reports. I'm hiring Betty as my investigator, and she's going to ferret out some eyewitnesses from around Grand Street. If you're indicted, your case will be assigned to a Superior Court judge, and you're going to plead not guilty." He added, "If you're convicted of homicide, anything could happen, Ida. You could pay a stiff fine, thousands of dollars. Or you could, conceivably, get a jail sentence. Ida, if they convict you of a serious enough crime, they may try to take the children away."

Ida's face paled, and then reddened, and then paled again, as if she were balancing the weight of her own shame against her fear of losing her children. "All right," she said. "I'll do what you say. Everything is moving so fast. I just don't feel like myself." Ida was embarrassed at how befuddled she sounded. She had found the courthouse that morning a nightmare: the language of the lawyers and judges was as unintelligible as a foreign tongue. Their cynicism baffled her; their rules made her feel powerless. In jail, she felt more at home. Jail, at least, was a small, enclosed place with a predictable regimen.

The prosecutor, F. X. Harkin, was an old personal friend of Rupert Dixon's. Harkin was a thin man with a pockmarked face who spoke in a sardonic tone indicating that he believed everything he said but hardly cared about it. After the grand jury indicted Ida Terhune for the crimes of reckless manslaughter and death by auto, he argued in Superior Court for an increase in her bail.

"This woman has no contacts in the area," Harkin told the judge. "In fact, until seven months ago, she lived in a place called Baton Rouge, Louisiana, where she apparently ran out on her husband of many years. She's held her current job for only a few weeks and before that reportedly 'never really worked a day in her life,' to use her own words to the police upon her arrest. And of course, the People intend to prove that she drinks. In short, she's a bad bail risk. Considering the seriousness of the charges—there's a dead body here—I think you should set an unreasonable bail." Harkin laughed at the phrase "unreasonable bail."

The judge, the Honorable Vincent Kiley, may or may not have heard Harkin. It was known in the Superior Court that Judge Kiley wrote murder mysteries in his spare time. At that moment, he was reading one. He did not do this discreetly: he propped the book on the end of its spine so that the court spectators could see the title, *The Dead Don't Care,* and the author's photo. As defendants approached the bench all that morning, Judge Kiley had seldom seemed to notice them. He had carried on a joking conversation with his clerk through several arraignments, rose and swiveled his swivel chair for almost a minute during another, and then signaled the bailiff to come and fix the chair.

When Harkin sat down, Mike Ribeiro stood without talking in front of the bench, until Judge Kiley, lost in his murder mystery, felt the uncomfortable insistence of Mike's silence.

"What are you waiting for, Mr. Ribeiro?" the judge asked then, tilting his book forward. "You apparently agree with Mr. Harkin that your client's a bad bail risk?"

"Your Honor, these trumped-up charges against my client, a mother of two who has never even committed a traffic violation before, an employee of our own Municipal Court—"

"Trumped-up?" Judge Kiley asked. He looked over his book at the defendant.

"There's no evidence my client killed the victim. He seems to have died of a heart attack."

"Yeah, his heart stopped when the car hit him," Harkin interjected. "And he had head injuries."

"The hospital reports show that his body was so full of cocaine you could have gotten high if he'd breathed on you."

"Well, he's not breathing now," Harkin noted.

"And the Breathalyzer tests were all well under acceptable standards."

"It seems," Harkin said, "that one of the officers sat on the Breathalyzer and broke it. The defendant told the police flat out that she'd been drinking from an open bottle in the front seat. She was driving a stolen vehicle."

"That was her car," Mike Ribeiro explained. "She had just found it after reporting it stolen, and the car thief apparently left a bottle behind."

"You might like this book, Ribeiro," Judge Kiley interrupted, holding up *The Dead Don't Care.* "You seem to enjoy fiction."

"Besides," Mike continued, "she's been indicted for reckless manslaughter, and there's no such thing as reckless manslaughter by automobile in New Jersey."

"Well, I see it as a personal challenge to indict a defendant for a nonexistent crime," Harkin said.

"What do you mean, there's no such thing as reckless manslaughter by automobile in New Jersey?" Judge Kiley asked. In the mystery novel he was writing, one of the villains had just killed a minor character by running him over with a cement truck. Judge Kiley was thinking of having the villain convicted of reckless manslaughter instead of murder. In this way, the villain could receive a middle-range sentence and get out of prison in time to kill the protagonist's brother a few years later.

"Your Honor," Mike said, as he thought: This won't be the first time I've tried a case in front of a complete idiot. "As you're already aware . . . " He pulled out a warped and water-stained copy of the *New Jersey Code of Criminal Justice.* Ida recognized the book, because it was the same edition she had used in the complaints office. She felt a pang of loss, realizing that her job would surely be taken from her. Mike paged through the code and then read. "Here it is. *'Death by Auto.'* A fourth-degree offense, which carries a presumptive penalty of no imprisonment and a maximum penalty of eighteen months in jail. *'Criminal homicide constitutes death by auto when it is caused by driving a vehicle recklessly.'* "

Mike turned to another page, and said, *'Manslaughter.'* A second-degree offense, which carries a presumptive penalty of imprisonment for five to ten years. *'Criminal homicide constitutes manslaughter when: it is committed recklessly.'* Your Honor, there's no difference between these two crimes, except for the car. If you recklessly kill someone with a car, it's a lesser crime. Obviously, the legislature was afraid juries wouldn't want to convict anyone of a serious offense that resulted from a car accident, because any juror would say, 'There but for the grace of God go I.' So they created a lesser offense where car accidents are concerned."

Ida barely followed her lawyer's arguments. The law had seemed so open and friendly to her in the complaints office, but now it seemed impenetrable and unfriendly. She recalled that the night before, she had dreamed about Judge Fournet. He had sat before her on a high bench in his panama hat, looking down at her sternly. Beside him sat Huey Long, dressed inappropriately in swimming trunks. His large hairy stomach belled out over his waistline. She had been shocked that the judge allowed Huey Long to expose himself in this manner. Ida had raised her hand, uncertain of what the proper decorum was for getting the judge's attention. She felt it incumbent upon her to protest Huey Long's appearance. But when she looked away from him and back, Huey had slipped into a white suit and held a cigar. He winked at her, and Ida quickly lowered her hand.

"Naw. Naw," the prosecutor was saying. "Mr. Ribeiro here is asking this court to make a controversial legal ruling. If he has trouble with what the law says, let him write a pretty appeal after the defendant's convicted."

Judge Kiley was not about to make a controversial legal ruling. He fixed his eyes on Ida as if she were placing an unreasonable demand on him, and Ida looked away guiltily.

"Your Honor," Mike Ribeiro argued, "the New Jersey legislature couldn't be that stupid. They couldn't have created two identical offenses with two completely different penalties."

"Who says the legislature can't be that stupid?" Judge Kiley asked. "And why don't we show a little respect for the grand jury? In any case, there's a dead body."

"You know the grand jury will do anything the prosecutor

tells them to," Mike Ribeiro answered. "They'd indict a bowl of rice and beans."

"Not just any old dead body," Harkin followed. "This lady killed the son of ex–mayoral campaign manager Rupert Dixon."

"One hundred thousand bail. Ten thousand bond," Judge Kiley pronounced.

"That's unheard-of for a vehicular homicide!" Mike protested.

"Down, boy. Don't raise your voice in my court."

"My client can't possibly come up with that kind of money. You've seen the statement of her assets. She's the sole supporter of two children."

The bailiff approached Ida with handcuffs, and she submitted timidly.

"She should have thought about that when she mowed that poor fellow down," the judge answered.

"Aw, come on, Judge. Let's wait for the trial," Harkin said good-humoredly.

◆ Antonio

Ida had found her first night at the penitentiary somewhat horrifying, although she did not wish to complain. Especially to someone like her cellmate, Pamela, who apparently had been in jail a number of times. The guards had taken Ida's purse and dumped it out, thereafter making a list of all its contents, right down to her empty tampon holder. Three different officers had searched her, running their hands over her as if she were a prize show dog. One guard laughingly suggested something called a "cavity search," but by the time Ida understood what he meant, another guard had arrived, announcing that the women's wing of the penitentiary was overcrowded and that all female arrivals were being sent to the psychiatric wing. The new guard did not search Ida, but he took her pantsuit belt and her shoelaces, "so that you won't hang yourself," he explained, and then transported her upstairs in an elevator.

The inmates had not proved to be as dangerous as Ida might have expected, and even the ones said to be crazy seemed fairly ordinary and were difficult to tell from the regulars transferred from the women's wing. (The occupant of the cell next to Ida's lay with her face to the wall all day, which was exactly what Ida felt like doing.) The lack of privacy resulting from her cell's exposure to the hallway that ran down the middle of the cellblock disoriented Ida. However, Ida saw that inspections occurred by schedule and that Pamela apparently had worked out an arrangement with the guards by which they had agreed not to really search her cell all that thoroughly. Pamela was respectful and courteous to Ida, turning to the wall when Ida undressed.

Pamela would not reveal the cause of her arrest, telling Ida only, "I don't think you could stand to hear it, honey." Ida was curious but did not think it would be proper to pry. She took comfort in the fact that Pamela had committed an offense so unspeakable that she would not judge Ida for having killed someone. Although Pamela did have some surprising quirks. For example, she spent hours devising astrological charts for herself and other inmates, with notations such as "Mercury is in retrograde and you'll feel the call of the wild soon" and "With the lunar nodes moving into your solar 3rd and 9th houses, you must remain madly possessive of your things." She offered to draw a chart for Ida, but Ida demurred. Pamela also smelled like a men's locker room, something that puzzled Ida until Pamela showed her a gallon-sized glass bottle under her cot, filled with a substance she called "pear jack," which she claimed was made by fermenting canned pears and apricots with the aid of rubbing alcohol and then straining the results through Wonder bread.

"Isn't that poisonous?" Ida asked.

"Have some," Pamela answered, pouring some pear jack into a plastic cup for Ida. Pamela was a small, sinewy woman, and her tendons stood out from her arms as she poured. She had a blue cast to her long black hair and wore blue mascara, something Ida had never seen. Why would someone want blue eyelashes? Ida accepted the cup of pear jack, sensing the warmth and generosity of the gesture, but she allowed the cup to remain untouched in her hand while Pamela opened a box of dominoes and divided them on an upside-down checkerboard. Eventually, after a few rounds of dominoes, Ida set down the cup, and Pamela absentmindedly lifted it and sipped until it was drained.

Ida had never learned to play dominoes until now and was surprised by the game's simplicity. Pamela loved dominoes passionately, and as she played, she liked to discuss domino strategies and divulge her knowledge of the law, which seemed extensive to Ida. Pamela also enjoyed giving legal advice, and several inmates a day sent her notes asking about their lawyers and legal procedures, often requesting their daily horoscopes as well.

"Don't put your double six there—save it for later," Pamela told Ida. "Take my word for it, a double six is good luck: it means you'll get out of here. This place is just for people who haven't been tried yet but can't make bail and for petty offenders," Pamela explained, dropping a domino after Ida's. "Serious offenders go to Trenton. The word is out that this pen's so overcrowded the Municipal Court judges have been told to give everyone suspended sentences." Ida had not been aware of this fact when she was working at the Municipal Court. "Except for the shoplifters, because the third time you're caught shoplifting in Jersey, you have to serve time. So here the law types are, letting out all these downgraded rapists and robbers on suspended sentences, and the jail's chock-full of people who swipe candy and hairpins."

"That hardly seems fair," Ida said politely.

"That's why there's so many women here, since shoplifting's a female crime," Pamela continued. Ida thought uneasily of Sherry. "Men rob and burglarize, women shoplift. Men deal drugs, women get arrested for being look-outs. Sex segregation is what it is. Discrimination. You know the way men are the presidents of companies and women are just executive secretaries? Well, crime's no different. We're always on the edges of crime, the same as we are with everything else." Pamela smiled to herself, as if she might be an exception to this rule. She dropped a domino next to Ida's and said, "Ha! Snake eyes! A brilliant move! You can tell I'm a Scorpio. You're playing just like a Libra, and it's not surprising. It would be hard to invent outer circumstances more alarming than the recent passages of Saturn in your Seventh House and Neptune in your Sixth."

Ida felt she had little knowledge to offer Pamela in return. Ida had already told about her trip north, downplaying the part in which she and the children had been trapped in the hurricane, because it seemed unnecessarily dramatic. Ida suppressed an impulse to mention her father and Huey Long. She had had another dream about Huey Long the night before, in which he had escaped from a mental asylum and appeared in his pajamas before the governor's mansion to announce his reelection. "Liar! Liar! Liar!" Ida had heckled him, although in fact he had been reelected. She awoke to realize that she would never, never again take joy in her vicarious association with Huey Long. She felt that he had personally betrayed her.

"I'm worried about my children," Ida ventured after setting down a domino. She hesitated to talk about Skeet and Sherry, because she missed them so much she could hardly bear to think about them. "I've never been apart from my children for a whole day since they were born."

"I miss my boy too," Pamela said. She pulled a photograph of a toddler from under her mattress. "I was laid up in bed for five months when I was pregnant, and they delivered Timmy by caesarean. My husband, Pete, didn't give me any emotional support all that time—he didn't want a kid. 'So what do you want?' I used to ask him. 'You have a new car. You have a condo with a deck.' I can't believe how much I love him. Timmy, I mean." Pamela picked up Timmy's photograph and kissed it. "Can you believe this face?" Pamela held the photograph in front of Ida. "He's so beautiful."

Ida thought Timmy looked wrong somehow—his eyes were too wide-set, and his skin was sallow. "He's sweet," she pronounced.

"He weighed two pounds two ounces when he was born.

They had to shave off his hair and feed him intravenously through the head. Now he's in the ninety-ninth percentile for his height. When they arrested me, they confiscated him and stuck him in foster care. Who's going to take your kids while you're in here?"

A wave of anxiety drowned Ida, and she could not answer.

"Sorry. New topic," Pamela told Ida. "Well, maybe you'll get your bail knocked down. Who knows? I'm not going to see the light of day until I serve out my sentence." Again Ida suppressed the desire to ask Pamela what offense she had committed. "I'd do anything to get out of here and see Timmy."

For breakfast, Betty took Skeet and Sherry to the Family Diner at Grand and Barrow streets. It was the tenth day in a row they had eaten there. Ida's children sat next to each other, funereal and polite, saying nothing and ordering only cinnamon toast. Betty could not persuade them to eat anything else.

Betty leaned back in her chair and let the feeling that had been dogging her all week settle. She was worried sick about Ida. That was part of it, but not the part that was getting to her. When Betty was not sure what the source of a feeling was, she liked to sit still and let it soak into her bones until she could say what was troubling her. Light and shadows played off the leaves of a ficus tree in the restaurant's corner, flickering on the ceiling like countless gods talking. She longed for Ida, that's what it was. More than she would have thought possible. How could someone as oversheltered and narrow-minded as Ida Terhune be so essential? It's that Ida knows who she is, Betty thought. She may be a funny lady, but look how her children need her.

Betty lacked Ida's constancy and tenderness. She could show Sherry how to answer a catcall with finesse, how to braid tinfoil into her hair, and how to dance the mambo without a partner, but she could not teach her how to feel safe. The night before, Betty had entered Skeet and Sherry's bedroom to tuck them in and overheard Skeet talking to himself, staring at the ceiling. When Betty got close, she heard him saying, "Skeet Skeet Skeet Skeet Skeet," as if doubtful of his own existence.

"We have to go," Sherry told her. "It's past school time."

Betty walked the children to Immaculate. Betty had chided Ida repeatedly when she announced her decision to send the children there. Ida had explained that parochial schools cloistered children from the real world, letting them enjoy their innocence as long as possible. Betty had told her, "Shit on toast, Ida. What's so awful about the world? What's so great about innocence?" But Betty felt relieved as she led the children past Sister Andrea, who barked at them for being late.

Skeet worried that Mrs. Feeley's interest in crime stories would lead her to exhibit the *Jersey Journal* article about his mother's accident to the third grade. For days after he had discovered the newspaper stuck in Betty Trombley's drawstring bag, he had entered Mrs. Feeley's class on tenterhooks. Although Mrs. Feeley had not yet referred to the newspaper article, Skeet believed she must know about his mother. Adults had a way of finding out such things. When she finally confronted Skeet and his sister, publicly or privately, he needed to be prepared.

Three weeks after his mother's arrest, Mrs. Feeley pretended to notice for the first time the Albert Payson Terhune book Skeet kept on his desk. She questioned him about it, looking at him oddly, and then said, "Please bring your tray up to the classroom today during lunch period." The rest of the morning, Skeet felt a gnawing in his stomach, wondering what Mrs. Feeley would say about his mother.

Right before lunch, Skeet chose a secret name for himself: not Skeet or Skeeter or even Mosquito, but *Antonio,* an extravagant-sounding name, possessed by no one he had met in Baton Rouge but that he had heard called over Columbus Avenue by an unseen mouth to an unseen ear, disembodied as a spirit. *Antonio* was the name Joseph knew him by. It was the name whose mystery and power required that no human speak it directly to him. It was a name that Skeet suspected would take him to places he was not allowed to visit but must visit.

Antonio was a risk taker, an adventurer, a warrior with only a dog as a companion. Antonio was certainly prepared to deal with Mrs. Feeley. At lunchtime, he found the teacher seated at her desk. She nodded to him and indicated that he should pull up a chair. His book lay before her on her desk.

Buddy boy, I wish you was here to bite her, Antonio beamed to Joseph.

Antonio had cut off the bottom six inches of his clip-on tie with a pair of scissors. He had hoped that Mrs. Feeley had called him in to reprimand him about this infraction. However, she looked directly at the tie stump without remarking anything. Still hoping she wanted him for some ordinary reason and not to discuss his mother, Antonio ventured, "I smacked Caleb because he and Sherry was already fighting it out on the playground because Sherry told Caleb he wasn't going to squeeze her neck one more time." Caleb was a sorry specimen: he had had an operation in second grade, which had left a large, U-shaped scar on his chest, and if anyone ever hit him after he attacked that person, he would shriek as if murdered and yell, "You hit me in my operation! You hit me in my operation!" He was a merciless bully, nonetheless. Many times Antonio had baited him on the playground and wrestled him to the sticky tar of the blacktop in hand-to-hand combat.

Mrs. Feeley answered, "*Were,* young man."

"What?"

"They *were* fighting it out on the playground."

"That's right. Because he squeezes Sherry's neck every morning. That's why Sherry whomped him on the head with his own clarinet case."

Mrs. Feeley abruptly changed the subject. She had not called him upstairs because of the fight. He steeled himself.

"It's nice that you've taken the trouble to join me for this little kaffeeklatsch," Mrs. Feeley began. "I know that you're related to this famous man." Her fingers drummed nervously over the figure of the collie embossed on the Albert

Payson Terhune book. "But for some reason you've chosen not to tell me." She smiled down at Antonio. It was a simpering, incomprehensible smile.

It would not have occurred to him to think that Mrs. Feeley was simply unusual. Many of the adults in his experience had acted unpredictably. After Mrs. Hardy exhibited her scar to the third grade to show them how all children are torn as babies from their mothers' sides, he had been baffled to learn that she had been fired for this conduct. He was always surprised to discover that some adult had been acting ignobly in the eyes of other adults. For example, he had met Lotta Stroke on at least a dozen occasions, when alone with Harlan Pinkerton, and she had treated him well and Antonio had liked her. Later, however, Harlan would swear him to secrecy, forbidding him to mention Lotta to his mother, as if Lotta had overstepped some invisible line adults were prohibited from crossing. This information had made Antonio like Lotta even more. As he had no reason to tell his mother about Lotta, he never did.

During the remainder of the lunch period, Mrs. Feeley talked chattily and ate with enthusiasm. Her lunch consisted of little crackers called Sociables, shaped like playing card symbols, spread with liverwurst and topped with green, onion-centered olives. Antonio resisted when she offered him one. He was relieved when the bell rang and Mrs. Feeley excused him for recess.

As he stood to leave, Mrs. Feeley lifted up the Albert Payson Terhune book.

"I'm sure you don't mind if I borrow *Bruce,*" she said. To Antonio's astonishment, Mrs. Feeley opened her top desk drawer and dropped in his book.

When school let out, he accompanied his sister to Mrs. Tutwiler's apartment after picking up Joseph. Mrs. Tutwiler told them that Betty Trombley was meeting with their mother's lawyer and would be home in a few hours. Mr. Ribeiro rarely came by, now that he was involved in their mother's case. Skeet began to associate him with her absence: he seemed a messenger from the law, with its police and courts and jails. When Mr. Ribeiro did drop by, to speak with Betty Trombley, Skeet avoided him.

Politely nodding when Mrs. Tutwiler instructed them to stay within seeing distance, Antonio struck out for the boat colony. Sherry followed, melodramatically singing "The Red River Valley," one of Mrs. Feeley's favorites. As they passed the junkyard, the three dogs did not run out to bark at them. Joseph dropped the object he had been embracing in his jaws (an unopened can of Vienna sausage) and sniffed the air in front of Antonio, as if troubled by the unnatural quiet. *Although I, Antonio, am fearless, boy,* he beamed to Joseph, *do not hasten to bidmeado. Can't we bidmeado together?*

Antonio told his sister stoically, "Feeley took my book that Mr. Ribeiro gave me. The dog book." He suddenly felt furious: Mrs. Feeley had swindled him.

Sherry stopped singing and raised her eyebrows. "That old witch better give it back," she said.

As they approached the junkyard, Skeet imagined rounding the corner and finding his mother perched on the aluminum seat of Henry Purdy's skiff. "Skeet, honey," she would call to him, "I've decided to hide out here awhile. You can visit me whenever you want." Skeet pictured her waving ecstatically to him, climbing from the boat and running toward him. Skeet thought of how dogs greeted people, jumping on them to knock them over, turning circles in the air. It would be nice if people acted that way. *Woof! Woof!* Skeet thought as he neared the boat colony. *Here I am!*

But when the path turned and Skeet saw the scenery before him, his daydream left him: the canal, iridescent with oil, stretched out emptily. Wood splinters and flotsam bobbed here and there on its surface. The boat colony was gone. Every man, every boat, right down to the last small skiff. The empty oil drum, and the police light he had hidden under it a few days before, were gone, and so were the cinder blocks the colony's residents had liked to sit on. A few spare ribs and hog hooves from the March pig roast littered the ground where lard-filled barrels had once been, but the barrels had vanished.

Joseph sniffed the earth. *The enemy has been here, old pal,* Antonio told him. *They have carried off our ships.*

To Antonio's consternation, Sherry started to cry. Her arms stiff at her sides, her chin jutting forward, at first she just sobbed, saying, "Where are the boats? How can that old witch just take your book?" She raised her voice and said next, hoarse with anger, "Where's Mama? Where's Mama?" Then Sherry cried loudly, howling.

Antonio almost leaned forward and took his sister's elbow. He felt a temptation to encircle her shoulder with his arm, but he also felt pinned to where he stood, uncertain what to do next. Skeet felt powerless to do anything.

Joseph barked at two uniformed guards as they rounded a stand of marsh reeds. Sherry stopped crying when she saw the guards. They waved the children away.

Immaculate had no gymnasium. Occasionally, a gym class was permitted in the local park when the teachers were tired and the weather was good. The following day, there was a spirit of elation in the third grade after Mrs. Feeley announced that the last hour would be a gym period. However, the sky darkened as the day progressed, and Sister Andrea announced over the intercom that all gym classes would be canceled.

At the beginning of the last period, Mrs. Feeley smiled conspiratorially at Skeet, nodding to him as she withdrew a red-bound book from her top drawer. She explained to the class that the book was by a famous New Jersey writer named Albert Payson Terhune.

"I know the author intimately," Mrs. Feeley told the third grade, "and this is a copy of a book he gave me personally. It is called *Bruce,* and it is about a dog of war." From her desk, she lifted a road map, which rustled thunderously as she shook it toward the class to make it unfold. She held the map against the blackboard and said, "This is Sunnybank, where the great author lives." She had drawn a red circle in the middle of a green area.

"Mr. Terhune inscribed this book for me with his own

hand," Mrs. Feeley said next, laying the map down on her desk without refolding it, so that it flopped over the desk's sides. She picked up Skeet's book, opening it before the class to reveal a large black signature that had not been there before. Skeet leaned forward: Mr. Terhune had the same perfect rounded handwriting as Mrs. Feeley. Hadn't Mr. Ribeiro said that Albert Payson Terhune was dead?

Mrs. Feeley read from the book, abridging and paraphrasing some pages in the first chapter. Eventually, she put down the book and simply told the story as it was written, or perhaps merely as she would have written it. It was, in any case, a gripping story: Bruce, a messenger dog for the American troops in World War I, was hit by seven bullets when passing an enemy encampment. Mortally wounded but persevering, Bruce arrived back at the American camp and was able to lick the hands of his favorite American infantryman before expiring. The soldiers, despondent and weeping, built a dog-sized coffin, laid his body lovingly inside, and carried the coffin on their shoulders to a dog-sized grave. But then, just as the pallbearers reached Bruce's tombstone, they heard a knocking and scratching inside the coffin, as if Bruce's spirit were struggling to free itself. The soldiers, awestruck and a little frightened, opened the coffin lid. The powerful collie was alive.

"I will read further from this on another occasion," Mrs. Feeley said, snapping the book closed. The third grade expressed disappointment; various moans arose from the back row. Skeet was impressed by the story. He wanted his book back: it was his.

He watched with dismay as Mrs. Feeley returned *Bruce* to her purse. *Dog, come get my dog book,* Skeet beamed. He imagined Joseph trotting into the room and dragging Mrs. Feeley's desk through the classroom door and down the stairs, out into the rainy day.

As if in response to his thoughts, Mrs. Feeley closed the classroom door. She faced the third grade, held her finger to her lips, and said to her students in a loud, rasping whisper, "Now I will tell you a real horror story."

She turned off the lights. The classroom filled with the gray duskiness of the day outside. "All right," she said. "If you must know." She arranged the papers on her desk into three piles and looked out the windows at the drizzling rain. "At one time in my life, I lived in New Zealand and was a married woman."

Mrs. Feeley paused, allowing this information to sink in. "I was married for thirteen years to a man named Harris Feeley. One morning I awoke and said to him, 'Rise and shine, Harris, it is a new day.' I reached out and touched my husband gently. He was quite cold. He had died during the night. Perhaps I had been sleeping for several hours next to a dead person. The shock of it quite unhinged me for several months."

The children waited in deadly silence for Mrs. Feeley to continue. Sherry hoped that a ghost story of some kind would follow. But nothing did. Mrs. Feeley arose, turned the lights back on, said, "All right now, out with your spellers," and wrote the week's word list on the blackboard.

The remainder of the afternoon, Skeet simmered until he grew enraged about Mrs. Feeley's appropriation of his book. He resolved to confront Mrs. Feeley after school and demand that she return what was his. Antonio would ask her politely for the book, but if she did not comply, he would take it by force.

By three o'clock the sky had cleared, and Antonio's mind also had cleared. He told his sister to walk home without him, and after Mrs. Feeley led the third grade downstairs following the dismissal bell, Antonio returned upstairs to the classroom to wait for her. He waited for what seemed like a long time, perhaps an hour. He pulled out his map of Grand Street and admired it: it was better than any adult could have done. He had used a ruler to make the streets perfectly straight, and their names, from Grand Street to Newark Avenue, were spelled out in neat capitals. If only he had been with his mother on the night of the accident, she never would have gotten lost.

He drew several maps of New Jersey on the chalkboard, in which he depicted the state as an oblong with a collie in the middle. Mrs. Feeley's purse still sat on the desk, and thus Antonio was certain she would have to return. However, Antonio grew impatient and decided to take matters into his own hands.

He walked to the teacher's desk and opened her handbag; he saw several square plastic boxes full of pills. The book was not inside. Antonio sat back down. After awhile, he rose again, this time circling behind Mrs. Feeley's desk and looking in the drawers. One drawer held a metal box containing several dozen note cards with fingerprints on them. Another was full of objects Mrs. Feeley had been confiscating over the past few months from her students: comic books, Matchbox cars, a toy lipstick, and a squirt gun. The book was not in any of the drawers.

Antonio sat back down. He waited with a patience that came from his long and demanding training as a warrior. Outside, the sun's rays reddened and slanted into the classroom. Dust motes danced in the air.

Antonio heard the tapping of Mrs. Feeley's high heels on the school stairs. Her devil's-food-cake hat popped in at the doorway. She stopped abruptly.

"Skeet!" she said, smiling her incomprehensible smile.

Antonio rose. "I want my book."

Mrs. Feeley cocked her head and looked at him questioningly.

"My Albert Payson Terhune dog book. It's mine," Antonio said.

"Oh, yes. Of course, yes," Mrs. Feeley said. "Have you been waiting here all this time for it? Oh, my." She picked up her purse and her plan book and walked quickly toward the classroom door. "It's in my car," she said. "I hope you don't mind that I chose to entertain the class a little today with it. I thought I might entice you into reading it if I livened it up a little."

Antonio wondered at her lame explanation for taking his book. He followed Mrs. Feeley down the school stairs and out a side exit, to an orange Volkswagen. When they reached the car, Mrs. Feeley turned to him and asked, "Would you like a ride home?"

He knew not to get into a strange car; Mrs. Feeley herself had warned him. He saw his book on the dashboard. He opened the car door, sat in the front seat, and placed the book in his lap. At the moment Antonio entered the car, he knew that something outlandish, thrilling, and unacceptable might occur, but Antonio did not feel endangered.

Mrs. Feeley turned on the ignition, and the car rumbled under them. It would be dark before any of the adults returned home to find Antonio missing. He closed his eyes and pictured Mrs. Feeley kidnapping him, driving him to Sunnybank. The navy-blue sky arched overhead, and the stars waggled around him, the highway winding its glittering asphalt into Albert Payson Terhune's driveway. Collie dogs chased the car.

Mrs. Feeley double-parked in front of the Grand Street building. Antonio, book in hand, opened the door and climbed out of the Volkswagen. Mrs. Feeley told him goodbye in an overly cheerful voice. After he shut the door, the teacher drove away. The apartment building's top windows glowed dimly under the broken street light. He felt lost and disoriented and unconnected to the world, which suddenly seemed too large and unmappable without his mother in it. He mounted the stairs slowly, heard barking upstairs, and oriented himself toward Joseph.

Mr. Rodriguez, almost invisible where he sat in darkness on the stoop, greeted Skeet and communicated that Betty Trombley would be home late—she was visiting Skeet's mother at the penitentiary. Supper was ready for him and Sherry at Mrs. Tutwiler's. No one thought to ask him where he had been.

◆ Gloria

After Mike Ribeiro's repeated attempts to reduce Ida's bail had failed, Betty wrote to Aunt Rosine and Uncle Porter, telling them that the children needed to stay near their mother during the trial and that both Skeet and Sherry seemed confused and lost. Aunt Rosine could not take a leave from her job, and so it was decided that Uncle Porter should drive the pickup to Jersey City. He was still laid off and could do the same kind of tinkering work anywhere that he did in Baton Rouge.

Porter arrived on Grand Street in early afternoon, when no one was home, and he wandered around, staking out the neighborhood. He walked about a mile and a half, until the April cold began to bother him through his thin jacket (he hadn't needed a jacket more than a few times in his life). He bought some fried crab at Curry's fish market on Pacific Avenue, strolled along a boarded-up and burned-out section of Communipaw, and circled back to Grand Street. He thought Jersey City was kind of average ugly, like the poorer parts of Baton Rouge, but it had pockets of fine things here and there: Curry's fish market, butchers with good prices on spare ribs, a hardware store called Borinquen Home Improvement Center, which had impossible-to-find items like wooden mortars and miniature copper piping elbows. And there was a nice junkyard right within throwing distance, with all kinds of machine parts.

After his walk, Porter opened his bag of cooked crabs and sat on Betty Trombley's front stoop, waiting for the children to come home from school and cracking open his crabs. He threw the shells into a cardboard carton where he had two dozen live crabs he'd bought for dinner. He was the kind of man who liked to eat the same thing over and over until he grew sick of it and then move on to something else, and anyway, Skeet and Sherry loved crabs. And, he remembered as he poked through the shell of the biggest crab, Betty couldn't cook to save her life. She preferred to use food as a weapon for killing off anyone who expected her to do his cooking. Porter had almost choked to death once on a pile of her half-cooked black-eyed peas, shriveled and hard as gravel.

It had been a few years since Porter had seen Betty Trombley. It had been over ten since he'd seen her with her clothes off, but it had taken a lot out of Rosine to let him travel up to Jersey City, knowing he'd probably end up under the same roof.

"I'm trusting you, Porter," Rosine had told him, with a look of complete mistrust that made him feel sorry for her, strangled by her, certain of his faithfulness, and filled with longing for Betty Trombley, all at once. Betty was the only woman he'd ever been with who was anywhere near his size. His whole marriage, he'd made love staring at a pillow or into a wall or up onto the ceiling. He hardly remembered what it was like to lose yourself in someone's eyes while you lost yourself between her legs.

"Come on, Rosine, I'm too old for that kind of thing. And

Skeet and Sherry will be there. And all anyone will have time to think about is how to get Ida out of the mess she's in."

Rosine might have been appeased, but she didn't answer, probably out of pride. She just slipped over to another subject. "Maybe you'll want to tell Ida that snippet Honey Perkins has moved in with Harlan on Tulip Street. She's pressing him to divorce Ida fast, they say. Left her own husband, a lawyer, they say. They say she's after Harlan's money."

Porter had put his arm around Rosine and squeezed her to assure her everything was OK, or probably OK anyway. "I don't know about all this gossip," he told her, "but I do know that Harlan's money has always been made up of other people's money, and when the smoke clears, that gal's likely to find that whatever she's got her hands on is just a picture in a trick mirror and that suddenly Harlan's got everything of hers besides."

As Porter sat on Betty Trombley's front stoop, he wasn't sure he would tell Ida about Harlan and Honey Perkins. It just didn't seem all that important in the scheme of things.

When the children rounded the corner of Jersey Avenue onto Grand Street, they saw Uncle Porter. Something about his monstery hugeness tugged at them like a familiar but nameless person in a dream. They watched him lean over a bright-orange crab, its steam rising around him in the hard cold sunlight. They walked faster.

"Hey!" Porter called, standing up. He waved, wiggling the crab in his hand.

Skeet and Sherry stopped about ten feet away, looking wary. They did not fully believe Betty Trombley's assertion that they would not be sent back to Tulip Street, and the children wondered if Porter had arrived to retrieve them. Skeet and Sherry had considered running away temporarily, maybe hanging out in the boat colony. However, that had been before the boat colony disappeared.

"Crabs is sure stupid," Uncle Porter said, sitting down and reaching into the bag in front of him. "Best way to catch a crab is just to drop down a piece of bacon on a string. No crab can resist the smell of bacon. He'll just hold on, and you can pull him up, ten, twenty, forty feet onto a pier, and he'll never think to just let go; he'll only get mad at you for pulling him up. They's whole kinds of people won't touch crab 'cause they think crabs is so nasty. They nasty, all right, too nasty to live. Only thing to do with a crab is to eat it." Porter held out a steaming crab and stuck it in Sherry's hand. "Hey, Sherry," he said. "Hey, Skeeter." Skeet watched his sister's face, relief washing over the expression that had been frozen there for too many days to count. Porter reached his arm behind Skeet's back, drawing Skeet to his side. Porter plunged his hand again into the brown bag. It rustled as if alive. Skeet grew still, as still as Joseph when he suddenly ceased to pant. Porter withdrew a live crab. "See, this kind of crab is brown and blue before you cook it, but they go bright red as soon as they hit hot water. Nothing in the world but shellfish will do that—who knows why. I'm gonna be living up here with you until things get straightened out with your mother."

Porter stayed. He stayed for the first week, when the frozen sewer water in the basement of the Grand Street apartment thawed to sludge, and he stayed a second week, after Rupert Dixon turned off the heat and hot water to force Betty Trombley and Ida Terhune's children out of his building. Porter introduced himself to Angel Rodriguez, because it made Porter nervous to live in a place where he did not have at least one other man for company. Then, while Betty was out meeting with Ida's lawyer, Porter enlisted Angel's help in moving everything out of Betty's apartment and into and on top of his pickup, and the men carted her possessions in six trips to a building ten blocks away, on the corner of Pacific and Communipaw.

Joseph sat in the pickup's cab, between Angel and Porter, sniffing the coonhound smell of the upholstery. He had followed Porter and Angel up and down the stairs of the Grand Street apartment, dragging several objects that had been under Skeet's bed to the pickup. When they arrived at the new apartment, Joseph dragged the same objects from the truck over the new apartment's threshold.

Porter drove Angel back to Grand Street and made one last trip by himself. He threw the remaining objects that had been under the children's bed into a box to transport to Pacific Avenue. Porter was surprised at the variety and unusual nature of things tangled up in the yellow scarf: a box of condoms, an amethyst ring, a collapsible cup and a Swiss Army knife, a bar of soap with a Playboy insignia on it, a burned matchstick half wrapped in pink foil, a shriveled brown root, pinking shears, a bottle of Jean Naté bath oil, and a letter addressed to Ida, from Carlotta Stroke, of all people. Porter read the letter, shook his head, and chuckled. "Sounds just like Lottie."

He found the children's photograph of his brother, expensively framed, and wondered who had given Skeet and Sherry the frame. The picture had been taken right after Dewey married Ida. He had loved her so much that he sold his favorite hound, a blue tick called Midnight Becky, just to pay for a hotel suite in Hot Springs on their wedding night. Ida's father had offered to foot the bill if she took her honeymoon in Baton Rouge, but Dewey said no. He couldn't stand the way Mr. Daigle boxed Ida in, spending heaps of money to make her do what he wanted her to and never what she wanted. Like sending her to that Catholic school where girls never saw a boy. If her grandmother had not gone behind Mr. Daigle's back and kept Ida home so many days they had to expel her, Ida might have ended up a nun, locked away in some nun house somewhere. Her grandmother used to let Dewey in the back door when Mr. Daigle was out.

Porter's recollection of Dewey's sweetness caught him off guard. He felt the loss of his brother as abruptly and fiercely as if he had suddenly slipped when using a tool and cut himself. Porter wrapped the photograph back up in the yellow scarf.

Porter drove down to the Salvation Army and picked up a few extra pieces of furniture he thought he wanted: a tangerine-colored couch, the only thing long enough for him to sleep in; two sets of bunk beds, one for Skeet and Sherry and one for Ida and Betty (that would save floor space); and a table with a nifty top that revolved like an oversized Lazy Susan.

After Porter had transported these items in two trips to the new apartment, he hand-lettered a sign and stuck it in the window:

PORTER TERHUNE
WILL FIX YOUR HOUSEHOLD APPLIANCES
NO ESTIMATES, IF IT DON'T WORK
YOU DON'T PAY

When he had finished, Porter drove back to the Grand Street building, seated himself in the barber's chair, read the sports section of the *Jersey Journal,* and waited for Betty Trombley to come home.

Joseph sat beside the chair, communicating through his eyes with Porter. Porter's coonhounds were the same. They expressed all their feeling through their eyes, not their mouths. They used their bell-like voices mostly to say only bold things, to set off alarms and throw off any feeling that was too strong—when they were impatient with joy or overfilled with sorrow. He missed his dogs, Porter Jr. and Porter III, and knew they were dying with longing for him at that very moment.

When he had read the entire sports section twice, Porter heard Betty Trombley skipping up the stairs. She was moving so fast that she was halfway across her living room before she stopped and looked around.

"What's going on here, Porter? Where is everything? Did Rupert Dixon do this?"

"It's not seemly for you to keep fighting with a landlord when his son just got killed, Betty."

"Tell him that! I just got a court order to make him turn the heat back on. What'd he do with my possessions?"

"Nothing, Betty. I moved us. I don't want the children living here anymore, and right now I got to focus on Skeet and Sherry, not keeping the hot water on."

"You might have talked to me first."

Porter scratched the back of his head and allowed himself to grin. "No way would I have got myself into discussing anything with you, Betty. You always could argue the Pope right out of his pointy hat. There's not a word in my head that would stand up to a word in yours. Only way to deal with a gal like you is to just do." Porter got out of the barber's chair, withdrew an adjustable wrench, and began unbolting the chair from the floor. He thought he'd take the rinsing sink too. He decided to come back for the wall-to-wall mirror, because he was not equipped to transport it at the moment.

Betty leaned against the mirror with her arms crossed. "OK, where we living?"

"Right near Curry's fish market on Pacific. It'll be fine. They got great crab."

In May, while the children pretended to be asleep in their bunk bed, Betty told Uncle Porter, "Mike's trying to maneuver for a better judge. The prosecutor and the judge are both real dickheads." She then said, "Isn't it something how so many men's names have come to mean 'pecker'? I mean, there's Dick and Peter and John Thomas. And Johnson. 'His Johnson's hanging right out his pants,' for example." The children heard Uncle Porter's low, monstery laugh. "There's a whole slew of men's names no one with sense would want to be called anymore. But not one woman's name has come to mean 'pussy.' Now, why is that? I mean, no one says, 'Put your Peter in my Veronica.' Or *Gloria*. Why not Gloria? That seems like a great word for it. How do you explain it? Maybe it's because Johnsons move by themselves, almost like independent people, while female private parts are too private, even invisible. Well, there really is no satisfactory explanation."

Betty listened to herself going on and on. What she needed was something to keep her busy. Something more than working as Mike's investigator on Ida's case, which was proving to be a frustrating and vain exercise. Something that would keep her busy forty hours a day so that she could keep her mind off the one thing preoccupying her, which was fucking her brains out with Porter Terhune. She was not under any circumstances going to allow that to happen. She would watch every step, because if she didn't, she would sleep with him or he would sleep with her. Ida would never understand, Rosine would be hurt, Porter's marriage would be messed up, and Betty would be starting something she did not know how to finish. However, every time she looked at Porter, her liver leapt up to her throat like a porpoise.

As if to make it clear that he was not reading her mind, Porter said, "Betty, I still don't know why you left that man you up and ran off with who brought you here."

Betty answered, "He didn't like my grits."

The children's uncle snorted.

Betty could feel that tentacle wrapping around her, hot and stinging like a man-of-war jellyfish's. The blood pushing too fast into her heart. She didn't remember: she *felt* what she had felt like twelve years before, when she'd lain next to Porter on the mattress they'd dragged onto the porch to snag a breeze. That feeling where she would have walked on boiling water to get to him, if necessary. That feeling which would have led her to promise anything—to let her life curl around his like a cat, to keep his house and tend his children, counting the minutes until he came home, while he hunted with Dewey through the swamps. That would have led her to relinquish everything until she disappeared into one sorry waiting woman whose lungs filled with stove smell, whose hands shaped themselves to mop handles, who thanked him for whatever money he gave her and schemed for more whenever she needed it. Who still wondered, had she been wrong? Because Rosine had worked and had traveled for her job—things other husbands just did not allow back then. But, Betty reminded herself, he's been here less than a month, and he's already moved me out of my own home, without talk.

"What's going on in your head?" Porter asked. Betty looked up. Her eyes were the exact color of old pennies and just about the only thing about her that never changed. Every time he saw her, she was two inches shorter or taller from the shoes she wore, or she had a different hairdo or had dyed her hair. Porter wasn't even sure what color her real hair was. Ida was the only person who'd ever stayed close to Betty for a long time, but it was clear enough why that was: they were just the same underneath. Both of them wanted the world to keep its distance. They just went about getting what they wanted differently. Ida hid from the world like a mole, and Betty scared it off by fighting everything in her path like some raccoon with rabies.

Betty was relieved when Skeet and Sherry came into the kitchen before she had to think up an answer to Porter's question.

Skeet mounted the barber's chair, which was newly bolted to the kitchen floor, and demanded breakfast. He felt a tension in the air between Betty Trombley and his uncle, and it made him uneasy. *I, Antonio, would like some pork sausage. And you, Joseph, are you awake?* Suddenly, Skeet was seized by a terror that Joseph had died in his sleep. Skeet jumped down from the barber's chair and returned to the bedroom, where the dog lay on his sister's top bunk. Skeet climbed the bunk bed's ladder and saw that his sister had hung Betty Trombley's earrings made from blue-jay feathers on a nail-head in the top rung. One of Betty's vests, covered with tiny mirrors, lay curled beside Sherry's pillow. Skeet touched the dog's wet nose, but Joseph did not awaken. Skeet picked up an earring and held it before Joseph's muzzle, until he could see the dog's breath tickling the feather. Joseph's chest rose and fell like a dependable machine.

Skeet returned to the kitchen and set to work on his map of the old Grand Street neighborhood. He had added details, including the Rambler in the junkyard. He especially liked the new picture of Joseph guarding the entrance to Betty Trombley's building. Skeet had decided to leave in the boat colony, although it was no longer there. He would continue to add to the map until he felt he had not lost anything in the move to the corner of Communipaw and Pacific: everything worth knowing about Grand Street was there on the paper before him. And Skeet preferred the new apartment anyway. He liked living on a street that had the word "paw" in it.

When Sherry wandered into the living room, she sat on the floor beside the couch. The couch was occupied by parts of a ceiling fan, carefully spread on the tangerine-colored cushions. With Uncle Porter there, things seemed to take on the sultriness of Louisiana. The humidity seemed denser, and people seemed to walk more slowly, and the objects of Porter's work inhabited all corners of the apartment. The fan relaxed on the couch; a newly oiled sewing machine crouched on top of the refrigerator, as if ready to pounce; a Mix-o-matic from the Sisters of Charity at All Saints Convent basked in a spot of sunlight on the revolving table, the machine's bolts and washers laid out in order of dismemberment.

Sherry picked up one of the fan's parts, a twisted piece of unknowable use, and put it in her jumper pocket.

"Don't take that, Ladybug," Uncle Porter told her. "A machine don't work if it's missing anything at all." Sherry reddened and returned the part to its resting place on the couch. "I'll handle the sausage. You go off to work," Porter told Betty. Betty vanished into the back hallway.

When she reappeared, Porter read aloud the badge from the public defender's office that Betty had pinned to her jumpsuit: BETTY TROMBLEY: CRIMINAL INVESTIGATOR.

"It makes me look more official," Betty explained.

Such desire welled up inside Porter when he looked at her badge that he felt as if he were being taken over by a different creature, like the Incredible Hulk on television. Porter watched Betty wistfully until the front door boomed shut behind her. Rosine had sent him a card the day before, whose purpose, he knew, was to remind him of his ties to her. He had missed Rosine when he opened the card: she let him be himself. She didn't expect him to work to death, and he didn't expect her to wait on him. She could be a little bossy, but then, she had good sense. Nevertheless, he didn't trust himself at all around Betty. If he could just hold out until Ida made bail, he'd be all right. So much depended on Ida. It would be impossible to carry on once she returned. Still, he wished Rosine hadn't sent him the card.

Skeet heard Joseph hit the floor in the bedroom, and his nails clicking on the linoleum as he entered the kitchen. The dog followed Uncle Porter to the refrigerator and watched as he sliced sausage patties from a roll of spiced pork. It was the same thing they had eaten for breakfast every morning since Porter arrived, and Skeet liked the predictability of his uncle's cooking. Skeet imagined himself not as the son of Ida Terhune but as the son of Porter Terhune and Betty Trombley. The idea both frightened and pleased him. He struggled to picture his mother, but he felt such longing and panic that he stopped himself.

When Skeet stood close enough to Porter, the panic receded. He brushed Porter's sleeve as his uncle dropped sausage patties into a black skillet and turned on a burner. The orange flame struggled upward momentarily, like a crab on its back, grasping at the air.

Betty checked the mailbox: she thought she had glimpsed a letter from Rosine through the slit the day before. Now, when she opened the box, she saw the Louisiana postmark, and a lump formed in her throat. But when she turned the letter over, she saw it was addressed to Ida and bore the name Honey Perkins. Betty pocketed the envelope for Mike to bring to Ida. He was meeting with her at Hudson County Penitentiary later that day in the hope of convincing her to let Porter pay her bail. Ida's savings would barely cover half her bond. Porter and Rosine had offered to take out a second mortgage on their house, but Ida had refused to accept their offer. Betty could just imagine Mike trying to argue Ida into changing her mind. Ida would never budge. Her principles (never borrow money, never be a burden to others) wouldn't let her.

Betty headed toward Grand Street. She missed the joy of battling with Rupert Dixon. She knew that Angel, carrying out her smart idea, had taken to leaving plastic gallon jugs of sewer water in front of Rupert's corner store every morning. Angel also had scouted around the building for witnesses to the accident, but like Betty, he had had little success. This fact seemed the most preposterous of a strange season. Here was Ida Terhune, the most innocent adult Betty knew, but there was not one person who could testify to her guiltlessness at the most important time of her life. The prosecutor apparently had quite a few witnesses: Rupert Dixon's chauffeur, who claimed to have seen the accident (although tenants said that Rupert and his Marquis had not been around that evening), police witnesses who were saying Ida was drunk, and medical experts. And the only person who could speak in Ida's defense was Ida herself. The whole trial would be such a gross distortion of life that Betty could barely stand to think about it. She would try talking with Wilma Tutwiler to see if they could scare up some more leads.

Rumors were flying around Grand Street, but whenever Betty followed them to their sources, they became attenuated and finally evaporated. She had heard, for example, that Henry Purdy knew who had stolen Ida Terhune's car and that the car thief had left a bottle of wine in the front seat. Betty had followed the story from a high school student on the fourth floor of the Grand Street building, to a man who delivered cars to the junkyard, to a man who worked as a patrol guard near Liberty State Park, who said he had seen a person matching Henry's description accompanied by an impossibly tall, thin, red-haired youth near the boat colony. But the boat colony was gone, and Henry with it. Betty could get no further. Her desire for Porter and her longing to get Ida safely home intermingled into one great yearning that propelled her toward Grand Street. Ahead of her, Betty saw white signs with RENT STRIKE in black letters filling the windows of her old building.

Porter's voice resurfaced in Betty's mind: "I got to focus on Skeet and Sherry, not keeping the hot water on." I'm such an idiot, Betty thought. It's all my fault Ida's in this mess. I never should have asked her to live in one of Rupert Dixon's buildings. If I'd found her someplace nice, she wouldn't have crossed paths with Chicken. I never should have invited her to Jersey City. Look what I've done to her, and she's my oldest and best friend! Only someone as unchanging as Ida would hold on to me.

Remorse for ruining Ida's life stopped Betty dead where she stood, in front of the F. H. Eggers memorial. She stared at Joseph's pawprint and recalled Skeet before the accident, snickering over dinner, telling Sherry he had made a dog monument.

Betty squatted down and placed her fingers in the circles of Joseph's pawprint. Once, Betty had watched Porter pulling splinters from the pads of one of his dogs' feet. The pads had been gray and rough as asphalt, and the dog had lain there, perfectly trusting, her coppery eyes focused on Porter. Betty had felt like that so few times in her life, she could barely conjure up the emotion. A longing to feel comfortably vulnerable overtook her. She removed her fingers from Joseph's pawprint.

Wilma Tutwiler had heard all the details of Ida Terhune's case from other tenants, and the whole thing made her feel sad. Wilma was in bad spirits anyway, because she had stayed inside all April, warming herself at a space heater, heavy with memories. Since Betty Trombley had left the building with that tall man she couldn't keep her eyes off, conditions had deteriorated even more. Rupert Dixon had not turned the boiler back on, and the cold was too much for Wilma. It sank into her joints and filled her chest with phlegm and dulled her thoughts. Yesterday, when Wilma Tutwiler had walked down the stairs, she had felt her age for the first time in eighty-four years.

That was when Wilma noticed Henry Purdy's ghost in the lot behind the building. Until then, no one had known he had died: he was too young for anyone to have wondered, even for a moment, if he might be dead. Some tenants thought they had spotted him on the hazardous-waste site near the canal since his escape from the Municipal Court holding pens. Others speculated that he had taken his skiff across the water and was camping out at Ellis Island, which was still closed to the public.

Wilma Tutwiler was standing on the planks, looking out into the back lot's cesspool, newly filled by the April rains, and cursing it, when she saw Henry standing thigh-deep in water.

"Henry, are you crazy?" she called out to him. "Anything could be in that water. It's probably typhoid and TB and yellow fever out there." He stared at her without answering. "Henry, what are you doing?" she asked, to see whether she had his attention.

"Hey," he said in a watery voice, raising one hand and continuing to look at her.

The planks bounced. She heard footsteps behind her, and Angel Rodriguez's whistle, but before she could turn to greet Angel, Henry changed to a transparent watery green and then faded to nothing.

"I believe I saw Henry Purdy's ghost," Wilma told Angel.

"That's not Henry's ghost. That's Henry," said Angel. "I heard he's hiding out here for a couple days. They took apart that Jersey City Riviera boat colony, and he's keeping his skiff here until he decides where to go."

However, when Angel glanced out back, he did not see Henry or his boat. Angel followed the floorboards to Henry's dam, looking through the large hole Chicken had knocked in the doorway's brick wall. The apartment appeared to be unused. A terrible smell emanated from a blue cooler someone had left inside—something apart from the usual sickening smell of the sewer water. Angel crawled inside to investigate.

"I thought I was feeling my age," Wilma said to herself.

Wilma had not seen Henry again all that day, but late in the evening she heard a knock on her door, and Henry was standing there. She invited him in, and he sat quietly on her couch, staring at her with his forlorn, heart-shaped face, which had always reminded her of her brother, who had been killed in a cave-in during the latter days of the Holland Tunnel's construction.

"I sure feel sorry for that Mrs. Terhune lady and her kids," Henry began. He then confided in Mrs. Tutwiler that he had left the scene of the pig roast shortly before the accident occurred. He had seen Chicken bending inside the back of the van, his face lit by the interior light. Henry had crept behind him and seen several five-gallon kerosene cans in the van. Henry guessed that Chicken had come to commit arson that very night, so that Rupert Dixon once and for all could rid himself of the Grand Street Tenants Association, which had come to be such a thorn in his side. Chicken had closed the van's back door with a secretive look and walked backward into Ida Terhune's car. Henry wished that he could bear witness at Ida Terhune's trial, but if he appeared in court, he was sure to be arrested. The city was out to scapegoat someone for vandalizing the Municipal Court building, which had suffered tens of thousands of dollars in flood damage. Henry could not allow himself to be returned to Hudson County Penitentiary, and, he explained, he never voluntarily entered a courthouse, as a matter of principle.

When he was finished, Henry sat uneasily on Mrs. Tutwiler's couch, jiggling his leg vigorously and turning down her offer to have some tea. Wilma Tutwiler had already heard several tenants discussing the contents of the van after the accident. People had spied a dozen hefty steaks piled in a cardboard box in the back compartment—why Chicken would need so many steaks remained a source of mystery and gossip. Mrs. Tutwiler thought Chicken had probably achieved his hugeness by devouring large quantities of red meat. A wildfire rumor spread that Chicken had been so high on cocaine he'd dropped several steaks right on the F. H. Eggers memorial. Some tenants claimed to have seen what looked like spilled sugar but could have been cocaine lying next to a steak left in the van. All of these things had disappeared by the time the police thought to inspect the vehicle.

Wilma fell asleep in the armchair, and when she awoke, Henry Purdy was gone and had locked the dead bolt behind him—which evoked her curiosity, since the dead bolt could be turned only from the inside. She walked downstairs to her chair near the pay phone, to await Betty Trombley's visit. Wilma had plenty to tell her.

Betty saw Wilma Tutwiler seated in a chair positioned near the pay phone. Wilma stretched her legs in front of her to catch the sun on the first warm day of spring, her head cocked to the side as a young woman yakked on the phone. Betty thought she'd exhange information with Wilma for about an hour before heading to the Quality Inn to give Mike Ida's mail. Maybe I'll just seduce Mike in his hotel room, Betty thought. He's the kind of guy who would never say no. I'm so horny I could scream.

◆ Madame Bovary

Mike Ribeiro felt driven in his effort to rescue Ida Terhune. She seemed just as driven in her effort to thwart him. He had explained to her that a client who enters the courtroom in handcuffs is severely disadvantaged in the eyes of the jury; she should make bail any way she could. Now she sat before him, reading her mail, as if the matter were closed.

"You don't want to walk into the courtroom looking like a criminal," Mike told her. His shirt was rumpled, and he had something Ida could not identify in his hair—a white string or a piece of down.

"I am a criminal," Ida answered. "And I have no right to take my relatives' money." Ida opened her letter.

Dear Ida,

I am writing to let you know that I've left Harlan. Larry took me back. I don't see how you stood that stingy rat all those years. How come you let him stay in your house? Did he tell you it was his? That's what he told me, but he's full of it. Larry said no bank would give Harlan credit and that you must have made a huge down payment. Larry says even if you didn't, the house would be half yours when Harlan divorced you. Let me know if there's anything I can do to help you get even.

Yours truly,
Honey Perkins

What did she mean, she'd left Harlan? Ida did not even know Honey Perkins had designs on Harlan. Ida felt so distant from Baton Rouge: the letter seemed to belong to another life. Without tucking the letter into its envelope, she handed it to Mike.

"Is what she says true?" Ida asked. "Could I borrow against my own house?"

Mike scanned the letter. He was surprised by such a voluntary relinquishment of privacy. He had always seen Ida Terhune as an intensely private woman. "I'll look into it. My guess is, you probably couldn't borrow against your house if your husband is contesting your right to it. But I really don't know much about Louisiana, except that it has some strange statutes based on the Napoleonic Code. I can check with an old law school buddy who practices in New Orleans."

"That would be fine. I guess I'll need a Louisiana lawyer eventually in any case, for my divorce," Ida answered. "That letter feels like it's addressed to someone else," she added, "to me before I had ever done anything wrong. Before the accident, I always felt as if I'd never done anything wrong." She looked flustered.

"A sort of Madame Bovary," Mike said unthinkingly, "only it's homicide instead of adultery, and purely accidental and with the aid of intoxicants." Ida looked at him with a puzzled expression. Was adultery still a crime people were arrested for? Apparently, she was not his first female client. Had he also offered to defend Madame Bovary for free? Ida had refused his offer, and she felt uncomfortable when he refused in turn to bill her for his services until the trial was over. However, after some consideration, she had accepted: he was just being gentlemanly. Asking someone else to pay her bail, however, when she had only herself to blame for the trouble she was in, was another matter entirely.

Mike felt powerless and irritable when he left the penitentiary, and it was in this state that he conceived the idea of preparing a real family dinner for the Terhune children. He arrived at their door, a new pressure cooker gleaming under one arm and two shopping bags held in the other. He announced that the children needed a big meal and a man to cook it. Porter told him it wasn't necessary: they were just going to have crab in the living room. Still, Mike insisted that he would stay all evening and take care of everyone. He reached for the children with the most nurturant gestures.

Skeet shrank bank. He did not like seeing Mr. Ribeiro, who appeared now only when he was laden with bad news about Skeet's mother: delays in her case, failures to have her bail posted, the lack of witnesses on her behalf, things Skeet had never heard of before but that had come to consume his thoughts.

Mike spilled the shopping bags on the kitchen table, unwrapping paper parcels of what the children identified as pigs' ears and pigs' feet, sausage and fatback. Joseph circled him, growling with his mouth closed, his tiger stripes rippling. Mike threw off his jacket and emptied a whole bag of beans into the pressure cooker, then turned the heat on high. The pot hissed dangerously, shooting a geyser of steam toward the ceiling. A bubbling red bean froth splattered the stovetop and the linoleum around the oven. He browned two cups of rice in a skillet with garlic and soy oil, set a pot of water on the stove, and threw in the rice without waiting for the water to boil.

The children were tired. Skeet wanted a bowl of cornflakes, but Mike commanded him to wait, not to spoil his appetite. Guests would be arriving soon. He had invited an old client and some Grand Street tenants, to liven things up. Mike withdrew several large onions from his grocery bags, five bottles of rum, and half a dozen bunches of collards. He urged the children to pull off the leaves and slosh them in the sink.

"Wash the collards good, each and every leaf, and then roll the leaves like this on your knee and hand them to me." Mike held up a bunch of collards with a flourish, Betty and Sherry watching as he demonstrated, wrapping four or five leaves together on his knee into a tight column. "Just the way Cuban women roll tobacco leaves on their thighs into the best cigars in the world." Skeet ducked away, but Betty and Sherry imitated Mike as he hovered over them.

Sherry stuck a roll of collards in her mouth, pretending to smoke. Mike took the rest of the rolled greens and sliced them thin as coleslaw and then dropped them in a towering pile onto the countertop. He cut up so many onions that tears rolled down Skeet's cheeks.

"Don't get snot on the collards," Mike told him. "Or if you do, don't tell anyone."

Sherry watched Mr. Ribeiro remove from one brown bag a pile of roots exactly like the one she had once taken from Shop-Rite. He sliced the manioc into pieces the size of french fries and threw them into a skillet of hot oil. Smoke billowed from the skillet, stinging Skeet's eyes, and oil spattered across the floor onto the table near Skeet's map of his old Grand Street neighborhood. He retrieved his map and crawled into the barber's chair.

"No time to sit still. I hear the guests arriving!" Mr. Ribeiro told Skeet. "Brush your hair and take off your shoes. We all need a party." He held an unopened rum bottle in his hand, extending it toward Skeet as if he expected him to do something with it, then whirling around when the doorbell rang.

Betty opened the door. Wilma Tutwiler and Angel Rodriguez stood outside, followed by an old client Mike introduced as Mr. Soap, a small, meticulously dressed man wearing a tailored suit and a porkpie hat. He removed the hat, revealing a bald head as shiny as a newly waxed floor.

"Come in—make yourselves at home!" Mike told them. Porter stepped aside as Mike walked backward into the kitchen. Betty escorted the guests into the living room. Mike threw open the cabinet doors, looking for glasses, lit flames under the remaining burners, and placed a skillet over each. He coated the skillets with oil, heaped coils of onions into them, and piled the greens on top. Porter stood to the side, his hands in his pockets, and frowned. He knew there was only one way to cook collards: toss them in a pot with a ham hock and boil the hell out of them.

"Just a little while more," Mike announced to everyone, brushing against Skeet in the barber's chair. "Who wants frozen daiquiris?" he shouted. He knocked a tray of ice cubes on the counter, clattered the ice into a blender, and turned it on. Skeet covered his ears. Mike pulled frozen strawberries from a bag and sloshed them in the sink. He lifted the lid to the blender and tossed in the fruit.

Red juice sprayed over the counter before he clapped down the lid. A mess had gathered around him: sliced onion, a dropped manioc root, and shreds of collards lay all over the floor. Rivers of bean froth hardened on the side of the stove. Mr. Ribeiro had thrown his jacket onto the counter, and one sleeve reached dangerously close to one of the stove burners. An ice cube clattered across the linoleum, and Joseph chased it under the table.

"A map of the crime scene!" Mr. Ribeiro leaned over the barber's chair, startling Skeet. "We can use it as an exhibit in your mother's trial!" Before Skeet realized what was happening, Mr. Ribeiro took the paper and laid it on the counter. When Mike turned around, Skeet rescued the map before the puddle of strawberry juice trickling onto the floor touched the paper. He held the map in his hands, wondering if it really could help to save his mother. He tucked it into the pocket of Mr. Ribeiro's jacket and folded the jacket over the arm of the barber's chair.

"Try this unspiked daiquiri," Mr. Ribeiro told Skeet, handing him a slushy drink, and giving another to Wilma Tutwiler, who frowned with disappointment where she sat on the sofa: she could hardly smell the liquor. Skeet licked the tower of ice in his glass, and rum burned his tongue; he had gotten Mrs. Tutwiler's drink by mistake but said nothing. Mr. Ribeiro scraped chair legs over the kitchen floor as he moved the kitchen table to the center of the room. A pot boomed onto a hot plate, and silver rang into place. Uncle Porter loitered in the living room, his hands still in his pockets.

Mike sat at the head of the table, smiling at the people in the living room. He raised a frozen daiquiri and shouted, "The feast is prepared! Eat, eat, eat!"

Mrs. Tutwiler got up first. She headed for the rum bottle and poured a generous amount into her biteless drink, stirring the remaining ice slush into the liquor. Skeet and Sherry sat down next to one another, and the adults settled around Mr. Ribeiro. Skeet offered his glass to Sherry. She took a swallow and raised her eyebrows at him. He grinned back.

"It's too bad I couldn't find the ingredients to make *caipirinhas,*" Mike announced.

It was evident to everyone, even the children, that he was waiting for someone to ask him what *caipirinhas* were, but for an awkward moment, nobody did. Wilma Tutwiler's arthritis was bothering her, and she was concentrating on her drink, waiting for that precise moment when the pain in her knees would suddenly become distant. Angel Rodriguez knew that *caipirinhas* were a Brazilian drink, a simple combination of lime juice and water and cane liquor. When he had been to Brazil as a young man, Angel had lived for two months in the town of Florianópolis with a woman who kept three monkeys and twelve toucans for pets. He had drunk *caipirinhas* with her every day, but it was a sweet part of his past, and he liked to savor it rather than talk about it.

"This makes my frozen bones feel good," Mrs. Tutwiler announced, tapping the rim of her glass.

"It was so cold this morning even the lawyers had their hands in their pockets," Angel followed.

Porter laughed.

Betty was about to ask what Mike was yearning for someone to ask, but something stopped her: an uncharitable impatience with the way he had centered himself in the room. She missed Ida, and there were moments when everyone else seemed intolerable to her. But then she saw that this whole big dinner, like Porter's arrival, was centered around Ida's absence. Their lives seemed to revolve around the loss of her like a whirlwind around its empty eye.

"So what *is* a kayperwhatsit?" Mr. Soap asked encouragingly, making Angel think of a politician's brown-nosing shoulderman.

"*Caipirinhas* are Brazil's national drink," Mike Ribeiro explained happily.

"To Mikey Ribeiro," Mr. Soap declared, raising his glass. "The best goddamn criminal lawyer this side of the Pulaski Skyway. If you want my opinion, I'd still be in Trenton State Shithouse if it wasn't for him."

"What's wrong with twelve lawyers up to their necks in cement?" Angel asked Porter.

"What?"

Mr. Soap rubbed his hands over his shiny head as if polishing it.

"Not enough cement," Angel answered.

Mike Ribeiro laughed heartily. "Here's a better one," he proclaimed. "New York and New Jersey were allowed to choose between having the most lawyers and having the most toxic waste dumps. So why did New York end up with so many lawyers?" Mike continued before anyone could answer: "New Jersey got first choice."

"Ho ho," said Mr. Soap. "Ho ho. If you want my opinion, a good criminal lawyer is the best insurance there is."

Wilma Tutwiler asked Mr. Soap about his health, hoping he would ask about hers.

Sherry took two more gulps of Skeet's drink and passed it back to him. A cool, pleasant burning flooded her that felt like the liquid embodiment of her mother. Sherry slid back in her chair and watched the adults lazily.

"It was some fight," Mr. Rodriguez was telling Uncle Porter. Mr. Rodriguez was filling his glass for the third time,

Sherry noted, and leaning so far back in his chair it looked as if it might tip over. "That dog shot out after Chicken and never cared he was ten times his size. Never even noticed. He just fixed on to that boot like there was nothing connected to it. Maybe that's the way to fight—you just hold on to a small piece of a big thing, and don't let go, and hope the big thing will come with it."

"Joseph is a magnificent canine," Mike said. He tilted his glass toward Joseph, who lay next to Skeet's chair. *"Saúde,"* Mike said. "That," he told Skeet, "is Portuguese for 'Cheers.' "

"Sow-oo-gee," Skeet repeated. Joseph thumped his tail and barked with his mouth closed.

"Joseph *never* liked Chicken," Sherry said. "The minute he saw Chicken's fat behind, he laid back his ears."

"Doggo sense," Porter said, warming up to the conversation and his drink at the same time. Looking at Skeet, Porter said, "All us Terhunes got it. You got doggo sense too. That's what your daddy called it. It's this: You know how you sometimes meet somebody. Your dog's standing next to you. When you lean forward to shake the man's hand, he smiles at you. But your dog, his hair goes up on his back and he leans forward and he goes 'Gruff!' and chomps that fella's leg. That dog knows that man's slick. The one time your daddy met them Pinkertons, that's what he told me. 'Doggo sense,' is all he said." Porter sliced a piece of pork on his plate and popped it into his mouth. He saw that he had eaten all his collards. Well, they were pretty good, he had to admit.

Skeet took several swallows of his daiquiri. The rum's warmth curled inside his chest, lodging under his heart.

Mrs. Tutwiler looked around the table and realized that everyone, including the children, was drunk.

Betty watched Mike beaming at them all and scooped some of her frozen daiquiri into her mouth: the liquor melted her irritation. She had confidence in him as Ida's lawyer. He had just the right combination of charm, flamboyance, and total lack of morals to be a good defense attorney. When she had talked over Ida's case with him, he had turned over every fact of the accident with enthusiasm, and he knew the law cold. He quoted whole paragraphs verbatim from statutes and cases when explaining his strategies. Betty had been impressed by his thoroughness and logic. Perhaps people who were chaotic and messy on the outside needed minds that were orderly and efficient. Betty tasted her drink again and smiled at him. Mike grinned back wolfishly.

Tomorrow, he knew, he would convince Ida Terhune to let her bail be paid. She would not be so hard to conquer. He already felt victorious.

"My friends couldn't believe it when I married Pete," Pamela said as she divided her dominoes with Ida. "He was so handsome and tall! And a good earner. And no hangups. He never didn't get it up—I say it's because his pecker wasn't connected to his head or his heart; it just sort of worked involuntarily."

Ida blushed. Then she wished that she were Pamela, someone easygoing and experienced, and not herself.

Pamela offered Ida a cup of pear jack, sliding it across the upside-down checkerboard.

"I don't feel I should," Ida confessed. "I told you I'm in jail for running over someone while I was drunk-driving."

"Well, you're not driving now," Pamela answered. "Boy, I can't imagine killing someone *by accident.* When I do something big, I plan it out ahead of time. My girlfriends used to say, 'Pamela, Pete doesn't talk. How can you marry someone who you can't discuss things with? Doesn't it bother you that you can't talk to him even about the news?' I've always kept up with the news. I was watching the Ayatollah on television before my arrest, and he had on this dress the selfsame pink I'm wearing now. It's true: Pete never read or watched the news or anything. He always said he didn't feel close to anybody. 'What do you mean?' I'd say. 'What about your best friend, Errol?' 'We're too different,' Pete would say. 'Don't you ever feel close to me?' I'd ask him. 'Sometimes,' he'd say, 'but you're different too.' I told him, 'But what if everyone was just like you, how would that be?' The idea of it makes my teeth hurt."

Ida and Harlan had never talked about anything, but she and Dewey had. They had discussed everything from how to fry eggs to how they wished to be buried. Dewey had liked to bother her by saying that he wanted to be composted and plowed into the okra plot. Ida was seized by a painful longing for Dewey. She found that the more Harlan relinquished his hold on her, the more Dewey surged into her thoughts, as if he, too, had been held down by Harlan all those years.

"I'm a widow and a divorcée," Ida offered, feeling as if she had realized this for the first time. It seemed odd to her. "That makes me sound like I must know a lot, but the truth is, I don't know the first thing about men. I don't really know anything about anything."

"Right on!" said Pamela. "Who does?"

Ida certainly hoped most people knew more than she did. She had always assumed they must. She had relied purely on her sense of duty and right and wrong to guide her through life, and it had never failed her. Until the accident.

"You really should attack your hair," Pamela advised. "My hair used to be the same mouse color, but now I always make sure I have blue highlights." She slipped her hand under her mattress and showed Ida a box of black hair coloring. "Mrs. Clairol's in prison—someone let her out!" Pamela cackled, returning the box to its hiding place.

"My lawyer wants me to let my relatives pay my bail," Ida ventured.

"Great. I can't understand why you're in here, if all you did was run over someone while you were driving drunk."

"I don't think it's right to make others pay for my mistakes," Ida said matter-of-factly, setting down the double-blank domino. When she looked up, Pamela was shaking her head. Even Ida heard how prim she sounded.

The guards shut off the overhead light, and the domino game had to be abandoned. Ida was sorry. She did not look forward to going to bed: she hadn't slept through the night in weeks.

When Ida had slipped under her covers, Pamela said, "Make bail whatever way you can. It could be months before they get around to trying you. Longer with Judge Kiley. My advice to you is: Pluto's about to head into a five-month retrograde, so charge through your eighth house in a fiercely happy frame of mind. Take the money and run, run, run. It's too bad you won't let me do your chart." Pamela was quiet for a moment, and Ida heard her tossing and turning under her covers. "Anyway, Ida," Pamela concluded, "the last thing you want is to be led into the courtroom in handcuffs. You might as well bring your own rope and hang yourself right there."

Hadn't her lawyer told her something just like that? Ida lay awake, wrestling with her values. How could she ask Porter and Rosine to remortgage their house? They hardly had anything. Surely, though, it would be all right for them to do it on Skeet and Sherry's behalf. But if Ida accepted, how would she know she hadn't just done it to save herself? Thoughts whirled inside her like clothes in a dryer. She would do what Pamela thought best. Ida was thankful to have someone to advise her when she had no idea herself what was right.

Mike Ribeiro decided to pay Ida's bail, although this violation of the lawyer's Code of Professional Responsibility, if made known, might well result in suspension of his license to practice. "Just keep this between us, Betty," he said as he handed her a ten-thousand-dollar check enclosed in a letter requesting her "investigative services." His wife had complained that he gave away too much money to friends and clients—"as if you have a will to impoverish yourself," she had asserted.

"Lawyers are strictly prohibited from paying bail, because of conflict-of-interest problems," Mike told Betty cheerfully. "It's presumed that a lawyer who does won't argue ardently enough against his client being jailed during trial if the prosecutor later requests bail to be revoked." He told Betty to wait a few days before paying Ida's bond and explained that he would actually continue to pay Betty $125 a week off the books to work for him. "There's no need to let Ida know about this," he concluded.

Betty did not find Mike Ribeiro's conduct unethical, although she did find his flagrant disregard for the rules of his profession remarkable. Perhaps he was the kind of person who liked to believe himself above the law, or he liked to court punishment. Not that it was her business; Betty was glad Ida would be released.

In the end, Mike's bail money proved unnecessary. On the Monday after his check cleared, when Ida entered the counsel room, prepared to ask her lawyer to accept help from her relatives, Mike grabbed her hand and said, "Ida, I have amazing, wonderful news. A federal investigation has resulted in Judge Kiley's indictment! For racketeering!" Mike laughed. "At first, Judge Kiley told *Jersey Journal* reporters that he'd refuse to leave the bench even if he was convicted. He'd preside until his last appeal was exhausted! But it seems his lawyers have persuaded him to take a leave of absence at the Jersey shore until his case is resolved."

Ida did not see what was so funny.

"Your case has been reassigned to Judge MacFarland. You couldn't have had better luck. This is going to be a real trial." Mike sounded almost as if he expected Ida to cheer.

"What difference will it make?" Ida asked. She was guilty, wasn't she?

"What difference will it make? It's a gift from heaven!" Mike beamed at Ida as if he himself had engineered Judge Kiley's absence. "To begin with, your trial date will be moved up, and Judge MacFarland will surely reduce your bail," Mike continued. "I'm going to be back here in no time with an order of release." And he proved right. A few days later, Judge MacFarland reduced Ida's bail to $15,000, or $1,500 bond. Ida paid her bail from her savings, and Betty returned Mike Ribeiro's money and never mentioned their arrangement to Ida.

When Ida stepped onto the front steps of Hudson County Penitentiary, Mike Ribeiro strutted proudly beside her, hooking his arm around hers. Ida had been in jail for two months, and a paralyzing shyness grabbed hold of her. She felt as if everyone on the street would know what she had done and that even if they didn't know, it didn't matter: she knew. She hardly approved of herself.

Pamela leaned out a barred window over them and shouted, "Don't rob any banks, Ida!" Ida waved, and part of her wanted to rush back inside instead of braving the world. She felt guilty for leaving when Pamela was forced to stay behind.

Ida was not even sure who she was anymore. Sometimes she felt like two people: her old self, whom she thought of as the real Mrs. Terhune, and her new, after-the-accident self, whom she thought of as an impersonator. Someone not at all like her. Someone who lay awake at night, thinking: but it wasn't my fault, and even if it was, it's the only really bad thing I've ever done, and many people drive drunk their whole lives and are never caught—cowardly protestations she would not have countenanced in anyone else, which left her appalled at her hypocrisy. Sometimes, in her worst moments, she blamed Betty for her arrest: if it hadn't been for her, Ida would be the same person. She would never have come to Jersey City.

She struggled to retrieve the feeling of being Mrs. Terhune. But then the weight of her guilt became so overwhelming that she felt she had to put it down, like a shopping bag she could not carry one step farther. It wasn't that she was trying to rationalize what she had done, it wasn't that she was a hypocrite or an impersonator. She was just tired; she could not go on carrying the shopping bag. Ida missed Skeet and Sherry with such desperation that it embarrassed her.

"Are we going to stand on the jailhouse steps forever?" Mike prodded. "Although we certainly have plenty of time to spare. I processed your release papers hours faster than we expected. Porter didn't want the children to get restless waiting at home for you, so he and Betty planned to take Skeet and Sherry to the docks behind the Colgate factory after school. But it looks like they won't have to wait at all," Mike added in a self-congratulatory tone. He led Ida toward his car.

"Betty thought you might want to stop on the way to shower and change your clothes before seeing the children. She sent you these. Not that you don't look fine already. You look very pretty." Mike handed Ida a grocery bag. Ida opened it and saw her cranberry-colored pantsuit, its stifling polyester: she felt as if it would crawl onto her and enshroud her. She closed the bag.

"I hope you don't mind just stopping at my room at the Quality Inn to pretty up."

Ida felt uncomfortable at the idea of entering a man's hotel room. But somehow, she felt she had no right to be affronted—she, a murderess! Surely a criminal couldn't object to so small an impropriety.

Mike saw that Ida was blushing at his flattery. Did she think he had made a pass? He himself felt something bordering on moral obligation when a woman made a sexual overture; he did not believe it was right to turn a woman down, and there had been extremely few instances in his life when he had. He certainly would not injure someone with feelings as delicate as Ida Terhune's by turning her down, were she to make a pass at him. On the other hand, Ida Terhune was not the kind of woman you could imagine making a pass at, as it was very easy to imagine her being offended by a pass.

Mike's car was illegally parked in a space reserved for prison staff. He opened the door for Ida and pushed an unpaid parking ticket off the front seat, onto the floor. When they were both inside the car, he said, "With your trial date set for a week from now, we've got plenty of time to get ready."

"But I'm guilty," Ida told him. "I'll end up back here anyway."

Mike started the car and stepped on the gas pedal. "You're not guilty." He said this unequivocally, knowing this was what she required, but thought to himself: justice is in the eye of the beholder. In every trial, there was the prosecutor, out to prove the accused was a criminal deserving of punishment; the victim's family, who wanted revenge or reparation; the defendant's family, for whom justice was meaningless if it was not tempered with mercy. And there was the judge, who wanted the truth to warp itself to the curlicues of the law. Then there was each juror's view: each juror brought with him his own agenda and prejudice, his own shortsightedness and wisdom. Every offense could be looked at a hundred different ways, and it was Mike's job to see all hundred, to stand inside the prosecutor and judge and every juror. And from each Mike would have to see Ida Terhune.

He felt intoxicated by the challenge. He saw Ida as a struggling mother of two children who had the misfortune of being in the wrong place at the wrong time. He saw her from the eyes of Chicken's wife, as an irresponsible drunk who had killed her young husband and whose children had set their dog on him only months before. Mike saw Ida through the prosecutor's eyes—as his easy prey, a powerless, ignorant woman who could be railroaded into a guilty plea or tried to conviction, releasing Harkin from whatever favor he owed to Rupert Dixon and adding to Harkin's stellar conviction record. (He bragged he could convict any innocent man you handed him.) Mike saw Ida through the eyes of the indignant journalist who reported her case—as yet another drunk driver who imperiled the public at large and mandated the toughening of drunk-driving laws.

Who was Ida Terhune? This was really the question presented by her trial, the question at the heart of all the legal issues the jurors were asked to determine. It was Mike's task to mold her for the jury. He could hardly wait.

Ida entered Mike's hotel room with temerity, wading self-consciously through his masculine clutter. She tripped over his paint-by-numbers picture of the Virgin Mary, sent to him by one of his clients in prison, a hit man who had been arrested on federal charges immediately after Mike secured his acquittal for murder.

Ida thought that her attorney was staring at her strangely. Did he expect her to sleep with him? She entered the bathroom and closed the door behind her.

On the bathroom counter were a copy of the *New Jersey*

Code of Criminal Justice, thoroughly soaked, a half-empty bottle of Napoleon brandy, soap-on-a-rope, a Scrabble board with a half-finished game on it, a pair of Betty Trombley's peacock-eye earrings, and one of Betty's crazy scarves, peacock-colored. (She must have been here, working with Mike on Ida's case.) Ida lowered the toilet lid and sat down. What would she say to her children? Ida felt nervous about meeting Skeet and Sherry. Would they forgive her for being gone? She was so overwhelmed with longing for them that she could barely unbutton her clothes. Ida had never felt so wobbly inside. Surely, Skeet and Sherry would notice, and this would frighten them. Once, Ida had had an infection of the inner ear, which deprived her of her balance, so that when she stood, she tilted crazily to the right, lurching into doorframes and walls. She remembered looking up after a fall and seeing the astonished and horrified faces of her children. How dare you lose your balance, they seemed to be saying. We trusted you!

As Ida stood, she almost knocked the bottle of Napoleon brandy to the floor. She picked it up. Then she uncapped the bottle and took a whiff: it reminded her of her father, who had loved cognac.

And it reminded her of Pamela. Ida stepped into the shower. She missed Pamela. She was the only real friend Ida had made since Honey Perkins. Perhaps it was because Pamela had been trapped with her and had no choice but to befriend her. And jail had broken Ida open somehow. Her arrest had so robbed her of her bearings that she could not protect herself from confiding in Pamela. And she had turned out to be much nicer than Honey Perkins, who had not proved to be much of a friend at all. Ida had been so standoffish with Pamela! She should have asked what crime Pamela had committed. Surely, she would have liked to unburden herself too. What if she hadn't because she feared Ida would shun her? Ida hoped not. Why hadn't she let Pamela do her horoscope chart? It might have been fun, and Ida would have had something to remember Pamela by. And would it have killed her to drink just a little of Pamela's pear jack, as a way of making them closer? Hadn't she, Ida Terhune, already committed the worst transgression that could possibly result from consuming liquor? What could she possibly have had to lose?

Ida leaned out of the shower and unwrapped the paper from one of the Quality Inn's bathroom glasses. She watched her hand—a ridiculous hand, with dimples over the knuckles—reach forward as if it belonged to someone else. She poured herself a little Napoleon brandy. She sniffed the brandy again, and the image of Roy Daigle arose in her mind's eye like a genie. He had been a man of strong, overbearing odors: he smelled of cigars and cognac, the fresh seafood he brought home for the women to cook, the Curiously Strong peppermints he liked to suck at all times of day, and the leather chairs he sat in, which had absorbed his sweat and the mugginess of Baton Rouge summers.

Ida took a sip of Napoleon brandy before washing herself with the soap-on-a-rope. Oddly, the cognac tasted like a smell: the flavor settled in her nose. And she liked the taste—it was better than champagne. She shampooed her hair. It was the first private shower she had had since her arrest. Occasionally, she stopped to sip the brandy. The more she sipped, the less wobbly she felt inside.

When Ida emerged from the shower, she took a good look at herself in the mirror. They had taken down the mirrors in the women's bathroom at Hudson County Penitentiary. She wondered if this was true of all prisons. It had been strange never seeing herself; it had made her feel disembodied. Did prisons do this on purpose, to make people lose their sense of who they were? Pamela had kept a compact mirror hidden under her mattress. Ida poured some more brandy and took a large swallow, which scorched the inside of her nose and the back of her throat. If a person went years without ever seeing her reflection, would she forget herself?

The face that gazed back at Ida hardly resembled her. There were no hairdressers in prison, and she had been reduced to combing her hair to the side. Without her usual bouffant, she looked girlish and frivolous. She'd have to get Betty to do her hair. Ida had lost too much weight, but she was as bosomy as ever. She was proud of her bosom. She lifted her glass in a toasting gesture. There was the café au lait mark over her left nipple, which no one alive knew about except Harlan Pinkerton. At least Harlan had never failed to get an erection. Perhaps, Ida speculated, this was for just the reasons Pamela had spoken of with regard to her husband, Pete—because Harlan's thingdoodle (which was what he liked to call it) wasn't connected to his head or his heart; it was just sort of freestanding. Often, he had referred to it as "Ole Jim," as if it were separate from him and he were no more responsible for its conduct than a stranger's.

Ida watched a blush spread over and hide the café au lait mark: she was the only person in the world whose own thoughts could make her blush! She took another large swallow of cognac. She didn't miss Harlan at all; she missed Dewey. On her wedding night, her heart had beat so violently she could hardly sit down, and so Dewey had gone at her standing up. "Doggie style," Dewey had whispered in her ear, bending her down, and she remembered feeling that this was not the way a girl should do it the first time. The first time, certain ceremonies should be followed: they should have been lying in a newly made bed, with her on her back, not on all fours like some female coonhound. But when he had finished, she would not let him go until they had done it twice more, once with her draped over her father's suitcase.

Ida had not slept with anyone for a long time, and if she went to prison, she might never do it again. She took another swallow of brandy. What would happen if she just stepped out into the hotel room, without her clothes on, and asked her lawyer to seduce her? She herself had no idea how to go about seducing a man. What was it that Mike Ribeiro had said about his client Madame Bovary? Her name made Ida think of a fortune-teller or a woman who ran a saloon.

Mike tried to wait patiently in his hotel quarters. He heard Ida moving around in the bathroom, the shower running for almost twenty minutes, the tinkling of glass on glass, the rattling of the Scrabble pieces he had left in the box after abandoning his game of Scrabble solitaire the night before. He expected Ida to emerge any minute, but she didn't. He thought of knocking on the door but restrained himself.

Then he noticed that the paper bag containing Ida's clothes was still outside the bathroom. Of course, she was too shy to emerge and get them.

He picked up the bag and tapped on the door.

He had expected Mrs. Terhune to reply from behind the closed door, but instead she opened the door, wrapped in a towel. She held a glass of his Napoleon brandy. He had been under the impression that Ida Terhune did not drink: perhaps she had just tasted the brandy out of curiosity. She was built rather delicately and did not look severe at all, with her hair flattened by the shower. She stepped toward him and then stopped, looking at him as if she expected him to do something. He was surprised by her forwardness and directness: you would have thought Ida Terhune was the kind of woman who would need to take things slowly. However, she was not. After he had kissed her once, Ida simply removed her towel and led him to the bed.

Neither of Ida's husbands had ever given much thought to foreplay, and in her experience, kissing was usually followed directly by intercourse. Ida helped Mike Ribeiro remove his clothes, pulled him against her, and rocked into him. He held himself aloft, admirably, without smushing her the way Dewey had, and obviously enjoying himself in a way Harlan had not. He thrust deeply in her, calling out so loudly it caused her to remember that she had not known men cried out in bed: she thought only women did and then much more quietly. If she had not drunk so much Napoleon brandy, she might have been embarrassed by all the noise he was making. He sounded as if he were being murdered. The thrusting felt wonderful, nevertheless, reaching so deeply into her it was as though he had located her center. She felt Ida Terhune leave her body; she felt herself wash over herself in layers until she vanished.

Mike Ribeiro had never gone to bed with a woman who fainted when she came, although he had heard of such women. He was relieved to come almost a few moments after Ida fainted, as it would have felt a little strange to continue. He lay beside her and waited for her to regain consciousness. He was sweating like a pig. Perhaps he should take a shower before she awoke. He speculated that women who were naturally reserved were often the most passionate and abandoned in bed. Although women who were not reserved at all, such as Betty Trombley, were also full of surprises. As he stood up and bent over Ida, he thought she looked lovely where she lay, and he resisted the temptation not to cover her. As he showered, soaping himself happily with his soap-on-a-rope, he plotted out his trial strategy for Ida Terhune's case.

What could have come over me? Ida thought when she awoke hours later, with her head surprisingly, disappointingly, clear. It was two o'clock, and her children would be out of school in a half hour. Mike Ribeiro was not in the room. She wrapped herself in the bedspread, nonetheless, and headed for the bathroom. The floor was flooded, and the soap-on-a-rope lay in a mushy heap on the tiles. Ida tidied the bathroom, recapping the Napoleon brandy, returning the Scrabble squares to their box, and spreading out the *New Jersey Code of Criminal Justice* to dry on a towel. She hung the soap-on-a-rope anew from the shower head, and again she showered. She had not even used a contraceptive. And she was not unencumbered! What could have gotten into me? she thought, feeling again like her old self and feeling sorry to feel like her old self.

She had to prepare for meeting Skeet and Sherry. She dressed carefully, pulling her knee-highs up so that there was no sag at the ankle, and buttoning all the buttons on her pantsuit jacket. Only her hair was wrong: it looked like a crazy person's, the slept-on sections sticking straight out. She picked up Betty's peacock-colored scarf and wound it in a band above her forehead. She looked presentable.

Mike returned from his favorite Cuban-Chinese restaurant, La Delicia China, opposite the PATH station, bearing tins of *ropa vieja* and paper cups of espresso. When he entered his quarters, he was sorry to find Ida fully dressed. She probably feels shy, he told himself as he offered her a cup. I may be the first man she's slept with other than her husbands.

Ida had no appetite, but she drank the black coffee until she felt jittery. Mike chatted about the food and her case as if he had not been lying on top of her, moaning like a bloodhound, only three hours before. He told her about the terms of her bail, the homicide law, and all the parts of a criminal trial: jury selection, the lawyers' openings, the presentation of the evidence, first by the prosecutor and then by the defense, the lawyers' summations and the judge's instructions on the law, the jury deliberations and verdict.

Finally, Ida stopped him, saying, "Thank you for a wonderful morning. However, I don't think it would be prudent for me to sleep with my lawyer again before the trial is over. I need to focus on the matter at hand for my children's sake." She felt wounded when Mike agreed with her. He patted her hand, as if it were any other hand, and told her, "Of course, Ida. Whatever you say." She wished that he would argue a little. Perhaps it was just a matter of masculine pride.

When they arrived at the docks, Ida saw Skeet and Sherry first. Skeet stood on the edge of the dock between Porter and Mr. Rodriguez, gesticulating excitedly at the water and lowering a piece of bacon on a string. Sherry was encouraging Skeet's dog to pick up a large crab that stood poised on the dock. The crab raised its claws defiantly, scuttling toward Sherry. Porter lifted her up as she shrieked in mock fear, and Joseph pounced on the crab, raising it deftly. The crab's arms extended outward from the dog's mouth, so that from where Ida stood, Joseph looked as if he had tusks. Skeet shouted, pulling up another crab, and Sherry and Betty gathered behind him to watch. Both of Ida's children looked perfectly happy. Why, they didn't miss me at all, she thought. She felt excluded.

She collected herself and walked onward. She had to restrain her emotions to keep from overwhelming Skeet and Sherry. She wondered if she had slept with her lawyer purely out of a need to soften the intensity of the feelings she had known would overcome her when she first touched her children again.

The children spotted their mother at the same time. They did not rush to greet her: Sherry leaned into Porter, and Skeet stooped down to pat Joseph. But Skeet and Sherry's reticence distinguished them as her children and set Ida at ease. She thought: Hanging back is one thing I understand. Ida peered in the yellow bucket and saw that it was alive with crabs, gurgling and stepping on one another.

Sherry watched her mother wrinkle her nose. "Crabs is nasty," Sherry said. "Too nasty to do anything but eat."

"You're going to have to toss these back in," Ida said. "Crabs have too many germs for you to eat them from dirty water like this. They carry hepatitis." She immediately regretted dampening their fun.

Betty came to her rescue. "It's true. The Hudson's too full of junk out this way, and crabs always eat the sickest stuff they can find." She poked at a crab with her purple high-top tennis shoe and told it, "You're pure toxic waste and rat turds inside, aren't you, you little fucker?"

"Betty, you never change," Ida said.

The children hauled the bucket to the edge of the pier, as if thirsting for some reestablishment of rules around which to orient their rebellions. Skeet tilted the bucket and held it over the edge of the dock. The crabs moved inside like an angry swarm of wingless insects. Skeet lifted the bucket from behind, and the children watched, joyously, as the crabs whirled through the air and vanished into the dark water.

When Skeet straightened, lifting the empty bucket, he turned and saw Mr. Ribeiro and remembered, as quickly as he had forgotten, that his mother might be taken from him again. His joy altered, treacherously, into dread.

As Ida watched the last crab fade into the muddy darkness, she could not help thinking of what she had done in the hotel room: the image of her lawyer, when he had first removed his clothes, came to her as if it were swimming up from the murky river bottom. She could still feel the Napoleon brandy tingling in her nostrils.

◆ The Jury

Porter had remounted the wall-to-wall mirror expertly over the newly installed rinsing sink in Betty's kitchen. After Betty convinced her that the barber's chair was securely bolted to the floor, Ida agreed to ascend the chair to have her hair done for court. Even when Ida was seated, Porter continued to test the bolts with an adjustable wrench, to reassure her.

From where she sat above him, Ida could see Porter's neck nape, which reminded her so much of Dewey that she almost cried out. She noticed then that Betty was also watching Porter, and Ida sensed the electricity between them. I hope for Rosine's sake nothing's happened, she thought.

"You should look conservative for court tomorrow," Betty told her. "I'm going to give you one of those bouffants that look like football helmets."

"Oh." Ida sounded disappointed. "I thought maybe I'd try something slightly different. Just for a change," she added apologetically. "Maybe you could highlight my hair a little. It looks so mouse-colored."

"We could put a little henna in it."

"Sherry gave me these as a present," Ida said, removing a pair of earrings from her pantsuit's jacket pocket. Betty recognized the blue-jay feather earrings she had been missing for some time. "I was wondering if you could run something bluish through my hair to match them."

"You must be kidding, Ida," Betty said.

"Don't people with black hair sometimes tint their hair blue?"

"But your hair isn't black. It's brown."

"It's mouse-colored." Ida sighed.

"Naw, it's more like muskrat," Porter told her.

"It's Ida Terhune–colored," Betty said. "Christ, Ida, I missed you so much. Things just didn't hold together right with you gone. Don't ever run off and leave us again."

"I didn't run off—I got arrested," Ida corrected.

"Just don't get convicted," Betty answered.

Ida experienced a sinking feeling. The idea of sitting in a courtroom, all eyes on her, made her feel like hiding in a cave.

Betty sensed Ida's apprehension. "I could try rinsing your hair with Grecian Formula and see what happens. It's sort of blue, and it won't darken your hair too much if I water it down."

"Never mind, Betty," Ida said. "It was a silly idea. You're right: I should look respectable for court."

"Look, Ida, tomorrow's no big deal. They're just picking a jury." She squirted a very small amount of Grecian Formula into a bottle of water and attached a rinsing nozzle. "Just imagine what a Jersey City jury is going to be like," Betty told Ida. "They'll be even nuttier than we are."

Judge Lesley MacFarland knew that she was a formidable-looking woman, broad-shouldered in a way that made her robes look truly majestic. A red dress glowed like an ember above the collar of her black gown. She surveyed the courtroom, noting to herself that recently, whenever she tuned in to a television crime drama, it seemed a black actor was playing the judge. Now, why was that? It certainly was no reflection of reality, since black judges were still an oddity. She and Shirley Tolentino were the only black judges in the history of Hudson County. Perhaps the networks felt awkward about handling black characters. Perhaps white people felt guilty about their obsession with empowerment and liked to think of a black person judging them, as long as she was purely fictional so that they had absolute control over her.

While Judge MacFarland waited for the lawyers to arrive, she read over the questions the prosecutor and the defense attorney had submitted for her to direct to the prospective jurors during her voir dire. As usual, the attorneys were several minutes late. Once, she had thrown a pair of tardy lawyers into the bullpen. She hoped Mr. Harkin and Mr. Ribeiro wouldn't tempt her.

The defendant, a bewildered-looking woman with a tall hairdo that had a purplish cast to it and odd earrings that seemed incongruous with her generally stuffy demeanor, entered the courtroom behind her lawyer and seated herself at the defense table. She turned to her attorney and asked, "When is the judge arriving?"

"She's here," Judge MacFarland said, leaning forward on the bench.

Ida was mortified. She had never seen a black judge before. She turned around and whispered to Betty, "You could have told me the judge was black!"

"I didn't think to," Betty answered.

"How could you not think to?" Ida said, exasperated. She added, "You don't always have to appear to be right on. A black person would have mentioned it, I'm sure."

"Right on?" Betty answered.

Judge MacFarland ignored this exchange and waited for the prosecutor Harkin to seat himself.

When he turned around to locate his adversary, Mike saw

a middle-aged woman with loofah hair sitting beside a girl he recognized as Chicken's wife. Mike propped up his briefcase to shield Ida from seeing them. Rupert Dixon then entered the courtroom and, leaning before the older woman, said something under his breath that made the girl angry. He raised his voice to a loud whisper, pointing to the courtroom doors, and the two women rose. He waited for them to exit and followed them out. Perhaps Rupert Dixon feared that facts would emerge at trial about Chicken and himself that he did not want his family to hear.

After Rupert Dixon disappeared, the prosecutor opened his briefcase and removed a can of V-8 juice and a glass. He poured himself some juice and stirred it with the end of a ballpoint pen, watching the red whirlpool.

"Mr. Ribeiro," Judge MacFarland said. "I'm reserving decision on your motion to dismiss the reckless manslaughter count. This is an issue of first impression in New Jersey."

"Your Honor," Mike answered, "the New Jersey legislature couldn't be stupid enough to create two identical crimes with completely different sentences."

Judge MacFarland considered this statement and said, "Of course they could, Mr. Ribeiro. Of course they could. Anything is possible in the Garden State. However, if you wish to elaborate in a scholarly written memorandum, I would be glad to see one."

"If I could just argue orally on my motion for a moment," Mike said.

"No," the judge answered. "I've heard that you're quick on your feet, Mr. Ribeiro. However, I am not interested in off-the-cuff arguments at this time. Shall we proceed with the voir dire?"

As the prospective jurors reported their occupations, Judge MacFarland watched Mrs. Haskel, seated at the far extreme of the empanelment area, a stuffy, middle-aged woman with a brooch and a frosted hairdo. The judge would bet her bottom dollar that when the smoke cleared, this woman would be on the jury. The prosecutor would throw off people in the helping professions: teachers, social workers, anyone who had a soft spot or liberal leanings.

The defense attorney would throw off bankers and professionals and look for people he assumed had tasted injustice and were likely to view the police with suspicion: unemployed men, people from neighborhoods where the police were especially corrupt. Black and Hispanic people. Of course, the defense attorney, like the prosecutor, would engage in all kinds of racial stereotyping. In a case like this, with a white defendant, Mr. Ribeiro might just try to get an all-white jury. In the end, what always remained were jury pool members so unpeppery that neither side would challenge them. The woman with the brooch was the most certain candidate. She reminded Judge MacFarland of the defendant.

Mrs. Haskel glanced imperiously at the name tag of the prospective juror with bushy brown hair who sat next to her, and said in a loud whisper, "Mr. Corso, stop fidgeting! You keep bumping my seat." Mr. Corso glared at her and continued to fidget, apparently with purpose. Judge MacFarland saw the defense attorney look sharply at both of them.

"Corso and Haskel," Mike wrote on his pad, underlining the names twice. Long ago, Mike had decided that the best strategy in choosing a jury, especially in a close case like Ida Terhune's, was to find two jurors who were sure to dislike each other. Who would be sure to argue with each other, no matter how obvious a point might be. Two such jurors could be counted on to resist coming to an agreement about anything, including a guilty verdict. He might need to hang the jury.

Mike took copious notes while Judge MacFarland quizzed the prospective jurors as to whether any of them were members of organizations that fought for stricter drunk-driving laws or had themselves been victims of drunk or negligent drivers. Mike had not requested that the judge ask whether any jurors had friends or family who had been injured or killed by drunk drivers, because he knew from experience that there was probably not a person in the room who could answer such a question in the negative and he did not see any point in calling this fact to the jurors' attention.

When the judge asked if any of the potential jurors had family members involved in law enforcement, Mike took fewer notes. In his early career, Mike had sought to exclude people related to policemen from his juries. Over the years, however, he felt that such jurors were most likely to know intimately of instances in which police had lied or falsified evidence or done much worse. Now he tended to leave such people on the jury: he just liked to know who they were.

The prosecutor sipped his V-8 juice and noted each juror's profession, race, or ethnicity, and whether or not he or she was a home owner: the victim's father was a notorious landlord in the downtown area's black and Hispanic neighborhoods. Harkin hoped to pack the jury with white home owners and to challenge as many black and Hispanic jurors as possible without being accused of racial prejudice. He was somewhat more cautious than usual, as this was his first experience arguing before a black judge. Nevertheless, Harkin intended to go for jurors who he felt were easily impressed by authority, who would believe the police. Like Germans, for example. And maybe West Indians. Harkin wanted the big blond German man, Mr. Thiele, and thought he might get around the black problem by selecting Mr. Edgar, who had some sort of island accent, and Mr. Ortiz, who wore a hat with a Cuban flag on it. Harkin considered Puerto Ricans trouble, but Cubans could be counted on to be tough on law enforcement.

Mike Ribeiro thought he should get as many young men on the jury as possible: young men were likely to have driven drunk sometime in their recent pasts. Mike also thought men in general would be more sympathetic to Ida Terhune than women. Women tended to drink less than men and to judge other women more harshly. He also feared that some of the black jurors might be put off by Ida Terhune's southern accent if she testified, which he intended to discourage her from doing in any case, since she was so convinced of her own guilt. He noted the black prospective jurors by placing checks beside their names.

Judge MacFarland noticed him examining the black

jurors' name tags. She smiled grimly to herself and said, "All right, you two lawyers." She waited for the defense attorney's attention. "I will permit you each ten minutes to ask the jurors further questions. Ten minutes." Although the judge was not required to allow the lawyers to supplement her voir dire, she had been so efficient that she would have plenty of time to spare before lunch. In addition, she thought it would afford her an opportunity to see what kind of characters she would be dealing with during Ida Terhune's trial.

Harkin refilled his glass with the V-8 juice remaining in the can. He took a large gulp and swirled it around in his mouth, puffing out his hollow cheeks. Approaching the prospective jurors, he dedicated himself to ascertaining whether any of them had drunk-driving records. "Now, there probably isn't a person in this room who hasn't tied one too many on before getting into a car," Harkin began, smiling amiably at the jury pool. But as he had anticipated, the prospective jurors were reluctant to agree with him when questioned individually—after all, he was a prosecutor. Two prospective jurors were compelled to admit they had been stopped for drunk driving. Three others had family members who had been convicted of drunk-driving offenses. And one had been arrested for driving drunk to an AA meeting.

After Harkin had crossed these people's names off the sheet he was holding, Mr. Corso said tendentiously, "You should be going after those drug dealers, not honest drinkers."

Harkin suspected that Mr. Corso was being purposely obnoxious in order to get himself excused from jury service.

"I do, Mr. Corso, I do go after those drug dealers," Harkin answered, not looking at Mr. Corso but assuring the entire jury pool of the nobility of his profession. "And I've never gone after an honest drinker. I'm sure we're all honest drinkers here. What's an honest drinker? Well, I can tell you what an honest drinker is not. An honest drinker is not someone who would cruise right into a person in a car and just keep going—"

"Objection. Mr. Harkin is misleading us," Mike Ribeiro

protested. "This case has nothing to do with hit-and-run driving."

"No, he's not misleading anybody," Judge MacFarland said. "Mr. Harkin, I expect you to act like an honest drinker yourself and not let things get too out of hand, ever, in my courtroom. Is that clear?"

Mr. Harkin winked at Mr. Corso and sat down.

Mr. Corso hated being winked at: he found nothing more patronizing and insidiously coercive. He refrained from smiling and hardened his expression.

Mike approached the prospective jurors, commented on the weather, and questioned them in a conversational tone about what they would be doing for their summer vacations. He turned to Mr. Ortiz, who reported that his favorite dog had been killed by a car the summer before. Mike asked him what kind of dog it was and whether he had a dog now. Mike then talked with several prospective jurors about their pets.

"You may proceed, Mr. Ribeiro," Judge MacFarland said.

Mike rested his gaze on a petite elderly woman with "Mrs. Bugg" printed neatly on her name tag.

"Mrs. Bugg, when you go to the grocery store to buy eggs, do you just stick the carton into your shopping cart or do you open the carton and check to see that none of the eggs are broken?"

"I open the carton and turn each egg over, one at a time, to make sure it's not cracked on the bottom," Mrs. Bugg answered.

"And you, Mr. Corso?"

Before Mr. Corso could answer, Judge MacFarland interrupted. "I gave you ten minutes, Mr. Ribeiro. I'd like to get this jury empaneled before the end of the century. Please, ladies and gentlemen, answer the defense attorney's questions as speedily as possible."

Mr. Corso felt offended by the judge's comment, which he believed had been directed at him. This was altogether unfair, since she had interrupted him before he had spoken. One thing he could not stand was to be interrupted.

"I always check my eggs," he asserted forcefully before Mike Ribeiro could return to his questioning. "I run my hand over them, first in one direction, like this"—Mr. Corso demonstrated, moving his arm over an imaginary egg carton—"and then back like this, in the other direction."

"I'm glad to hear it, because that's just what I want you to do in this case," Mike told the jury. "I want you to turn over every fact the prosecutor gives you and examine it carefully. Every single one. Don't let him sell you a carton of rotten eggs."

"Oh, come on," Mr. Harkin said. He tilted his glass so that the last swallow of V-8 juice disappeared.

Mike Ribeiro moved on to the next juror, having achieved his purpose. Any juror chosen now would believe he or she had been deemed the kind of person who would not buy a carton of eggs without looking at it. Every juror would examine the facts carefully, trying to prove that he could not be fooled by bad evidence.

Ida realized that she had never checked every egg, one by one, in her life. In fact, she rarely even opened the carton before she bought eggs.

Mike concluded by asking what person each prospective juror most admired. One of the younger men present, Mr. Spinelli, named the boxer Jersey Joe Walcott, and Mr. Thiele, an eyeglass repairman, named Spinoza. Mike asked a few more conversational questions about the jurors' pets, until Judge MacFarland motioned for him to desist.

When he emerged from the judge's chambers with the prosecutor a few minutes later, Mike's list read:

> Juror #1 (Mr. Clark): appeared to make pass at both Ms. Jankowski and Ms. Bonilla.
>
> Juror #2 (Ms. Bonaparte): brother is officer. She does not like police dogs.
>
> Juror #3 (Ms. Bonilla): churchy; Manila Ave. home owner & landlord; owns three dogs.
>
> Juror #4 (Ms. Sparks): pregnant juror; black; downtown renter. Likes some dogs.

Juror #5 (Mrs. Haskel): old pruneface. Never owned a dog.

Juror #6 (Mr. Thiele): eyeglass repairman. Likes Spinoza.

Juror #7 (Ms. Jankowski): bookkeeper; quiet; hard to figure; renter.

Juror #8 (Ms. Bugg): lead egg-turner.

Juror #9 (Mr. Edgar): church caretaker; black; downtown renter.

Juror #10 (Mr. Corso): on the defensive; looking for a fight. Wife just left him. Would like to get a big dog.

Juror #11 (Mr. Spinelli): very young. Served four years in military.

Juror #12 (Mr. Ortiz): drunk? Hates all lawyers. Hates criminals. Hates the police. Hates everybody. Likes dogs OK. Dog killed in car accident.

"Well, what a fine-looking jury," Judge MacFarland said. "I see no reason why we can't begin with the trial first thing in the morning. And Mr. Harkin, I'll thank you not to bring food into my courtroom. Tomorrow, a glass of water will do just fine. Mrs. Terhune, I expect you to be here at exactly nine o'clock tomorrow and not a second later."

All the jurors stared at Ida, summing her up.

Skeet lay in his bunk, listening to his mother talk about jail as if she had returned from an adventure to a foreign land. She stood on the bunk bed's ladder, leaning over Sherry's mattress and telling her, "They put me in the part of the jail with crazy people!" Sherry tittered. "My cellmate was a lady named Pamela who wore blue mascara. It made her look like a pixie. I once asked her what crime she had committed and she just said"—Skeet's mother altered her voice to make it harsh and rumbly—"'I don't think you could stand to hear it, honey.'" Skeet's mother and Sherry laughed together.

Skeet did not like his mother pretending to be someone else. "Well, you'd be interested to know what Pamela told me," she continued. Again she changed voices. "'Shoplifting's a lady's crime. Men burglarize and rob people; women shoplift. Sex discrimination is what it is.'" Skeet wished she would just sound like herself. He was glad that her hairdo was back to usual. She had looked scary when she showed up at the docks with Betty Trombley's scarf twisted around her head. He did not like the new bluish tint in her hair.

"Sherry, I stole something not very long ago," his mother whispered, jiggling the bed as she leaned closer to Sherry. "I once walked right into a lady's home, without knocking, and I saw she had an ostrich egg with a picture painted on it of a house with sunflowers around it. I wanted it, and I took it. I felt she had taken something from me, and that I was justified, so I did not really think of it as stealing, but I guess it was. When I told Pamela, do you know what she said? She said, 'Right on, Ida, right on!'" Again Sherry laughed at her mother's rumbly voice. "I wish I had that egg now, Sherry. If I did, I'd give it to you. It was just the kind of ridiculous, gaudy thing you would have liked."

After she had tucked in Sherry, Ida descended the ladder and tucked in Skeet. She wanted to speak to him, but he appeared to be asleep. She wanted to reassure herself that he had not been changed too much by her absence, that he was the same precious Skeet she had left behind and done without for so many weeks. Skeet purposely kept his eyes closed as she hovered above him. He felt her lightly rearranging his covers. Ida was tempted to wake him by fluffing his pillow, but decided this would be selfish. She kissed the air above his head.

Ida would be on her own in court. Porter was staying at home to attend to the children, whom Ida had forbidden to watch the trial. Mike intended to call Betty as a witness, and she would not be permitted into the courtroom until after she testified. It was the eve of trial, and Ida felt as expectant as if it were the night before an important holiday. And she felt terrified.

Part V

THE TRIAL

◆ The State's Case

The State of New Jersey, as personified by F. X. Harkin, rose. "Men and women of the jury," the prosecutor began, "I will prove to you that the defendant got herself drunk, got into her big car, mowed down a man, and killed him. Listen to the facts carefully. Turn them over, like eggs in a carton." F. X. Harkin winked at Juror #10, Mr. Corso. "Once you have, you'll feel comfortable in performing your duty and returning a guilty verdict."

As the prosecutor read the indictment and described the evidence he intended to introduce, Juror #11, Mr. Spinelli, thought of the time he and two army buddies had hijacked a jeep from Fort Dix and driven it into a lake forty miles away. They had drunk one six-pack after another, and by the time they reached the lake, Spinelli was drunker than he had ever been in his life. He was so drunk that he had wondered why people ever bothered to stay sober: the stars wobbled overhead, the piney air was sharper than turpentine in his lungs, he and his buddies sprang from the jeep as it soared off a promontory into the lake, landing facedown, with its parking lights flashing eerily in the water. Spinelli and his buddies had hitchhiked back to the base that night, and amazingly, were never caught. It was the most amazing thing Spinelli had ever done. Spinelli hated the army, and the rest of the time he was in it, whenever an officer screamed at him, he had consoled himself with the image of the army jeep flashing beneath the water. It was fucking amazing.

"Finally," Harkin concluded, "the decedent's father will testify that he was asked to come to the hospital and identify the body, and that he did so, and that it was the body of his only son." Harkin gazed solemnly at the jurors. Juror #3, Mrs. Bonilla, looked teary-eyed. Harkin sat down.

That night, at Wednesday-night prayer meeting, Mrs. Bonilla would pray for Ida Terhune's soul to be saved from the everlasting damnation it might well deserve. At the end of the state's case, when Rupert Dixon would fail to appear at the trial of the person who had killed his only son, Mrs. Bonilla would be horrified. At that time, she would pray for the elder Mr. Dixon's soul to be saved as well.

Mike Ribeiro surveyed the jurors, lined up like twelve eggs in a carton. He walked to the jury box, placed his hands on the rail before it, and leaned forward. Juror #5, Mrs. Haskel, leaned backward. From that unnatural angle, she noted for the first time the disagreeable fact that she and the defendant had dressed almost identically, in mint-green pantsuits. However, the defendant was also wearing some odd kind of earring made out of blue feathers, which Mrs. Haskel would not have been caught dead in.

"Ladies and gentlemen of the jury," Mike began. "Before you pass judgment, I simply want you to ask one question, privately, of yourselves. What is the worst thing you have ever done?" Mike returned to the defense table, rustled some papers in his briefcase, and gave the jurors time to think.

Juror #7, Mrs. Jankowski, thought to herself: I once fell in love with a married man, stole him from his wife, and then, after his wife got cancer two months later and died, I left him.

"And then I want you to ask yourselves: Is the act the defendant has been accused of any worse? And yet the prosecutor is asking you to condemn her, a mother of two. Are you prepared to condemn her?"

"That'll be enough of that, Mr. Ribeiro," Judge MacFarland said.

"Mrs. Terhune," Mike began, "came to Jersey City in July of last year, hoping to improve things for her two children. Her dear friend, Betty Trombley, had told Mrs. Terhune she could make a good life with her family here. She'd never been out of Louisiana before. She was provincial and sheltered." Juror #8, Mrs. Bugg, noticed the defendant stirring peevishly behind her lawyer. "But one thing Mrs. Terhune was skilled at was driving. She'd never gotten so much as a parking ticket before. And she had a good car, left to her by her late husband when she was widowed while still pregnant with her second child. Her journey was perilous: she drove by herself, she stayed where she could afford to, not always in the safest places—she even drove through Hurricane Marguerite, which destroyed so many southern coastal towns last year.

"When she arrived here, everything she owned was in four suitcases. But she had her car, she had her children. And once she came here, she made good. She made us, the citizens of Jersey City, proud to receive her. Here in our city, she blossomed. She got her first job right in our Municipal Court."

Juror #6, Mr. Thiele, tried to picture the defendant blossoming. He could not: she looked grim and sour in her high-piled hairdo. Although her feathery earrings did soften her appearance somewhat.

"Mrs. Terhune was a soldier of the law, and she worked hard, performing her duties fairly and competently, in our Municipal Court's complaints office. It was to her that victims turned as she listened to them with compassion and encouragement. When she returned from work, she took care of her children. Life was a challenge at home. The landlord, Rupert Dixon, had allowed the building to fall into disrepair; health violations plagued his building, his thugs terrorized the tenants—even Ida's children."

"Objection," Harkin said boredly, not rising from his blond-oak prosecutor's table.

"Ladies and gentlemen of the jury," Judge MacFarland instructed, "as I already have instructed, defense counsel's opening statement is not evidence. Nor is the prosecutor's. In reaching your verdict, you will consider only the evidence—the testimony and exhibits presented by each side."

"But Ida Terhune persevered. She scraped up enough to send her children to parochial school. She is a woman of high moral principles, and she wanted her children to share those principles.

"She was making it.

"And then terrible things started to happen—call it bad luck, call it the cruelty of fate. Her car was stolen, the car her beloved husband, Dewey, had left her, the last relic of the happy days of her marriage. And afterward she went out to dinner at the My Way Lounge with her dear friend Betty, her only friend in the city—they had helped one another through thick and thin—and they quarreled.

"It was one of the moments in life when you say, Why was I ever born? What is it all for? She left the restaurant in despair."

Ida had always considered her feelings to be somewhat of a mystery, because of her private nature. Her lawyer's insight into her character impressed her: it was as if he had read her like a book.

"And then the cruel hand of fate again intervened in Mrs. Terhune's life. She saw her car. Her stolen car. The one that her beloved husband, Dewey, had left her. The last thing she had from him.

"She took a deep breath. She peered inside. Was the thief nearby? In the window, she saw a bottle of wine, racing-car magazines, a baseball mitt. Boys' things. She took a chance. She put her fear aside. She got in the car and drove toward home. She was going to fight fate. She wouldn't be beaten.

"She didn't know that her headlights weren't working; perhaps they had been broken in the theft. It was that time of evening—we all know it—when it's not day anymore but not yet dark. When you say to yourself, Should I turn my lights on yet? You look around, don't see any other cars with lit headlights, and think, I'll wait a bit. But Mrs. Terhune, always a safe driver—she had two children—turned her lights on. She didn't see her headlights reflecting off the pavement yet, but it was only dusk.

"Mrs. Terhune drove along under the street lamps of Newark Avenue. She turned right onto Grove Street. She headed home, happy, with her car. She turned the corner onto Grand Street.

"The corner street light on Grand Street and Orestes Cleveland Road had been broken for some time. Now evening had descended. She saw dark pavement, unilluminated by headlights. She wondered if her car's lights were broken. At that instant, fate struck. Why Ida Terhune? Why did it choose Ida Terhune? Why not you or me? Because fate doesn't care where it strikes. Fate doesn't choose. It doesn't ask, Is this fair? Does she deserve it?"

Juror #7, Mrs. Jankowski, scrutinized the defendant: her head was cocked toward her attorney, a perfectly trusting expression on her face. When was the last time she, Violet Jankowski, had worn that expression when she watched a man? Perhaps she had looked that way at her father when she was eight years old.

"Ida Terhune felt a collision. Her head struck the steering wheel, shocking her, leaving her woozy. But, an expert driver, she managed to steer to safety, to turn toward the curb.

"Then sirens, like the hounds of fate, raced down her street. Police encircled her. They yanked her out of her car. They never asked if she was injured. They never thought to treat her with delicacy. You must be drunk, they said.

"Big, rough hands grabbed her and forced her into a patrol car. The door shut behind her. The police drove her to jail. They threw her inside. Animal, they said. Criminal.

"Is Ida Terhune a criminal?

"No. Righteousness cries out for you to remedy this injustice! Send Ida Terhune back to her children, who lie awake crying for her, having lost a father already. Come to her aid where the agents of the law have failed us. Her fate is in your hands. Rescue her."

F. X. Harkin called Rupert Dixon's chauffeur, a barrel-chested young man with dark hair and dark glasses, as the state's first witness.

The chauffeur looked at Judge MacFarland and then Harkin and asked, "Where's the honor?"

"I'm the judge," Judge MacFarland said. "State your name for the record."

"Oswald Small."

Harkin began: "Where do you work, Mr. Small?"

"I drive the Marquis. I'm Rupert Dixon's man. Chauffeur." Mr. Small's voice had a peculiar lack of intonation. Mike had noted a similar flatness of affect in one of the contract killers he had defended. "Mr. Dixon owns a store on the corner of Grand and Orestes Cleveland," Mr. Small droned on, "so when he's downtown for any reason, I usually park the car there and hang out."

"Excuse me," Judge MacFarland said. "Mr. Small, if those aren't prescription sunglasses, please remove them. They are not appropriate dress for a court of law."

Mr. Small took off his sunglasses, revealing startling violet eyes with long lashes.

Juror #9, Mr. Edgar, thought he recognized the chauffeur as one of the thugs who had terrorized two parishioners in the church where Mr. Edgar worked as a caretaker. He wondered if he should volunteer to disqualify himself, but then decided against it: perhaps God had a divine reason for placing him on Ida Terhune's jury.

Harkin continued: "You were parked near the corner of Orestes Cleveland and Grand Street on March twenty-third?"

"Naturally." Mr. Small's tongue stumbled over the word. Juror #8, Mrs. Bugg, watched Mike lean forward and scrutinize Mr. Small.

"Did you see Clark Gable Dixon that night?"

"Chicken was across the street, closing the back door of his van." Mr. Small stared at the floor as if he had forgotten what he was saying. He drew himself up abruptly. "Yup. That's what he was doing."

"By 'Chicken,' you mean the decedent?"

"None of us knew him by any other name. This is the first I heard 'Clark Gable.'"

"Where was he standing? Like this, behind the van? Or was he partway out in the street?"

"Oh, no, he was right behind the van. Near the curb. He was a very careful man. Very careful."

"Objection."

"Just answer the questions, Mr. Small," Judge MacFarland said.

"And honest. Also, he was a wonderful family man," said Mr. Small, as if he had rehearsed his testimony beforehand but was unsure exactly at what juncture he was expected to assess Chicken's character.

"Focus on the questions, Mr. Small," Judge MacFarland said. "Mr. Harkin, I caution you not to elicit testimony regarding the decedent's character." She looked at Mike Ribeiro, anticipating an objection, but he simply nodded. He was glad for the prosecutor's indiscretion. Ordinarily, Mike could not have questioned anyone about a dead victim's character, but now that Rupert Dixon's chauffeur had opened the door, no holds were barred. Mike had quite a few facts he wanted to elicit about Chicken. As a rule, Mike objected only to the most egregious prosecutorial misconduct, because the jurors often misunderstood and thought the defendant was trying to hide something by objecting.

"And what did you see next?"

"I saw a car come careening wildly around the corner."

Perhaps I was tipsier than I realized, Ida thought. I don't remember driving that fast.

"Did you notice anything else unusual?"

"It was dark, but the headlights were off."

Mike surmised that the chauffeur knew about the headlights from Ida's own statements to the police after her arrest.

"The car struck something and veered off to the side. People started shouting. Also, Chicken was going to enroll in Saint Peter's College this fall."

"The witness will answer only those questions put to him," Judge MacFarland again intervened.

"What did you do then?" Harkin prompted.

"I got out of the Marquis, and at first all I saw was that big car stopped in the middle of the road. A New Yorker. It'd take a car that size to kill someone the size of Chicken. A big Chrysler or a Cadillac. Maybe one of those foreign station wagons that look like turned-over refrigerators."

"After you emerged from your car, did you see Clark Gable Dixon?"

"Yeah. Chicken was lying on his side near his father's store. It was a terrible thing to see. And I saw that lady—"

"Let the record reflect that the witness has pointed at the defendant," Judge MacFarland interjected. Ida looked with embarrassment at the hands sitting in her lap. She was guilty: it could not have been clearer.

"—I saw her sitting drunk in the front seat of the car that hit Chicken."

"Objection," Mike Ribeiro said. "There's no foundation for this witness claiming the defendant was drunk."

"Sustained."

"What made you think she was drunk, Mr. Small?"

"When she got out of the car, I could smell her. She smelled like cheap wine. And she was walking funny, like a drunk person. There was a bottle of cheap wine lying on the car seat."

"That will be all," Harkin said. It was an open-and-shut case. He sat down, winking at Juror #10, Mr. Corso. Mr. Corso's bushy eyebrows drew together under his bushy hair, and he scowled.

Mike Ribeiro estimated that most of the chauffeur's testimony had been fabricated. Betty Trombley had canvassed the area near the corner for witnesses, but there did not appear to have been anyone present at the very moment of the accident: two people who had rushed to the scene after they heard the crash had reported that Chicken and Ida Terhune were the only people in sight. No one had mentioned any chauffeur.

Mike removed from his briefcase a map Ida recognized as Skeet's handiwork. Mike leaned the map against the briefcase and smiled at it. He then studied Mr. Small and smiled at him.

"Your Honor, I'd like to introduce this map into evidence to aid the jurors in picturing the scene of the accident." He handed the map to F. X. Harkin, who returned it without interest. "It looks accurate," Harkin said. "The state has no objection."

Mike gave the map to the foreman, saying, "Ida's nine-year-old boy drew this. Isn't it nice?" Several jurors leaned forward. "That's his dog, Joseph, there—do you see?"

Harkin understood then that the defense attorney had entered the map as a ploy for sympathy, for the sole purpose of presenting the jury with a physical reminder that the defendant had children. Juror #8, Mrs. Bugg, saw the prosecutor suppress a look of irritation.

"All right, Mr. Ribeiro," Judge MacFarland said. "Let's get on with your cross-examination."

When Mike rose, Mrs. Bugg noticed there was a green spot on his shoe. Could it be pea soup? she wondered.

"Mr. Small, you look a little sleepy. Are you sure you can keep your eyes open for the rest of your testimony?"

"Objection."

"Get on with it, Mr. Ribeiro."

Mike stared at the air above the witness and appeared to conduct an argument in his head. He raised one hand as if illustrating a point, and then dropped his palm as if the point had been proved.

"Did you know Chicken Dixon well?" Mike cross-examined the chauffeur.

"We grew up together."

"Please try to speak clearly. I'm having trouble understanding you. Can you tell the jury what kind of employment Chicken had at the time of his death?"

"He worked for his father."

"Do you know what he did for his father?"

"No."

"He never discussed his work with you?"

"No."

"He was your close, childhood friend and he never discussed the nature of his work with you?"

Harkin whirled his index finger in the air.

"Sustained. Asked and answered," Judge MacFarland said.

"Do you think that his work may have been of a less than legal nature?"

"Sustained," Judge MacFarland said when Harkin again raised his finger.

"Now, you say you saw Chicken Dixon right before the car hit him?"

"Sort of."

"What was he doing out there?"

"He was getting something inside his van. It was parked there."

"Can you please repeat that more clearly? Can the jury understand Mr. Small?" Mike turned toward the jury with a solicitous look. "Please try and enunciate. Was the street dark?"

"Yeah. The street light there was broken."

"He was standing in the middle of a dark street, right near the intersection of Grand and Orestes Cleveland?"

"Just for a second."

"Is your speech slurred, or do you always talk like this?"

Harkin waved his hand.

"Sustained. Mr. Harkin, see if you can summon up the energy to voice your objections. This is not an auction house; this is a court of law."

"What was he looking at inside his van?"

"I don't know."

"You don't know. He didn't mention to you what he'd come down for that day? Do you know if he had poisoned meat in there?"

"Objection. There's no foundation—"

"Sustained."

"Poisoned meat for a dog?"

"Sustained. Mr. Ribeiro! Ladies and gentlemen of the jury,

what comes from the mouths of lawyers is not evidence. Only the witness's testimony is evidence."

"You say that the defendant was 'walking funny' when she got out of the car?"

"Yes."

"How far away from her were you?"

"About fifteen feet."

"You could smell her breath from fifteen feet?"

"Yes."

"You have a good nose. You testified that her car's headlights were off?"

"Yes."

"And the street light was broken?"

"Yes."

"But you could see the defendant was walking funny? And that a bottle on the car seat contained 'cheap' wine?"

"Yes."

"You have good eyes too." So the fuck what? Mike's wife suddenly loomed up, a jarred-loose memory he could attach to no particular setting. So you poked holes in his story. How do you know he's lying? You can poke holes in any story.

"Your work for Rupert Dixon, Chicken's father, is your sole source of income?"

"Yes."

"No more questions. Oh, except for one. What is the name of the drug you took this morning?"

Mr. Small tried to catch the prosecutor's eye. Harkin focused on some motion papers in front of him.

"What's this?" Judge MacFarland asked, leaning over Mr. Small from the bench. "Did you enter my courtroom on drugs?"

Mr. Small answered, pointing at the prosecutor. "I'm legal—ask him!"

"What did you take?" Mike repeated. "Thorazine?"

"My client," Harkin now volunteered, "has a legal prescription for tranquilizers."

"Is this true?" Judge MacFarland asked. "You are taking a legally prescribed sedative?"

"Mr. Small," Mike asked, "has the prosecutor drugged you?"

Mr. Small again tried to catch Harkin's eye but failed.

"Mr. Small," Mike resumed, "did the prosecutor tell you to take a sedative before testifying? Are you ordinarily a volatile person?"

"Objection," Harkin said in a bored tone.

"Approach the bench," Judge MacFarland commanded. In tones too low for the jury to hear, she said, "What's going on here, Mr. Harkin?"

"I just want to know," Mike said loudly, so that the jurors were sure to overhear, "whether the prosecutor has drugged his witness because he was afraid the witness might display a violent temper under cross-examination."

"Mr. Harkin, is there anything to this accusation?"

"Of course not," the prosecutor said. "Mr. Small is a naturally calm person. He's just nervous about appearing in public."

"There better not be," the judge said.

"Your Honor," Mike pressed, "I'd like to make a motion for a mistrial. Regardless of whether this witness drugged himself or was drugged to subdue his explosive personality"—Mike's voice rose on the last two words—"his ordinary demeanor is being obscured by the drug, impairing the jury's ability to assess his credibility."

"Motion denied," Judge MacFarland said. "However, I will instruct the jury that they may consider Mr. Small's use of sedatives in assessing his credibility." As Mr. Small stepped down, the jurors watched him intently. "Mr. Harkin, my courtroom is my kingdom, and when I'm here, I expect everyone present to act better than he or she may be used to doing. I expect the highest level of decorum and the diligent pursuit of justice. This I expect without the use of artificial stimulants or depressants, is that clear? I do not consider a nod to be an acceptable answer from an adult human being who possesses the gift of speech."

"Yes," Harkin stated.

"Yes? Yes, what?"

"Yes, I will respect your standards, which are admirable,"

Harkin said, poker-faced, so that it was impossible to read either sarcasm or sincerity into his words.

"I will be searching for signs of that admiration, Mr. Harkin. Proceed with your next witness."

Ida recognized the police officer who took the stand, a husky man with large hands. She felt the imprint of his grip on her upper arm. The sudden recollection of the moment when she had been shoved into the patrol car made her flinch inwardly, and the feelings of that moment returned to her: the bafflement and fear and sense of strangeness that had begun then and had never relinquished hold on her since.

When questioned about Ida's appearance at the time of her arrest, Office Starkweather responded, "The defendant was swaying and leaning against me. And she had slurred speech."

Ida reddened. The image of her swaying and leaning against Officer Starkweather was more than she could bear.

Juror #3, Mrs. Bonilla, saw Ida Terhune redden and felt sorry for her.

"And when I shined my flashlight into her eyes, her pupils contracted slowly."

When the police-officer brother of Juror #2, Ms. Bonaparte, got drunk, he liked to shine his flashlight into his own eyes to demonstrate to anyone who cared to listen that his pupils were contracting too slowly, and to explain that this was a sign of drunkenness police were schooled in. The image of her obnoxious brother making an ass of himself overpowered Ms. Bonaparte, and she laughed out loud.

"The jurors will be orderly," Judge MacFarland said.

Officer Starkweather looked toward the jury pool, bewildered. "And the defendant's eyes were bloodshot. And she was shouting and using abusive language."

Why, he's making that up, Ida thought.

"What else led you to believe the defendant was drunk, Officer Starkweather?"

"The defendant herself stated, point-blank, that she had been drinking."

"And did you find any alcohol in the car?"

"We sure did. An opened bottle of Boone's strawberry wine."

"And where was the victim?"

"He was lying half on the sidewalk."

"Did the defendant appear to be aware that she had struck another human being?"

"No, she did not."

"No more questions."

Ida realized that one of the women jurors whom she had thought to be merely plump was actually pregnant. She appeared ashen and raised her hand to her mouth as if nauseated. Ida flashed her a reassuring look and then feared this would be mistaken as a calculated attempt to influence the jury. However, the juror did not appear to notice. She withdrew her hand, rested it on her stomach, and smiled at nothing, as if she had felt her child turn within her. Ida recalled the first time she had felt a baby move in her, before her initial miscarriage. It had been a happy, otterlike movement. She had been unable to give that child life, but it had given her a notion of life at its quickening, perhaps the dearest gift she had ever received, and also the cruelest.

Juror #7, Mrs. Jankowski, watched the defendant and saw that her mind was wandering. Mrs. Jankowski was relieved, as she had allowed her attention to stray a little as well. When the defendant's attorney approached the police witness, Mrs. Jankowski sat up straight and leaned forward with an exaggeratedly intent expression.

"Officer Starkweather, did you perform a Breathalyzer test on Mrs. Terhune?"

"Yes."

"And how did it register?"

"Below the legal limit, but it turned out the Breathalyzer wasn't working."

"In fact, you performed a test twice."

"Yes."

"Did my client cooperate?"

"Yes, but like I said, the Breathalyzer didn't work. We've been having trouble with them."

"Did you report that your partner sat on it?"

"Yes."

Juror #2, Mrs. Bonaparte, laughed.

"Were you ever informed that the defendant, this swaying, cursing, staggering woman with slowly contracting pupils, drank at most one or two glasses of champagne? That's some champagne. I'd like to get my hands on that champagne," Mike concluded gaily. "No more questions for this witness."

After Officer Starkweather stepped down, the prosecutor called several medical experts, who testified at cross-purposes, some opining that Chicken had died from the car's impact and others attributing his death to a heart attack brought on in part by cocaine abuse. At first, the jurors paid attention: they seemed interested to learn that Chicken had been full of cocaine at the time of his death. However, the coroner, who was no longer excited by the idea of death, droned on in a sepulchral monotone as he deciphered his illegible handwriting for the prosecutor, so that by the end of his testimony, several of the jurors were fighting off sleep. Juror #5, Mrs. Haskel, prodded the foreman, Mr. Clark, at one interval when his breathing became audible and threatened to evolve into a snore.

The defense attorney cross-examined the coroner: "And what does this writing say here?"

"Lungs—unremarkable."

"And here?"

"Esophagus—unremarkable. Liver—unremarkable. Genitals—unremarkable. Pancreas—unremarkable."

As the coroner continued to testify in detail about the procedures he had followed and the tests his chemists had made, Juror #8, Mrs. Bugg, wondered whether her husband would notice that she had thoroughly cleaned the bathroom that morning. Probably not. Not only had she scrubbed inside the toilet, under the lid, and in the difficult-to-reach places at the lid's base, as well as the parts where the toilet attached to the floor; she had Windexed the mirror, scoured the bathtub, wiped the sink with ammonia, removed the dirty towels and hung up new ones after burnishing the towel rack, and mopped the floor after scrubbing between the tiles with a toothbrush. Dr. Bugg had never cleaned a bathroom in his life, although occasionally he would swish the toilet brush around in the bowl with a martyred expression. Surely a man who had an M.D. from Albert Einstein could figure out how to clean a toilet if he cared to.

Following the experts' testimony, Harkin announced that the victim's father had not yet arrived to testify that he had identified his son's body. The jurors grew solemn. After some discussion, the court declared a recess for lunch. However, after lunch, Harkin approached the bench, and the jurors heard him say, "Apparently, he could not make it because he's involved in an important business deal." The defendant's lawyer answered, "When his tenant threatened his property interests, he was ready to come to court on a moment's notice—but then, that was his pocketbook, and this is only his son, Chicken, we're talking about."

The judge turned to the jurors. "Pay no attention to what the lawyers say up here. Cover your ears with your hands, turn your heads, think of other things: this does not concern you," she instructed. "Juror #12," Judge MacFarland told Mr. Ortiz, "I meant that figuratively. You may remove your literal hands from your literal ears."

Harkin left the courtroom and twenty minutes later reemerged with a pale, thin man who took the stand and introduced himself as Bob Paper, an employee at Rupert Dixon's corner store. Mike remembered seeing the clerk once before, when Sherry had been stopped for shoplifting. Bob Paper looked like a faded version of Rupert Dixon himself, as if Rupert suddenly had been stripped of his confidence, his shrewd grin tautened into a line of despair. On the clerk's temples were two peculiar red circles of what looked like rouge to Juror #7, Mrs. Jankowski.

Bob Paper answered all questions with extreme brevity. He eventually communicated that he had accompanied the victim's father to Jersey City Medical Center and there identified the body with him. Harkin also asked the clerk whether he knew what Chicken had been doing outside near his van at the time of his death.

Bob answered that Chicken had been investigating a former tenant. "Named Henry Purdy. Because it looked as if he was using the F. H. Eggers memorial as a urinal." Bob almost appeared to smile as he said this, but the smile was so fleeting and subdued that none of the jurors could be sure.

"Mr. Paper," Mike asked on cross-examination, "are you related to the decedent's father?"

"Maybe," he said.

"Just answer the question yes or no," Judge MacFarland instructed.

"Maybe yes, maybe no," he said, looking at the floor.

"Your Honor," Harkin objected, "there seems to be some controversy within the family about Mr. Paper's lineage, if you get my drift."

"Move on, Mr. Ribeiro," Judge MacFarland directed.

"So, Mr. Paper, maybe you're related to the deceased and his father, here. Let the record indicate that the witness has just nodded.

"You'd say about anything for your maybe brother, wouldn't you?"

Bob appeared to contemplate the question seriously and answered, "Nope." The witness stared at his hands, with a small, introverted smile.

"Do you know what Chicken had out there in his van?"

"Nope," Bob repeated, shaking his head.

"You didn't hear anything about cocaine or poisoned meat? Or kerosene?"

"Objection. Hearsay and asked and answered," Harkin said.

"Sustained."

"Not from him," Bob answered.

His short answer suggested a mountain of knowledge to Juror #9, Mr. Edgar, who did not particularly care about legal rules and who resented the prosecutor's efforts to withhold information from the jury. Had Chicken been a thug together with the thug chauffeur? What was he doing with dog poison and kerosene? What kind of man would have a father who refused to come identify his body at a homicide trial? Imagine being the son of a slumlord, Mr. Edgar pondered. Imagine your father training you to be a thug for his own private business purposes. Mr. Edgar felt a flicker of sympathy for the victim, Chicken Dixon.

Ida turned around and noted for the first time that several members of the tenants association were seated in the rear pews of the courtroom, watching the case. For just an instant, Ida felt that a trial was sufficient punishment in itself for any criminal. It was terrible to sit in the defendant's seat, all eyes on her, accusing and judging and disapproving. The single human being in the courtroom who was on her side was her attorney. She scooted her chair closer to Mike Ribeiro's, taking comfort in his presence.

◆ The Defense Case

Judge MacFarland called a brief recess to allow the jurors to stretch their legs and in order to take the defense attorney aside to ask him if he had a clean tie. A few moments later, Juror #6, Mr. Thiele, saw the defense attorney in the bathroom, attempting to scrub a spot on his tie with a paper towel. Mr. Thiele was tempted to offer him his own tie and would have, but for the judge's instructions forbidding jurors to speak with the lawyers. Once back in the jury box, Mr. Thiele saw the defense attorney reenter the courtroom, his tie looking clean and uniformly black. He approached the jury box and gave the jurors a hearty smile. Mr. Thiele alone knew that the tie was soaked from top to bottom and that this accounted for its uniformity of hue and apparent stainlessness.

The defense lawyer announced that he would call his expert witness, and a lean old man wearing a jumpsuit that said *Exterminator Angel* in bright-orange stitching over the pockets took the stand. After several objections from the prosecutor, Judge MacFarland qualified the witness as an expert on insecticides and poisons.

"Mr. Rodriguez, where do you live?"

"I live right off a basement flooded with sewer water, in a building owned by Rupert Dixon."

Juror #3, Mrs. Bonilla, gasped, and several courtroom spectators, as well as the judge and the jurors, looked at her. Mr. Rodriguez smiled, glad that he had succeeded in producing a ripple. However, Mrs. Bonilla had not reacted to his testimony. She had remembered abruptly that she had never turned off the burner under her glass coffeepot that morning. She remembered turning off the kitchen light but had no recollection of checking the stove.

"Did you visit the accident site on the morning of March twenty-fourth?"

Should she raise her hand and ask the judge to allow her to call to her next-door neighbor, so that he could peer through the kitchen window to see if the burner was on?

"I walked around, yeah. Only I didn't know about Chicken getting killed yet. I saw all these people standing around Chicken's van, so I crossed the street to see what was up."

No, maybe she had turned the burner off. It had happened before: hadn't she run home more than once, thinking the stove was on, and in fact she had remembered to turn it off? She had just forgotten that she remembered, instead imagining the heated dry glass exploding all over the kitchen, setting her house aflame and killing the children in the family who rented the top floor, trapped alone while their mother shopped.

"Mr. Rodriguez, would you mind telling the jury whether you saw anything remarkable near the decedent's van following the accident?"

Of course she had turned it off. However, as soon as the judge called a recess, Mrs. Bonilla would phone her neighbor to make sure.

"There was steak all over the Eggers memorial, just to the left of the van. Big pieces of porterhouse."

"Objection," Harkin said sarcastically. "Mr. Rodriguez is not a butcher. He's an exterminator."

"Overruled."

"Did you see anything else unusual?" Mike Ribeiro continued.

"Well, awhile later, after I heard about Mrs. Terhune's accident, I looked in the empty apartment next to mine for a guy named Henry and noticed a blue ice cooler that had not been inside there before."

"Can I ask if you saw what was in the cooler?"

"Yeah. I saw it was poison."

"As an exterminator, can you tell us something about the nature of that poison?"

"Well, it was basically rat poison. A kind I don't like to use."

"Can you tell us why?"

"Strychnine, that's why. Some people like to lay it out to kill rats, but I don't use the stuff because dogs and cats scarf it down sometimes."

"Do you have any opinion about what kind of animal in the building anyone might have wanted to kill?"

"I think Chicken brought it to kill Joseph."

Judge MacFarland interrupted. "Are you asserting that the decedent was contemplating a homicide?"

"Joseph's the dog," Angel explained. "Mrs. Terhune's kid's dog. The dog had won a fight against Chicken a few weeks back."

"Objection!" Harkin said. "There's been absolutely no showing that the victim had anything to do with the cooler."

"I forgot to say," Angel Rodriguez told Harkin, "that cooler's from Chicken's father's store. I've seen it a million times. It used to belong to the man, Persaud, our landlord stole the store from. Persaud kept curry and ginger beer in it. What's more, I saw Chicken hanging around in the apartment next to mine the same evening as the accident. I thought he was up to no good."

"Your Honor," Harkin protested, "I want his testimony stricken as inflammatory and irrelevant. Even if Clark Gable Dixon was there that day, I'm sure he was just killing rats."

"Not likely," Mr. Rodriguez answered. "He never cared about the rats there before. I always had to deal with them."

"So it's true there were rats in the basement where the rat poison was?" Harkin asked.

"Is Mr. Harkin cross-examining my witness?" Mike asked.

"Mr. Harkin, you wait your turn," Judge MacFarland told the prosecutor.

"So," Mike asked Angel, "there are rats in the basement?"

"Not anymore. The basement's flooded with sewer water. A rat couldn't live down there. He would drown."

"The children's dog doesn't live down there, does he?"

"No. He lives on the third floor. But I forgot to explain that the reason I went in the place next door was because there was an awful smell in there. Something besides the sewer water, I mean. What it was was rotting steaks, inside the cooler, next to the poison. Smelling like dead people. Same as the steaks I'd seen outside the van. Porterhouse. That's the reason I thought of Chicken when I saw them. He must have gone out to the van to fetch the last pile of steaks he was going to salt down with rat poison. He must have been so busy thinking about getting back at that dog that he didn't see the car coming."

"Objection. This 'poison expert' "—Harkin rolled his eyes to show he thought the idea of Mr. Rodriguez being an expert funny—"is straying outside his realm of expertise."

"Sustained. Are you finished with this witness, Mr. Ribeiro?" the judge asked. "You are? Well, Mr. Harkin, here's your chance," she said.

"Mr. Expert," Harkin said, remaining at his blond-oak prosecutor's desk, as if Mr. Rodriguez were not worth the effort of a close examination. "You said the apartment belonged to a man named Henry. How do you know the steaks and the poison weren't his?"

"I said it was Henry's apartment. I didn't say he lived there. Our landlord, Rupert Dixon, ran him out. Chicken beat down his door with a pickax, and then they trumped up some case against him and got him arrested. That was after they turned off the heat and hot water in Henry's apartment."

"Objection. Inflammatory and irrelevant," Harkin interrupted.

"Sustained."

Angel turned toward the jurors and added, in a pleading voice, as if he thought they could do something about it, "Henry just wanted to get the goddamn sewer water out of the basement."

"Sustained and stricken."

"And the sewer water is still there, after all this time."

"Sustained, sustained," Judge MacFarland said.

Angel fell silent and leaned back, studying Harkin's face. Then, suddenly, Angel leaned forward and barked, "I know you!" He had saved this surprise for the end; he'd seen no point in letting the defense lawyer in on it until now.

Harkin did not answer.

"I've seen you in the back of the office at Rupert Dixon's store. The victim's father's store."

"Investigating the case," Harkin said impatiently.

"Nope. This was about a year ago. I saw you talking to Rupert Dixon, when his son, Chicken, was there."

"I'm done with this witness," Harkin said.

"The prosecutor will approach the bench," Judge MacFarland said. "Are you friends with the victim's family, Mr. Harkin?"

"Who doesn't know Rupert Dixon?" Harkin answered.

"I don't," Judge MacFarland said. "Do you have any ongoing business dealings with Mr. Dixon?"

"No."

"Ha!" Angel said.

"Mr. Rodriguez, we do not allow witnesses to editorialize," Judge MacFarland followed. "However, Mr. Harkin, I intend to make inquiries."

"I move for the prosecutor to recuse himself," Mike Ribeiro said, loud enough for the jury to hear. "He appears to have a conflict of interest here, which may have compromised his integrity."

"Motion denied. You may step down, Mr. Rodriguez. Proceed with your next witness, Mr. Ribeiro."

To think, Ida reflected wonderingly, that Chicken might

have killed Joseph if I hadn't run into him. Ida pictured Joseph, with his tender black eyes, and for a moment, wholly inappropriately, she was relieved that she had prevented Chicken from killing the children's dog.

Angel stepped down from the witness box, his head held high. He smiled at Ida and was surprised when she smiled back warmly.

All of the jurors turned as Betty Trombley strode past Angel, wearing clogs that added two inches to her stature and resounded like gunshots on the court's floor.

The judge recalled her meeting with Ms. Trombley at the Municipal Court several months before. Ms. Trombley had stood in the judge's chambers, reporting with absolute merriment on the corruption and incompetence of the public defender's office. At that time, Ms. Trombley's hair had been bright red rather than the coppery brown color it was now, and she had been wearing an artificial fur of some kind. Jaguar. She was now dressed equally oddly—in a man's suit and tie that showed up the defendant's lawyer, whose suit was wrinkled in the back beyond explanation. Perhaps it was difficult for a woman that tall to find the clothes she needed.

"Miss Trombley, please state your occupation," Mike Ribeiro began.

"I'm your investigator. I'm the investigator on this case."

"Do you also know the defendant, Ida Terhune?"

"Yes. She and her children live with me in Jersey City. I've known her for twenty-seven years."

"You were with Ida Terhune on March twenty-third?"

"We went out together to the My Way Lounge at about four o'clock."

"Did you observe whether the defendant had anything to drink?"

"Yes, because I was there to celebrate, and I ordered a bottle of champagne. I know that I drank around two glasses before it was gone, so Ida couldn't have had more than one or two glasses."

"Was this during the course of a meal?"

"Yes. We both had eggplant parmigiana."

"Did Ida appear to be drunk?"

"No."

"Not even a little tipsy?"

"No."

"Did anything unusual happen during the meal?"

"Yes. I started a quarrel, and Ida left early, at about four forty-five."

"Have you ever heard Ida Terhune use abusive language?"

"Oh, no. She can't abide people swearing. Every time I swear, she makes a face."

Ida doubted that she made a face *every time.*

"Have you ever seen Ida drunk?"

"Not as an adult, no. She almost never drinks. She doesn't even like beer."

"How long did you say you'd known Ida Terhune?"

"Twenty-seven years."

"Thank you. That will be all."

"Mr. Harkin," Judge MacFarland said, "I will thank you to stand up in my courtroom while you cross-examine defense witnesses. I was hoping you would come to this realization yourself while questioning the poisons expert, but as you apparently did not, I am helping you to come to it now."

Without betraying the least sign of embarrassment or capitulation, Harkin rose, walked over to Betty Trombley, and said, "That's a pretty little accent, Miss Trombley. Are you a native of Louisiana, like the defendant?"

"No, I'm from Bumfuck, Idaho," Betty answered.

Juror #12, Mr. Ortiz, laughed too loudly.

"The witness will act with decorum in this court," Harkin said, as if acknowledging the judge's stated views.

Juror #8, Mrs. Bugg, noted that the defendant in fact made a face when her friend used foul language.

"Tell the prosecutor not to come on to me," Betty Trombley answered.

"Let's proceed," Judge MacFarland said.

"So, Miss Trombley," Harkin recommenced, "you went out to celebrate at four o'clock."

"That's what I said."

"Just answer 'yes' or 'no.'"

"You were asking a question?"

"What were you celebrating?"

"I was celebrating quitting my job," Betty answered.

Judge MacFarland raised her eyebrows.

"And you and the defendant got into a drunken brawl?"

"Objection."

"Sustained."

"That's a pretty strange question, Mr. Harkin."

"You speak when you're spoken to," the prosecutor answered. "How did the defendant act during the quarrel, Miss Trombley?"

"Speak when I'm spoken to?"

"How did she act during the quarrel?"

"How did she act?"

"Was she loud and abusive?"

"Loud, like you're talking now?"

"The witness will stop badgering the prosecutor," Judge MacFarland said. "Just answer the question."

"Not Ida. Ida's never loud. She just clammed up and walked out."

"What were you fighting about?"

"We weren't fighting."

"You were quarreling."

"I was trying to. But we didn't fight. Ida doesn't fight."

"The court will instruct the witness to cooperate."

"Cooperate," Judge MacFarland said.

"What was your little quarrel about?"

"Huey Long."

"Huey Long?"

"Huey Long."

"You were arguing about a man?"

"Asked and answered," Mike Ribeiro objected.

"Overruled."

"You don't know who Huey Long is?" Betty answered. "The governor of Louisiana? You didn't know that Huey Long was the governor of Louisiana?"

"You were arguing about state politics?"

"No. We were talking about Huey Long."

"Please move on, Counselor," Judge MacFarland instructed.

"You testified that Ida Terhune had quite a bit of champagne that afternoon?"

"No. I testified that she had about one or two glasses. Over a meal."

"The My Way Lounge is a bar, isn't it?"

"It's a lounge."

"Two single women alone at a bar? No one offered to buy you drinks?"

"We weren't alone. Mike was there."

Harkin whirled around. "Mr. Ribeiro?"

"Defense counsel will approach the bench," Judge MacFarland said sternly.

Harkin frowned and caught the eye of Juror #5, Mrs. Haskel. Mrs. Haskel frowned.

"Mr. Ribeiro," Judge MacFarland said, "is there a conflict of interest here? Am I hearing that you might have been a witness in this proceeding?"

"No, Your Honor. The only thing I might have testified to was whether the defendant had been drinking. But to be honest, I wasn't paying attention to what she was having. If called, I couldn't have reported anything relevant."

"You didn't buy the defendant any drinks?" Harkin asked.

"No. Ask your witness Ms. Trombley."

"It seems clear, Mr. Harkin, that Mr. Ribeiro's testimony would have been at most cumulative. However, Mr. Ribeiro, I am not at all happy that you concealed this from the court until now. Not at all happy."

"This is unethical!" Harkin pronounced, loud enough for the jurors to hear.

"Continue with your examination, Mr. Harkin."

"Miss Trombley," Harkin resumed, "did the defendant's attorney, Mr. Ribeiro, buy her a drink?"

"No. She wouldn't have accepted anyway. She only drinks champagne."

"Was the defendant's attorney drinking?"

"He had a bourbon."

"He didn't offer her a sip from his bourbon?"

"She doesn't like bourbon. She can't stand the smell."

"Why did the defendant's attorney take her to a bar? Is the defendant having a love affair with her attorney?"

"Objection!" Mike Ribeiro answered.

The jurors saw Ida turn crimson.

"Sustained!"

"No," Betty Trombley said.

"No?" asked Harkin. "They're not in love?"

"Objection."

"Sustained. Mr. Harkin, you watch it."

"The defendant doesn't like bourbon? But she likes wine and champagne?"

Juror #7, Mrs. Jankowski, continued to look at Ida Terhune after the other jurors had stopped.

"She doesn't drink wine."

"Not even Boone's strawberry wine?"

"Does she look like the kind of person who would drink Boone's?" Betty said, turning toward the jury.

Juror #11, Mr. Spinelli, laughed knowingly.

When Ida looked up, Mrs. Jankowski was still staring at her.

"When did you next see the defendant?"

"Not until days later. We didn't know what happened to her. I got home at nine o'clock, and she wasn't there. She'd already had the accident."

"You stayed at the bar with Mr. Ribeiro from four forty-five to nine o'clock?"

Betty hesitated.

"Did either of you accompany the defendant to her car?"

"No."

"Someone at the bar could verify that you were both there until nine?"

"We left around six."

"What did you do from six o'clock to nine?"

"Objection."

"Overruled."

"We went to the Quality Inn."

"To do what?"

"What do you mean, to do what? You mean, to sleep with him? Say it straight, Mr. Harkin."

"All right, Miss Trombley, did you have sexual intercourse with defense counsel?"

"Not exactly. Not on that night."

"Objection."

"Sustained. Mr. Ribeiro, approach the bench."

Betty saw a startled, wounded look cross Ida's face. Does Ida have a crush on Mike? Betty wondered.

Mrs. Jankowski saw the defendant look away as the witness tried to catch her eye.

"Mr. Ribeiro," Judge MacFarland asked, "do you have an ongoing relationship with this witness?"

"Your Honor, I disclosed to this court earlier that she's my investigator on this case. I do not have an ongoing sexual relationship with this witness at this time, no."

"It was just a one-nighter, and not that night, either," Betty explained to the judge, speaking loudly enough for Ida to hear. I was just trying to keep from sleeping with Porter, Betty wanted to tell Ida.

"My God, Mr. Ribeiro," Judge MacFarland said. "Let's finish up here, Mr. Harkin."

Ida felt stunned. She certainly could not say she was surprised that Betty had had a fling with Mike Ribeiro. However, she felt stunned. Once again, Ida noticed Mrs. Jankowski looking at her. Ida thought defensively, I'm not in love with him. I was only about to fall in love with him. She felt herself blushing, nevertheless, and she was embarrassed by the delicacy of her feelings.

The prosecutor continued: "Miss Trombley. You're the defense attorney's investigator?"

"That's right."

"You'd do anything to help him win a case, wouldn't you?"

"He doesn't need help," Betty said.

"No more questions."

"Wait," Betty Trombley said, turning to the jury. "I just want to say Ida Terhune is a wonderful mother to her children—"

"Objection," Harkin said.

"Sustained."

"They're crying themselves to sleep every night for her,

and they need her back," Betty continued, looking at each juror in turn.

"Sustained. Miss Trombley, when I say sustained, I mean it."

"And I just don't see what else matters," Betty concluded.

"One more word, and the judge will hold you in contempt," Harkin said.

Betty folded her arms, looking contemptuous.

"That's for me to decide, Mr. Harkin. Ladies and gentlemen of the jury, you will disregard the witness's outburst. That last testimony is stricken." Judge MacFarland pounded her gavel and called a recess.

Mrs. Bonilla asked the bailiff's permission to use the telephone outside the courtroom, and he accompanied her there while she telephoned her neighbor to assure herself that her stove had been turned off.

Ida chose not to refer to the unsettling part of Betty's testimony in her meeting with Mike Ribeiro when the court recessed. However, for the first time, Ida did not feel content to let him elicit her side of the story from other witnesses. She insisted on testifying, a turn of events he had continued to hope would not develop.

"I have the right to tell what happened," Ida said, perched on the torn leather chair in Mike's office. She insisted with a vehemence that Betty feared was fueled by the revelation of her roll in the hay with Mike. She should have kept her distance and suspected that Ida might fall for someone like Mike. She watched Mike trying to cajole Ida into changing her mind. Betty had never seen Ida really fight before. Ida leaned forward in her chair, nodding as she spoke but then repeating her view.

"It's just not necessary," Mike told her. "We don't have to prove anything. Only Harkin does. And what does he have? A drugged thug and a lying policeman." Mike had explained to Ida countless times the right to silence guaranteed by the Fifth Amendment.

"I was there," Ida said. "I know what happened."

"You were there," Mike answered. "And you have an opinion about what happened. You have one possible viewpoint. You don't know."

"I'm not a crazy person. I know," Ida said. "I and Chicken Dixon are the only people who know. And he's dead. I believe he's left a widow and child behind." Ida held back tears. She felt as if Mike Ribeiro had swindled her somehow. If he had not insisted on refusing payment until the trial was over, she would have demanded her money back. But it was her own fault. Hadn't she seduced him into seducing her? She should have assumed that Betty, who slept with anything that wasn't tied down, would have had sex with him by now. Ida had acted with reckless abandon, and now that her feelings were hurt, it was her just reward. She experienced such deep embarrassment that she felt immobilized, stuck to her chair.

My God, Mike thought. She's going to hang herself.

"You told me," Ida said, "that the decision of whether or not a defendant should testify was ultimately up to the defendant, not his lawyer. And I'm going to testify. If you won't call me, I'll ask the prosecutor to." Ida stared at Mike with a resolute look. Why, Ida thought, he was probably never even interested in me. If it hadn't been for the Napoleon brandy, I never would have thought otherwise.

"So you're just going to throw the Fifth Amendment to the wind, is that it?" Mike asked.

"That's right," Mrs. Terhune told him. "To the wind."

◆ Fifth Amendment Thrown to the Wind

Once Ida took the witness stand, an uncomfortable period followed before the clerk swore her in. First, a bailiff entered the courtroom and whispered a message to the judge about another case. The judge conversed with him while Ida remained on the stand, vulnerable and inspected by the jurors. She sat up straight, smoothed out her pantsuit, and felt herself turn red. What could the jurors think of her?

To be honest, she herself did not know what she thought of Ida Terhune anymore. There had been a time when she possessed a very definite sense of who she was, but this sense had left her after the accident. She felt like a shapeless person, a whirl of thoughts and morals and emotions. There was no center to her, just an emptiness surrounded by confusion. Was this what people felt like when they changed? She did not know. She did not think she had ever changed before.

Before she came to Jersey City, she had felt daunted at the prospect of opening her front door to step into her own yard. Well, she had walked through her front door, and look what had happened: things worse than she could have anticipated, even in her wildest dreams.

"Mrs. Terhune? Mrs. Terhune? You will please raise your right hand," Judge MacFarland said. In a moment of disorientation, Ida held up her left hand. She apologized and held up her right as the clerk asked her to swear to tell the truth. Ida repeated "So help me God" with a solemn expression, trying to show that she took the duty of testifying seriously. When Mike rose and faced her, Ida sat up stuffily in her chair.

Juror #6, Mr. Thiele, felt that there was something overbearing about the defendant, dressed in her cranberry-colored pantsuit and leaning forward rigidly as the clerk swore her in. The earrings Mr. Thiele had admired earlier were gone, and her imperious expression reminded him of his Aunt Alice. Aunt Alice, whom the family called Deutschland, Deutschland uber Alice behind her back. Perhaps Mrs. Terhune, giddy from alcohol intoxication, had acted out her belief that the apparently dangerous Clark Gable Dixon deserved to die. She looked like the kind of woman who might take it upon herself to mete out punishment.

Mike Ribeiro had prepared Ida for her testimony for several hours the evening before, but he had never felt less sure of a witness. He saw now that he probably should not have slept with both his client and his investigator *before* the trial, but looking back on it, what else could he have done? In each case, he had been utterly moved by his feelings of the moment.

"Mrs. Terhune," he began formally, "do you have children?"

"Yes, I have two children."

"Where are they now?"

"They're in school." Ida suddenly needed to see Skeet and Sherry, to check their faces to make sure their eyes were still that dark, identical green. If only she could hear, just for a moment, Sherry's high, raspy singsong and Skeet's drawly, exasperated little voice.

"Mrs. Terhune, are you feeling well? Do you wish to step down?" Mike Ribeiro asked.

Ida waved him on with an impatient look.

"Who's caring for your children at this time?"

"Their uncle came up from Baton Rouge to look after them during the trial."

"What will happen to them if you don't come home?"

The defendant looked as if she would cry.

The prosecutor objected and the court sustained, instructing the jurors that their function was simply to determine guilt or innocence and not to consider sympathy for the defendant or the punishment that could result. But Mike had accomplished his purpose: keeping Ida focused on the consequences of imprisonment to her children and away from her conviction that she was guilty.

Juror #8, Mrs. Bugg, noticed that the defense attorney had removed his wedding band: she clearly remembered seeing a gold ring on his left hand the day before. Why had he removed it? Had his wife left him in the middle of trial? Or was he trying to impress the jury that he was no adulterer, just a lawyer who slept with his witnesses?

"You're a widow?" he recommenced.

"Yes," Ida answered, although she thought that introducing herself in this manner was misleading, because she was not sure she was technically a widow after remarrying. Mike did not ask about her second marriage.

Juror #7, Mrs. Jankowski, felt sorry for Ida Terhune. Mrs. Jankowski recalled the time when she had first been rendered a single woman. Then she remembered how she had felt when she finally found her current husband. The first night they spent together, she was not even sure she remembered where that part of her was anymore. It had been almost four years, and she swore she thought it would be like a rhinoceros trying to enter a pinhole, but then it had felt better than she remembered, and essential, the most essential thing in the world. As if she had been holding her breath all those years. As if she had learned to live without breathing since she had left Tom. Which is exactly what she had done, because a person can live without almost anything if she has to.

"Mrs. Terhune," Mike continued, "had you ever been arrested before the accident?"

"No. I've never even received a ticket for a moving violation."

"Were you drinking on the night of March 23, 1983?"

"Yes. I had two and one-fourth glasses of champagne over dinner."

"And what happened next?"

"I had a disagreement with my best friend, and I left the restaurant. I walked around the downtown area. I got—" Ida stopped herself. Mike had counseled her not to volunteer that she was lost: the jury might interpret this as a sign of drunkenness. This did not seem entirely right to Ida.

"And what happened then?"

"I found my car. I had reported my car stolen, and there it was, right next to a high school. I didn't know whether to call the police or just get in the car, but I decided to drive it away. I was afraid the thief would return and take my New Yorker if I left to telephone for help. Or that he would see me near the car and come over and shoot me. Or at least rob me of my purse. Hadn't he already taken my car?"

"Please keep your responses to your attorney's questions focused and brief," Judge MacFarland instructed.

"Ida, was there a bottle of wine in the front seat?"

"Yes, there was."

"Do you drink wine?"

"No, I don't like the way wine tastes." She recalled, however, the startling aroma of Napoleon brandy and felt that her answer, while it might have been the whole truth a mere month before, no longer was. "However—"

Mike cut her off. "Did you notice if the car's headlights were broken?"

"No, I did not walk to the front of the car before I got in."

"Was it dark outside?"

"It was just turning into evening."

"Did you switch on your headlights?"

"Yes, I turned the knob that turns them on."

"And did the lights come on?"

"At the time I thought so. They had always worked before."

"Now, when you rounded the corner onto Grand Street, did you see anyone in front of your car?"

"No, I did not."

"Can you describe general visibility at that time?"

"I could see very little. You see, the street light on the corner doesn't work, and so when I approached the corner, I saw there was no light hitting the pavement, and that's when I knew the headlights were broken."

"What happened next?"

"Something struck the front of my car. I was jerked forward, and my head hit the steering wheel, and I turned to the right."

"When the police arrived, how were you feeling?"

"I was groggy."

"Had you felt groggy before your head hit the wheel?"

"No."

"Thank you, Mrs. Terhune. That will be all." Mike was relieved. He had sufficiently circumscribed her testimony to prevent her from volunteering any information that might be self-condemnatory.

Now Harkin rose, shaking his head as if he hadn't believed much of the defendant's testimony and doubted any sane juror would, either.

"Mrs. Terhune, did I hear you testify, 'Something struck the front of my car'?" Before Ida could answer, Harkin turned to the jury and said, "I once read a funny little list of car insurance claims printed up in the local paper, sent in by a claims adjuster. One of them read, 'I was just driving along, and suddenly a telephone pole appeared from nowhere and ran into my truck!' "

Mr. Clark, the foreman, laughed.

Now Harkin spun around to the defendant, who appeared predictably unsettled after being the butt of a joke. "So, about this drinking?" the prosecutor began.

Harkin liked to defuse the defendant's testimony in any drunk-driving case by asking whether he was drunk. When the defendant said he was not drunk, Harkin would then ask, "So you're familiar with what it feels like to be drunk?" If the defendant answered yes, Harkin would imply the defendant was accustomed to drinking in excess. If the defendant said no, Harkin would say, "So you like to insist you've never been drunk?"

"Mrs. Terhune," the prosecutor began, "you were drinking on that fatal night?"

"Yes, I had had two and one-fourth glasses of champagne."

"And were you drunk?"

Ida did not answer immediately but tried to recall what Mike Ribeiro had told her. He had instructed her to say that she had been drinking but she did not believe she was "intoxicated" in a legal sense; that she understood the phrase "under the influence" and that she categorically had not been under the influence. He had told her that when Harkin asked whether she had practiced her answers with her attorney, she should answer: "My lawyer and I discussed my testimony, and he counseled me to tell the truth."

The prosecutor's ill-intentioned smile caused Ida to remember Harlan Pinkerton, whom she had scarcely thought about in weeks. Harlan's presence suddenly seemed palpable, as if he stood looking critically over her shoulder while she typed up one of his real estate documents. "You think you're so high and mighty and perfect," he assessed her.

"Yes," Ida said. "I believe I must have been."

Before her answer had fully registered, Harkin rushed on: "So you're quite familiar with what it feels like to be drunk?"

"No, I am not very familiar with what it feels like to be drunk," Ida answered. "I believe I had never really been drunk as an adult, before that night. Afterward—"

"You're asserting that you were intoxicated?" Harkin asked, realizing his mistake.

"Asked and answered," Mike Ribeiro objected.

"Sustained," Judge MacFarland ruled.

Harkin regrouped. "What makes you think you were drunk?"

"Well, for one thing, before that evening, I had never committed a moving violation. But that night, I committed two. I drove the wrong way down a one-way street and—"

"Objection, Your Honor," Mike Ribeiro said, exasperated.

"The prosecutor is exploring an area I did not address on my direct."

"I'm afraid the defendant opened the door here, Mr. Ribeiro," Judge MacFarland said. "You may continue," she told Ida.

"I also ran a stop sign from behind," Ida confessed. "Two other vehicles honked at me. I remember this distinctly, because I'd never been honked at before in my entire lifetime."

The thing that I feared most has happened, Mike Ribeiro thought, and in a form far worse than I could have imagined. She has single-handedly provided all the evidence the prosecutor needs in order to convict her.

Harkin turned to the judge and then to the jury, with a weary smile indicating that the jury might as well return their guilty verdict there and then: his work was over.

Juror #10, Mr. Corso, looked at Juror #5, Mrs. Haskel, and saw her purse her lips in reprobation as she examined Ida Terhune. At that moment, Mr. Corso decided that he was deeply impressed by the fact that Ida Terhune had seen the smallest mistake as evidencing her drunkenness. She must truly be a stupendous driver. For that reason alone, she deserved to stay on the road. Obviously, she was simply unlucky. Mr. Corso had driven drunk quite a few times in his life and had never been caught. He found it unfair that on the one occasion she had driven drunk, Ida Terhune had had the misfortune to kill someone.

"Mrs. Terhune," Harkin said. "I just have one more question. Is there anything else you'd like to say?"

"Oh, yes," said Ida. Do I finally get to speak in my own words? Ida thought with gratitude. "What I'd like to say is that I have heard the testimony of all the witnesses, and there is no doubt in my mind that I was at fault. However, I wish to mention that I don't think the police officer or the chauffeur were entirely truthful."

The prosecutor and the defense attorney objected at the same time.

"Sustained, sustained," Judge MacFarland said. She rustled her papers irritably. It was a terrific challenge at times to be one of the few competent judges serving on the Jersey City judiciary. Could it make a difference, when the only purported eyewitness drugged himself, the police falsified evidence, the prosecutor and the defense attorney both had possible conflicts of interest, and the defendant tried to prove the state's case?

"Your Honor," the defense attorney said, "I'd like to declare my client a hostile witness."

"Excuse me?" Judge MacFarland replied.

"I'd like to declare Mrs. Terhune a hostile witness against herself," Mike continued.

"Mr. Ribeiro, let's save the melodrama for 'Perry Mason.' I will allow you some leeway in leading your witness on redirect, but I hardly feel such an extraordinary measure is necessary. In fact, it might be unprecedented in the history of the law."

Mike rose and cast Ida a piercing, angry look that discomfited her and reminded her of Roy Daigle.

"You're a pretty judgmental woman, aren't you, Ida?" he asked her.

"I—" Ida answered.

"I mean, if you were sitting over there"—he gestured toward the jury box—"you'd convict yourself without even hearing the evidence, wouldn't you? You'd probably revel in it. Why, you'd demand the death penalty."

Until that moment, it had never occurred to Ida that she might be executed.

"You're really out to punish Ida Terhune, aren't you? Guilty until proven innocent, right?"

"Objection."

"Sustained. Argumentative. You don't have to answer that, Mrs. Terhune." Judge MacFarland saw the defendant crumbling. The judge felt on edge: she was profoundly aware of the cruelty of cross-examination, its potential for so subverting the confidence of some witnesses that they lost faith in the validity of their own perceptions.

"The truth is, Ida, you just can't bear the idea that a man has died and there's no one to blame for it, can you? You'd like someone to pay, even if it has to be you."

"Sustained," Judge MacFarland said, although Harkin had not objected.

"The truth is, Ida, you don't really remember drinking two glasses of champagne, do you?"

"What?" Ida answered.

"Can you tell me what kind of champagne it was?"

"No."

"No?" Mike barked. "No?" Ida shrank back. "You have no recollection whatsoever? Was it Wild Duck? Could it have been Budweiser?"

"Perhaps it was Budweiser," Ida answered.

Several jurors laughed loudly. Others giggled or chuckled or guffawed. Ida felt deeply humiliated. What had she said wrong?

"What about the color? Was it pink champagne?"

"I don't remember," Ida said meekly.

"You don't remember?" Mr. Ribeiro raised his voice. "You don't remember what kind of champagne you were drinking or even what color it was, but you remember you drank"—he pronounced the end of his question in a parodic squeaky female voice—"*two and one-fourth glasses?*"

Ida did not answer.

"You heard Betty Trombley testify that she drank over two glasses?"

Ida nodded.

"What if I told you the bartender is prepared to come here to court to say that those bottles only hold three glasses?" Mike asked, although he had never talked to any bartender. "That he is prepared to take off from his job to sit right there where you're sitting, and to testify to the whole world that you couldn't possibly have had more than one glass?"

Ida looked bewildered. "I couldn't have?"

"Ida, why would you perjure yourself?" Mike leaned forward so that his face was barely six inches from hers, and she felt cowed. He looked like a troll, with his unruly, warthoggish hair.

Ida found herself inventing facts to protect herself, to shield the truth from him. "I thought all champagne bottles held four glasses," Ida said, although she had never believed this. She had no idea whether champagne bottles were uniform in size or differed.

Mike made an impatient, dismissive gesture. "Perhaps you don't remember how much you drank. Given that your recollection is less than flawless, do you concede it's possible, Ida, that you had only one glass?" He backed away, and Ida breathed deeply.

"Yes, it might perhaps be possible."

Betty Trombley felt an unnameable sensation cloak her. She sat still, waiting to identify it. Her uneasiness turned into a subtle horror. How had Mike undermined Ida Terhune? Betty thought: Mike really could be dangerous. I'm glad I got between them. Ida could never hold her own against a man who could do that. She needs someone gentle, like Dewey. Or Porter.

Ida sat hunched forward, her shoulders drawn together. She looked confused and exhausted.

Mike returned to the defense table, and his demeanor became affable and gentle. He shuffled some papers absently and said, "Yes, Ida, maybe you were too hard on yourself."

Ida felt grateful that Mike had returned to the table and lowered his voice.

"Ida, how did you feel when you found your stolen car?"

"I was very happy." Her voice sounded almost girlish with relief.

"Were you nervous about driving the car away?"

"I was a little flustered, yes."

"Is it possible that in your state of excitement, you were so flustered it affected your driving in the first few minutes, when you drove the wrong way down the street?"

"Yes," Ida conceded.

She realized then that Mike had rescued her. She thought: he's saved me from the clutches of Mrs. Terhune. The oddness of the thought made her smile, inappropriately. The juror dressed in the beige pantsuit looked at her disapprovingly.

"Ida, before the accident, had you ever been drunk in your entire adult life?"

"Before? Never as an adult. However, once, when I was

fourteen," she added, taking Mike off guard, "I and my best friend, Betty Trombley, each consumed three large tumblers of my father's bourbon, and we became quite drunk. I believe I came near death. I've never been able to stand the smell of bourbon since. And I've never ever gotten tipsy since then, until—"

"How do you know you were drunk that time when you were fourteen?"

"I lost consciousness. My grandmother found me passed out on the living room floor."

Juror #11, Mr. Spinelli, hooted. Judge MacFarland looked at him pointedly.

The image of Ida Terhune passed out on Mike's bed at the Quality Inn flashed before his eyes. So she hadn't lost consciousness from the force of his passion! It had been the Napoleon brandy. She must have felt out of sorts and nervous after her release from prison and treated herself to too much cognac. Or perhaps she had just wanted to celebrate her release. Oh, well. He had thought he was such a Casanova. He shook his head and laughed.

"I see no need to laugh so boisterously, Mr. Ribeiro," Judge MacFarland said.

"So, Mrs. Terhune," Mike continued, "do you think it would be fair to say that your experience in assessing whether or not you're drunk is somewhat limited?"

"Yes, that would be fair," Ida answered.

Mike sat down, thinking: Well, I've discredited my own client. Once again, his occupation had required his personal martyrdom for the sake of a client: his devilish conduct had been the only means of undoing the harm Ida had done herself.

On redirect, Mr. Harkin smiled at Ida and said, "Mrs. Terhune, you testified that before that night you had never committed a traffic violation. Do you consider yourself a careful driver?"

"Yes. I'm a very good driver. Ten months ago, I safely steered my car through a hurricane."

"Through a hurricane? Weren't you nervous in that hurricane? Did it made you feel flustered?"

"Oh, yes. I was terrified. My children were in the car. The wind whisked our trailer away."

"But you didn't run into anything then. You didn't run over anybody then, did you?"

"No," Ida answered.

"Ah," said Harkin, winking at Juror #10, Mr. Corso. "No more questions."

Mike decided that he should call Wilma Tutwiler as a witness, after all.

The following morning, Mrs. Tutwiler, her gray braids coiled around her ears like ram's horns, took the stand. She could not remember when she had last traveled as far from Grand Street as the courthouse. Her journey imbued her with a sense of mission, and she intended to enjoy fully the drama of her surroundings. She knew a few facts that would add a little life to the trial.

She pronounced her name in her surprisingly deep voice. It echoed off the back of the courtroom and settled in the alcove behind the jury box.

"Mrs. Tutwiler," Mike Ribeiro began, "did you see the accident that occurred on March twenty-third?"

"Yes, I did. I saw every bit of it."

Harkin, who had been pouring himself a glass of water from a pitcher and ignoring the witness, looked up suddenly. Mrs. Bugg thought she detected a fleeting expression of mild outrage before the prosecutor's poker face resettled into its accustomed expression of indifference.

"Can you relate what you saw?"

Mrs. Tutwiler paused, as if summoning up a memory of the event. In fact, she had just recognized Juror #2 as the granddaughter of Sergeant Bonaparte, notorious in his day for making out-of-towners pay cash for traffic tickets. Mrs. Tutwiler cleared her throat and said, "I was going to buy groceries. As I was heading for the corner store, I stopped to look across the street, where Chicken Dixon was. I saw him crouched behind his black van."

"Why did you stop?"

"I figured he was up to no good."

"Objection."

"It's pertinent, Your Honor," Mike Ribeiro said. "I mean to show that this witness had good reason to be watching Chicken carefully at the moment of the accident."

"Proceed."

Mrs. Tutwiler also recognized the foreman, Mr. Clark, as the man who had carried on affairs with two different women in a Bright Street building and whose goings-on had caused quite a stir among neighbors, since neither of the women knew about the other. Mr. Clark apparently came to one woman's apartment for a late dinner and spent the evening while her husband worked the late shift at his job. Early in the morning, before the husband returned, Mr. Clark would slip downstairs to the second woman's apartment, where she would serve him breakfast, her husband having departed for his work. In this way, Mrs. Tutwiler mused, most of Mr. Clark's meals were provided for.

"Mrs. Tutwiler?"

"I was afraid," she resumed, "that Chicken might have come to poison the children's dog, so I crossed the street and crept up behind him, stopping about ten feet away. Mrs. Terhune's boy has this little dog, and about a month before, Chicken had threatened the children with a crowbar—"

"Objection!" Harkin shouted.

"Mr. Ribeiro, you'd better be heading somewhere good with this," Judge MacFarland said.

"And shortly after that, he threw a pickax at us, so the dog bit him. I thought Chicken had come back to our street to kill the dog. He was his father's henchman. His father is our landlord. So I crossed the street to watch Chicken carefully. I got up right behind the van."

"Did Chicken notice you?"

"Yes, he did. He shut the van door so that I wouldn't see what he had in there, but by then it was too late."

"So that you wouldn't see the poison?"

"So that I wouldn't see the kerosene. He had cans and cans of kerosene in the van."

"Kerosene."

"Yes. You see, his father is what you would call a slumlord, and it wouldn't have been the first time one of his properties went up in smoke."

"Objection, Your Honor. This witness has no basis for such a farfetched conclusion!"

"Sustained. The jury is instructed to completely disregard the witness's last statements. Mr. Ribeiro, behave!"

"What did Chicken do next, Mrs. Tutwiler?"

"He slammed the door and walked right into the middle of the road."

"And then what happened?"

"A car hit him."

"How was that car driving?"

"At an ordinary speed. Slower than most cars that come down Grand Street."

"Do you think that anyone driving at that slow speed could have avoided hitting Chicken?"

"No. It would have been impossible. He just jaywalked into traffic. They say, you know, that he was on drugs," Mrs. Tutwiler commented. "I would also like to add that one of our old tenants, Henry Purdy, knows the man who stole Ida Terhune's car, and that man left a bottle of wine in the front seat and shorted the car's headlights when he hot-wired the car."

"Objection. Hearsay!" Harkin said angrily.

"Sustained. The jury will absolutely disregard that statement as well."

"Thank you, Mrs. Tutwiler, for your invaluable insights," Mike said, returning to the defense table.

Wilma Tutwiler had added the last part herself, on an impulse. It was a very good explanation for why the lights had not worked and for the presence of the wine bottle in Ida's car: Wilma had heard two Grand Street tenants discussing the possibility. It was the least she could do for the children.

Harkin had no doubt that Mrs. Tutwiler had invented every word of her testimony. He had watched witnesses lie enough in his life, often at his own behest, that he had developed an instinct for detecting lies. He also did not believe that anyone was a good enough liar to withstand thorough cross-examination.

Harkin looked Mrs. Tutwiler directly in the eye. She gazed back at him, unperturbed. Everyone on the block knew that Ida Terhune may have saved the Grand Street tenants from being burned in their beds. As to whether or not Ida Terhune had driven carelessly, or Chicken had placed himself in her path, Mrs. Tutwiler didn't really care. There was a greater truth overriding the smaller ones, and that was the one she was there to defend.

"Mrs. Tutwiler, you're a pretty old woman, aren't you?"

"You think I'm pretty?" Mrs. Tutwiler said, her lips parting in garish coquetry under her ram's horns.

"Do you see well?"

Mrs. Tutwiler thought she recognized the pregnant juror also, but she could not place her.

"Mrs. Tutwiler? Did you understand the question?"

"Of course I understood. I see perfectly well. I have hawk eyes."

"You said earlier that you were on your way to the corner store that evening?"

Now she remembered the juror. She was the schoolteacher who had scandalized the board of education by showing her eighth graders how to use condoms. She had rolled several over the school broom's handle and was rumored to have instructed, "Leave plenty of room at the tip." She had promptly lost her job, but she had caused quite a stir, telling *Jersey Journal* reporters that she had just wanted, for once, to graduate her entire group of eighth-grade girls. Well, look at her now. She must have left the condoms behind with the broom.

"Mrs. Tutwiler?" Harkin asked, turning to the jury and winking at Juror #10, Mr. Corso, as if to convey a private joke about the witness's evident senility.

"Restate the question," Judge MacFarland said.

Mrs. Tutwiler said, repeating the prosecutor's question before he could, "You asked if I testified earlier that I was heading to the corner store. That's exactly what I said. Don't you remember?"

"What were you going to buy?"

"I was on my way to buy pork and beans."

"You often bought pork and beans at the store?"

"Every Friday."

Harkin asked, although he had no reason to know what Dixon kept in stock, "What would you say if I told you that Rupert Dixon's store didn't sell pork and beans?"

"I wouldn't know about that. I wasn't going to his store. I said I was going to *the* store."

"Then why did you tell the jury that you were heading for his store when the accident occurred?"

"Of course I was heading for it. It's at the corner. I have to pass his store in order to get to the Shop-Rite on Grove Street. I do my shopping there, because Rupert Dixon charges too much and because I don't like the way he treats the people in his buildings. I make a point of never shopping at his store. If you ask me," Mrs. Tutwiler concluded, "I think we were pretty lucky Chicken got stopped that night. I may be old, but I'm not ready to be fried to a crisp like a piece of bacon."

"Objection," Harkin said. "And that's enough from this witness."

"Sustained and stricken," Judge MacFarland responded.

Juror #4, Mrs. Sparks, felt her unborn daughter awaken and turn a somersault inside her. This world's a rough place, girl, Mrs. Sparks thought. You better be tougher than this Mrs. Terhune lady. You better come out ready to fight.

Summations and Charge

During his summation, Mike carefully reviewed the prosecutor's case, highlighting its weaknesses. He avoided mentioning Ida's testimony, as if it had never been spoken.

F. X. Harkin delivered the most intemperate summation Mike Ribeiro had heard in his fifteen years of practice. During Harkin's speech to the jury, Mike made twenty-seven objections, twenty-six of which the judge sustained. Eventually, he desisted, fearing the jurors might believe that he was trying to prevent them from listening to the other side of the case.

The jury ignored his objections and the judge's remonstrances. The grounds for the objections seemed remote and legalistic: the prosecutor was straying outside the four corners of the evidence, shifting the burden of proof to the defendant, vouching for the credibility of his police witness, expressing his personal opinion, denigrating the defendant and ridiculing her attorney, making inflammatory arguments, and mistranslating Latin. The jurors just wished the judge and the defense attorney would stop interrupting so that they could hear.

"Ladies and gentlemen of the jury," Harkin began, "it's my job as the prosecutor to summarize all the evidence the state has assembled, in order to help you arrive at the proper verdict. But I don't think in this trial I have to bother. Instead, I'd like to summarize the defense case, for its entertainment value.

"The defendant wants you to believe that she left a restaurant immediately after consuming more alcohol than she claims she's ever drunk at one sitting as an adult, but that she was not drunk. She wants you to believe that she just happened upon her own stolen car, and that there just happened to be an opened wine bottle in there, but that she did not drink any of the wine. She wants you to believe that she went the wrong way down a one-way street and ran a stop sign and drove for several blocks without her lights on, but that she was not drunk. She wants you to believe that Officer Starkweather got up there on the witness stand and for no apparent reason lied through his teeth when he said she was reeling and staggering and reeking of alcohol and cursing at him. She wants you to believe that the victim, who had managed to live a good thirty years up until then, just strolled in front of her car. She must think you're pretty stupid.

"'I wasn't drunk,' she says. 'I was just flustered.'"

Ida shifted uncomfortably, thinking: I never said that!

"She wants you to believe that this vicious, senseless crime could have been committed by any one of you, this wasteful crime, resulting from the selfishness of a drunk who puts her own love of inebriation above human life. She'd even suggest that, well, maybe it was her fault, but Clark Gable Dixon was little better than an animal—a Chicken—wasn't really worth keeping alive. He poisoned dogs. He was his father's toady. He used cocaine. She even suggested he was an arsonist. Kill him before he kills us!

Maybe those were her very thoughts as she sat behind the wheel.

"You know better than to think any human being deserves to die, deserves to be mown down by a drunk. That's why you cry out with righteousness. Poor you: you've had to stand there and listen to this.

"I guess her smart lawyer is looking for one juror who will run amok and say, 'I believe her! I believe this woman!' Well, this jury was chosen very carefully. There isn't one bad egg on this jury."

Harkin paused and winked at Juror #10, Mr. Corso.

"Imagine how Clark Gable Dixon felt at the moment the car ran into him. He thought of his wife. His infant son. He felt terrible pain. Is he an animal? Did he deserve to feel that pain? Did he deserve to be cut down in the flower of youth?

"Now I'll tell you what really bothered me. The way the defendant wants us to think Officer Starkweather was a liar. Maybe she described him to herself using even worse language. She swears she never swears. So, 'That dirty rotten cop,' she says. 'He'd risk his career to fabricate evidence.' Ladies and gentlemen, Officer Starkweather's just doing his job. He isn't coming here asking you for a promotion and a medal. You're not going to make him police chief. He's just doing his job. He's evenhanded. He's fair. If there's a hero in this case, it's him.

"You hear the defense attorney objecting. Well, maybe he's right to object, but I can't help myself. I'm boiling with indignation. When I feel strongly about something, I speak my mind.

"Should we be scared to walk the streets? I'm not sure I want to live in this town if the law says: sure, go ahead, get in a car in pitch darkness, leave the lights off, run all the stop signs you want to, drive the wrong way down the street, tie a few on. Kill anyone you don't like.

"We don't know much about this defendant, ladies and gentlemen. She's from another state, somewhere way down South. Maybe someplace where everyone drives drunk and no one cares. They just teach their children to jump out of the way when a car heads for them. Maybe she's run into someone before, and how would we ever know it? Have we been following her around behind the wheel all her life? Apparently, she'd have you believe anything. She's driven through hurricanes." Harkin guffawed.

"Don't let her get away with this. Don't let her. Don't let her twist the truth and tell you that police who stop drunk drivers are the bad guys. Don't let her smart lawyer fool you out of using your common sense. Turn over every egg carefully. Look at the facts.

"What is a verdict? Verdict is from the Latin word *veritatum,* 'very truthful.' You tell the world what the truth is. We're counting on you.

"Guilty, guilty, guilty, guilty, guilty!"

When Harkin had finished, Mike rose and said, "I'd like to make a motion for a mistrial, based on Mr. Harkin's outrageous prosecutorial misconduct during summation."

"I will hold my decision on your motion in reserve until the verdict," Judge MacFarland answered. "However, some curative instruction is in order. Ladies and gentlemen of the jury, the prosecutor's summation is not evidence. When you go into the jury room, I expect you to base your deliberations on the testimony of the witnesses and the defense and state's exhibits. I expect you to ignore any statement Mr. Harkin made that was followed by a sustained objection and stricken from the record."

But the jury could hardly remember which of the prosecutor's statements had not been stricken and which had. His speech had been moving and uplifting. The jurors felt swayed, exhilarated by the thought of Ida Terhune's guilt, and might well have convicted her within a matter of minutes, had they been released at that moment for their deliberations.

However, following summations, something happened that the jury had not anticipated. Every juror had watched courtroom dramas on television, but even the best of those had failed to reveal that every criminal trial terminates in a lengthy and laborious charge by the judge on the law applicable to the case. Judge MacFarland charged the jury for a full ninety minutes. She told them about the role of the judge and the jury, the assessment of witness credibility, interested witnesses, the value of the grand jury's indictment, the presumption of innocence, and the prosecutor's burden of proof and reasonable doubt. She defined every element of the crimes charged, and then she summarized her definitions. She explained legal principles of causation. She instructed the jurors that the victim's negligence, if any, was not a defense to the crimes at issue, but that the jury could consider it in determining whether the defendant had caused the victim's death. She instructed them how to assess the prosecution's failure to call a witness. She charged the jury on circumstantial evidence and expert testimony.

Even the most attentive of the jurors grew impatient after half an hour of this. None of the jurors heard the full charge. The foreman, Mr. Clark, listened carefully to the descriptions of the offenses' elements but then fell in and out of attentiveness through the rest of the charge. Juror #7, Mrs. Jankowski, whose mind had been wandering through much of the trial, did not hear any of the charge. For all the jurors, by the end of the judge's legal instructions, the invigorating effects of the prosecutor's speech had dissipated. The law, tedious and weighty and dull, had filled the jurors' ears and entered their hearts and left them all feeling restless.

◆ Deliberations and Verdict

Mr. Clark, the foreman, seated himself at the head of the table in the jury room, beaming at the jurors with the perfect smile of a denture wearer, his toupee a toffee brown several shades darker than his graying temples. At his right hand sat Mrs. Haskel, her pocketbook in her lap, a silver scarf draped around her neck and weighted in place with a bulky silver pin. Beside her sat Mr. Ortiz, who had a strong masculine odor that caused Mrs. Haskel to purse her lips. Mr. Ortiz emptied his left pocket and deposited a trombone's mouthpiece and a pile of linty peppermints on the table. Beside him, Mr. Thiele, the eyeglass repairman, cleaned his spectacles with a diaphanous white cloth.

Mr. Corso had established himself across from Mrs. Haskel, his bushy hair partially smoothed down, one bushy eyebrow rising above the left rim of his glasses, which rested crookedly on his nose. Mrs. Bonaparte pulled up a chair next to him, her perfume, Enchantress, causing Mrs. Sparks to choose the chair farthest from her, for fear that the fumes might injure her unborn daughter. Mrs. Sparks had designed her own maternity dress and matching hat from orange-striped kente cloth; she refused to wear the ridiculous matronly clothes stores pushed off on pregnant women. Mrs. Bonilla, sitting down beside her, complimented the outfit immediately, wishing she had it in her to costume herself with such haughtiness. Her smoky lavender secretary's dress, ornamented with a single gold cross, made her feel self-contained and obedient. Often she felt that the personalities of her clothes overshadowed and controlled her own personality. Even her favorite gold pin seemed diminished by Mr. Edgar's large brown leather cross, suspended on a piece of black rawhide from his neck.

Mr. Edgar seated himself at the end of the table opposite the foreman. Dressed in black, Mr. Edgar also wore a round pin with a black-and-white photograph of Malcolm X mounted under plastic. His cross had snagged on the pin and appeared to be wrestling with it. Mrs. Bugg thought the photograph must be of one of Mr. Edgar's children and found it touching. Mrs. Bugg planned to visit her grandchildren that evening; she had dressed cheerily in a bright yolk-yellow-and-white polka-dot dress, white straw hat, and matching white wicker purse that contrasted remarkably with Mrs. Jankowski's large patent-leather handbag, which lay bulging and half open before her. Mrs. Jankowski looked at herself in her compact and smoothed a fine peach-colored dust over the strawberry mark on her chin. Mr. Spinelli, his Grateful Dead T-shirt's rainbow tie dyes offending Mrs. Haskel's sense of decorum, admired Mrs. Jankowski's profile.

Mr. Clark clacked his dentures and began. "Well, I don't think this will take more than an hour or so. Is there anything to discuss, or should I just take a vote now?"

"Wait—I have to say I don't really understand all this," said Mrs. Bonilla. "Do they mean that you can be convicted of manslaughter just because you get in a car accident? There but for the grace of God go I."

"What do you mean, 'there but for the grace of God'?" Mrs. Haskel asked before Mr. Clark could respond. "Are you in the habit of driving drunk?"

"She was hardly drunk," Mr. Spinelli said. "She'd hardly had anything to drink." He thought of the army jeep with its parking lights glittering lakeward. Now, that was drunk. Beautiful, beautiful drunk.

"The police officer testified she was intoxicated," Mrs. Haskel insisted.

"Ha!" Mr. Corso said enigmatically, staring directly at Mrs. Haskel.

"I remember driving once at night with my lights off," said Mrs. Bonilla. "I'd hate to think I might have gone to prison just for running into somebody. I'd hate to imagine myself up there on that witness stand. Poor Mrs. Terhune."

"That's absolutely true," said Mr. Edgar in a soft voice.

Mrs. Bonilla looked at him gratefully. "I'd just hate it," she said.

The foreman passed the exhibits to the left and indicated that they should circulate around the table: there were several medical records, the map of the crime scene, and an autopsy report.

"The defendant is a terrible sourpuss," Mr. Thiele offered.

"She belongs in jail," Mrs. Haskel affirmed.

"Ha!" Mr. Corso repeated. "That's funny."

"Just what do you mean, Mr. Corso?" Mrs. Haskel asked.

"*You* belong in jail, Mrs. Haskel," Mr. Corso answered with a leer.

"Lay off, Corso," the foreman, Mr. Clark, intervened. "So we're going to acquit her, right? It seems to me she did everyone a service by knocking off that Chicken guy."

Mrs. Sparks, who was examining the exhibits, exclaimed, "He was going to kill the children's dog!"

Mr. Ortiz responded with a growling sound. Mrs. Bonilla drew back, unsure how to interpret the growl.

"As far as I'm concerned," Mrs. Sparks said, "a man who would poison a dog has sunk as low as a person can sink."

"He went at the children with a crowbar," Mr. Corso said. "I'd say that's lower."

"The victim is not on trial here," said Mrs. Haskel.

"How do you know he went at the children with a crowbar?" Mrs. Jankowski asked.

"The old lady said it. Don't you remember?" Mrs. Bugg answered.

"My mind must have been wandering," Mrs. Jankowski confessed.

"We need to turn over every egg carefully," Mrs. Bugg asserted.

"All right, girlies," Mr. Clark said, clacking his dentures. "I'm the foreman. Let's talk in an orderly manner."

"Don't call us girlies," said Mrs. Sparks. "You may address me as Ms. Sparks."

"And my name is Ms. Bonaparte. That's M-i-z-z, Ms."

"And none of this 'Mister' stuff for me. My name's Spinelli. Just plain Spinelli."

"The defendant had a bottle of wine in her car. She had already drunk half of it," Mrs. Haskel asserted.

"No way," said Spinelli. "You heard the old lady say it belonged to the guy who blew the fuse to the headlights when he hot-wired her car."

"That old woman was mentally deficient," said Mrs. Haskel.

"Ya ya," Mr. Corso said.

"She seemed like a sweet old lady to me," said Mrs. Bonilla.

"I fully agree," Mr. Edgar followed. Again Mrs. Bonilla smiled at him gratefully.

"The police officer was an idiot," said Ms. Bonaparte. "He lied his little head off."

"Cops!" Mr. Ortiz exclaimed.

"And that chauffeur was lying too. What a thug!" Ms. Bonaparte said. "He probably killed someone yesterday."

"Probably cut off someone's head and threw it in a vat of acid in Bayonne," said Mr. Ortiz.

There was a silence while the jurors considered Mr. Ortiz.

"I just can't see sending that lady to jail," Mr. Edgar offered. "What kind of sentence you think the prosecutor wants to give her?"

"That poor prosecutor has terrible skin," Mrs. Jankowski said. "He must have had a tragic time as a teenager."

"Maybe that's why he's such an asshole!" Mr. Ortiz said, a little too loudly.

"It's the nature of the job. Imagine making your living punishing people," Mr. Thiele observed.

"What about the other guy, the defendant's lawyer?" Mr. Clark asked. "A real snake oil salesman."

Mr. Thiele told Mr. Corso, "I could fix that for you." Mr. Thiele pulled out a small black leather case from his shirt pocket. He opened the case and withdrew two minuscule screws, a miniature screwdriver, and a clear plastic nose-piece.

"My glasses?" asked Mr. Corso. He took off his glasses, revealing both bushy eyebrows under his bushy hair.

The jurors watched as Mr. Thiele attached a new nose-piece to Mr. Corso's tortoiseshell rims. Mr. Thiele's own spectacles were two lozenges of glass, frameless, connected by a bright wire gossamer.

"You do this for a living?" Mr. Corso asked.

"Just like Spinoza," said Mr. Thiele.

"Spinoza?" asked Spinelli.

"A philosopher," said Mr. Thiele. "He ground lenses for a living." He added dramatically, "He died from breathing in too much lens dust." Mr. Thiele replaced his small tools in their small case and handed Mr. Corso his glasses.

"Great!" said Mr. Corso, craning his neck back and forth to see how well his glasses stayed on his nose.

"Hey, knock knock," the foreman, Mr. Clark, said. "Knock knock."

"Who's there?" asked Mrs. Bonilla agreeably.

"Spinoza."

"Spinoza who?"

"Spinoza five minutes we've been repairing Mr. Corso's glasses. Let's get back to deliberations."

Mr. Thiele chuckled. Mr. Clark clacked his dentures and smiled proudly at his joke.

"So what kind of sentence you think she'd get?" Mr. Edgar repeated.

"The judge clearly instructed that we were not to consider punishment," Mrs. Haskel asserted. "It is not our concern. We're just supposed to decide whether or not Mrs. Terhune's guilty, so that the judge can punish her."

"Oh, I think it is very much our concern," Mr. Corso said. "I'm not going to have ruining that woman's life on my conscience. You all do whatever you want," said Mr. Corso. "I'm not convicting her. My vote's decided."

"You can't do that!" Mrs. Haskel said.

"Let's all try to be open-minded as long as we can about this," Mr. Clark interceded.

"Well, then," said Mrs. Haskel, "*my* vote is cast too. And I'm not acquitting."

Ms. Sparks rested her head on the table. "All I want is to find a nice, quiet toilet where I can vomit."

"You poor honey," said Mrs. Bonilla. "I have a friend in her third trimester, who keeps saying, "It's getting so there's not enough room in here for the both of us. One of us has got to go, and it ain't going to be me."

"When I had my last baby," said Ms. Bonaparte, "I swore that next time I wouldn't enter a delivery room without a gun. You have to protect yourself against those doctors! The things they put you through, jabbing you with needles and cutting you up. You defend yourself!" she exhorted Ms. Sparks.

Mrs. Jankowski volunteered, "This friend of mine had to have this procedure done. Curettage, it was called. Where the doctor stitches your cervix closed so that the baby doesn't fall out."

"Just don't ever let them trick you into one of those amnios," Ms. Sparks answered, sitting up straight but then hunching over the table again. "It's the closest thing you can get to a rabies shot without actually being bitten by a mad dog. They jab this two-foot needle into you and suck your juices out. Of course, they tell you that it doesn't hurt. 'Only a pinprick,' they say. Then when you're lying there, feeling like they've run you through with a bayonet—"

"My friend who got the curettage," Mrs. Jankowski resumed, "said they stuck her in her spine and turned up the table she was lying on, so her feet were up in the air, so that the doctors could just peer down into her while they were sewing her closed. And meanwhile, she could feel the painkiller creeping down her spine, down her stomach, down her waist—what was left of it—down her chest, pushing all of the feeling out of her. And all that time, she was so afraid she might let loose without even knowing it and, you know, cut a—"

Mr. Thiele laughed.

Mrs. Haskel pretended not to listen but looked pointedly at the foreman, Mr. Clark.

"All right," said Mr. Clark. "We should be able to get out of here in an hour or less. This hardly looks like a complicated case. If these vagino-Americans here could just focus on the matter at hand."

All of the women jurors turned toward Mr. Clark. Ms. Bonaparte fastened on him a look of pure hatred. Mrs. Bonilla blushed.

"The way I see it," said Mr. Thiele, "maybe she's a sourpuss, but she's a pretty careful driver. I can't see condemning her. So she had some champagne. So what?"

"You said it," Spinelli seconded.

"Excuse me," said Mrs. Bugg. "I don't think that police officer was telling the truth. How could someone get so drunk from a little champagne that she had bloodshot eyes and staggered?"

"All she had was two glasses," said Mrs. Bonilla.

"Two and one-fourth," Mrs. Bugg answered. "Or perhaps it was one or less."

"That defense attorney never talked to any bartender about a champagne bottle holding three glasses," Mr. Clark said. "What a snake oil salesman." The foreman added, "There's a great game on tonight. I hope we can progress through this speedily so that we can get home in time to see it."

"Why should we take the defendant's word for it?" asked Mrs. Haskel. "For all we know, she'd had ten whiskeys."

"Yeah, sure," said Mr. Corso. "Maybe she took heroin too."

"She looks like she could use a few whiskeys," said Mr. Thiele.

"You said it," Spinelli seconded.

"That police officer was full of shit," said Mr. Ortiz, again talking too loudly.

"My brother the police officer," Ms. Bonaparte offered, "told me he always testified exactly the same way in all drunk-driving cases." Everyone turned toward her. Sensing she'd been recognized as an authority, Ms. Bonaparte continued. "He always says the defendant was staggering, his speech was slurred, his eyes were bloodshot and watery, he cursed at me, that sort of thing. It's standard police bullshit. I mean, if that officer had testified that the defendant had *fallen out of her car, singing to herself,* say, I might have believed him. If he'd said something original. But he just used the ole boilerplate."

"What's boilerplate? I'm afraid I missed that."

"Pay attention, Mrs. Jankowski," the foreman, Mr. Clark, said.

"The defendant doesn't look the type to curse at a police officer, that's for sure," said Mr. Thiele.

"You said it," Spinelli agreed.

"I once cursed at a police officer," said Mr. Ortiz.

"So is she guilty or isn't she?" Mr. Clark urged. "Let's see, we got manslaughter, and we got death by auto."

"I always thought manslaughter sounded worse than murder somehow," Mrs. Jankowski said. "It's the 'slaughter' part."

"Hooo!" Mr. Ortiz said, drumming on the table with his palms.

"Well, it's *not* worse than murder," Mr. Thiele said.

"It just sounds worse," Mr. Edgar added.

"Well, which is worse, manslaughter or death by auto?" Mrs. Bonilla asked.

"They do seem kind of the same to me," said Mr. Thiele. "For one, you cause death by being reckless. For the other, you cause death by being reckless when you drive."

"Which one gets punished worse?" Mrs. Bonilla asked.

"We were instructed not to consider punishment," Mrs. Haskel said.

"Well, manslaughter is a second-degree crime, and death by auto is a fourth-degree crime," said Mr. Clark.

"Is it like burns?" Mrs. Bonilla asked. "The way a third-degree burn is worse than a first-degree burn?"

"No," said Mrs. Haskel. "It's the opposite. First degree is the worst."

"You'd know," said Mr. Corso.

"We'll ask the judge to tell us," said Mr. Clark. He scribbled some questions on a white square of paper and then reread them silently to himself, erasing words here and there, taking his time. He held out the paper, examining it ceremoniously. Then he rose and handed the paper out the door to the court officer and signaled the jurors to file into the courtroom after him. They paraded into the jury box with Mr. Clark at the head, clacking his dentures, and reseated themselves.

"The jury has issued two notes," Judge MacFarland announced. The first says, 'Can we find the defendant not guilty of death by auto but guilty of manslaughter?' The second says, 'Which is worse, second or fourth degree?'

"Ladies and gentlemen of the jury, on the facts of this case, it would not be possible for you to find that the defendant did not drive recklessly but that she acted recklessly. The answer to your first question is therefore 'no.' In response to your second question, manslaughter, the second-degree offense, is the more serious of the two charges."

When the jury had returned to deliberations, Mike Ribeiro said, "Your Honor, I renew my motion to dismiss the manslaughter count. Obviously, the jurors are confused. I have written a memorandum, which I am now submitting to the court."

Judge MacFarland accepted the memorandum and glanced briefly at a paragraph:

> The present prosecution frustrates the legislative intent that reckless vehicular homicide be prosecuted under the specific statute created for that purpose and the language of N.J.S.A. 2C:11-5 admits no other reasonable interpretation than its substitution for N.J.S.A. 2C:11-4(b), in this circumstance, because the Legislature added the element of the automobile.

Sometimes when the judge stared at the language of the law, it seemed vacant of meaning, like the words of an alien species who wished to imitate humans but really did not understand the nature of speech.

"What's so confusing?" Harkin asked. "Manslaughter is manslaughter, and death by auto is death by auto."

The judge paged through the memorandum until the foreman, Mr. Clark, reappeared at the door to the jury room with a third note, which the court officer passed to the judge.

Judge MacFarland called the jurors back into the courtroom. She stated, "The foreman has issued a note that says, 'Your Honor, we're unanimously deadlocked.' "

The judge announced that the jurors would be sequestered overnight and urged them to continue their deliberations with open minds the following day. Mrs. Bugg expressed dismay that she would not be able to visit her grandchildren that evening.

In the morning, Judge MacFarland informed the jury that she had dismissed the manslaughter count. She explained: "A judge is required to assume the legislature does not mean its laws to be ridiculous." Ida felt little relief that a legal technicality had saved her. She desired exoneration after judgment, although she did not believe she deserved it.

Juror #6, Mr. Thiele, thought that the defendant looked tired. Her high towering hairdo was toppling and appeared to be tangled with her feather earrings, which she had resumed wearing.

Once the jurors had entered the jury room, Mr. Clark commanded, "Let's get down to business. We missed a good game last night. All we have left is death by auto."

"How can the judge do that?" Mrs. Haskel asked. "I thought she got to name the punishment but we decided whether or not the defendant was guilty."

Mr. Corso leered at his coffee.

"I hardly feel as if any of it's worth my time now," said Mrs. Haskel. "Obviously, the judge doesn't take us very seriously." She then said, turning to Mr. Edgar, "No offense, but

I don't think that judge knows what she's doing. There are so many black people who have qualifications. I can't approve of making someone a judge just because she's black."

Mr. Corso sipped his coffee noisily.

"She's a perfectly good judge," Mr. Edgar answered dismissively. Addressing the jurors generally and apparently choosing not to respond further to Mrs. Haskel, Mr. Edgar said, "I'm sure we're all aware that Rupert Dixon, the victim's father, is a well-known slumlord downtown. I believe there was a fire last year in one of his buildings in which an entire family died. I was distressed to learn that his son was carrying cans of kerosene at the time of his death. I have asked myself many times whether many people would have perished that night if Clark Gable Dixon had not, and whether the defendant, Ida Terhune, was not in some way a messenger from the angels. Sometimes it is difficult to understand the workings of God, or even to identify evil and good when we see it. Perhaps Mrs. Terhune was a sheep in wolf's clothing."

A short silence followed, during which the jury considered Mr. Edgar's statement.

Mrs. Haskel intruded on the silence, announcing, "I'm going to abstain from voting."

"You can't abstain," Mr. Thiele said.

"Why not?" asked Mrs. Bugg. "The judge only said that the vote had to be unanimous. She didn't say we all had to vote."

"All right," said Mr. Clark.

"That's wonderful!" Mr. Corso cheered sarcastically. "You abstain!"

Mrs. Haskel sulked through the remaining deliberations.

"So let's take a vote on whether or not the defendant was drunk," said Mr. Clark. "The way I see it, if she wasn't drunk, she wasn't reckless, either, so we can kill two birds with one stone."

Mr. Ortiz leaned forward and laughed drunkenly. The smell of Wild Turkey filled the jury room.

"That's not exactly true," said Mr. Thiele. "You can drive recklessly without being drunk. You could also be drunk without driving recklessly."

Mr. Clark felt somewhat offended at Mr. Thiele's invasion of his territory. He was, after all, the foreman. "So was she intoxicated?" he resumed.

"Just a moment," said Mrs. Bugg. "We haven't turned over all the eggs yet. I'd like to say something I've been thinking about. First, I'm a small woman, a little smaller than Mrs. Terhune, and it takes very little to get me intoxicated. However, I have always found that I could drink two glasses of wine at an Italian restaurant without becoming inebriated, because of the heaviness of Italian food. The defendant's friend testified that they both had eggplant parmigiana. The evening after Mrs. Terhune's testimony, I decided to have dinner at the My Way Lounge, with two and one-fourth glasses of champagne, and I did not feel intoxicated at the conclusion of the meal. As you must already know, eggplant parmigiana is a rather heavy dish if made properly. The correct way to cook eggplant, of course, is to roast it in the oven before mixing it with other ingredients, and to use plenty of olive oil. However, there are those who choose to cook it in oil over the stove first, which makes the eggplant taste singed. It is my opinion that the My Way Lounge does follow the former method. The dish was quite tasty, and the escarole excellent. So my first point is, how could Ida Terhune have been drunk after eating eggplant parmigiana at the My Way Lounge?

"Now, the second thing is, those streets down by Second and Brunswick are impossible. They all point in the wrong direction. I've driven the wrong way down them many a time, and I know from experience that it's a simple matter to run a stop sign when you're seeing it from the back. You'll notice that the defendant drove in rush hour along Newark Avenue and had no mishaps whatsoever.

"Therefore, the only evidence of drunkenness is the testimony of the police officer," Mrs. Bugg concluded.

"Who lied his little head off," Ms. Bonaparte followed.

"Cops!" said Mr. Ortiz. The smell of Wild Turkey again enveloped the jurors.

"And of course," Mrs. Bugg added, "the elderly witness said that Mrs. Terhune was driving slowly and that the young man simply stepped out into traffic."

"Well, I think a lady's view on this issue is controlling," Mr. Clark said. "Do any of the ladies disagree?"

"I can't see taking a mother away from two children," said Ms. Sparks.

"We don't know that the judge would give her a long prison sentence," Mrs. Haskel responded.

"I thought you were abstaining," Mr. Corso told her.

Mr. Ortiz leafed through the pile of exhibits, paused at the map, and peered at the small picture the defendant's son had drawn of his dog in the bottom left-hand corner: a stumpy-nosed dog with crossed eyes and bowed legs and a wiggly tail. It would be nice to have a tail.

"I felt so sorry for her when she realized her friend was having a love affair with the lawyer," said Mrs. Jankowski. "That's punishment enough. The defendant is obviously in love with her attorney."

"Maybe we should send her to jail to keep her away from him," Mr. Clark joked. "What a snake oil salesman."

"All I can say," said Spinelli, "is that she doesn't know what it means to be drunk."

"Well," Mr. Edgar said, "what if we all just sit quietly for ten minutes and arrange our thoughts? Then perhaps the foreman could take the vote."

As the foreman, Mr. Clark again felt his territory was being trod upon. "All right," he said. "We'll take exactly seven minutes."

Mr. Edgar sat back and envisioned Ida Terhune as an unwitting savior of her building's inhabitants, as a martyr, almost. Beside him, Mrs. Jankowski thought of how alone and frightened Mrs. Terhune must feel. Then Mrs. Jankowski's mind drifted, and she thought of how lonely she had been during the four years she was on her own, how loneliness had made her feel larger than herself, how her skin had seemed too tight, painful to wear. Beside her, Ms. Sparks sensed the baby turning inside her, and she recalled the moment when the victim's father had failed to appear in court. She contemplated Mr. Edgar's statement about the slumlord and tried to picture Ida Terhune as a sheep in wolf's clothing, but the image would not come to her.

Mrs. Haskel grieved over her failure to put the defendant behind bars, where she could be kept from harming others in the future. Mrs. Haskel wished she could have been the judge in the case. She knew she would make a good judge. Mr. Corso pictured himself as the judge in a trial where Mrs. Haskel was the defendant, and smiled. There was no question in his mind that Mrs. Terhune was harmless and ordinary, hardly worth the hoopla of the trial.

Ms. Bonaparte imagined herself being tried for the crimes of Ida Terhune. She, Ms. Bonaparte, would have handled things differently. She would not have allowed the prosecutor to manipulate her into a confession. She would not have dressed in such a stuffy manner, and she would have smiled more often at the jury, exuding an aura of self-confidence. But then, she probably would not have driven a car at night without realizing that the headlights were broken. Nor would she have admitted anything to the police, ever. Ms. Bonaparte disapproved of Ida Terhune for being such easy prey, for being a victim from the moment she had been accused of being a perpetrator.

Mrs. Bonilla pitied Ida Terhune, poor soul, thinking that for the rest of her life she would walk around burdened by guilt, the victim's death weighing on her conscience. Mrs. Bonilla said a prayer of thanks to God that she was not Ida Terhune. Mr. Ortiz said a prayer of thanks that the trial was over. The effects of the Wild Turkey he had drunk that morning were beginning to wear off, but soon, soon, he would be out in the crisp May air, away from the imprisoning jury room and its eleven jurors, who with their silences had summarily judged him without any of the consideration they accorded the defendant.

Spinelli wondered how Mr. Ortiz had managed to get hold of hard liquor when the jurors had been sequestered all evening. Perhaps if the jurors had been allowed to pass around a bottle of whiskey from the beginning, they would not have been so full of themselves and would have reached their verdict sooner. Spinelli hardly thought there had been anything to discuss: if Ida Terhune went to prison for drunk driving, you might as well throw in all of New Jersey. She looked liked the kind of woman who would be a lot happier drunk than sober, and it was a shame that she probably would never know it.

Mr. Thiele felt uncomfortable with the whole idea of sitting in judgment on someone. If anyone asked him, he would say that he thought prosecutors on the whole were sadists, lusting after punishment, and that defense lawyers lacked any moral sensibility, but judges were the worst. Imagine the ego you would have to carry around to think you were wise enough to condemn and incarcerate another member of the human race. As a juror, Mr. Thiele was content to examine the facts but not to judge. He believed that Ida Terhune probably had been drunk when she drove into the victim. She may have had only two and one-fourth glasses of champagne, but then she wasn't accustomed to drinking. She was a careful driver by habit but had driven with some recklessness immediately after getting in her car and had failed to notice that her lights were not operating until she had driven a number of blocks. She had probably hit the victim not because he was in the road but because, without lights, she hadn't seen him. Mr. Thiele thought that she was probably guilty under the law; however, he didn't particularly care. Spinoza would not particularly have cared. Mr. Thiele doubted Ida Terhune would ever drive drunk again. In fact, she was safer on the road than most people. He didn't believe in punishment for its own sake, although, as her attorney had asserted, the defendant probably did: if she had been sitting on her own jury, she undoubtedly would have convicted herself. Mrs. Haskel would not have felt so alone.

Mrs. Bugg was certain of a verdict of not guilty. Her arguments had been logical, well-reasoned, and persuasive. She felt that, in a sense, Mrs. Terhune was Mrs. Bugg's own creation. Because of her, Mrs. Terhune would be seen as an innocent person who had suffered a terrible misfortune rather than as a criminal who had committed the most horrible of offenses, homicide.

The foreman, Mr. Clark, clacked his dentures as he mused, distracting and irritating Ms. Bonaparte. Mr. Clark also believed that he had orchestrated the verdict. He had never cared, from the beginning, which way the vote went, but it was important to him that no jury of his hung itself. He felt he had handled things deftly and was proud of his success. He was glad that Mrs. Haskel had agreed to abstain.

The jury entered the courtroom, with Mr. Clark at the front, clacking his dentures. After the jurors were seated, Mr. Clark rose, and without waiting for Judge MacFarland to ask for the verdict, he said in a stentorian voice: "We the jury find the defendant, Mrs. Terhune, to be absolutely innocent."

◆ Epilogue

June filled Jersey City with the overexuberant smell of asphalt from the refineries bordering Hudson County. Air conditioners struggled fruitlessly, water pressure dropped in tenements as fire hydrants twisted open, and Henry Purdy's cosmos flowers reseeded themselves, multiplying and struggling over the hot vacant lot, blazing and swirling.

Porter Terhune stopped at Grand Street to pick up Angel Rodriguez. Porter waved to Wilma Tutwiler, who sat in her chair near the pay phone, eavesdropping on a desperate teenager who was plotting with his girlfriend to run away from home. Cosmos flowers shimmered along the sidewalk cracks in front of Wilma, so that she seemed to be riding on a float of fluorescent blossoms. Angel walked the floorboards over the flooded basement, took the steps three at a time behind her, and climbed into the back of Porter's pickup with Betty Trombley and the Terhune children.

Ida sat in the cab next to Porter. Betty had convinced her to wear a tie-dyed sundress and a pair of sandals with plastic daisies on them, and Ida felt self-conscious, although more comfortable than she might have in a pantsuit and pumps. She felt all the more self-conscious because Mike Ribeiro would be at the riverside docks. He had acted with great delicacy around her since the trial and never alluded to the incident in the motel room, but nevertheless she sensed he was still interested in her.

She was apprehensive about her continuing romantic feelings toward him. She still felt so wobbly inside, uncertain of who she was or where she would find herself next. More and more often recently, the odd notion that she might not want to remarry kept tangling itself with her normal thoughts. Odder still, she found herself wondering if Mike Ribeiro was the type of man who might not enjoy a casual love affair. Perhaps she should just keep going in the direction she had started and see where it took her. Mike had rescued her, after all, and she was curious what he would prove to be like without the aid of the Napoleon brandy.

"Mama looks like a kook in that dress," Sherry told Skeet, smiling as if this were a compliment. Skeet frowned, but he really did not care anymore about how his mother looked: he was just glad she was back for good. Still, it was a little hard to adjust to her Betty Trombley hairdo, flat on top and shaggy in back, and when he closed his eyes and pictured his mother, she looked the same as she used to: a lady with a high hairdo and a drip-dry mint-green pantsuit.

Porter drove toward the docks in Paulis Hook, passing Persaud's Corner Store. Rupert Dixon stood in the doorway, watching a twelve-man construction crew back a cement mixer toward a site twenty yards from the F. H. Eggers memorial. Large green-and-yellow letters reading DIXON CONSTRUCTION spun around the mixer as if powered by a lethargic whirlwind. Rupert chewed absently on a pencil stub, and his eyes narrowed while he watched the progress of the vehicle. He was planning to run for mayor against the incumbent in the next election, as the anti-machine candidate. He saw Porter pass before the cement mixer but did not recognize his pickup truck.

Mike Ribeiro had attempted to retrieve the New Yorker from the municipal lot where it had been impounded. For weeks, red tape impeded him. While Ida was being tried, the car had been marked for a police auction, as unclaimed stolen property. After Mike managed to claim the car, a ticket for reckless driving had been issued in Ida's name and the New Yorker was again impounded under the scoff law. Through an inexplicable omission, she had not been charged with the more serious traffic offense of drunk driving. Mike accompanied Ida to traffic court, where he argued that her acquittal of the crime of death by auto rendered the ticket for reckless driving unlawful, a violation of the constitutional principles of due process and double jeopardy, but Judge Polk pounded his gavel and pronounced Ida guilty. In the end, in order to retrieve her New Yorker, Ida had to pay a stiff fine and the added costs of impoundment.

When Betty and the Terhunes had arrived at the municipal lot to retrieve the New Yorker, they discovered that its windshield had been shattered.

"It's like a broken leg in a horse," Porter told Ida. "You just got to put that car down." No one mentioned the crumpled left fender, where Chicken had run into the car.

The children opened the New Yorker's doors and sat inside. Sherry removed the bull's-eye cigarette lighter from its cylinder in the dashboard and placed the lighter in her pocket. Skeet sat before the steering wheel, pretending to drive, his arm half outside the window.

"Don't stick your elbow out too far, or it might go home in another car," Sherry said, and the words seemed more ghoulish to Betty than they ever had.

Ida had felt less upset about the damage to the New Yorker than she might have expected. She wasn't certain she wanted the car anymore. It reminded her not only of her old life but also of the moment when her old life had ended. She had stared at the New Yorker as solemnly as if it were her own grave marker and asked Porter to sell it to the junkyard.

Now Porter's pickup hit a deep pothole on Grand Street as he turned left, heading for Exchange Place. "You could drown a mule in that hole on a rainy day," he told Ida.

Rumors had spread that streets now identified by their

historic potholes would be paved and widened, that a shopping mall would be built near the Holland Tunnel, that the rat-infested docks behind the Colgate factory and at Liberty State Park would be turned into boardwalks with picnic areas, that realtors would descend on downtown Jersey City like jackals and advertise apartments at a thousand dollars a month or even higher, outrageous, unheard-of prices for downtown renters, who had never paid more than four hundred dollars monthly for family-sized apartments.

In the back of the pickup, Betty was telling Angel, "This new kind of landlord is a different animal. You got your slumlords and your gentrifiers. This one's a gentrifier. That means that instead of making money off running down buildings, he's going to fix up our buildings. Then he'll push us all out, one by one, and get rich people to move in. Just watch. They'll start with those brownstones over by Van Vorst and Hamilton parks. Every last one of those tenants down there is going to be evicted by the end of two years."

"It'll never work," Angel answered. "Jersey City is not Hoboken. It's too ugly here. The ugliness of things is what we've got going for us. Those New York investment bankers and lawyers and stockbrokers are going to take one look at what it looks like over here, and they're going to turn tail."

When Porter's pickup reached the Hudson, the sun was already slanting across the river away from Manhattan, reaching for Jersey City. Manhattan looked unreal, as if it floated on the water.

"It's the best view of New York City from anywhere," Angel said, "but no one ever sees it except the dock rats."

Mike waved to them from the dock. He had parked his car in a towaway zone and left the door open. He leaned over a metal pressure cooker and poked at the contents. He was happy to see Ida Terhune and her children. He had feared after the trial that Betty and the Terhunes would abandon him, but they had not. He had been at the dock for two hours that morning, waiting for them, and had caught such a horrifying number of crabs he wondered if he had hit some sort of crab hive swarming around on the river bottom. He had thrown most of them back so that he wouldn't discourage the children from spending a long time crabbing after they arrived.

Skeet and Sherry ran to the dock and looked in the pressure cooker: a half-dozen crabs scrambled inside, feasting on raw chicken bones.

"I didn't want to break their hearts by taking the bones away," Mike said. "And they didn't seem to want to give them up."

"Crabs don't have hearts," Porter told him. "But we brought lots of bacon anyway."

Porter frowned: he saw that the lawyer was wooing Ida through her children, and he struck Porter as a man desperate for a woman, something that made Porter uncomfortable. He sensed that the lawyer had gone after Betty as well as Ida, and Porter had thus placed the lawyer in his mind as one of those men who used the shotgun style of courting—he just hit on every woman he saw until one of his birds dropped. Well, it was his business, especially since Betty did not seem to have any real sustained interest in the lawyer. (That was one thing Porter could count on: at least Betty would never pair up for good with another man.) Besides, Ida could use some warmth in her life, and if she and the lawyer had a love affair, it would keep the lawyer away from Betty.

The children tied bacon strips to long strings and tossed them into the Hudson. Joseph stood with his toenails hanging over the dock's edge, sniffing the bacon's trail longingly, yearning for the feel of something in his mouth and watching for the first crab.

"Smell that?" Ida told Angel. "That's toothpaste."

Angel breathed in, and a minty taste burned his lungs. He thought that Ida Terhune was altogether more likable, now that she had murdered someone. She seemed more relaxed.

"Ellis Island is over that way," Angel told her. "You can't see it from here, but it's there, right around the bend." He thought it was funny that she stared at an empty stretch of water off to her right when he had finished speaking, to demonstrate her interest in what he had to say. He had never known anyone as ridiculously polite as Ida Terhune.

Betty sat down on a cinder block and saw, in front of the Colgate factory, two long red couches and several armchairs, arranged in a half-circle around a coffee table. A barrel blackened by smoke stood beside one of the sofas. Betty flashed Porter such a sudden, toothy smile that he was afraid he would get an erection, and he turned toward the river to pretend to admire Manhattan.

The children overheard Mike Ribeiro tell their mother, "I talked to my law school buddy in New Orleans. He thinks you might be able to keep the Tulip Street house." Mike admired Ida Terhune's slender feet in her funny plastic sandals.

Skeet felt a chill in his spine that failed to travel upward: instead, it settled like a lump of ice over his tailbone. Sherry felt strangled by velvety hands. It was as if Harlan Pinkerton were standing on the dock between the two children: he rose up in their imaginations, not as a presence, but as an absence, a feeling of grabbiness and stinginess that caused them to draw toward each other and withdraw into themselves. They had been so relieved after their mother came back at the end of the trial, but neither of them trusted the permanence of things anymore. They both believed with conviction that they could wake up tomorrow in a different place, surrounded by different people, and that not once would anyone consult them to ask their opinion about anything.

"If that's true," their mother answered, "maybe the New Orleans lawyer could help me arrange to sell the house. I'm going to stay in Jersey City." The city had given Ida back her job at the Municipal Court: it didn't seem to bother anyone that a person working in the complaints office had been indicted for homicide. Ida could not face the idea of Louisiana. Back there, people would mistake her for what she had been. They would never suspect that she'd killed someone.

"I'll be sorry to leave you here," Porter said. He turned and looked at Betty.

What did he mean? Ida wondered. That he regretted having to go, or that he felt sorry for them because they were staying in Jersey City?

A skiff rippled like a mirage on a hot road over the sun's red rays reflected in the river. Ida glimpsed, or thought she glimpsed, Henry Purdy, oars in hand, paddling toward Ellis Island. His figure grew smaller and smaller, until he disappeared into a patch of light burning on the water.